Brothers in *Arms*

A Black Watch Security Novel

Kristen Casey

The Black Watch Security Series

About This Book

Wyatt Oaks did not see Jesse Burke die, but he endured the same devastating skirmish, and it deep-sixed his SEAL career.

He only remembered the soldier because he'd spoken to him for a few hours weeks before, one drunken night on leave. That connection barely made them acquaintances, and certainly not friends.

So why does he feel such an obligation to the wife and small son the Army captain left behind? Wyatt heard about them exactly once. He should be able to forget them. What's more, the fact that his new employer, Black Watch Security, is in the midst of taking down a corrupt senator with a vendetta against his team, means Wyatt *needs* to forget them.

He isn't the forgetting type, however. And once he discovers that Burke's widow knows more than anyone could guess about that infamous ambush and what the dirty senator wrought there—he realizes he just might have to become more than another brother-in-arms Leah and her son don't need. He might need to be their guard, their shield, their safe harbor...

Wyatt might have to become their everything.

Content Guidance

I want my readers to always feel comfortable picking up a Kristen Casey romance, and I recognize that certain topics and scenarios can be challenging to encounter when reading for pleasure. As an avid reader myself, I want to give you the tools to keep yourself safe.

If you would like detailed content information for any of my titles, please scan the QR code or click on the link below, and you will be directed to a dedicated page on my website that lists this information.

In addition, if you encounter a situation in any of my titles that is not listed (but you believe should be), I encourage you to reach out to me at *KristenCasey* [dot] *com* to recommend adding it.

Thank you.

https://www.kristencasey.com/content-guidance

Prologue

Tate

TATE WATCHED THE spring snow falling outside the huge plate glass windows, contemplating whether he wanted to start a fire now or wait until the sun went down for maximum romantic effect.

His coffee had gone cold way too fast, but it was his third that afternoon so that was probably for the best. Next to it, his phone vibrated insistently.

Lyla was across the cavernous room at a desk facing another wall of windows, and the steady clicking of his wife's keyboard testified to how inspiring she seemed to find this place. Tate had no doubt her next murder mystery would be set in a snowy location just like this one.

It was probably weird that he found that kind of hot.

His phone buzzed again. Technically, he wasn't supposed to be working during their little getaway. Lyla was clearly doing it, though, so there had to be some wiggle room, right?

He grabbed it and connected the call with his usual, "Monroe."

"I did it," his tech guy, Noah, gasped. "I finally cracked that bastard, and found out who owns the shell company shielding all those real estate holdings."

"Meaning, the estate where Dan Cox held Kim hostage." Tate leaned in, fascinated by the development.

Kim Sutherland was a Dallas socialite who'd briefly dated one of their targets and was now engaged to a Black Watch operative named Bennett Shaw. She'd been kidnapped a few months prior, and held at an estate in tony Montecito for days before they'd found her.

They already knew who'd done the kidnapping, but Noah had been working for weeks to discover who actually owned the posh accommodations. The guy was right to be excited by his find, too—it brought them one step closer to discovering the head of the beast they'd been chasing, so they could lop that fucker off.

"There are other properties, but yeah."

"Nice work," Tate said. When Noah didn't go on, he smirked and added, "You gonna share that information with me, or just gloat for a bit?"

"No, I think I've got most of the gloating out of my system. But you're not going to believe who it is."

"Somehow, I bet I—"

"It's Leon Doggett!" he blurted breathlessly.

Tate blinked. It'd been a while since he'd seen Black Watch's resident computer genius this hyped, but then, establishing a direct link to yet another family member of Senator Roy Doggett's corrupt escapades over the last few years *was* a notable breakthrough.

Thanks to Kim and her man Shaw's efforts, they now had Roy's stepson Dan doing time along with his filmmaker ex. The net was tightening bit by bit on Roy himself, and now, it appeared Ole Roy's brother Leon could also be a person of interest.

Tate couldn't say that was a shocking development, and there was still a long way to go before they could prove that Leon— Hollywood producer and all-around dirtbag—was actually involved in Kim's kidnapping, but at least they had another avenue to explore.

On the downside, now they had another avenue to explore. One more lane to follow, in an expanding, chaotic city map of a case that just kept getting more complicated.

Tate would stay the course, though. Eventually, he and his men would figure out who was truly pulling the strings and bring that person down. Given the way last year's ambush in the tiny village of Nabarut, Qahat had unfolded, he was personally betting on a dirty puppeteer in the Special Warfare chain of command.

He needed proof, however, and it'd been a slog trying to piece it all together.

The rub was that even if they were successful, other bad apples would inevitably bubble up to assume that person's place, and at this point Tate doubted that the SEALs who'd originally taken the fall to cover whatever undercover deal had been done in Nabarut would ever be returned to their rightful spots on the Teams.

At least he'd be able to say he'd gotten some justice, though—for the SEALs who'd become the heart of his company, and for his old Army unit, Echo Company, which had been decimated in the ambush's crossfire.

"I can tell you're amazed, but I assure you it gets better," Noah said.

Tate sniffed in amusement. "I have no doubt."

"Seeing Leon's name got me thinking. So, I crossed Doggett's official financial statements against property records in Texas, where the Doggetts' listed residences are, and Louisiana, where Landry Cox and Mrs. Doggett's family used to be based, and also in West Virginia, where Dan moved the Landry headquarters a few years ago. I found a bunch of parcels held under entities with very similar names to the shell company Leon's using. I'll follow up on the particulars, but I thought it was pertinent. Maybe one of them is where they've been hiding the girls."

And there it was, the most time-critical part of their investigation. For all his team's efforts, they still hadn't been able to locate the twelve teenage girls who'd been snatched from their tiny Qahati village during the skirmish that had kicked off this investigation almost two years ago. It'd been stressing him and his team out. *All* the way out.

"Could be. Worth ruling out, in any case." Tate checked on Lyla, who was still typing away, though a bit more slowly now. "Was that all, or did you have something else?"

"Nothing concrete. I'm playing with some ideas, though. Thinking about ways all this stuff might fit together."

"Any breakthroughs?"

"Maybe." Noah hesitated, then admitted, "I thought that next, I'd look at ties between these companies and the one Senator Doggett was using to funnel government arms contracts to Landry Cox. If we can somehow prove where the funds flowed…I don't know, maybe we could nail down if someone paid for those girls. Or even who paid."

"That's good. I like that. *Follow the money* is a classic."

With Landry Cox's former CEO, Dan Cox, cooling his heels in the clink for kidnapping, the arms manufacturer had scaled down the AR-15 production lines that Dan had been spearheading and keeping a low profile. That was undoubtedly Lena Cox Doggett's doing, who'd inherited the company from her grandfather and run it successfully, before passing it on to her son when she'd married Roy.

"Right." Noah paused, took a deep breath, and plowed on. "Last thing I have is Kim's hard drive. Thanks to the bank records she gave us, I've been able to identify several women that Dan took on dates around the time Kim figured he was cheating on her. And get this—at least four of them have a connection to each other."

Tate frowned. "How so?"

"It popped right up when I searched them as a unit. They're all listed together on the roster of a bible study group at Camp Pendleton."

"Pendleton." Tate glanced at Lyla, whose fingers froze on the keys of her laptop, and whose back now looked decidedly stiff. *Shoot.*

"Son, that's a Marine base," he said unnecessarily.

"It sure is. And I bet you know which Army unit was training there two years ago."

Lyla spun in her seat and eyed him with a little scowl. Therefore, while Tate really wanted to jump up and pace around so he could process this information, he kept his posture relaxed and settled deeper into the leather armchair next to those floor-to-ceiling windows.

He was supposed to be unwinding in a winter wonderland this weekend. His wife would kill him, bring him back to life, then re-kill him if she thought he wasn't following orders.

Tate said, "I can guess," though he knew. *He knew.*

"Yup. Echo Company, last seen at the ambush of Nabarut."

"Imagine that."

It was the best he could come up with on the fly. His former infantry unit hadn't done much in the last year-and-a-half because their ranks had been decimated during the fighting. His friend Tank had died, along with many others Tate had served beside for years.

The only reason he was sitting here in this luxury lodge in the mountains, tucked away with the gorgeous woman he got to call his wife, was because Tate had been stuck at home recovering from a TBI when his unit had deployed.

Lyla arched a warning eyebrow at him, not buying for one second that this was a run-of-the-mill social call. *Smart girl was smart.*

Tate gave her a cheeky wink and figured he'd better wrap things up before he found himself in the doghouse later instead of Lyla's bed.

"That reminds me—what is our boy Oaks up to this week? He still sniffing around Burke's widow?"

Tate had only met Captain Burke in passing a handful of times back in the day. The man had been Tank's brother-in-law, so they'd crossed paths here and there within the unit. But Burke had also been an asshole, rest his soul, so Tate hadn't been terribly inclined to further their acquaintance.

The fact that one of his operatives was currently laboring under an inconvenient fascination with Burke's widow seemed destined for complications. Tate was coming to understand that *any* time one of his operatives took a shine to a woman, things were bound to get messy—but that seemed like it would go double for Wyatt Oaks, a **charmer** of the first order.

Decidedly not the kind of personnel situation he'd anticipated when he'd set up the Black Watch Security company all those months ago.

Noah cleared his throat, a tell if ever Tate had heard one. "That's being handled."

"He's sitting right next to you, isn't he?"

"Not *right* next to me."

"Do I need to get involved?"

"No sir. We'll take care of it."

"I'll bet."

A mutinous silence settled over the line. A loyal, stubborn, mutinous silence.

Tate grinned.

His wayward SEALs were coming along nicely, absorbing Noah into their team like the guy had always been with them. He'd done well putting them together. In another few months, he could probably introduce one more, and expand their capabilities even further.

His gaze drifted back to Lyla, who gestured pointedly for him to hang up.

Tate rested his phone against his shoulder and mouthed, "What's it worth to you?" He grinned wider when his wife's eyes narrowed.

She stood abruptly, and began unbuttoning her flannel pajama top as she prowled closer.

Now Tate was the one clearing his throat. "Okay well, keep me in the loop," he said quickly.

"Hoorah," the kid responded, a split second before Lyla snatched the phone out of his hand, disconnected the call, and tossed it to the couch behind her.

"No working on vacation, Mr. Monroe," she purred dangerously.

Tate pulled her into his lap and pushed her hair over her shoulder, murmuring close to her ear, "Said the woman who probably just knocked out three chapters on her computer."

"Look, murders don't just write themselves."

"Does it take place in a snowy cabin? Does the husband make it?"

"Wouldn't you like to know?"

"I would, yes. It feels like alarmingly pertinent information."

"Who was on the phone?" Lyla countered. "Noah again?"

"Mm-hm."

"You know what the price is for taking work calls this weekend?"

"I do," Tate smiled back. "And I am so ready to pay."

Chapter One

Wyatt

HE SAW HER coming, stomping toward Joe's nondescript sedan with hell on her heels—and yet somehow Wyatt still managed to be surprised when Leah Burke rapped sharply on his side window.

Once he recovered, he sat up straight and adjusted the brim of his ball cap, then slowly lowered the passenger window. He had no idea what to say.

Luckily it didn't matter, because Leah had plenty of ideas for both of them.

"I've had about enough of you," she spat. "I don't know whether you're staking out me or my kid, but it ends now. The next time I see you in this neighborhood, I'm calling the cops and filing a report."

Shit. She'd marked him again. And Mrs. Burke was quite upset about it.

"It's not like…that," Wyatt muttered, as his hand made a vague swipe through the air that felt oddly disconnected from the rest of his body.

"Oh yeah? Then what is it like?"

It appeared his time for dithering was up. *Might as well cut to the chase.*

"I wasn't trying to scare you," he said. "I knew your husband. Well, kind of. He told me about you guys, and now that he…" Wyatt stopped and lamely cleared his throat. She knew what her husband was. "Anyway, I thought I should see if you were doing okay—if you needed anything."

Leah glared at him. "So, you figured lurking was the way to go? You could've asked directly."

Wyatt nodded. She was right, of course. Why hadn't he?

And, for that matter, why had he made an effort to show up at different times, in different cars, only to park in the same spot, directly across from her front door, on every visit?

He might as well have begged her to notice him. To challenge him.

"Well?" Leah demanded.

Could he even call her Leah? Was that presumptuous if they'd never been introduced?

"I wasn't sure I should intrude," he explained.

Lame. So very lame. He hated the feeling. Hated himself at that moment.

Leah Burke let out a very heavy sigh, as if everything about him and this situation exhausted her.

"You've been here since at least six." She rolled her eyes at his no-doubt stricken expression. "Yes, I saw you."

"Was I really that obvious?"

"You do all tend to look the same."

"There have been others?"

"A few."

"Jesus. Okay." He was a fool. A royal, decreed-by-God fool. "I'm really sorry I worried you."

"I mean, how did you think it was going to look?" she wondered. "I live alone with a small toddler. You've been staking me out."

"True, but—" Wyatt tried to readjust in his seat so he could face her, but his frame felt too big, too awkward for the space. He didn't fit, but what else was new.

Leah eyed him critically. "Alright, could you just..." She hmphed in irritation, raising her palms like he needed to settle down. "Just get out of the car, okay? We can talk in the yard."

"You sure?" He glanced down the street, eyeing his exit route. "I can get out of your hair. I don't want to—"

"I'm sure. You're not coming inside, though. Don't even ask."

"Roger that."

As she backed away, Wyatt took a minute to stare out the windshield, swallowing back his sudden flurry of nerves. All this time, he'd been telling himself he would approach her when the time was right, but now that Leah had made the first move, he was no longer sure if that had been true. Maybe he would've just kept watching her, getting a weekly hit of someone else's life.

A life that might never be his.

Still, with her gauntlet thrown, he could hardly take off now. And truth be told, he was curious. Rabidly so.

Leah retreated across the street as he got out, then onto her stairs when she got a look at his full size. Even though he'd stood slowly, and attempted to infuse every inch of his body with deference, her eyes still widened as she assessed his height. His breadth.

Mrs. Burke hadn't expected him to be quite so large.

He got that a lot.

"I'm not going to try anything," he swore. "I would never hurt either of you."

Instead of reassuring her, the assertion only seemed to piss her off. "Damn right you won't," she snarled, then urged him forward with another wave. "Come on. Let's get this over with."

Wyatt crossed the street slowly, keeping his distance, trying to look nonthreatening.

She puffed out her chest and affected an annoyed demeanor, but her darting gaze made him wonder if this was Mrs. Burke's version of *fake-it-till-you-make-it.*

"Alright spit it out," she demanded once his shoes hit her lawn. "What's your story?"

"I met your husband overseas last year. He talked about you guys. Showed me pictures. When I heard what happened to him, I thought I should see if you two needed anything."

"By loitering."

Her dry as dust tone made him smile. "As I said, I didn't know if I should intrude. I only met your husband the one time. It's…maybe it's not my place and you have all the help you need."

"Yet again…try asking instead of skulking."

Wyatt shrugged. "I *am* sorry. I honestly didn't think you'd notice me out here." *A lie, but was it for himself, or her?*

She huffed. "Mr.——?"

"Oaks. Wyatt Oaks." He whipped out his military ID and held it toward her. It was a little outdated, but it wasn't like his new employer was in the habit of handing out company IDs at the end of orientation. They were supposed to be *shadowy* or whatever, now that they were a part of Black Watch Security.

Civilian rules were taking some getting used to.

"I don't remember hearing your name around base, Mr. Oaks." Leah bent forward and peered at his ID, her brow wrinkling in a little frown. "Wait. You're Navy, not Army."

"I was. I'm out now."

"So, you weren't in Jesse's unit. Where exactly did you meet him?"

"On leave in Dubai. Half of Echo Company must've been in that bar. It was a scene."

She studied him, from his hat to his running shoes, then grudgingly nodded. "They were in Dubai a week before they…well." Leah swallowed. Her voice went flat, nearly emotionless. *Nearly.* "You obviously know what happened next."

Wyatt nodded. "Actually, I was there, too. I tried to find him, but…" He shook his head. *Fuck a duck, this was hard.*

Leah's dark eyes locked onto his. "I'm sorry, did you say you were *there?* As in, at that village, *there?*"

He managed to combine a shrug and a nod into some new, painfully awkward gesture. He hadn't had a prayer of finding Jesse Burke in the melee that'd been Nabarut, but he'd tried. He'd fucking *tried.* Not that it would make any difference to this woman.

Wyatt was at a loss. He shouldn't have come here. She'd been through enough.

Her troubled gaze flicked to the side, landing on the front windows of the duplex connected to hers. There was an older woman lingering in there, observing the proceedings. Wyatt had seen the blinds shift when Leah marched across the street.

Mrs. Burke had clearly noticed the woman, too, and maybe she didn't like her because she tensed up. Or rather, tensed up more.

After a moment of indecision, she shoved her phone at him. "Take a picture of your ID."

Wyatt complied, guessing where she was headed.

She examined the picture, deemed it satisfactory, and scowled again. "If I let you in—"

He put up his hands and smiled. "No funny business. Hands where you can see them. Swear on my mom."

"Alright, settle down. Don't make me regret this."

She scaled her stairs, opened the door and held it wide, then pointed him to a family room off to the left when he entered.

Wyatt stepped over a couple of toys on the rug and parked his butt on an armchair next to the couch.

"You want something to drink?" she asked. "I was just having coffee."

"No, I'm fine. Thank you."

Leah hesitated, but eventually went to fetch her mug before sitting at the farthest end of the couch. She stared at him suspiciously for a long moment, then broke the silence like she was preparing to conduct an interview.

Or perhaps an interrogation. He had to admit, he liked her determination.

"Okay, let's…let's just start over," she said. "You said you met Jesse, and that the rest of his unit was there. Did you…did you talk to anyone else? Or just him?"

Wyatt thought back. "Uh…there was also a guy called Tank. He didn't stick around, though—he was mostly hanging with some other dudes."

Leah startled, then tried to cover by shifting restlessly and putting her mug down on the coffee table. She reconsidered quickly, picking it up again and taking a long sip.

"You knew Tank?" he guessed.

"Yeah. He was my…" She choked a little, blowing out a short breath. "…my brother."

Wyatt couldn't help it—he glanced at the old-school gold star banner hanging in the front window. One banner, two stars, two devastating losses.

His heart ached for her. "Ah, damn. I'm so sorry."

Leah eyed the banner, muttering, "They would've made fun of me for hanging it. I guess that's why I did it. It's kind of like getting the last laugh. Screw them, right?"

Wyatt held still, not sure how to take that.

She flushed a little and peeked at him. "Sorry. Theo always used to say that when people got on my nerves. *Screw them.* All the time, no matter what anyone did. He just didn't care."

"Theo?" Wyatt prompted.

"Sorry, my brother. Tank. He was a hothead and an ass, but he was still my big brother, you know? Protective. He hated that…" She stopped and shook her head, cutting off whatever she'd been about to say. "Anyway, my son Teddy is named after him and our grandpa."

"I'm sorry for your loss." Wyatt looked at his shoes, giving her what privacy he could.

She waved away his condolences, along with her brief flash of emotion. "Tell me about meeting Jesse."

"Uh…four of us were there on a short R&R between deployments." Wyatt paused to check Leah's face, but the spare explanation seemed to suffice. "Two of my buddies decided to turn in early when they saw all the grunts in the place. I didn't blame them—it was a recipe for trouble, and we were hoping to keep it chill. But my best friend and I stayed anyway, and had a couple beers. At some point, he left to scout out the food situation. Maybe he met someone. I don't know. I didn't see him until I went back to our room later that night."

Wyatt shook himself out of his memories and refocused on Leah. "Jesse was next to me at the bar. He introduced himself and Tank. Maybe some others. But Tank left pretty quickly, as I said."

Leah's gaze was distant. "They didn't get along."

"That's hard," he said.

She gave him the barest nod, like she could see right through him. Wyatt had no idea what he was talking about—had zero experience navigating siblings and spouses. It didn't seem fun, though it *was* interesting.

Who'd been the problem, he wondered? Jesse, or Tank?

Leah waited a minute for Wyatt to say more, then sighed impatiently. "Mr. Oaks, I'm sorry to be short but I have other things to accomplish this morning and a short window of time before I have to go pick up my son, get him some lunch, and hope his good mood lasts long enough for me to buy groceries before his afternoon nap. If you have something more to say to me, please get it over with."

There it was again. Why was he so enamored of her officiousness? It made no sense. He should have been put off, but instead he was…intrigued.

"The truth is…" He stopped, glanced at his watch and calculated how long he had before Leah needed to get in her car and make the drive to her kid's preschool, then tried again. "The truth is, I didn't know your husband well. We only talked that one night, and the next time I heard about him…"

"He was dead."

Was she so matter of fact because she was trying not to cry? Or was it something else? Something was happening here that Wyatt did not understand.

He said, "Yeah," and strangely, his explanation seemed to relax her a little. Some of the tension dropped from Leah's shoulders as she drained her mug and leaned forward to set it carefully on a coaster.

"You said you were part of the fighting," she prompted. "In Qahat."

"Some of us, yes. My team was tasked with evacuating high-profile U.S. nationals who were on the scene."

Leah frowned at him until, all at once, understanding dawned on her face. "Oh, Christ. You're one of those SEALs, aren't you? The ones that senator from Texas is so hot to trot about."

Wyatt nodded. All his fantasizing about what he would say to this woman had long since evaporated, leaving him a half-mute, stammering knucklehead. Where was he even going with this? Why was he here?

Leah had been pretty from afar, but God, she was even more beautiful up close, and sharp as a blade, to boot. He'd lost the plot, big time.

"Mr. Oaks…no offense, but why are you here? Because if it's just to try and score with the lonely widow, you need to leave. I do not have time for this."

"It's not that," he said in a rush. "I live nearby. And with you and Teddy on your own, I thought…"

"What did you think?" she demanded in frustration.

"I thought I could lend a hand. Mow your lawn or change your oil or whatever. Whatever you need help with."

"I was an Army wife for years. I take care of that stuff just fine on my own."

"All of it?"

Her eyes were fierce. "Yes."

"Okay, but you said yourself that you're busy. It couldn't hurt to have an extra set of hands here and there. I have time. I'm happy to pitch in."

Mrs. Burke examined him coldly, not buying what he was admittedly so bad at selling. "Did Jesse put you up to this?"

"No. Of course not. Like I said, we barely knew each other. He probably had ten other dudes in that bar alone he would've asked before me."

Leah frowned in disbelief, weighing his words and fiddling with the trim on the arm of the sofa.

He'd watched her for weeks, wavering about whether to approach. Her presence now shouldn't be sending shivers along his limbs, like she was giving off a low-grade electric charge.

Shouldn't, but was. God, he felt like a ghoul.

"Truly," he told her. "We got to talking and hung out for a few hours, give or take. He bragged about you and your son a lot—showed me photos, even. He was very proud of you guys."

"Yeah, he sure was," she said bitterly.

Wyatt blinked. Call him crazy, but he was beginning to think the Burke marriage hadn't been all sunshine and roses, and he didn't know how he felt about that.

He felt something, though. Something…sticky.

"When I heard he didn't make it, I don't know why, but I couldn't stop wondering about you and your boy. I just…I felt like I had to check on you. Make sure you guys were tight up here. And if you've got it handled, then so be it. But if this is pride, and you don't…I wish you'd let me help."

Leah chewed on her lip and studied him. At length, she seemed to come to a decision. "Alright, you know what? You want to help us? Fine. Come back Saturday at 4. The lawnmower's not working, and I can't figure out why. If you can fix it, I'll make you dinner."

Wyatt did his best to mask the relief that swamped him. "You got a deal."

Chapter Two

Leah

LEAH STOOD IN her yard and stared at the stop sign at the end of the block where moments ago, Wyatt Oaks had turned and driven away.

The olive-green muscle car he sometimes used had been missing today. Instead, he'd arrived in a random, forgettable sedan, as if that and a baseball hat would be enough to conceal him from her.

She shook her head, not sure whether to be insulted that he thought she had no situational awareness, or amused at how little effort he'd made to hide while he scoped her out. He'd shown up, what? Ten times, now?

He was a SEAL. He'd made next to no effort.

He'd *wanted* her to see him, and she had. Every time.

Even now that they'd spoken and he'd left, it didn't quite feel like he was truly gone. It felt as if she could still see his sparkling green eyes and mischievous smirk hanging in the air, like a less-sinister Cheshire cat grin.

She could feel him, shimmering just out of reach.

Which, really, was straight-up foolishness. Leah didn't know him at all, and she had to get a grip.

As she turned toward her steps, she casually scanned the yard and house, not letting her eyes land on anything in particular. Even so, she was able to pinpoint what she was truly looking for—her landlord was gone from her front window.

That was good. Biddy had always been nosy about their comings and goings, and lately hadn't proved to be terribly sympathetic about Leah and Teddy's new circumstances.

She had a feeling that the less the woman knew about Wyatt, the better. Odds were good she'd noticed him hanging around, though, and wouldn't be too keen on many more visits.

That was a problem for another day, however.

With one last glance down the street, she ducked inside and turned her attention to getting her day back on track. As it stood, she had just enough time to still make it to the pharmacy and hardware store before picking up Teddy.

As she gathered her things, she stopped near her laptop and considered bringing it, in case she had a few minutes before the preschool let out to get some work done in her car.

She decided against it, though. Her morning was already running behind—no need to make it more hectic by cramming in extra tasks. Once Teddy went down for his nap, she could get on top of the claims she needed to process for the day, and if she was still behind after that, there was always the evening to get caught up.

Leah left their breakfast dishes in the sink, set the alarm, and headed out.

At the pharmacy, Teddy's allergy medicine was on sale, and so was his sunscreen. *Done.*

The hardware store was another matter. She forgot her list at home, so she ended up wandering the aisles, getting distracted while she tried to remember what she'd come for.

Her thoughts kept straying to Wyatt's visit. In retrospect, she felt a little guilty that her effort to be assertive might've come off as mean, but she hadn't been lying when she'd told him there'd been others.

There had been. At least three that she could recall, guys from the unit who'd flirted relentlessly with her before Jesse's death, and who'd made a habit of showing up at her door whenever her husband was away, under the flimsy guise of camaraderie.

She'd had their number, eventually. It'd taken her longer than it should have to discover how Jesse boasted about her to his buddies, cultivating a certain zoo-like interest in his wife because he enjoyed the attention. And it'd hurt when she'd first realized what was going on—that his friends hadn't been trying to help her because they were, in a sense, all a big family.

No, they'd heard her husband's tall tales and wanted a piece of the action.

There'd been some who'd taken it too far, and since Jesse wouldn't knock it off, it'd been up to Leah to make sure his friends got the message that she wasn't interested in extracurriculars.

Friendly rebuffs hadn't gotten her anywhere, but staying aloof had. Except maintaining a reserved façade had eventually turned into a box she had trouble breaking out of.

Some guys, of course, had been easier to dissuade than others. Few had ever crossed any outright lines, but the accord often felt precarious, and the men kept showing up—especially now that she was technically single again.

They didn't know her—didn't care who she was as a person at all. She couldn't be sure what her husband had told them about her, but she could guess. And there were days when she wanted to kill Jesse all over again for putting her in this position.

Wyatt, though…he was different. Leah couldn't put her finger on why. Sure, it was possible he'd come to ogle Jesse's 'beautiful bride' like all the others, maybe shoot his shot—but it hadn't felt that way. He'd seemed…gentle. Respectful. Earnest, even.

Even when he admitted to seeing her picture back in Dubai, he hadn't made it about her looks at all. And when she'd called him out for all of his skulking, he'd been sheepish, not defensive. Like it hadn't even occurred to him how that might scare her.

Coming from a man of his size and obvious strength, that had to mean something.

Leah thought about his long legs, tucked carefully close to his chair but still eating up so much space. His massive sneakers—laces casually untied like he'd shoved his feet into them and run right out—his broad shoulders and brawny arms, forearms deeply tanned where they'd rested on his thighs.

Wyatt wasn't overly bulky, but he was clearly capable of doing some damage. And yet, Leah had felt safe with him. God only knew why—all those special ops guys were a little scary, and she'd heard tales of what SEALs were capable of. Jesse had spoken about them like they were universally cocky, arrogant reprobates, and if it took one to know one, then he ought to know.

Mr. Oaks, not so much. At least, not in her house.

He wasn't just any SEAL, though, was he? Wyatt was part of the team that'd been splashed across the nightly news for months, then booted from the Navy for fumbling their mission in the same hot zone that had killed both her husband and her brother.

Leah was still a little bitter, though not terribly surprised, that the media coverage had focused on the few men who'd emerged from that skirmish relatively unscathed, instead of on Echo Company, who'd done more than anyone to try to save the people in that Qahati village. It was the Army that had made up the majority of the casualties that day.

Not the fancy documentary crew, not the senator and his entourage.

Not even those supposedly formidable SEALs.

Now that Leah had met Wyatt, however, she wondered how accurate that reporting had been. He didn't seem like the type to let ego get in the way of duty. From what she'd seen, it'd been the senator who'd acted like the world revolved around him—superior, egotistical, and condescending.

It didn't make any sense.

Even so, she probably should've sent Wyatt on his way like all the others, and kept him far away from Teddy. It remained a bit of a mystery why she hadn't.

Stopping in the middle of yet another long aisle of bolts and brackets, Leah spun in a bewildered circle and looked down at the little plant that had made its way into her hands at some point. She was going to have to pay for it, then return on a different day with her list. Without it, she had zero clue what she was supposed to be looking for.

On her way to her car, she conceded that if Wyatt was so bent on helping her, then the lawnmower was the perfect thing to task him with. She'd read the manual from cover to cover, watched countless DIY videos, and had taken three cracks at fixing the freaking thing already. She'd run out of things to replace, refill, or readjust.

If she let it go much longer, Biddy was going to get on her case about the grass, and no one—but especially her—had time for that. She was done.

Saturday at 4 it was, then.

Maybe that made her nuts. Who knew. Her brother had used to tease her when they were young, saying she was too trusting of people. Leah hadn't seen the harm until she and Jesse had been married for a while, and she'd come to understand exactly who she'd tied herself to.

The blow had been deep, and now…now Leah didn't know what to think anymore. She *pretended* to know, but she didn't feel sure about anything.

Sure, she told everyone she had things handled, but that was a lie. Some days, it felt like a scream was building inside her, one so big if she let it out it might never end.

It was so much harder doing things on her own when she knew no one was eventually coming home to spot her. For all his faults, Jesse had been a good dad. But he wasn't ever coming back.

Not in a week, or a month, or even six months. There was no respite coming for Leah, and the weight of that knowledge was beginning to crush her.

She was barely thirty. A mom and a widow already. She'd managed to hold things together so far, but the structure felt unstable—as if one thing tilting askew would send the whole 'edifice crashing down.

She'd been careful, so careful to avoid that. Teddy's well-being came first, and that was that.

Except, as she'd sat across from Mr. Wyatt Oaks, secretly admiring his forearms while he begged her to let him be of assistance, a rogue thought had sidled into her brain and refused to be dislodged.

Would she ever go on a date again? Or kiss someone? Was that an impossibility or…not?

Leah looked to the little plant she'd dropped in her cupholder for safekeeping, but it held no answers for her. *Imagine that.*

As she drove toward Teddy's preschool, she checked the time. Wonder of wonders, she was still a little ahead of schedule, despite her aimless meandering—ahead enough, in fact, that she could probably squeeze in time for a little treat.

Thanks to their new budget, treats were normally restricted to weekends, paydays, and particularly awful PMSing days. Today was none of those things, but she still pulled into the bakery a few doors down from Teddy's school, locked her car, and went inside.

Wyatt's visit that morning had thrown her off in a big way. The system was breaking down all over the place and if she was going to be expected to soldier on, Leah needed more coffee and a dose of the woman who ran this place.

Liz was the owner, and a force of nature, officiously upbeat as she served customers and bustled around behind the counter. The woman unapologetically took up space—amply plump, with a cloud of shoulder-length black curls, warm terracotta skin, and dancing brown eyes.

Her customers adored the way she doled out quick pep talks with her throaty laugh, along with her mouth-watering pastries and bracing coffees. Leah could hardly qualify as a regular, but she admired the way the woman moved with economy and grace, exuding confidence, claiming her beauty with gorgeous makeup and impeccable outfits under her retro aprons. She was charismatic, impossible to look away from.

Liz held court behind that gleaming counter like a queen, and her welcoming optimism gave Leah hope for humanity, and hope for herself. If Liz could do it, day after day, surely Leah could too.

If only she didn't get tongue-tied when faced with the proprietor's magnetism. How could she toss off a quip with the same breezy attitude as Liz, when lately she was never sure if it was going to come out a bit too real?

Somehow, "He's dead, but he was a bastard anyway," wasn't quite the opener she was hoping for.

As it happened, Liz made it easy for her today. Of course she did.

When Leah reached the front of the line, the owner extraordinaire sparkled slyly at her and said, "Well hello, Ms. Leah. It's looking like a chocolate croissant and cinnamon latte kind of day."

"Is it that obvious?"

"Your hair's down and you found your mascara. Lip gloss, too. I think we saw someone we liked today, didn't we?"

Leah had to laugh. The woman didn't miss a trick. "Wow, you're good."

"Got that right," Liz clucked.

She checked behind her, but there was no one in earshot, so she leaned closer. "I had a male visitor earlier," she confided with a happy shrug. It felt good to let the secret out and suddenly, Liz felt like the perfect recipient. Who else was she going to tell?

"Judging by that blush of yours, I'm gonna go out on a limb and guess he was a cute one." The baker spun to the side to grab

Leah's croissant from the case, and called out her coffee order to one of the baristas.

She rang her up at the register, and Leah handed over her cash.

"Humor me," Liz said as she sorted through the change drawer. "Exactly how cute was he?"

Leah thought back to Wyatt's eyes, bright green against his tan and so perfect paired with his sandy brown hair. She bit her lip and smiled.

"*Really* cute."

"As cute as your little mini-me?"

Leah warmed with the knowledge that Liz remembered Teddy, too, like maybe they were more connected to the community all around them than she sometimes felt.

"Different kind of cute," she smiled.

"Good for you. Get that hottie." Liz accepted a to-go cup from her barista and handed it over. "And here you go. Have a spectacular day, one baddie to another."

LATER, WHEN TEDDY was cleaned up and fed and sacked out in his bed like a little angel, Leah posted up on the couch with her laptop and *intended* to start working.

Instead, she called up her browser and began searching the internet, diving deep into a rabbit hole of articles about the team of SEALs Wyatt had been a part of. She'd known the general outline of what happened during the skirmish in Nabarut because of Jesse and Theo. However, she hadn't quite put together the context of it all, or the details of the other participants.

The girls' school, the famed beauty of the village women, the documentary that—according to a defunct blog called *Global Lens*—had turned into something very different…it all seemed like an odd place for a Texas senator to show up glad-handing, even if he had been trying to run for president.

Familiar resentment reared its head, along with confusion. Why had the senator and his stupid toadies merited an elite team of special operatives to escort them to safety, when there'd been no backup available to shore up Echo Company?

Jesse and Theo's unit had gone in to protect that village from some trigger-happy warlord, not to preen in front of cameras. If anyone had deserved help, surely it'd been them.

Leah reminded herself that none of that was Wyatt's fault, though. He didn't get to pick and choose his missions any more than the infantry did. And he *had* said he'd looked for Jesse amidst the fighting.

Hell, for all she knew, that was part of the reason his extraction plan had gone awry.

She shook her head, exasperated with herself. Instead of following vague trails all over the web, she needed to get her butt in gear and get to work.

If the insurance claims didn't get processed, she didn't get paid, and not getting paid meant not keeping a roof over Teddy's head or food in his mouth. Not to mention, she was damn lucky to have a job that let her work from home most of the time so she could save on childcare.

Saturday, if she got the chance, she would just ask Wyatt his side of the story. She could make a decision about whether to see him again once she'd heard his answer.

Chapter Three

Wyatt

WYATT SPENT THE morning inventorying gear at one of Black Watch's hidden command centers, in an unremarkable warehouse tucked into a nothing-special industrial park on the fringes of San Diego—presumably banished because he'd been tagged as too 'antsy' to sit at one of Noah's precious computers any longer, safely looking up stuff on the internet.

It was ridiculous. He'd told Leah he would be at her house at 4, and he did not intend to be even a second late. There were things he had to pick up before then, and stuff he wanted to do to prepare. Did he really need to be counting tactical vests and med kits for hours on end?

Not to mention the fact that Noah and Joe appeared perfectly content to live off gallons of coffee while the kid's fingers flew across his keyboard at lightning speed, and Joe's performed a sorry hunt-and-peck routine on his. Wyatt had long since burned off the breakfast he'd eaten hours earlier, and was seriously due for a refueling.

Fortunately, they eventually got tired of his pacing and complaining, and agreed to relocate to the apartment. Wyatt immediately hit the kitchen, throwing together a sandwich from last night's leftovers, while Noah headed back to Bennett's old room. He'd moved in weeks ago, but was still in the process of unpacking.

Joe, on the other hand, seemed content to keep working. Upon arrival, he'd parked himself at the kitchen table, pulled out his laptop, and doggedly kept at it with the browser Olympics.

Wyatt had to admit, he *was* a bit curious about what Bruiser was on the trail of, so on his way to the couch he stopped to peer over Joe's shoulder.

The screen's display was unexpected, to say the least. "Bible study?" he chuckled. "Finally decided to get right with Jesus?"

Joe grunted. "What makes you think I'm not already right with him?"

"Let's call it a hunch."

"Rude."

Wyatt jerked his chin at the laptop. "What, then? You're looking for a church girl?"

"At Pendleton. Really." His tone was dry as the Sahara.

He gave it a minute, but when no further explanation seemed to be forthcoming, Wyatt settled into the chair next to Bruiser's and leaned in closer to examine his buddy's screen.

"So…we're investigating bible study groups at the Marine base…why?"

Joe backed out of the page he'd been perusing and clicked on the next link in the list. "You know those chicks Noah found on Kim's hard drive? The ones she thought Dan Cox was fooling around with?"

The senator's stepson had clearly not understood the gem of a woman he'd landed when he'd begun dating Kim. He'd started screwing around on her within months, and she'd kicked him to the curb shortly after. She'd landed on her feet, though—she and Bennett were as happy together as steak and potatoes.

"Yeah?" Wyatt said slowly.

"Well, Noah thinks the sidepieces might all have something in common."

He looked between his buddy and that laptop, blinking in disbelief. "A love of the Lord?"

"Right?" Joe chuckled. "Go figure."

He shook his head. "You're saying that Cox is literally a bad enough date that he's been driving his exes to repent?"

At this, Noah bustled out of his room with a few collapsed boxes, which he set next to the front door, presumably to recycle later. "In theory," he said.

"Dude, Cox literally drugged and kidnapped Kim, and held her hostage. How much more of a red flag do you need him to wave?" Joe huffed.

Wyatt ignored the jab, eyeing Noah instead. Noah, in turn, came over to study the paragraph highlighted on Joe's laptop.

"But in practice…" Wyatt nudged him.

Noah frowned and told Joe, "Keep looking. I feel like we'll know it when we see it."

Bruiser sat back and crossed his arms across his chest. "Right, but what are they even gonna put on the website? I wouldn't be advertising that shit, I gotta tell ya."

Wyatt cleared his throat, certain he'd missed some crucial element of this conversation. "In practice…?" he repeated louder.

Noah blinked and turned to him, pushing up his glasses thoughtfully. "In practice, I think it's all connected. Dan's supposed hookups, the missing Nabaruti girls, and the Pendleton bible study group."

Wyatt reared back in shock. "You…we…" he shook his head, trying to clear his thoughts. "We've been looking at trafficking, I thought. Are you saying this was some kind of missionary thing? Kidnap and convert? Use the girlfriends to find their victims?"

Noah smiled. "No, nothing like that. Just wait. The other guys will be here in a few, and then I'll explain everything."

Joe grunted again, but this time it sounded different. "Look at this," he barked suddenly.

Noah peered at his display, a slow smile growing on his lips. "*Cavalry Coalition*. Ten bucks says that's the one."

BUCK AND BENNETT arrived a while later, already deep in conversation. By then, Noah had gone back to unpacking and Joe had moved from the table to doze off in front of the muted TV.

Wyatt sprung up from the couch when they breached the threshold and darted forward, hoping to get his own business out of the way before everyone started talking at once. Noah's conspiracy theory du jour was all fine and well, but he had pre-existing plans. *Important* plans.

And time was running short.

"Finally." He grabbed his keys and bee-lined for Bennett. "Hey, do you need your truck later? I wondered if we could trade rides this afternoon. I promised a friend I'd help them out."

Easy didn't hesitate. He simply pulled his keys from his pocket and handed them off. Which, come to think of it, said a lot about their friendship, didn't it? Dude loved his truck like it was his child.

"Clean it up when you're done," Bennett smiled, taking a sandwich section neatly from Wyatt's fingers and biting into it as he wandered toward Joe.

Bruiser, always a light sleeper, was asleep no longer. "Friend? What friend are you making promises to?" Joe glanced around the room, then eyed Wyatt darkly. "We're your friends. Here in this room."

Everybody in the place went still, until Noah darted up, blinking at Wyatt and snapping his fingers like he'd suddenly remembered this very thing. "Your friend from high school, right? The one with the, uh, the bed he needed to move?"

Wyatt turned to the guy and smirked. The cover wasn't perfect, but that wasn't the point. The dude had tried.

Buck only rolled his eyes, however. "Nice try, brother, but I think we're all clued in on who this friend is. About 5'9, long dark hair, killer body…and quite female. Sound familiar, Stitch?"

Wyatt drilled him in the chest with a finger, probably a little harder than strictly necessary. "How do you know all that."

"Listen, you used *my* truck for a drive-by last week. She's gonna start to recognize our rides, man."

"I'm not doing another drive-by," Wyatt protested hotly. When everyone laughed, he realized what he'd given away. "Anyway, I don't need to anymore. I met her. We talked."

Eyebrows shot up in every direction.

"Say what now?" Bennett finally drawled.

"Leah and I talked. Tuesday morning," Wyatt admitted. "I'm going over to help her with some yard work soon." He hadn't felt weird about it, only excited, until the moment those words left his mouth and the men around him let out a collective groan.

"Oh, so she's Leah, now," Buck said archly.

Joe pushed slowly to his feet. "Just to be clear," he said, his tone flat and face wiped of expression, "We are talking about Leah Burke, widow of Jesse Burke, the Echo Company infantry soldier killed in action in Nabarut. Mother of that man's child. *That* Leah?"

Wyatt swallowed at the look of betrayal on his best friend's face. He hadn't told Joe. He had never, not once in all the years they'd been teammates and brothers, from the first day of BUD/S to this moment right here, kept something like this from Joe Doherty.

He couldn't say why he'd done it, only that Leah felt different—like a secret meant only for him.

"Thought we were going to be leaving that shit alone?" Bennett inquired carefully.

"Apparently not," Buck fired back, never taking his icy blue eyes from Wyatt. "How much yardwork needs doing?"

Wyatt knew he'd fucked up. The guys should've been roped in on his intentions from the start. He felt small. Abashed. This was new.

"Not a ton. She said her lawnmower's broken, so I told her I'd take a look. Figured while I was there, I could lay a little mulch or whatever."

They looked him over, waiting for the rest.

"Listen, I didn't…I didn't plan to talk to her. It was just supposed to be like the other times, but she spotted me and came over to chew me out. She thought I was fucking stalking them—"

"You *were* fucking stalking them, numb nuts," Joe pointed out hotly.

Wyatt sighed and rolled his eyes. If Bruiser was moving on to tossing out creative insults, it was a fairly reliable sign his ire at being left out was beginning to fade.

"She didn't need to be worried I was some perv." He stopped and looked around the room. "I had to explain what was up. And dude, I didn't know her brother was KIA in Qahat, too. It would've been a dick move to not offer to help her out."

"Couldn't have planned it better if he'd tried," Bennett told Noah.

"Who's her brother?" Buck demanded, zeroing in on that little detail, as he often did. "Did you get a name?"

"Theo. Went by Tank. I actually met the guy in Dubai. Just for a minute, though. Sounds like he and the husband didn't get along."

Noah squinted at him. A second later, he pulled Joe's laptop closer and began typing rapidly. "Theo, Tank…who are you?" he murmured to himself. "Why do I know that name."

Buck took Wyatt's arm and led him aside, putting his body between Wyatt and the others. "Not like you to run solo missions on the side," he scolded quietly.

"I know. And I'm sorry. Like I said, it didn't go as planned."

"Given the way you've been acting, you should've expected something like this to happen."

"True."

"Which tells me you were hoping."

It seemed safer to stay silent on that point.

"I don't suppose there is any chance in hell I can convince you to walk away from this. It's a bad idea. Surely you realize that?"

"You, of all people, should not ask me to do that," Wyatt retorted. Buck was sort-of-not-exactly their superior in the new Black Watch framework, but the man was the last person on earth to be pointing fingers when it came to choosing a bad-idea woman.

He watched Wyatt for a beat or two, but eventually he nodded. "I've got lawn tools in the shed. I'll text Peyton and tell her to expect you."

Wyatt breathed a sigh of relief. "Thanks, man. I appreciate that."

Buck sighed, too, but he just sounded resigned. "I'd ask if you knew what you were doing, but…"

"Improvise. Adapt. Overcome," Wyatt interrupted, tongue firmly in cheek and ready to get on with it.

"…you'll figure it out," his buddy finished. "Or you won't. Either way, we're here."

Chapter Four

Leah

LEAH POSTED TEDDY at the front window to keep watch for Wyatt, assuming that would buy her some time to get the place in order now that her kid was up from his nap. Her plan to do it while he was sleeping had already failed—she'd conked out on the couch two seconds after she sat down earlier, thanks to a restless night of vaguely worrying dreams interspersed with anxiety thought spirals.

Luck was still not on her side it seemed, because Teddy sounded the alarm within minutes.

Damn it. Wyatt was early. *Really* early.

He'd exchanged the boring sedan for a new, expensive-looking pickup truck she was sure she'd seen before. Still no sign of the olive-green muscle car she'd noticed a few times, too, though.

Which vehicle, if any, was really his? Leah couldn't begin to guess, and procrastinating was not going to get this show on the road.

She marched to the door and opened it wide with a sigh, while Teddy nibbled on banana slices and pretended to play with his toy trains near the window. He hadn't expressed much of an opinion when she'd told him about the visit earlier, but he looked cautiously curious now.

"You're early," she called, once Wyatt jumped down from the cab.

"No, I'm not. I'm exactly on time." His tone was offended, but his expression was not. He had a blinding smile on his face.

He looked even cuter in his old t-shirt and gym shorts than he had the other morning in his hoodie and sweats. For some reason, that was incredibly irritating.

Leah felt hot and sweaty, and not a little hangry, after chasing Teddy around the community playground this morning and crashing on the couch for the last hour. And Wyatt's hyper-punctuality meant she hadn't had time to change.

"It's 3:40," she pointed out.

He checked his watch and shrugged. "Okay, so I'm five minutes early. Traffic was light."

"It's never that light. Besides, I told you 4." *Why was she arguing with him? The man was here doing her a favor.*

"If you're not ten minutes early, you're late," he intoned.

Leah tossed up her hands. "You're weird."

Teddy had sidled up at some point, and now he peeked around her hip. "You're weird!" he called, giggling like a goofball as he scampered back to the kitchen.

"Meet Teddy," she smiled, relaxing a little when Wyatt looked delighted. She checked the lock and pulled the front door closed behind her, then gestured to the gate at the side of the house. "Why don't you come out back? I pulled the lawnmower out of the shed for you."

Wyatt strolled to the truck's tailgate and dropped it. "I'll meet you there. I have a few things to unload first."

Leah frowned as she got a look at what he'd brought. "What's all that?"

"Some tools. Parts. Mulch," he listed.

"Mulch?"

His cheeks turned pink, and he shrugged. "It's spring. Time to mulch."

Leah felt a scowl hit her face. Mulching was hot, heavy, filthy work and she despised it—everyone did. "Why would you do all this? You were just supposed to look at my mower. What possessed you to get mulch?"

"Maybe I'm a stickler for landscaping."

"Right."

"Or maybe I'm just a nice guy," he tried.

"Oh, I'm supposed to believe you brought all this stuff out of the goodness of your heart? Please," she huffed.

Even as she said it, Leah knew she sounded rude and irrational.

On the heels of that acknowledgment, she realized she probably should've made herself a snack when she'd put together Teddy's. Some apple juice, at the very minimum, so she wouldn't act like such a jerk.

Wyatt, however, seemed unperturbed by her snippiness. His smile stayed firmly in place as he yanked the things still in the truck bed closer so he could hoist them out.

"It's true, my heart is good," he told her. "But I'd be lying if I said there weren't other mitigating factors at play."

Leah blew out a long breath, because there it was. She'd wondered if it was coming—the come-on, the one-liner, the indecent proposal—and she readied herself to reject him, as she had Jesse's other friends.

As she took in Wyatt's easy posture, undemanding smile, and dancing green eyes, the words died in her throat, though. As stunning as that development was, she was more startled to realize she had no idea what to say instead.

What eventually emerged from her lips was a weak, "Oh."

Leah shook her head. *Geez.* She was really off her game.

Wyatt did not appear to notice that, either. He simply winked and pushed a couple of empty plastic jugs into her hands. "Can you get these for me?"

He grabbed a toolbox and a tank of gas from the truck and jerked his chin at her gate. "Lead the way, ma'am. The sooner I wrangle that mower, the sooner we get to eat."

Leah blinked for a moment or two, then jerked into motion, leading him to the backyard, then over to her mower. He dropped his stuff next to it, curiously scanning their small yard and what he could see of the house. His interest made her antsy.

"So…this is it," she told him, redirecting his focus to the matter at hand, instead of Teddy's toys strewn everywhere. "It started acting weird a few weeks ago, and now it just won't start at all."

"No worries. I'll check it over and see what's what."

"It's not that old. It shouldn't have died already."

Wyatt smiled at her. "Okay."

"Do you even know how to fix a mower?"

"I do, actually."

Leah glanced away in frustration. He probably thought *she* didn't know what she was doing, but both her dad and her brother had made sure she could do basic maintenance around the house, and with Jesse deployed as often as he'd been, she'd had plenty of practice. She wasn't helpless.

Up on the porch, Teddy was standing at the screen door, watching them.

"Do you want to come out?" she asked.

He stepped outside warily. Teddy liked to size up new people for a bit before he let down his guard. He'd gotten that from her.

When he padded over to the top step in bare feet, Leah scooped him up, gave him a twirl, and settled him on her hip. He cuddled close, and her heart squeezed a little. He was getting so big—she didn't hold him like this much anymore.

She kissed his hair and brought him over to their guest.

"Teddy, this is Mr. Wyatt the Weird. He's going to help fix our mower and then eat dinner with us, okay?"

Teddy nodded.

"Hey buddy," Wyatt said, holding his hand up for a high-five.

Leah helped Teddy tap Wyatt's palm, but then Wyatt's gaze drifted to her forearm and his eyes went wide. He grabbed her wrist in a gentle but firm hold.

"Jesus, what the heck happened to you?"

Leah twisted it around to see what he meant. *Oops.* Her skin was covered in red, inflamed scratches, and when Teddy saw them, he immediately turned worried.

"Mommy?"

"Don't worry. I'm okay," she assured him.

The scratches hadn't looked that bad when they'd gotten back from the park. She'd put peroxide on them and moved on, forgetting all about them. In the meantime, she'd probably been itching them and making them angrier without realizing it.

Her son was so protective of her though, even as young as he was. Teddy was going to feel guilty about this. He squirmed in her arms, scrambling to be let down.

Leah set him on the grass, and hoped a little silliness would defuse the situation.

"There was a shark attack at the park," she told Wyatt matter-of-factly.

He looked between her and Teddy, totally buying in. "Seriously?"

"Nooooo!" Teddy giggled, bopping in place. *Victory.*

"You got me," Leah admitted. "It was really a bobcat. At the park. Super ferocious, right Teddy?"

Teddy grinned, shaking his head. "No, it was a bear!"

"A bear!" Wyatt exclaimed, hand over his heart in horror. *Oh, he was good.*

Leah nodded. "You heard him. It was super tall, too. Probably a rabid grizzly."

"Was it armed with sewing needles?" Wyatt took her arm and examined it carefully. His hands were warm and calloused on her skin, large but tender.

Leah tore her eyes away and nibbled her lip.

Teddy was laughing and hopping around the grass in his pudgy bare feet. She should make him put some shoes on, if there were going to be tools lying around out here.

Wyatt tugged on her arm to get her attention, subtly frowning to make his concern clear.

Leah shook her head and said, loud enough that Teddy could hear her over his chant of *lions and tigers and bears, oh my*, "Well, you know how ferocious bears are. They'll use whatever they can get their grubby paws on to attack people. Swords…sewing needles…even dead branches from a rose bush. You really don't want to get on their bad side."

"Ahhhh. I see," Wyatt's expression cleared in understanding. He glanced at her son. "That must've sucked."

She shot him an exasperated glance, which she hoped would translate to '*language*, you big dope', but it wasn't like Teddy was paying attention. She hoped.

Wyatt seemed to recognize that, as well. Fast as lightning, he pulled her arm to his lips and kissed it.

"All better," he murmured.

Leah stumbled back a few steps, flustered. He didn't push his luck, though. Stifling a grin, he crouched next to his toolbox and said, "Now, let's see what we've got here."

She kept one eye on Teddy and one on Wyatt as he methodically checked over the mower.

"I already replaced the spark plugs and topped off the oil and gas," she told him. "I also checked to make sure there was nothing stuck in the blades."

"Great," he said placidly.

"So why are you doing all that over again?"

He cast her a smile over his shoulder. "Just being thorough."

Leah bit back the instinct to defend her maintenance skills. Unlike Jesse, Wyatt probably wasn't trying to belittle her, implying that she couldn't be trusted to take care of a straightforward piece of machinery. He was simply stating facts.

As calm as she could, she asked, "Do you think the gas tank could've gotten flooded?"

"Maybe. I'll be sure to check."

"Okay, well…" She took a step away, and then another. "Let me know when you're done, I guess? Dinner will probably be ready in an hour or so. We eat pretty early so Teddy can get to bed at a decent hour."

Wyatt sat back on his heels and looked thrilled. "Can't wait."

Not sarcastic, just enthusiastic—like he'd been hearing tales of her cooking all over town and was ecstatic to finally get a chance to sample it.

Leah felt a twinge of regret. She ought to have made him something more interesting than steak and potatoes, but come on—was there any meal a guy liked more than that one?

With one last look, she called Teddy over to the porch. "You can stay outside, but only if you sit up here while Mr. Wyatt is working, okay? Some of his tools might be sharp."

"Or weird," Wyatt added with a grin.

Leah bit back a smile of her own. The guy was a natural. Of course he was.

Teddy parked himself on the porch, so she ducked inside to get him his sippy cup and a bowl of goldfish crackers. Holding his snack carefully in his lap, he munched on his crackers and watched Wyatt feed a dipstick into the lawnmower's gas tank, pull it out to examine it, and then rear back with a frown.

Wyatt sniffed it cautiously, and glanced up at them. After a moment or two of thought, he drained the gas tank into one of the containers he'd brought, eyeing the liquid with marked suspicion.

Suddenly, Teddy got up and hustled into the house.

"Is there something wrong with the gas?" she wondered.

"I'm not sure. It smells off, like…" He peeked at the back door, then looked away. "…uh, not gas."

"What do you mean, *not gas?*"

Wyatt squinted at her. "Is it possible something else got in there? Like…apple juice, or something?"

Leah squeezed her eyes shut, let her head fall back, and released a heavy groan. Once she could form coherent words, she gritted out, "My dad keeps telling Teddy he's the man of the house now. I know he means well, but Teddy keeps trying to help me, and he's *four*. He doesn't know what he's doing."

"And you can't exactly get mad at him."

"Nope. Not gonna lie, I'm kind of pissed at Grampa, though. I ought to make him pay for the new mower."

"Nah. I'll bring this one with me and get it fixed up by next weekend," Wyatt told her. "No harm done."

"Still, I need to say something to Teddy. He shouldn't be worrying about stuff like this. He needs to know I've got everything handled, and that he can stay a kid."

Wyatt watched her for a long moment, then got to his feet and wiped his hands on his shorts. "You're a good mom, Leah, and he seems like a great little dude. You guys will figure it out." He sounded so confident, she almost believed him.

In any case, she was grateful for the vote of confidence. "Thanks. You seem like a great guy, too."

WYATT TRIMMED THE shrubs, pruned the lemon tree, and mulched the beds in record time, then mowed the grass with the backup lawnmower he'd brought with him in case he couldn't fix hers.

She wasn't watching him work. She was only checking on his progress to time their dinner right. That was what Leah told herself, anyway.

Once he loaded everything back into the truck—his friend's, she'd learned—he washed up in her guest bathroom and changed into clean clothes.

Then, he ponied up to her dinner table like a kid in a candy store, staring at the plate she set in front of him with avid eyes. As soon as she sat down herself and picked up her fork, he dove in, lavishly complimenting her cooking between hearty, happy bites.

"Oh my god," he breathed eventually. "I'm sorry I'm wolfing this down, but everything's so good."

"I'm glad you like it." Leah and Teddy peeked at each other with little smiles. "I really appreciate you taking care of the…" She tilted her head, trying to take in his machine-like focus on his food. "…yard."

Wyatt wasn't *quite* shoveling roasted potatoes into his mouth like he hadn't eaten in days—his manners still toed the line of politeness—but if she ever fed him again, she was going to have to cook much bigger portions.

The man could *eat*, and clearly loved to.

She watched in amusement as Wyatt picked up a spear of asparagus and tapped it against Teddy's like they were knights knocking swords. Her son giggled for about the hundredth time.

Teddy, she expected, was going to be a relentless fount of Wyatt questions and lore for the next several weeks. The two of them were getting along famously. *Inconvenient, that.*

Leah turned back to the table and scanned it again, unable to shake the sense that she was missing something important. The napkins, the salt and pepper, the…

Wyatt swallowed, cleared his throat, and pulled her from her mental recitation. "So, have you always been a vegetarian?"

She frowned at the non sequitur. "Pardon?"

"I just wondered if it was a religious thing, or a health thing. Or, well, I guess a lot of times it's an animals-are-too-cute thing."

"I'm not—" She broke off and scanned the table again.

In quick succession, Leah took in the steak knives positioned next to her and Wyatt's plates, the bowl of chimichurri sitting in the center of the table…and the glob of chimichurri he had spooned onto the side of his plate and was cheerfully mixing into his potatoes.

The salad was long gone. So was the asparagus.

She leaped out of her chair like she'd been stung. "Oh my god, the steak! I forgot to grill the steak!" Her heart rate kicked into rapid, panicked gear. *Shit. What was wrong with her?*

Wyatt dropped his head and chuckled, then slowly got to his feet with a quick wink at Ted. "Thank god."

"I am so sorry," Leah said in a rush. "I knew I was forgetting something, but I just couldn't figure out what it was."

If there was blame to hand out, she decided, it was kind of his fault. With all the flexing he'd been doing outside, no woman in her right mind would've been thinking clearly.

"Please don't worry about it," he told her. "You had your hands full with this guy. Just save it for dinner during the week."

Leah ignored him and scrambled for the kitchen. "It really needs to be cooked. It's been marinating all day." She gulped down her mortification and forced a smile onto her face.

Wyatt reached her in two long strides and held her in place, then tipped his chin back toward the table, and Teddy. "Stay with him. I'll cook the meat."

"But you've already—"

He gave her a quelling look.

"Okay, fine. The grill is—"

"I saw it," Wyatt smiled. "Don't worry, it'll heat up fast. It's all good, I promise."

She glanced at Teddy, who watched them with wide, interested eyes as he popped a piece of potato into his mouth and chewed slowly. Like he'd stumbled across a soap opera on TV, instead of his usual cartoons.

"I'm so sorry," she said again. "Let me at least pull it out of the fridge for you, and get out the tongs."

Wyatt gave her arm a small squeeze and nodded. "Sure. I'll fire up the grill."

Leah stood rooted as he ducked out the sliding door, fighting off the shiver his touch had elicited. He wasn't acting the least bit irritated. Relieved, perhaps, at the prospect of more food—but not mad.

His compassionate understanding was something new for her. Something…interesting. She peeked at Teddy, and wondered if he'd noticed it, too.

* * *

LATER, AFTER WYATT had scarfed down two bowls of cobbler and cleaned up the kitchen while Leah gave Teddy a bath, she walked him out to his truck.

That was when she realized, for the first time, that Wyatt had spiffed up *all* the yard in the front. Including Biddy's side.

"Oh, wow. You did the neighbor's, too," she commented, trying to keep the alarm from her voice and rendering it strangely flat.

"Yeah, I hope that's okay," he shrugged, eyeing his work. "I thought it would look more uniform. Do you think they'll mind?"

Almost definitely.

"Are you kidding? No way. I'm sure she'll be thrilled," she lied. Biddy was going to have a conniption, and probably accuse her of trying to knock money off the rent.

Wyatt looked unconvinced. "You sure?"

"Absolutely."

He gave her a warm, uncertain smile, and stroked her arm, his fingers lingering at her elbow before he pulled away.

"Okay, well—thanks again. For everything," she told him. She needed him to leave before Biddy stuck her head out and tried to start something with him.

"Thank *you*. I had a great time. I hope we can do it again soon," he said gently.

Then Wyatt slid behind the wheel and pulled away, taking all the sweetness and light he'd brought to her house with him.

Chapter Five

Wyatt

LEAH WAS LYING. When they stood in her driveway and said goodbye, she suddenly got cagey and then she lied to his face.

Wyatt couldn't figure out why it happened and after enjoying dinner so much, he had to admit that it hurt.

As he hit the freeway in Bennett's truck, he reviewed the visit in his head, ticking through step by step. As far as he could tell he hadn't screwed up, and everything seemed to have gone smoothly.

The landscaping was a breeze—no problems there. Even though he'd only ever lived in apartments, he'd worked on lawn crews all through school to earn money. Those guys taught him plenty about how to edge flowerbeds and repair tools, but they'd also taught him Spanish, how to flirt with girls, and how to stay out of trouble when trouble was all around you.

He'd been skinny as a rail back then, but their *esposas* had soon begun supplementing his mom's PB&Js, keeping him properly fed for the backbreaking work. Somehow, they'd all seemed to know about the sorry-ass white kid working with their men, and managed to keep him alive until payday each and every week. Foster *tías*, when he'd had none of his own.

Speaking of which, Leah had also cooked him a mean dinner in exchange for his yard work—particularly once her forgotten steak had joined the chat. She'd been understandably upset about the oversight but nothing too crazy, and she'd more than made up for it with a glorious berry cobbler for dessert. Wyatt's mouth watered as he glanced at the small container on the passenger seat, holding the extra portion she'd sent home with him.

It would have to wait until he got there, though. No way could he juggle a dripping spoon while navigating the I-5 in a borrowed vehicle.

With a reluctant sigh he refocused on the visit, searching for missteps. After dinner, he'd cleaned up the kitchen, and felt confident about how Leah might view his efforts on that front. His mother and the Navy had drilled proper cleaning protocols into him until it was second nature. Wyatt had definitely left that place cleaner than when he'd arrived.

It really wasn't until she'd walked him outside that the good vibes had faded. It wasn't as if Wyatt had tried to kiss her—though he would've liked to. No, Leah had been looking around the yard, checking out his handiwork when her whole demeanor changed, and sincerity hit the skids.

So maybe…the issue had less to do with him and more to do with the neighbor?

He wracked his brain to come up with any mention of who lived over there, but came up blank. He only knew there'd been an old woman in the window the first time he and Leah spoke, and when Leah had noticed her, she'd hustled Wyatt inside despite telling him he wasn't welcome.

She hadn't mentioned her otherwise. That wasn't a lot to go on.

If Leah let him come back—and Wyatt figured she probably had to, given that he'd promised to fix and return her mower—he'd try to find out more about the mysterious neighbor. If there was a problem, maybe he could help.

Until then, he simply wanted to bask in the lingering glow of the last few hours, to draw out the satisfaction he'd felt playing house with a beautiful woman and an extremely cute kid. He could only imagine what the happy hour crowd at Skippers would say.

At some point, he'd acquired a reputation as a player there, though pretending like it was anything other than his own actions that'd saddled him with it was simple cowardice.

Wyatt hadn't made a habit of hanging out with women who were the settling-down type. Odd, given how much he wanted to himself. It was almost as if a specific choice was being made, like he'd been purposely avoiding the one thing he desired most.

Maybe he hadn't been ready. Or maybe he feared a cycle repetition, instead of a cycle destruction. Either way, it was his fault.

Wyatt grunted, the cab of Bennett's truck feeling unfamiliar and surreal as the lane markers on the tarmac streaked past.

Before about the last week or so, he would've avoided dating a single mom or a widow like the plague—and certainly not a woman who was both. Who needed that kind of baggage in their life? He had plenty of his own.

And yet, none of that factored in with Leah and he couldn't say why. Wyatt had no idea why she felt different, or when that fact had filtered into his consciousness.

Surely it hadn't been the first time he'd laid eyes on her photo, back in Dubai—but perhaps one of the times he'd driven by her house, curious about how she was faring? When exactly had curiosity and duty evolved into…whatever this infatuation was?

He changed lanes and swallowed, unease threading through him. He was the party guy, not the family guy. *Right?* After all, a man had died to create the vacancy he'd stepped into tonight, and here he was, thinking he could get cute about it.

It wasn't like he was trying to roleplay his own dad. *No.*

He didn't even know if this was how his dad would've felt about his home life. For all he knew, the guy might've taken Wyatt and his mom for granted and stepped out on them.

But maybe…maybe pride and contentment would've rooted deeper, anchoring Ensign Gregory Oaks in his role as a husband and father?

Wyatt huffed and changed lanes again, skirting a vintage convertible and braking hard so he wouldn't miss his exit.

He would never know what his dad might've felt about life within their little family, because the man had died two months before Wyatt was born. Speculation was, and always had been, pointless.

With his mom now gone, too, there would be no wisdom shared about how to take care of Leah and Teddy, and no glowing memories to share with them one day—not unless Wyatt wanted to hit up the guys he still knew from those old lawn crews, he supposed.

They'd done enough, though. They didn't need him coming around pestering them again, not when they deserved to enjoy their retirements with their own kids and grandkids.

He left the freeway and steered Bennett's truck through the evening streets of San Diego, and made his peace with the reality of his situation. As he had so many other times in his life, he'd be figuring this one out alone.

HE TEXTED LEAH midweek to let her know that her mower was fixed, and she replied gratifyingly quickly with an invitation to dinner the coming Saturday. No convincing required.

It did a lot to dispel his remaining disquiet about how their last get-together had ended, but rather than have her shoulder the burden of feeding him a second time, Wyatt negotiated to bring them takeout this time around.

Getting takeout required adhering to certain rules, however, which he and Joe had developed over several years, and were in the process of explaining to Noah for the third time.

To his credit, the guy was doggedly attempting to absorb the guidelines so he could place their order for tonight's dinner, but the finer points seemed to be eluding him.

"But wait, why can't we just get burgers again?" Noah wondered.

"Because it's Wednesday," Wyatt explained. *Again.*

"And?"

"And we only get food from Asia on Wednesdays," Joe said.

Their newest roommate blinked for a few beats, but still looked mystified. "W…why?"

Joe huffed in irritation, but he launched into another reasonably tight recitation of their schedule. "You know how Stitch loves food, right? That's a given. But what many people don't know is that he doesn't like to get in a rut about it. That's why we started rotating around the world in a regular pattern. We assigned a continent to each day of the week, so when we eat out, we have parameters. It helps curtail arguments over restaurants, and no one gets tired of eating the same thing over and over."

Wyatt nodded. "In the process, we support many small, family-run businesses all around the metro area. Wins all around."

Noah looked from him to Joe, then back again. "What if eating the same thing is comforting? Or what…what if you don't feel like that kind of food that day?"

Joe shrugged. "There's no requirement to participate. Just eat whatever's in the house if you don't like it."

"Or…you could find a recipe from the correct continent that you *did* feel like, and cook that for the group. We should add that to the rules," Wyatt added thoughtfully. "Anyway, it's the perfect system. Plenty of variety within each landmass, and nothing gets overplayed."

"No getting bored," Joe agreed.

"Right. Or bickering over what to get."

Noah was not mollified, of course, not in the least. His scientific brain would not rest until he'd hammered out every last detail. "That's…wait, so you already know what you can bring to Leah's? Does this still apply when you go out with people? Like on dates?"

Wyatt glanced at Bruiser, and leaned in. "Yes," he admitted quietly, "but we keep that part kind of quiet."

Noah looked taken aback. "The dates don't know?"

Wyatt grinned and shrugged. "Nope. Not one has ever figured it out."

The guy blinked slowly. Blinked some more. Pushed up his Clark Kent glasses and stared off into space. At last, he capitulated to the majesty of the plan.

"I'm not gonna lie. I'm kind of impressed," he admitted finally.

"Because it's fucking genius," Joe grumbled.

Noah eyed them in fascination. "So, what's your favorite? Day, I mean?"

Wyatt didn't even have to consult Joe. There was no question. "Thursday."

"Which is?"

"Africa," he told him.

"That covers a lot of cuisines."

"You'd think," Joe nodded, "yet somehow, we always end up with Ghanaian food. Why do you suppose that is, Stitch?"

"Because I enjoy jollof."

"Oh okay, fucknuts. Sure thing," Joe snorted.

Noah peered between them. "What? He doesn't?"

Bruiser shook his head. "No, he does. But Wyatt also enjoys the drive to the restaurant, which takes him past some very interesting scenery. Nice freeway, good-looking strip malls, fascinating blocks of suburban architecture…"

Wyatt stayed mutinously silent, because that was uncalled for.

Joe continued, "Truly lovely townhomes…maybe a MILF or two…"

Oh, no he didn't. He snapped, "Bruiser, so help me God."

"But hey, what do I know?" Joe laughed, annoyingly smug. "The food is badass too."

Noah shook his head and focused on his phone, clearly hoping to forestall an escalation of bickering. "Okay, so if today is Asia day, we can go ahead and order Thai, right? I really want pad see ew from that place next to Ralph's."

"That works," Joe said. "Get me the pad thai with chicken."

Wyatt took a minute to check his own phone, but Leah still hadn't replied to his last text. He sighed. Maybe she was busy with Teddy.

"Do you still want something?" Noah prompted.

"Oh, yeah…let me check the menu again."

Joe groaned. "Dude, come on. We've been going in circles for half an hour. Just pick something for fuck's sake."

"Give me a minute. Geez."

While he made his choices, Noah mused, "So, when you go back to Leah's house this weekend, you'll have to bring something a kid would like, right?"

"We made Saturday Europe on purpose. I can bring pizza," Wyatt told him.

Noah nodded in approval. "Not bad."

"It's foolproof," he agreed. "And I'll have the dinner special with spring rolls, tom kha gai, and the drunken noodles with shrimp. Oh, and get me an order of kanom jeeb, too. And a side salad."

"Done," Noah said, a minute later. "Should be ready in twenty minutes. I'll go pick it up."

Wyatt handed him some cash, punched Joe's shoulder only semi-lightly over the MILF crack, and wandered back to his room to wait. In his wake, Noah and Joe started up again, hashing out the loopholes of eating by continent.

Wyatt stretched out on his bed, tucking his hands behind his head and studying the poster of La Jolla he had pinned to the wall above his TV. He'd grown up not too far away from where the picture was taken, and it was still one of his favorite surf spots.

That hobby was on his mom. She'd grown up outside Bloomfield, North Dakota, with miles of prairie stretching in every direction but she'd loved the beach and the ocean. Though they hadn't had much, she'd raised Wyatt as close to the coast as she could manage, bringing him to the beach and to swimming lessons at community pools as often as fiscally possible. Was it any wonder he'd ended up in the SEALs?

Like a lot of local guys, he'd taken up surfing when he'd gotten older, buying a second-hand board with his first landscaping money. His mom had loved to park herself on the sand and watch him in the waves. She'd been so proud of him.

He missed her. He stared at the photo for a bit, then closed his eyes and let his mind wander for a few minutes, but he couldn't relax.

Sitting up again, he grabbed his phone and checked again for a text from Leah. *Nothing.*

Did she and her son like to hit the sand sometimes? Did it matter?

Why was he so hungry to know everything about this woman, when so many others had failed to capture his interest? He couldn't understand it.

His phone dinged and he snatched it up again. One thumbs-up, agreeing to his pizza idea. That was it.

Disappointment swamped him.

Wyatt groaned and flopped back on his pillow. He was so freaking screwed.

Chapter Six

Leah

WYATT ARRIVED FOR dinner in the olive-green muscle car she'd seen outside her house a few times before, and Leah realized she must finally be witnessing him driving his own car. It suited him, she decided—fast and sassy and undoubtedly a blast to drive.

Teddy would probably lose his mind if he got to sit in it—and if she was being honest, she probably would, too.

She threw open her door to hear that engine growl, but Wyatt was already parked and strolling to his passenger side with a long, loping gait. As she watched, he retrieved three large pizzas and some stuffed brown bags from his seat.

"I come bearing gifts of cheese," he grinned when he spotted her.

Leah shook her head. "Not that I'm complaining, but how many people do you think you're feeding right now?"

He chuckled lightly and sauntered to the steps. "Well, hello to you, too."

"Hello, Wyatt. You are insane." She moved out of the way so he could squeeze through the door with his Jenga pile of takeout and inhaled deeply as he passed. "Smells good, though."

The man *and* the food.

Wyatt headed for the kitchen, calling over his shoulder, "It's from Carlo's. Best pizza in town. And for the record, better to have too much than too little."

"I'm half Greek, my guy. We have a lock on the whole 'too much food' thing."

He stopped at the counter, eyeing her curiously. "Really? That's cool. What's the other half?"

"American mutt."

"Yeah, same. I can see the Greek in you, though." He set down his load and sidled close to her. "Face like this belongs on a statue."

Wyatt's preposterous green eyes twinkled down at her as she gaped in shock. For someone so wary, she sure hadn't seen that coming. He was too smooth. *No fair.*

Leah pulled herself together, and tried to sound stern. "You tone that down, sir. I know the look of a hound when I see one."

He laughed but he stepped back before she could get uncomfortable, giving her space. "I think there was a compliment buried in there. In fact, I'm sure of it."

"Please. Like you don't know you're pretty." She scowled at his preposterously fake innocence. He'd probably been hearing about his looks for his entire adult life.

"Hello pot, I'm kettle," he fired back. "And for the record, pretty men get tired of being objectified just like pretty women do. You, of all people, ought to know that."

She waved her hand at him, all of him, trying to block out the charm and growling in annoyance when it didn't work. She was supposed to be offended by cheesy come-ons, wasn't she? Where was her trusty outrage?

"All I can say is, you better have a license for all that charisma, Mr. Oaks. It is lethal, and I have a child to think of."

"I sure do," he smirked, beginning to unpack one of the bags. "Keep it in my lockbox with my birth certificate and social security card." Holding her gaze, he lifted a finger and licked a dollop of red sauce from it.

Leah fought a shiver. She could not—would not—become a fool for this man. She'd learned all she needed to know about attractive soldiers and their slick lies from her husband Jesse. She'd sworn off military men when she'd buried him, because she'd known she would not survive a repeat performance with her soul intact.

"Ought to be on a list of controlled substances," she grumbled, pushing aside another bag with a spot of oil bleeding through its side. She was irrationally peeved by her body's reaction to Wyatt's deep rumble of amusement. "Database of biohazards, or something."

"I like to think I use my powers for good, not evil," he told her, reaching for the bag she'd shoved away.

"That's what all the guys say, right up until they crumple under the weight of the slightest bit of temptation. I'm not fooled." Leah felt a little guilty as the barb exited her mouth. Wyatt had been nothing but kind and helpful so far. She shouldn't be profiling him like this.

She shied away from his raised eyebrow and scanned the various containers now arranged across her counter. "Seriously, what *is* all this?"

"Appetizers, salad, sides, and dessert," he listed genially. "And forgive me if I'm overstepping, but I'm getting the distinct impression you haven't known too many nice guys in your life."

"My dad is a great guy," she protested. "My brother was pretty decent, too, once you got past how grumpy and bossy he was."

He waited for her to continue, both eyebrows climbing his forehead as Leah stayed silent. She moved a container of calamari aside so she could crack the lid on what appeared to be tiramisu, and took a little taste.

Wyatt cleared his throat and eyed her pointedly. "I know I shouldn't speak ill of the dead but…"

He paused again, giving her time to shut him down with a rousing defense of her former husband.

Leah found a plastic spork in his pile of napkins and plates and took another bite of the tiramisu. She pointed at it and moaned, "Oh, man. This is so good."

Wyatt snorted. "…but I guess that tells me everything I need to know."

Welp. No use sugar-coating things. It wasn't like he and Jesse had been friends or anything. Which was really nice, come to think of it.

"Imagine how I feel," Leah told him. She studied him over her second bite of dessert, but his motivations remained a mystery. "Speaking of fools…why are you trying to get involved with me? Do you not see that I come with a boatload of baggage here?"

He didn't dispute her brazen assessment. He only shrugged, "Maybe I'm just the fool for you."

Damn it. He was too good at this.

Leah rolled her eyes, but inside her chest, her heart did an ungainly flip. "And now you're quoting songs."

Wyatt smiled and hummed as he freed the last few containers, then neatly folded the paper bags and set them aside. He surveyed the counter, and began rearranging the various boxes into distinct dinner courses.

Leah's surly attempts to keep him at arm's length battled with a sudden, absurd desire to grab him with both hands and hold tight. It made no sense. None at all.

True, Wyatt had been an incredibly nice person thus far. He was thoughtful and capable and eager to please. However, her unwarranted instinct to reject his flirting made her suspect that she was not, in fact, over what Jesse's nonsense had done to her, despite more than a year of therapy.

That would be awful if true, the bitter pill topping off a whole sour gallon of suckiness. Would she ever be free of him?

The tiramisu's espresso turned acrid in her mouth. She didn't deserve this.

Wyatt was the first guy since Jesse had died that she hadn't been immediately repelled by, the first she'd even marginally considered trying to date—and the first she hadn't minded having around Teddy. If she kept up her current hot-and-cold behavior, it would be the same as shooting herself in the foot—the tried-and-true *hurt him before he hurts me* maneuver.

Something was truly wrong with her. And perhaps, something was wrong with him for wanting her.

Finished with his fussing, Wyatt caught her eye with another smile. "So, where's Teddy?"

Teddy. Always the perfect deflection. "He went down late for his nap. I'll go get him now." She pivoted toward the hall, grateful for the excuse to duck out for a minute and regain her wits.

"Leah, wait." Wyatt's hand on her arm was heavy and warm. "I'm sorry. I shouldn't be coming on so strong, and I shouldn't have brought up Jesse."

"No," she sighed, remorse washing over her. "You're completely fine. It's just…this is the first time I've even attempted to jump back in the pool, you know? I'm not trying to be mean or send you mixed messages, but I am obviously out of practice and trying to get my head on straight."

"It's okay. I get it," he soothed. "And look, I'm not going to pretend that I'm not interested in that way, but there have clearly been others and I'm not about to press my case if you're not in that headspace yet. Or ever, frankly. I would like to get to know you better, but only if you understand there's no rush and no expectations. You do what feels right for you, and if you decide you want me to get lost," he hesitated almost imperceptibly, his easy smile growing tight, "Then I'll leave, and you can go on with your life."

She squeezed his hand. "Wyatt, I don't want you to leave."

"I appreciate that. But I also don't want you to feel obligated to put up with me just because I did a little yard work for you. I didn't help because I expected some kind of quid pro quo thing."

"I know that." On impulse, she turned and wrapped her arms around his waist and hugged him quickly. It felt good. When had she last willingly embraced another adult?

"Let me go get Teddy before the food gets cold."

She avoided his eyes as she released him, not yet ready to see what might be written there. At the threshold of the hall her feet froze, and she turned back.

"Wait. Wyatt…I have one more question and then I'll let you off the hook."

"Shoot."

"Did you seriously come all the way up here and forget my mower?" Horror washed over her as she realized how bitchy she sounded.

His laugh was warm, though, and a devilish twinkle lit his eyes once more. "No, Leah, I did not," he said, his crooked grin cooling the flames in her cheeks. "It's in my trunk, I promise. I just need to reattach the handle, and you'll be good to go."

"Good save." Leah took a steadying breath and forced her shoulders to relax. "Beer and wine are in the fridge," she told him as she fled, "And the glasses are in the cabinet over the sink. Help yourself. I'll be right back."

WYATT AND TEDDY spent the meal making each other laugh, but instead of worrying over whether Teddy was getting too attached, or Wyatt was getting them to like him only to turn on them later, Leah forced herself to sit back and simply enjoy herself.

It was good for her son to see that more men than just Grampa could be friendly and not critical. It would be good for him to trust more, and to have that trust reciprocated with gentleness.

She wanted her baby to grow up and see good in the world, to appreciate what a gift it was. Right now, strange as it seemed, Wyatt felt like a gift.

She hadn't known him for long, but Leah could trust him, she decided. It was a risk, but a good one, supported by concrete evidence. If that changed down the line, she would reevaluate then.

She polished off the glass of wine she'd nursed through dinner, and began gathering plates.

Time would tell, she supposed, if Wyatt was really a walking green flag, or if she only *wanted* him to be. It was hard to believe that a man could be so wonderful and still want her around, but here they were.

He certainly wasn't in any hurry to leave tonight, that was for sure. As soon as she'd stood up, Wyatt had helped Teddy from his booster seat and let himself be led to the train table in the family room.

"Hang on," he called, when he noticed her in the kitchen straightening up. "Let me help you."

"No need." She lifted the plates in her hand and grinned. "Paper plates. Nothing to wash." And hadn't *that* been thoughtful of him.

As Wyatt lowered himself to the floor, crossing his long legs and attempting to shoehorn himself into the small area of carpet Teddy had allotted him, Leah winced in sympathy. He didn't seem uncomfortable, though. He simply accepted the toy train Teddy offered him and said, "Oh, this guy is *cool*. What's his name?"

On her return trip to the table, she called, "Hey, what do you want to bring home with you?" There wasn't as much left over as she'd predicted, but still enough to make up another lunch or two, at least.

Wyatt's gaze landed on her and darkened, going on a slow meander up and down her person. Leah narrowed her eyes at him, challenging him to step out of line with a toy in his hand and her son a foot away, until finally he relented with a rueful chuckle.

"Nothing," he told her, "You keep it."

Then she watched in surprise as Teddy ambled over to his little bookcase, selected a few favorites, and pressed them into their guest's hands before snuggling up against his side.

Wyatt's eyes lit with happiness as Teddy showed him which book to read first, and soon his deep, easy tenor began telling the story with far more expression than she often managed.

She shook her head, amazed. He was a natural, and it was possible her kid liked him even more than she did.

Leah reflected that Teddy never seemed to miss Jesse very much, and assumed it was because Jesse had been deployed for big chunks of his life. Now, watching him with Wyatt, she ached at the thought that Teddy might've needed something all this time that she couldn't give him.

It was only once she'd hustled back to the kitchen that something else occurred to her. Maybe the missing piece wasn't a male role model…maybe it was joy. After all, how often had she told her son, *no we can't play now, no it's time for dinner*, or *no we can't read, it's time for bed?*

Maybe Teddy just needed unfettered, unrestricted joy.

Leah choked back the tears that threatened. For everyone's sake, she needed to take this slow, but she was damned if she could figure out how she was going to make that happen.

* * *

AS WYATT PULLED away sometime later, Biddy Daniels emerged from next door, lips pinched, and a dowdy, fawn-colored cardigan clutched across her chest.

"That man again," she commented, coming to a stop on the front lawn next to Leah. "Who is he?"

A flash of movement in the front window caught her eye, and Leah turned to wave at Teddy. His eyes were dark and round, already looking concerned again.

She smiled, hoping he wouldn't pick up on her disquiet. He was so perceptive for such a little guy—too perceptive—and Biddy had never particularly warmed to him.

"He's just a friend," Leah told her evenly.

"A boyfriend, you mean."

"No, just a friend," she countered. "Though I don't see how that's pertinent."

"Seeing as how I rented to your husband with the understanding that you were a god-fearing family, I believe it is." Biddy shook her head and tutted, "Not one year in the ground. What did that poor man do to deserve such disrespect?"

Leah swallowed around the ball of nausea rising up her throat. *Don't say it.* Biddy would only tell her it'd been Jesse's right to treat her as he had.

"It's been eighteen months since my husband passed," she corrected, hoping she sounded civil, "And we miss him every day. But Wyatt knew him in the service, and promised Jesse he would look after us if anything happened to him. He's just trying to honor that commitment."

Biddy eyed her dourly. "Eighteen months? Your man died for his country, for you and his boy up there, and all you can muster is eighteen sorry months?" She shook her head in disgust. "This world. Everything has changed for the worse."

"Mrs. Daniels, was there something you needed?" Leah wondered. "I should get back inside and put Teddy to bed."

"I was right to replace you at church." Biddy continued, examining her critically. "And I would like to remind you that there's a morality clause in your rental contract. Read it. No more men inside the premises. I'm not running a cathouse here."

Leah blinked away the bitter tears she could feel stinging her eyes. The night had gone so well. She had fun. She ought to have known it wouldn't last.

"Neither am I."

"We'll see." Biddy turned on her heel and marched away, her spine ramrod straight and disapproval trailing after her like a plume of car exhaust.

A sound at the front window caught her attention, and Leah turned to see Teddy clutching his little train engine, showing her the book he'd made Wyatt read him at least three times.

He had fun tonight, too, and Leah wasn't going to stop seeing Wyatt just because some old bat told her to. Who did Biddy think she was?

Still, just to be safe, she made a mental note to pull out their lease agreement sometime this week, so she could be sure of what it really said.

Chapter Seven

Wyatt

DEEP IN ONE of Black Watch's nondescript bunkers, Wyatt tried like hell to maintain focus. Buck had called a meeting to brainstorm about the search for the missing Nabaruti girls, but the afterglow of playing house with Leah and her son the night before kept jamming up his synapses.

He couldn't stop thinking about how satisfying it'd been to eat together around their table, to read books with Teddy while Leah bustled around her kitchen, brewing coffee and plating the dessert.

He'd felt a certain caveman satisfaction in being the one to provide food for such a special little family, enough that it made him wonder if perhaps he had some kind of previously unrecognized breadwinner kink or something.

Exploring it would have to wait, unfortunately. The guys arrayed around the war room part of the warehouse were still talking, and he was quite decidedly not listening. Wyatt scrubbed a hand over his face, chugged the rest of his protein drink and zeroed in on the discussion.

"Twelve young women don't just vanish into thin air!" Buck bellowed in seething frustration. He paced an open stretch of floor near them. "Someone, somewhere had eyes on these girls, and I want to know who they are and when it was!"

Right. It seemed they were still rehashing the *Senator Doggett Does a Kidnapping* theme. Wyatt hadn't missed as much as he'd thought.

When they'd arrived earlier, he'd dutifully dropped into his favorite rolling desk chair while the rest of the team had scattered into the other assorted seating of the command center. Noah booted up his computers while they tossed around ideas, attempting to find a new path forward in the stagnating search for the missing girls.

Except he hadn't been able to stop himself from mentally disconnecting when the brainstorming produced a whole bunch of nothing revelatory. Tuning out their voices, Wyatt began daydreaming about Leah and where he wanted to bring her on their next date.

He'd touched her last night, briefly, in passing. Hands and arms. His skin prickled at the memory.

His mouth felt left out. Wyatt wanted to kiss that woman like he wanted to keep breathing. He had to think of somewhere romantic to take her that might encourage her to think along the same lines.

Buck was having trouble standing still, though. And, like every other man there, Wyatt could understand his vexation—those poor girls had been in the wind for far too long, and what they might be enduring didn't bear contemplating.

A wave of guilt washed over him. His inattention was inexcusable. Finding those kids was serious. Life-and-death. Planning out the timeline of his current infatuation—if that's what Leah truly was to him—was not.

Buck's agitated wandering came to a halt in front of the large whiteboard, and he stared at the squeaky-clean expanse for a long moment before gesturing impatiently. "Someone toss me a marker for this thing."

Noah found one on his desk and threw it over, and Buck turned to face them.

The LED lights high overhead made his unusual silver hair almost glow, giving him the appearance of a ferocious avenging angel. Wyatt had seen this expression on him before—they all had.

Buck was officially done with this shit, and some poor chump out in the world was going to feel his wrath, one way or another.

"We're going to walk through this motherfucker step by fucking step, and we are going to find these girls. Got it?" he barked.

Rumbles of assent sounded from around the room, though they'd been trying to do exactly that for over a year now. The delays, and the achingly slow progress, had them all on edge. At every turn, momentum had been stymied by their career and legal troubles.

Black Watch had given them free rein, though, and it was past time to use it.

"First, we have the people visiting Nabarut," Buck said.

Across the center of the board, he wrote the names of Senator Roy Doggett and his wife Lena, Roy's stepson Dan Cox, filmmaker Joely Spitz, and their various staff and crew.

"We have the senator doing his photo op," Buck listed, "his stepson along for the ride but mysteriously not on any guest lists, and the movie crew supposedly filming everything. Why are each of them claiming to be here?"

Noah piped up, "During the presidential primary debates, Doggett's opponent was harassing him about his record regarding education and women's rights. Remember? That was ostensibly why his PR team set up the glad-handing in Nabarut—they needed to counter the allegations with positive optics."

He went on, "Lena was present at all of his campaign events, so it makes sense that she was there. Same for the PR people and other staffers. On the face of things, nothing too fishy there."

"You'd think they could've found a stunt closer to home," Wyatt commented.

Buck nodded. "Exactly. Especially when you consider Roy's stances on the Middle East, and globalism in general."

Wyatt raised his brows at him. *Someone had been talking to his political scientist wife.*

"Okay, so there was obviously something else important about Nabarut, specifically," Joe said, picking up the thread. He looked slightly less haggard than usual this morning, dialed in like he hadn't been for a while now.

Wyatt eyed him. Maybe he'd gotten a good night's sleep for once?

"There sure was," Noah said.

"The girls."

"Correct."

Buck went on, "Now, Dan's reasons were a lot more tenuous. He claimed he was there unofficially supporting his stepfather, but between his position heading up Landry Cox Arms and the alleged backchannel dealing thanks to Roy's position on the Armed Services Committee, his presence there seems suspect. Add in his affair with Joely and it looks even worse."

Wyatt nodded, as did the others. Cox was a shitbird, no debate there. And after the way he'd treated Kim, it was a wonder Bennett hadn't put him in the ground a few months back.

"Ms. Spitz, of course..." At this, Buck paused, and Wyatt winced in sympathy. There'd been a brief dalliance between Buck and Joely in the days before the Nabarut ambush took place, and hopefully before she'd taken up with Cox—and everyone in the room knew how much he still regretted it. Not least because Joely had gone on to make such trouble for Buck's eventual wife Peyton.

"Ms. Spitz," he forced out, "was *supposed* to be filming a documentary about the girls' school opening. Thanks to empty promises of fame and fortune from the Doggett crew, that somehow morphed into a puff piece on Dan and Landry's expansion into the M16 market."

"Lest we forget, while she was accepting Cox's ring, she was also low-key banging his dad Roy," Joe snorted.

Buck looked faintly ill.

"But true love conquers all," Bennett countered with a smirk. "I believe those little jailbirds are still fixin' to wed. So, I guess you missed that boat, buddy."

Buck rolled his eyes, then drew some boxes and prison bars around Dan and Joely's names.

"Anyway," he groaned, "Next arrivals on the scene were al-Kadir and his motley band of fighters, followed by Echo Company trying to reign shit in." He wrote those names on the board beneath the others. "We know for a fact how all the original visitors left the scene, because we were the ones airlifting those fuckers out of there. By the end, most of Echo was in no condition to spirit anyone away, and neither were the villagers. The only people on-site with the ability to move those girls sight unseen were—"

"Kadir's guys," Joe finished, pointing at the board. "And it was probably pretty simple, too. The girls were conveniently gathered together for the opening, so they could've easily picked out the ones they wanted and carried them off."

"They must have had trucks waiting in the Boshad Pass," Noah surmised.

Bennett growled under his breath. "And they already knew which girls to take because Cox had headshots of them weeks before he even landed in Qahat. Where did he even get those pictures, by the way? Did someone take them as prep for the documentary?"

"Good question," Buck agreed. "But it does underline what was really going on here. Under the cover of the senator's photo op, they had a definite prearranged deal taking place. Cox's guns in exchange for the young women. Except, then Kadir's guys got out of hand, shit went sideways, and both we and Echo showed up to restore order."

"So," Noah mused, "When the plan hit the skids, did the girls stay in Qahat, or did they eventually make their way here like they were supposed to?"

Buck studied the board, drawing a couple of arrows and filling in details. "No, they didn't stay there. Doggett and Cox have been acting way too smug for the deal to have fallen apart. I think they got the girls. But where are they holding them?"

Bennett slowly pushed to his feet, scratching his jaw as he walked closer to the whiteboard, too. "These guys…they're old boy network, through and through. Roy, especially, is not going to risk any chance of blowback now that he's lost the primary and is hanging on by a thread in Texas. No, these fellas have connections, and they're gonna stick with the people they know and trust. I say we'll find those ladies in one of three places: Dallas, DC, or LA."

"Why LA?" Noah frowned.

Joe answered before Bennett could. "Because that's where Roy's brother Leon, the movie producer, is. Doggett visits him a lot. Plus, he's the one bankrolling the shell company holding all that real estate."

"They call it Linedance," Noah supplied absently.

Bennett nodded. "Right. And here's another thing. Dan used to ask Kim about her pageants and modeling all the time. I think…I think the girls must have been earmarked for more sophisticated clients. I think they were meant to be escorts for Roy and Dan's cronies. Leon's too, probably."

"Makes sense," Buck agreed. By now they all knew better than to second-guess one of Bennett's hunches—the man had a sixth sense that had saved their collective bacon more times than they could count.

"So, who did the glow-ups?" Noah wondered. "A bunch of village girls who didn't speak much English would've required serious finessing before they could work as arm candy at the level we're guessing."

Buck pointed at him. "Yes. That. Track down any and all females seen in the company of these people. Follow those trails. Get us some names. One of them will know how it's done."

"Hey…what if there are photos?" Bennett wondered. He tilted his head as he examined Buck's flowchart.

"What do you mean?" Buck demanded.

Easy stared at the board. "Well…we know Dan took several women out on the town more than once, right? Kim's hard drive gave us that much. But what if…what if Roy and Leon did, too? And what if some of those women are other victims, promoted to be part of the infrastructure?"

Joe scoffed, "Dude, his wife's money basically funded his political career. Without it, he's nothing. Roy wouldn't be stupid enough to step out on her in public like that."

Buck stared him down.

"Okay, fair. He's dumb as a box of rocks, and I forgot about Joely. But surely Roy's not reckless enough for there to be photos? Witnesses maybe, but photos?"

Noah smiled a troubling, sinister grin. "Leave that to me. If they exist, I will find them."

Lasered in now, Wyatt studied Buck's scribblings, unable to shake the sense they were missing something major. He went closer, his gaze following the various connections, around and around until…

"Wait, wait, wait," he blurted suddenly. "I have a question."

Buck jerked his chin at him, urging him on.

"Who were the girls *really* supposed to leave with?"

The low chatter around him stopped, his closest friends on earth—his brothers—all falling silent as a unit.

"The fighters," Buck said.

"No, seriously. Someone would've noticed if twelve village girls suddenly attached themselves to either the politico group or the movie group. And al-Kadir, for all his chest-thumping, is still just a local asshole. He doesn't have the reach to ship those girls out of the country." Wyatt looked around. "So, who exactly was supposed to get them where they needed to go?"

No one said a word as the old school clock on the wall ticked off the seconds.

"Listen, we're assuming the event in Nabarut was intended to be a quid-pro-quo of guns for girls, right?" Wyatt said. "Dan was presumably there to oversee the transfer of his company's new M16s to al-Kadir, who in turn was expected to perform what service, exactly? Because I don't think anyone with half a brain would've trusted him or his fighters to leave that village with both the guns *and* the girls."

"And as far as anyone knows, he doesn't have the ability to get them out of the country," Noah reiterated.

"Or even the general region of Nabarut," Wyatt agreed. "So, let's say his services rendered weren't meant to be abduction *and* transport, but only to provide cover for the actual abductors. Who were they?"

"Doggett? Or the film crew?" Bennett frowned. His expression said it all—he didn't believe either option was possible.

Wyatt shook his head. "No. Think it through. The Qahati authorities would've been awfully suspicious if either of them tried to leave with twelve more people or significantly more luggage than they'd arrived with. Along those same lines, though, how were the guns brought in? I was thinking they might've tried to disguise them as camera equipment or something, but...no. The documentary production wasn't big enough to obscure the number of crates that would've had to be moved."

Buck drilled him with an intense stare. "So, what are you saying?"

"Don't you guys think it's just a little bit odd that Echo happened to be right where they needed to be when al-Kadir got trigger-happy and all hell broke loose? Isn't that just a tad too convenient?"

Bennett dropped back into his office chair, leaning so far back that it creaked in protest. He glanced at Buck and drawled, "Uhhhh…yes?"

"Have we ever looked into what their actual orders were in the weeks leading up to the ambush?" Buck inquired. "Not what they told us after, or what the media reported. Why was Echo boots on the ground going in two years ago, and who would remember?"

Joe turned to study Wyatt carefully. "Are you saying you think Echo—"

"—was meant to be the middlemen? Yes," Wyatt agreed. "They're the only entity that had the means to deliver the guns, *and* transport the girls out of Qahat."

The room fell into weighty silence, broken only when Bennett muttered darkly, "Well, shit."

When Buck finally spoke up, Wyatt wished he'd never brought it up.

Their de facto leader drilled him with chilling, steely eyes and declared, "Someone—probably several someones—were dirty in Echo Company. We wanted a link to who fucked with us in WARCOM?" He stabbed at the whiteboard angrily. "Well, there it is."

Wyatt stared at his buddy and felt the blood drain from his head.

Echo Company was the former unit of Leah's husband and brother, both of whom sounded like real pieces of work, and neither of whom had survived the conflict. It was also the former home of their new boss, Tate Monroe.

Fuck.

Just then Noah stood, pleased as punch, like he'd been waiting for this exact moment all morning. "And now, let me tell you a little story about an unusual bible study group Joe and I found at Camp Pendleton," he announced. "It's called Cavalry Coalition, and I think it might be the key that unlocks all of this."

Chapter Eight

Leah

AFTER DAYS OF escalating flirting over text, Wyatt did something she should've seen coming and asked her out for a date the coming weekend. While Leah could understand why he might've thought that was a normal progression to whatever was going on between them, it was also a development she'd been hoping to forestall.

It was obvious he didn't grasp the complexities involved in a single mom intending to hit the town, and that was understandable, too. To her knowledge, he was not the parent of a small child, so how would he know?

He slipped in the invitation to dinner and a movie so smoothly, though, that Leah nearly accepted on the spot.

Nearly.

She caught herself just in time, and replied with what she hoped was a polite decline. Then she sat there like a capital-L loser, biting her lip and waiting to see how he took it.

After all, Wyatt had told her during his last visit that if she wanted him to get lost, he would. Turning down a date didn't seem quite the same, but it had to be close—the kind of thing

Jesse would've blown out of proportion for sure. Male egos being what they were, she suspected it would make other guys disappear like they'd never been there.

Wyatt, however, simply doubled down on his invitation, acting perplexed when she didn't fall victim to his charm offensive and coming perilously close to outright begging her.

Leah fiddled with her phone for a few seconds, agonizing about whether to cave and find a way to make it work later, then tossed the whole thing across the couch. Wishing things were different was a pointless waste of time. So was disappointment.

Eventually, Wyatt gave up on texting, and she couldn't say she blamed him for that, either. She probably would've done the same in his position. She was too much work right now, and there were plenty of unencumbered, uncomplicated fish in the sea. With his looks and personality, he probably knew a lot of them.

Except then, her phone began buzzing, insistently from across the couch. Leah stared at Wyatt's name scrolling across the screen for a long, tortured beat before snatching it up and shakily connecting the call.

He was a nice guy—he was not going to berate her. He wasn't going to lecture her or explain why she was lucky he was paying attention to her. Wyatt was not calling to gaslight her, and if he did, she would simply hang up and walk away.

Leah owed him nothing.

Besides, it wasn't like she didn't *want* to go out with him—she did. The problem was that reliable, trustworthy babysitters didn't exactly grow on trees and her kid's well-being was her prime directive, and the sooner Wyatt realized it, the better for all of them.

Leah took a deep breath, straightened her shoulders, and resolved to give him the honest lay of the land. He deserved that much from her, at least.

"Hello?"

"Hey, I had to…" he stopped and laughed nervously. "Are you not joking about Saturday? I can't tell."

She gripped her phone tightly, her heart rate ticking up and her body readying itself for a fight or flight despite her brain insisting there was no threat here.

Apparently old habits died harder than husbands.

Leah bit back the humorless laugh that tried to slip out. "I'm serious, Wyatt. Thank you for asking but I can't go."

"Okay." Then, like he couldn't resist, he tacked on, "Do you have other plans?"

"No. Teddy and I are staying home." She grimaced, hoping the clunky mention of her kid would clue him in.

No such luck. "Oh. So…you don't want to go."

"I didn't say that."

"Leah—" Wyatt took an audible breath and held it for a beat before continuing. "What's going on? Explain it to me like I'm five."

Ugh, that hurt voice. She was screwing this up. Wyatt's blunder hadn't been intentional, and she was doing a terrible job explaining.

She tried again. "Wyatt, I can't go out with you on Saturday, because I can't leave my four-year-old home by himself for hours while I go to dinner, have some wine, see a movie, and then make out in a car with some guy."

"I'm still just some guy, huh?" His tone was dry as dust. "Ouch."

"Focus on the main message please."

"I would like to do that," he told her genially, "but half my neurons shorted out when you mentioned making out in my car."

"Wyatt."

"Right. Teddy. You can't get a babysitter?"

He made it sound so simple. Leah tried to stay calm, but anxiety was blooming in her chest like wildfire. *Goddamn it, Jesse. Look what you've done to me.*

None of this was Wyatt's fault, she reminded herself. He didn't know how this talk usually went or that their whole conversation had her feeling frustrated and antsy, like her inadequacies were the problem and not the inescapable realities of parenthood.

"Come on. Get a babysitter," he laughed, when she didn't answer him. "We need some alone time to discuss these late-night texts of yours in more detail."

Leah's discomfort grew. She wanted to revel in the dark promise in his voice, but she chafed at his cavalier dismissal of her child. "No, I can't," she heard herself argue. "I don't know anyone."

"How is that possible?" he wheedled. "Can't you ask around and find a teenager who needs spending money? They've got to be a dime a dozen."

"*Mr. Oaks,*" she admonished him angrily.

"Yikes. I've heard that tone before."

She rolled her eyes. "Let me guess, from your mom?"

"Among others."

"Awesome, so you do this a lot," she said. "Well, then let me be perfectly clear. You will never, not ever, take priority over my son. Not your wants, not your needs, not anything. You are an adult, and Teddy is a toddler. He comes first for me, always, and under no circumstances will I be leaving him with some random stranger so you can make some moves on me."

"Leah—"

She cut him off, afraid if she didn't, she'd never get the rest out. "So yes, while I am acquainted with several people who would probably watch my kid if I asked, I do not know any of them well enough to be assured of his welfare in their care. I'm a good parent, and I do not intend to compromise my son's safety for your, or my, selfish whims."

Wyatt fell silent, absorbing her scolding.

She waited for him to pressure her, or perhaps blast her with resentment. This was undoubtedly the end of their little flirtation. Men didn't like coming in second. She'd learned that lesson well.

So, it was a bit of a shock when Wyatt finally spoke, sounding epically embarrassed and contrite. "Leah…I'm sorry. That was out of line, and I apologize. Of course, the little guy comes first."

"Teddy. His name is Teddy," she corrected.

"Right. Teddy comes first. Of course he does. I'm sorry I overstepped. I was having a great time with all the texting and got ahead of myself, but I of all people should've realized that you couldn't just drop everything without doing some prep work first."

He cleared his throat, like the apology felt unwieldy, or unfamiliar on his tongue. He didn't seem angry, though, so that was something. Still, what kind of supposed alpha male took defeat so well?

Wait. What had he just said?

"What do you mean, *you of all people?*"

"Raised by a single mom," Wyatt explained. "Once upon a time, I was Teddy."

"Ah." *Fascinating.*

"The fact remains that I think you're great and I'd love to keep getting to know you better." A smile crept into his tone when he tacked on, "Some parts of you more than others, as referenced in my text at 11:46 pm Monday night."

Leah pressed her lips together, refusing to buckle and admit she'd like to get up close and personal with some of his parts, too.

"So, let's figure this out," he went on. "I obviously have the more flexible schedule between us. If you tell me what you're comfortable with and how we can make an adult date work, I'll figure out the operational details. I want to show you a good time, not stress you out or make more work for you."

Leah blinked, trying to process what was happening. Once she realized where he was going with this, she blinked some more, impressed despite herself.

Wyatt wasn't mad and he wasn't accepting defeat—he was relaunching his attack from a different angle. A *better* angle. He sounded sincere and determined, like he actually…believed the words he'd spoken.

But could *she* believe him? What made her think this man was different?

A sudden thought occurred to her. "Is this some kind of weird game for you?" she inquired.

"No," he laughed. "This is me telling you I'm interested, enough that I'm happy to do this at your speed, and on your terms. If you are also interested, like I think you are, tell me how to make it happen."

Leah's gaze jumped around her family room, trying to make sense of his attitude—of this unexpected development. Wyatt was a unicorn. That was the only explanation.

"I'm sorry I was snippy with you," she said. "I just—"

"No backpedaling. I deserved it."

"Listen, I do want to see you, without having to censor everything we say because of Teddy. Please don't think I don't. I just don't know how to balance everything, or how much you will put up with before you get sick of me. I don't want to get invested, only to have it all—"

"I understand. I—"

A sudden wail sounded from Teddy's room. Leah shot to her feet. "Shoot, he just woke up. Now I have to go."

"It's fine. We should work this out in person, anyway. Where do you work? I can come up and meet you for lunch tomorrow."

Leah shook her head, trying to think over the noise her kid was making. "I work from home. I can take a break around 11, but I have to leave to get Teddy by 12:30."

"Done. I'll text you when I'm on my way. And Leah? Don't worry. We'll figure this out."

IT WAS NOON by the time Wyatt roared up to the curb the next day, an hour after they'd planned. He'd texted that there was an accident on the I-5, and wondering if he should still come. Leah was damned if she'd wave him off, though, not when they'd made it this far.

"I'm so sorry," he gasped, throwing open his door and bounding up her front stairs. "I got here as fast as I could."

"It's okay. I'm glad you made it."

"I didn't have time to grab us lunch."

"Are you hungry? I can make you a sandwich if you want."

"No sandwich." Wyatt followed her through the door, kicked it shut with his foot, and kept walking, crowding Leah into the far wall with his big body and a devilish grin.

"What are you doing?" she asked breathlessly. "Didn't your mother teach you not to stand so close to people?"

"I like your perfume," he said matter-of-factly, "It smells very good this close." A small frown marred his forehead as his hand coasted over her arm. "Is this okay?"

Leah hesitated. Her first instinct was annoyance, but as a shiver worked its way down her spine, she wasn't so sure. "Sort of? When you loom over me, it makes me feel…" She faltered, not sure how to put it into words.

'Small' wasn't quite right, not with the connotation he would assume. Unlike Jesse, Wyatt wasn't an intimidator—he was a nurturer, through and through. He wouldn't want her to feel inferior.

"What?" His voice had dropped low, like he wanted her secrets. His heavy hand molded around her hip. "What does it make you feel?"

She stared at the neckline of his faded t-shirt. "Small," she murmured, despite herself.

He stepped back, the indentation between his brows getting deeper.

Leah pulled him close again. "No, not like that. Small, like dainty. Like you could carry me wherever you wanted and not even break a sweat."

The feeling was a new one. At 5'9, she was far from petite, and hefting a solid four-year-old around had made her strong.

Jesse had a lanky build, and had only been a scant inch taller than her—one of the few ways they'd seen eye to eye.

Wyatt rested a forearm on the wall beside her head, crowding her a little more. "And you like it?" he rumbled.

His voice made her chest tight and her heart beat erratically, like it was skipping too fast, too crazy. Breathing seemed to require effort and thought. Leah sank into the sensation of her back against the wall, caged in, where he could *take*.

Where control was something she could relinquish if she wanted to.

She lifted her eyes to meet his heavy gaze. "I do."

Wyatt shifted a centimeter closer. "What else do you like?"

A frantic voice in her head screamed that telling him would give him too much power over her. Abruptly, Leah didn't care.

"Your shoulders. They're so broad. And your arms, the way they pull your sleeves tight. Your long legs, your strong thighs." Leah drifted a shaking finger up the side of his shorts, swallowing with effort. "I like your whole build. And your voice. And the way your eyes crinkle at the corners when you smile."

He bit his lip, smiling exactly the way she liked. "That's quite a list," he teased. "All physical. Are you objectifying me, Ms. Burke?"

"There are other things," Leah insisted. "Those just happen to be the ones staring me in the face right now."

"Hmm." It rumbled through his chest, and she felt it in her bones.

"That noise, too." She ran her hands up Wyatt's chest and rested them on his shoulders, brushing his neck with her thumbs and staring at the divot at the base of his throat. "That little sound makes me think filthy thoughts, Mr. Oaks."

Where was all this bravery coming from? Being alone with this man was clearly dangerous. She should be more careful.

His eyebrows jumped at her admission and his head dipped closer. "Do tell."

Two could play that game. "Why haven't you kissed me yet?"

His laugh was soft, a short whisper of warmth across her skin. "Because you don't want me to. Not yet."

"You are mistaken."

"When you want it, you'll beg for it," he claimed. "Or you'll just flat-out take it. Until then, I'm content to wait."

Leah pushed on his chest with a huff. "I don't understand you." He was a great big tease, damn him.

Wyatt laughed, immovable as a mountain. "I know what you're hoping for. You want me to make the first move, but I'm not going to. You want to know why?"

"Why," she grumbled.

"Because if I do, you'll be able to twist it later and make believe you weren't a part of it. You'll pretend it was something that happened to you, without your volition, outside your will. But if you make the first move, if you beg for it, desperate and needy, I'll know it's really what you wanted, and more importantly, *you'll* know it's what you really wanted."

Leah scowled, leaning into him. They were running out of time. "Wyatt, please. Too much analysis. I want you to kiss me *now*."

"Not yet, you don't. But you will." He smiled gently and eased back. "I have faith."

She shook her head, trying to make sense of his inscrutable strategy. "But…if you're leaving the first move up to me, why all the looming? Why all the little touches, and innuendos? And the texting. Oh my God."

"I said I was content to wait, Leah. I didn't say I'd make it easy on you."

She ducked under his arm with a frustrated growl. "You know, you're cute, but you're very devious."

He shrugged, unrepentant, that ever-present smile tickling the corners of his mouth.

Leah studied his expression, searching for insincerity, but it was as earnest as ever. Without giving herself too much time to think about it, she darted forward, landing a kiss on his lips that was supposed to be a test, but shifted without warning.

In the blink of an eye, Wyatt's big hands were buried in her hair, cupping her skull—and his tongue was plundering her mouth like he'd been starving for it. Just as suddenly, he pulled away, and a car door slammed in the driveway outside.

He tried to tuck her behind him, but Leah pushed past, heading for the door. "No, it's okay," she said. "When you got held up, I asked a mom in our carpool to bring Teddy home. So, we'd have more time."

"I see," he said.

"Wyatt, what was *that?*" she breathed. "Over there." She pointed a shaky finger at the wall, where he'd kissed the daylights out of her directly after saying he wouldn't.

The doorbell rang and he schooled his burning gaze quickly. "Let's call it incentive," he grinned.

Chapter Nine

Wyatt

H E'S NOT LISTENING."

"Sure, he is," Joe said. "Watch."

Wyatt ignored them as he clicked on another suggested page in his browser search results called 'Top Ten Dates for Parents'. It was recent, and local. *Looked promising.*

A hand appeared in front of his nose, snapping insistently.

"Stitch," Joe barked. "Hey. Fucknuts. Noah here thinks you haven't been listening."

With a sigh, Wyatt bookmarked the page and snapped his laptop shut.

He glanced between Noah and Joe, both standing next to the kitchen table and eyeing him expectantly. "Dude. Is this necessary? You know I'm listening."

Behind his chunky, black-framed glasses, Noah smirked, "No, you're not. You're knee deep in whatever that is." At this, he gestured to Wyatt's hands, resting lightly on the case of his computer. "Knowing you, you're probably researching top ten dates or something."

Joe mimicked the whistle of a falling bomb, muttering a wry, "Bullseye," under his breath at the end.

He had to chuckle at the accuracy, but eventually pinned Noah with a resigned stare. "We really gonna do this?"

"Yes," the guy fired back, arms tucked across his chest in the world's most defensive body language.

"Hell yeah, we are," Joe agreed, yanking out the chair across from Wyatt and dropping into it happily. "Hit it, brother."

Wyatt took a breath, briefly reviewing the facts in his mind to make sure he had it all ordered correctly. Then he pointed at Noah, "You've had suspicions about Echo for a while, so you looked into their social organizations and hangouts, searching for something that didn't feel kosher. You ultimately zeroed in on the religious groups, because they're run by outside entities and oversight is minimal."

"Ha!" Joe roared, "What'd I tell you? He looks sweet, but my boy's a fucking animal. Multitasks like a motherfucker."

Noah snorted, looking back to Wyatt for the rest.

He checked his watch, but he still had some time before he had to leave. He continued, "You believe the bible study you flagged at Pendleton is one critical element within a larger trafficking network within Echo Company. You found odd anomalies in the backgrounds of several participants, and significant overlap with the premarital counseling classes run by the same church. You also suspect the groups are being used to introduce and reintegrate former trafficking victims back into mainstream society."

It was clear Noah was onto something, too. The guy had developed theories about how the process worked, and though many of the women they'd looked into had been widowed in the Nabarut skirmish—and consequently moved away from base and the groups in question—there were still enough around that they could get corroboration if necessary.

"Okay, so you can parrot back what I said, but—"

"I'm wondering if the grunts in Echo helped connect potential grooms to the victims phasing out of the network and needing new, whitewashed identities," Wyatt told him. "Or were those hookups handled by someone else? If we could nail that down, it might eventually lead us to the Nabaruti girls."

He also wanted to know where he could find a reliable babysitter and a no-fail date night spot in the greater San Diego area, but he doubted either of his roommates would have the answers to those quandaries.

"You…you have?" Noah stammered.

Joe pointed at Wyatt. "Yes. The church organization running these things operates under the nose of base command, but it has unfettered access to the soldiers. With other churches managing similar programs too, it'd be the perfect way to hide in plain sight."

Noah threw up his hands and looked around, thoroughly exasperated. "Did you two plan this? Am I being punked again?"

"Bro." Wyatt shook his head at him.

Noah stared at him in consternation. "How long have you been wondering this? Why haven't you said anything before now?"

"I just thought of it now, while you two were bickering."

Noah glared back. "Fine. You know what? Fine." He pushed his glasses up his nose and dropped into the chair next to him. "If we can find a way to talk to some of the women who are left, maybe we can get one of them to tell us who's running the show and how it all works."

"And, where we might find the missing girls," Joe added.

"That too. I did some research," Noah explained. "And I think I found some former participants' social media accounts. I also found one listed on a DC restaurant's website, and another in a film industry paper."

"Were they perchance photographed with anyone we know?" Wyatt wondered.

"Some. Once I pull it all together, I'll send a blast to the team."

"Cool." Wyatt got to his feet, grabbed his laptop, and turned toward his room. "Great work, man."

Noah held up his hands in alarm. "Wait. There's more."

Wyatt's phone buzzed with a reminder, so he checked his watch again. Leah was making dinner for just the two of them tonight, and she'd planned it for *after* Teddy's bedtime. If he was going to make it on time, he had to leave now.

"Hold that thought," he told Noah. "We can reconvene later, but right now I need to take a raincheck."

Joe clasped his hands dreamily under his chin. "Ah. Young love," he sighed.

"Could you not?" Wyatt laughed.

Noah stood up, gripping the side of the table with a fair amount of angst. "No, but—"

"Text me if you've got names for those women you found. I shouldn't be home late."

"Why do you want names? Are you going to ask Leah if she knows them?"

"I'm…not sure." Wyatt ignored the troubled feeling tightening his chest and squinted at Joe. "Probably need to play that one by ear."

He hustled to his room before he could second guess himself, glancing back once as he stepped over the threshold to drop his computer on his bed.

Noah and Joe were sharing a heavy look, whispering heatedly about whatever he'd dipped out on. Whatever that "more" was, Wyatt had a feeling it was going to be a killer.

LEAH FLUNG OPEN her front door before he could ring the bell, and cast a quick frown at Wyatt's car before towing him back to the kitchen with a finger to her lips.

Once there, he whispered, "Was it okay for me to park in your driveway? There's not a lot of street parking with all your neighbors home for the night."

"It's fine," she told him quietly, though not terribly convincingly. "How was your day?"

"Uneventful. You?"

"Not too bad. Teddy went down without any problems, so that's good."

He held back and drank in the sight of her. Leah was wearing loose lounge pants that flowed around her legs when she moved, and a close-fitting top that occasionally flashed tantalizing slivers of skin at her waist.

As Wyatt watched, she shoveled a large slab of casserole onto a plate that was already piled high with salad, a thick slice of bread, and a few skewers of grilled meat and vegetables.

He grinned at the portion sizes. If the plate was meant for him, *someone* had clearly gotten a bead on his outsized appetite.

Leah stopped to assess her arrangement. "Hope you like pastichio," she said.

So that's what that was. "I do," Wyatt agreed, "Though I don't think I've enjoyed a version as good as that looks."

She smiled at the way he was ogling the mound of food. "Thanks for coming over this late. You must be hungry."

"Ravenous," he agreed. He shifted his gaze to her, and let it travel over her curves more openly than he usually did.

Leah stopped, slowly set aside her spatula, and leaned back against the counter, invitation writ large on her face.

Wyatt smirked at her expression. It seemed the control tower was approving his approach.

He moved closer—until their thighs were pressed together, and Leah had to tilt her head back to meet his eyes—and gripped the counter on either side of her.

She'd said she liked when he loomed. Well, Wyatt would tower over her if that's what she wanted.

She stretched up on her toes to touch her lips to his, and he was lost. For all his bold words about her needing to lead the charge, Wyatt folded like a deck of cards, and was surprised by the hunger that roared to life when he took her mouth.

For 32 hours, he hadn't been able to erase the small taste he'd gotten of her, and he groaned when this new hit of Leah flooded his senses.

She broke away with a quiet laugh, shushing him.

"Sorry," he grinned. *Could he have stopped himself? Not a chance.*

"No, I'm sorry we have to be so quiet. I really want that kid to stay asleep, if possible," she explained. "I hope this isn't too weird."

"I'll admit it's got a little something illicit I wasn't expecting." Wyatt nuzzled the side of her neck, gratified when her breath hitched.

"Is it giving you the ick?"

"I don't hate it," he admitted. "It kind of reminds me of making out in the back stairwell of my freshman year dorm, trying to make it to home base before someone busted in on us."

"Kinky," she drawled.

"More like desperate."

He dipped his head and kissed her slower this time, loving the way her body bowed against his and her hands grasped his waist. Right up until the angry sound of his hollow stomach rumbled through her kitchen.

Heat climbed his neck, and he prayed she hadn't heard, but Leah pushed him away with a rueful chuckle.

"This part can wait," she told him, pulling Wyatt toward her small kitchen table. "Eat first. Suck face later."

He studied the laden plate she plunked in front of him, estimating how long it would take to bolt it all down. *Five minutes? Maybe seven?*

"Don't rush," she warned, narrowing her eyes like she could see his internal calculations. "I'm not sure I can get a good enough grip on you if I have to perform the Heimlich."

Wyatt grinned as that softball sailed over home. "Oh, I bet you could grip me just fine."

Leah snorted and smacked him on the arm, but a blush crept up her neck that he definitely, desperately, wanted to see more of later.

THEY'D FINISHED EATING and were clearing their plates when the real world intruded once more on their little utopia. Wyatt's phone buzzed in his pocket, and dread descended over him like a shroud.

He knew who it had to be, and sure enough, when he glanced at the screen, Noah's name was trailing across it. He could hardly complain though—he'd asked for this.

As Leah stacked dishes in the sink, he considered his next move. If he ignored the text he'd specifically requested, they could go on with their night as planned. With any luck, dessert would proceed a lot like the appetizer had, and he might get to enjoy an hour or more of messing around on her couch before Leah finally kicked him out.

The problem was, Wyatt knew on some level he'd be thinking about Noah's text the whole time, and where was the fun in that? If he ripped off this bandage now, he could then stop worrying about it. He could go forth and plunder, as it were, unburdened by unsexy concerns.

A temporary setback for longer-term gain.

Decision made, he responded to the text with one of his own, and a second later, his cell rang with the incoming call.

"Shoot, it's work. I gotta take this," he told Leah. "Okay if I duck out back for a minute?"

The window over the kitchen sink was open. If he stood below it, she'd probably overhear everything he wanted her to.

"No need," she countered quickly. "You can use the family room. I'll stay in here and make us some coffee, so you have privacy."

"Thanks." He pecked her on the cheek and headed for the couch.

Wyatt answered with a casual, nothing-to-see-here, "Hey man. What's up?"

"You tell me," Noah retorted. "I texted you the names. Did you see them?"

"I did, yeah."

"And I am duplicating my efforts…why exactly?"

Wyatt caught a glimpse of movement in his periphery, so he said, "Kandace with a K. Okay. S, c, h…Schuler. Got it."

As expected, Leah ducked her head in a second later, so he held up a finger while he pretended to type the name into his notes app. "Kandace…Schuler," he murmured. Then Wyatt tucked the phone against his chest and smiled at her.

"Sorry, I thought you were done," she whispered. "Do you want regular or decaf?"

"Decaf. Thanks."

She hesitated, glancing at his phone with a little frown before slipping out again.

"Sorry," he told Noah. "You got anything else?"

"Questions. I have a lot of questions," he fired back. "And details you should know."

"We can deal with those later." Wyatt listened for Leah, but she was still rattling around the kitchen.

"Sure," Noah retorted drily. "Are we about done here?"

"Yeah, we're good."

"Great. Buck said he'd be here around 10:30, if your social schedule permits."

Wyatt bit back a grin as Leah peeked in again, holding two steaming mugs. He motioned her forward, told Noah, "Roger that," and ended the call.

"Sorry," he said, accepting the coffee and setting it on the table. "I don't work particularly regular hours."

Her brow wrinkled as she thought about that. "I don't think you've mentioned what you do, exactly."

He smiled as gently as he could, knowing she probably wouldn't like his answer. "This and that. How about you?"

Leah scowled, but she wasn't stupid. She had a good idea what that might mean, and she didn't press him. "I mostly process insurance claims," she said eventually. "I've been lucky that it's all remote for now."

Wyatt nodded politely, but damn if that didn't sound excruciatingly boring.

She cupped her mug between her palms and examined him. Her job was clearly the last thing she wanted to talk about. Luckily, it didn't take long before she blurted out, "Listen, I'm so sorry—I really wasn't trying to eavesdrop, but did I hear you say *Kandace Schuler* before? Do you know her?"

"I know of her. Why, do you?"

"I think so. Or someone with that same name, at least."

Shit. That was the opposite of what he'd wanted to hear. "Oh? How so?" he inquired.

"Jesse and I used to do premarital counseling for one of the churches on base. I'm pretty sure she was in one of our classes."

"Huh." Wyatt grabbed for his coffee and took a long gulp to cover the stab of unease her comment set off under his ribs. "Are you very religious, or…?"

The apprehension that Leah's life might in any way overlap their investigation made him faintly green.

"No, it was mostly Jesse's thing," she said. "He helped with the bible study sometimes, too. That's how we ended up renting this duplex. Mrs. Daniels—that's my landlord next door—runs the group."

Wyatt nodded, her elderly neighbor's chronic ill-temper taking on a new light.

"She had a different couple take over the counseling sessions once Jesse died," Leah continued. "But I guess it's just as well. Half the time, I didn't think the couples were going to last out the year."

"Leah—" He couldn't risk operational security, but he felt like he had to say *something* in response to that.

"No, it's fine. Is Kandace okay, though?"

"As far as I know."

She winced, just a little. "Is she in some kind of trouble?"

Wyatt took in her expression and *knew*. "Why do you ask?"

"Because…" she sighed, glancing around as if checking to make sure no one would overhear. She toyed with the handle of her cup, stalling, or maybe deciding if she wanted to share.

Eventually, she admitted, "The thing is, I saw her around sometimes. The guy she was supposed to marry died in Qahat, but even before the company deployed, when I saw her, she would often be with this other man."

He felt his eyebrows shoot up. "Oh?"

"Yeah, *oh*. He was a little older than her, not too much, but sharp-dressed and like, slick, you know? It feels mean to say it, but I kind of started to wonder if he might be her pimp, or a sugar daddy, or something like that. He seemed sketchy. I don't know. Anyway, I don't think she ever saw me, and I could never decide if I should bring it up in our sessions or not."

"Did you say anything to Jesse? Or Mrs. Daniels?"

"No." Leah turned a little pink at the admission.

Wyatt debated with himself about what to do next, but she'd brought it up, not him. Maybe it wouldn't look too odd if he tried for some confirmation. On a hunch, he called up a photo of Dan Cox on his phone and showed it to her.

"Any chance this is him?"

"Yes," she gasped, surprised. "Kandace fawned over that guy like you've never seen. Weird for someone trying to marry another person, right?"

"But you never ratted her out."

"Nope."

"How come?"

"Because I guess a part of me was worried that he was someone she needed to escape from, and that getting married was how she was going to do that."

Wyatt searched her wide, worried eyes. Leah had no idea how right she probably was.

What's more, the amorous mood of their little date was now officially dead in the water, and he had an impromptu debriefing to attend.

He groaned in disappointment and pushed to his feet. "On that happy note, I should probably get going."

"Aww, are you sure? I had dessert for you." She sidled close and slid her arms around his waist, batting her big brown eyes at him.

Wyatt smiled, smoothing her silky hair down her back and kissing her nose. "Don't tell me that. You'll never get rid of me," he murmured.

"We'll do this again," she suggested, giving him a little squeeze. "Tomorrow, even. If you want."

Heart lifting and hope restored, Wyatt told her, "Deal. Same time, same place," and gave her one last kiss.

BUCK WAS ALREADY at the apartment, beer in hand at the kitchen table, when Wyatt returned. Noah and Joe had a hockey game playing on the TV, but muted it once they noticed him.

"Noah told me about your little phone call," Buck commented. "What happened?"

Wyatt looked from face to expectant face. "You guys already knew that Leah and Jesse were doing the premarital counseling, didn't you?"

Noah nodded. "That's what I was trying to tell you when you left."

"I will not use her, so don't even ask."

Buck shook his head. "Not asking."

Wyatt stared at his relaxed posture, so at odds with the tight energy that usually thrummed through him. *Something was up.* "Should I be telling her what we're doing?"

He took a slow swig of his beer, making a show of contemplating Wyatt's question while Noah and Joe watched avidly from the sidelines.

Eventually, Buck answered, "Not yet."

"Will Leah and her son be in danger, if her husband was involved in this mess?" Wyatt tossed his keys on the console next to the door and stalked closer. "Because that is not something I'm okay with."

"Burke is dead," Buck shrugged. "Why would anyone go after her?"

"Because she was helping him with the supposed counseling. Because he was mixed up in that bible study, too. Because they'll wonder if she knows more than what she told me tonight."

Three pointed frowns pierced him, but it was Joe who demanded, "What did she tell you tonight?"

"That she used to see Kandace around town with a flashy dude who was definitely not her fiancé," he reported grimly. Wyatt shook his head, his stomach in knots all over again. "I showed her Cox's picture. She ID'd him."

"Really?" Noah hurried over. "What did she say? Did she—"

"What the f—"

Buck held up his hand, silencing everyone with a severe look. "We are not going to involve that woman if we don't have to. Okay? We'll keep an eye on it, but that's it. That's the best we can do for now."

Chapter Ten

Leah

LEAH WAS OFF-KILTER when Wyatt returned the following evening. He'd parked in her driveway again, but it wasn't like she could ask him to move—he'd been right when he said there wasn't any nonresident parking available on the street this time of night.

Seeing his car again would send Biddy into a tailspin, but what was done, was done. There was no saving it now.

Not to mention Teddy's bedroom fronted onto the street, and too many more slamming doors or rumbling engines were liable to wake up her son again. After what she'd gone through to get the kid bathed and asleep in the first place, Leah was not going to risk it.

She pasted a smile on her face and greeted Wyatt as normally as she could manage.

"Well, if it isn't Mr. Mysterious," she said, towing him inside and quietly locking up behind him before Biddy could interfere. "What brings you to our fair shores?"

He smelled fresh, like he'd showered right before coming over. Leah resisted the urge to plaster herself against him so she could sniff his neck. *One thing at a time.*

"Turns out, I was promised something sweet," he purred, sidling closer.

Leah glanced up the stairs and beckoned him deeper into the house. "Come back here. Teddy only fell asleep a little while ago. If he hears you, he'll never leave us alone."

He smiled as he followed her, whispering, "That wouldn't be the worst thing in the world. He's a cool little dude."

Leah cocked an eyebrow at him as she set out a couple of dessert plates.

Wyatt chuckled softly. "Okay, it's not my first choice, obviously, but still not the end of the world." He watched her for a moment, then lunged for the counter. "Dang, girl. You made baklava?"

"I didn't make it," she laughed. "No time for that. I got it at this bakery I know. They're not Greek but it's still pretty good, and I was going for the theme last night."

Wyatt rubbed his hands together, eyes glued to the brick of pastry she slid onto his plate.

"Do you want ice cream with it?"

"Is Cookie Monster blue?" he demanded, incredulous.

Leah rolled her eyes and pivoted toward the freezer, then jumped when, all of a sudden, she felt Wyatt's heat along her back, and his lips pressed against the side of her neck.

For such a big guy, he moved fast—and he hadn't made a sound. That realization, coupled with his peculiar reticence about his job last night, meant she probably ought to be hearing some alarm bells right about now.

All she could think about was getting his mouth on hers, though. Leah turned, slid her hands under the hem of his long-sleeved surfing t-shirt, and hummed at all the soft, warm skin she found.

Wyatt grabbed her around the waist and lifted her to the counter, then stepped between her knees. "First things first," he murmured, brushing his lips over hers.

Right off the bat, she misjudged things. She'd expected him to skip the build-up and head straight into a toe-curling lip lock, so when Wyatt instead led with a prim little peck, Leah met him with open lips and full-on tongue.

When he overcorrected, they knocked teeth.

She pulled back with a confused laugh, face flaming. "What is going on right now?"

"Sorry," he grinned. "Let's try that again. You, hold still." Then Wyatt cradled her face gently in his hands and leaned in.

His lips were careful at first, worshipping her with soft, slow kisses, like he had all the time in the world. He waited until a moan escaped her throat before his tongue sought entry, twining with hers in a hot, heady dance.

Leah tucked her feet around the back of his thighs as his hands found their way into her hair. Wyatt's mouth was hot. His skin was burning. She wanted to drown in this kiss and never come up for air.

How long had it been since she'd felt this way?

He pressed forward, angling his head to take the kiss deeper, when a sudden crack echoed through the kitchen, and a burst of pain arrowed through her skull. Wyatt inhaled sharply.

Had she bitten his lip in her shock? *Maybe.*

"Ow," she gasped, both for her and for him.

His eyes flew open in horror. "Oh my god, are you okay?" He pulled her away from the offending cabinet with a heavy hand on her shoulder.

Leah massaged the back of her head, trying to disperse the ache. "I think my head hit the edge," she whined. "Man, that hurt."

Wyatt grimaced, then bent and rustled through her freezer to find an icepack. "Did it break the skin?" He handed it to her carefully.

She hopped off the counter, sure she must be ten shades of crimson. Wyatt was smooth. She was…a cringy liability.

"No, I don't think so," she bluffed awkwardly. "No blood, no problem, right?"

He stared at her in concern. "Sure." After a beat, he reached for her arm, like he meant to turn her. "Let me take a look at it anyway."

Leah backed away, utterly mortified. "I'm fine, I swear. Let's just…take a breather and eat dessert. Once I stop seeing all these stars, I'll be good to go."

He didn't take his eyes off her as he retrieved some ice cream from the freezer. "Okay, but you go sit down. I'll bring our plates over," he commanded. "You keep that ice on your head, so it doesn't swell."

"Only thing not swelling right now is my ego," she grumbled, heading for the couch.

"Not the only thing," he muttered.

Leah squeezed her eyes shut in mortification. "Oh my god."

"I'm just teasing. Besides, that was my bad. After an Advil, a glass of wine, and some of this baklava, you'll be right as rain."

He grabbed the bottle of pills from the shelf over the sink, lined up two glasses, and popped the cork on the bottle they'd started with dinner the night before. Then he started digging through drawers, presumably looking for an ice cream scoop.

"It's in the drawer next to the stove," she prompted with a smile.

She might be a klutz, but apparently that was yet another thing that activated Wyatt's caretaking side. She couldn't say she minded. After so many years of playing that role without reciprocity, it felt new and novel—and so, so good—to be fussed over.

SOME TIME LATER, the icepack was melting in the sink, the wine bottle was empty, and the baklava demolished. Leah lay on the couch with her cheek on Wyatt's lap as he ran his fingers through her hair, over and over.

They'd talked about little things over dessert, but conversation had fallen away several minutes ago. It was a peaceful sort of quiet, though, like he was enjoying touching her. Like he didn't need words.

Eventually, curiosity overtook her. "What are you thinking about?"

Wyatt finished the last bit of wine in his glass and set it on the table beside him. "Honestly? Kissing you. Not sure whether you want to risk another concussion so soon, though."

"Wow, okay," she laughed softly. *Points for honesty.*

He peeked at her, brushing her hair off her forehead. "What about you? What were you thinking about?"

"Well, I can't remember, now. My brain's been taken over by a kissing montage."

"That's a good thing?"

"Yes, obviously."

Leah tried to turn so she could see him better, wincing when the lump on her head pressed painfully against the hard muscle of his thigh. It was a timely reminder that he was him… and she was her.

"Listen. Wyatt…" She hesitated, but perhaps it was better to get her concerns out of the way before this went much further.

"Leah."

"I get the impression that you're no stranger to the ladies."

His green eyes did a little half roll, half flutter—not quite dismissive, but not flattered, either. He wondered, "Not that I'm agreeing, but does it matter? I'm not seeing anyone else, and I'm disease-free if that's what you're wondering."

Leah blinked. That wasn't where she'd been going with this at all. "Uh, thanks. That's good. Me either. But what I actually wanted to tell you was that I, on the other hand, have not dated that much. I was kind of a wallflower in high school, and Jesse was my first and only college boyfriend."

Wyatt snorted. "If you were a wallflower, then I'm Albert Einstein."

"I suffered through an extended awkward phase before I blossomed. There is abundant photographic evidence, trust me."

"Seems unlikely, but go on."

"Let's just say…" She took a deep breath, not sure how to articulate her worry. "Jesse wasn't exactly breaking out the Kama Sutra, and now I'm…now I'm a single mom. I mean, I wouldn't trade it—Teddy is great. But I'm tired and grouchy like every night, and dating has been the last thing on my mind."

"Understandable." He was beginning to look wary, though.

Leah sat up carefully, and turned to face him. "What I'm trying to say is that between the two of us, you probably know what you're doing, and I'm almost certainly going to be a giant disappointment."

Wyatt's brows pulled down, like her explanation had only deepened his confusion. "Again, seems suspect," he muttered. "But is there a question in there somewhere? Or am I being let down gently?"

Leah huffed at his evident dismay. "Wyatt, I'm not trying to break things off, but I also know I come with a lot of hassle. You've been so good about it, but what if you put up with all my nonsense and I turn out to be a gigantic disappointment? I'm afraid to let myself get more invested if you're going to decide my mess isn't worth the trouble in a few weeks. Is that too much honesty so soon?"

He gaped at her, but his lips ticked up in amusement. "First of all, your candor is very refreshing. Authenticity is something I haven't seen a lot of lately, so definitely don't keep that under wraps."

He tucked her hair behind her ear, his fingers lingering for a moment before dropping away. "Second, what if you're not a *gigantic disappointment?*" He broke out the air quotes, making her smile. "What if you're the best I've ever had?"

"To use your words, that seems unlikely." Leah shook her head and laughed quietly. "I know it sounds weird. I convinced myself it would be wise to get ahead of things and manage expectations."

"Was that when you cracked your head on the cabinet or when you basically told me you think I'm a ho?" he smirked back. He shushed her when she tried to protest. "Here's a thought—why not expect that when the time comes, we'll figure out what works for us together?"

Leah sighed at his sheer reasonableness. "That makes sense. I just feel very out of practice." She pointed at the kitchen in illustration. "You saw what I did in there. I know I took a chunk out of your lip, in addition to knocking myself goofy. So, if we're headed in the direction I think we are, just know it might take me a minute to get back on the horse. To…up my game, or whatever."

"I can assure you, I will enjoy every second it takes for you to do that," he commented drily. "By all means, take alllll the time you need. Really explore the space."

She rolled her eyes. "Are you even listening to what I'm saying?"

Wyatt stroked his hands down her arms and intertwined his fingers with hers. "Yes, and I'm trying to tell you it's going to be okay. Don't worry about what you think I want, or whether you're going to measure up to some nameless women you imagine have been rocking my world. All I want today, tomorrow, and for the foreseeable future, is you. The real you. I don't expect you to improve yourself, or to show up in the bedroom with a PhD in boinking. And I'm not going anywhere because you have a kid. Okay?"

She blinked at his supremely unbothered tone. "Okay."

"How long have you been stewing about this?"

"Hour maybe?"

"On how many different days?"

Leah hit his arm with a chuckle. "Alright, you've made your point."

"Great. Then let's get back to my earlier thoughts."

"The kissing-related ones?"

Wyatt nodded slyly. "Come here, Nervous Nelly."

Leah hesitated, but realized a moment later that she truly felt zero indecision. His practicality had seen to that.

She shuffled closer on her knees, and let him guide her onto his lap. Once she was straddling him, he gripped her sides and dipped his head toward hers. He kissed her fiercely, like he'd been starving for exactly what Leah, and only Leah, had to give.

Her hands didn't seem to know where to settle and fluttered everywhere, electric shimmers alighting in her fingertips with every touch.

Wyatt's hands edged off her waist, one molding around her ass to press her closer, and the other inching up her ribcage until his thumb teased the side of her breast.

He pulled his mouth from hers, breath hitching, to rain hungry kisses along her jaw. His lips paused at her ear, hot with promise. "You taste like honey," he breathed, "So fucking sweet."

Molten heat streaked to her core when he devoured her mouth once more. His fingers tightened on her ass and Leah moaned, unable to control the tilt of her hips or the volume of her voice.

His Adam's apple bobbed as he held her still, despite the gratifying bulge pressing against the fly of his khaki shorts. Wyatt pressed his lips to her neck and held them there for a long moment, before he reluctantly lifted her to the side and stood gingerly.

"I should leave before this gets out of hand," he said shakily.

Leah supposed she should be grateful that one of them was thinking clearly. She needed to be responsible about this. Wyatt's kisses didn't exactly encourage cautious thinking, however—they beckoned a girl right to the precipice of Reckless Canyon.

And she *didn't* feel grateful. She felt disappointed.

"Again?" she pouted. "What did I do? Why are you running away again?"

He stood a couple of feet away, back to her. At length, he half-turned and let out a self-deprecating laugh. "Honestly? I'm freaked out about how this got out of hand so fast. I meant to take it slow, and now I'm not sure how to act."

She scowled in consternation. "What? Why?"

"Leah, you literally just told me you feel out of your depth with me, yet somehow, I thought it was a good idea to order you into my lap and maul you. If I leave now, at least I can tell myself I was mostly a gentleman."

"It's not like you twisted my arm, Wyatt. I came of my own free will."

"Let's be clear, there was a really unfortunate lack of coming," he snorted, stepping closer. "I'm just…I'm worried now that I'm moving too fast, or coming on too strong. This should happen at your pace, but I can't seem to keep my mitts off you." His burning eyes scanned her face, snagging on her lips and making her shiver.

"No one forced anyone to do anything," she told him. "We are consenting adults, and I liked everything we did immensely. Did you?"

"It's all I'll think about until the next time I see you," he admitted ruefully. "You know you can tell me to cool my jets any time you want, right? You don't need to worry about that with me. No means no."

"Good to know, and I'm not worried." She patted the couch next to her, but Wyatt only stared at the place he'd been sitting suspiciously. Like he didn't trust himself, or maybe blamed her furniture for his lack of self-control.

"Do you have somewhere else to be tonight?" Leah asked him.
He shook his head.

"Can I convince you to stay for another round?"

Wyatt's smirk was instant and devastating. *The hound.*

"Perhaps." He gave her a calculating once-over. "Can I petition for a change in location?"

Her eyebrows shot up at the thought. "Depends. What did you have in mind?"

"Well, as long as we're being honest and no one's feeling pressured, I'll admit I want you in my bed. However, since that's not an option at the moment, I'd settle for your bed."

Leah opened her mouth, intending to buy herself some time to think that through. Instead, a breathy, "Oh," emerged of its own volition.

"I'm not asking for sex tonight," he clarified. "I'd just like some room to do a little orienteering." His gaze set off sizzling shocks of want under her skin as she considered what that might mean.

Her pulse thrumming in her ears, the taste of him still on her lips, Leah said, "I'm listening."

Who was she kidding, though? She knew perfectly well that Wyatt's suggestion was too tempting to resist. She didn't think she'd ever experienced how she felt with him—his kisses were like a drug, making her feel light, yet languid. Powerful, but pliant.

It was no decision at all to slip off her shoes and quietly lead him upstairs to her room.

She had to keep checking if he was still behind her. There was no way a man of his size should've been able to move as silently as Wyatt could, but he ghosted past Teddy's room like a wraith and before she knew it, they were safe behind her closed bedroom door at the end of the hall.

Leah turned the lock after a moment's consideration, on the off chance her son came looking for her. Teddy would be confused if he encountered the resistance, but she'd still hear if he called for her. Better that than finding Wyatt in here, doing…

Well. Leah knew what she wanted that to be. *Her.*

Chapter Eleven

Wyatt

ANY REMAINING APPREHENSION Wyatt might have been feeling about staying with Leah and engaging in yet more amorous congress melted away at the sight of her palpable excitement. He'd thrown down a gauntlet, intending to test her resolve—but she picked it up, put it on, and charged headfirst into battle.

Guess she hadn't minded the tonsil hockey on the couch, after all.

Her steps were light as he followed her up the stairs and into her room. She had a goal in mind, that much was clear. Once she'd locked them in, she led him to the armchair near the foot of her bed and pushed him into it.

Leah braced her hands on the armrests, leaned over, and kissed him. Then, before he could get too invested in that, she knelt between his legs and shot him a self-satisfied little grin.

Wyatt cocked an eyebrow at her. "What are you up to?" he asked, though all signs were clearly pointing in a direction he hadn't even considered moments earlier.

"Oh, I think you know," she murmured, running her hands up his thighs.

The breath in his lungs didn't seem to know whether it was staying or leaving. Same went for whatever wits he'd once possessed. Wyatt could only watch as Leah inched his shirt up his chest until he obliged her by shucking it off, and again as she made quick work of tugging off his shorts.

She palmed him through his underwear, humming low in her throat when the material under her hand quickly grew damp. She didn't mess around too long, though. Soon, she was pulling down his briefs so she could wrap her fist around him.

Wyatt swallowed with difficulty, his throat alarmingly tight. Like his lungs. Like his dick. Every neuron in his brain was screaming for her to…

Like she could read his mind, Leah licked her lips, pressed closer between his legs, and took him deep into her mouth. He sank lower in the chair and groaned, then struggled to stifle another when she made a sound of warning.

Quiet. He had to be quiet.

But fuck, her mouth was hot and tight and wet—and Wyatt wanted her with an ache bordering on desperation. Leah sucked him down, over and over, her hand moving in time with her mouth, and if she kept up the pace, he was going to blow his load in about 5 seconds.

She'd left the lights on. He couldn't tear his eyes away. Wyatt pried his hand from the arm of the chair and touched her shoulder. "Hey. Do you wanna take a break? I'm not gonna last much—"

Leah snagged his hand and placed it on the back of her head, pressing it against her scalp. Once he'd gotten the message, she went back to gripping his thigh and hummed around his cock like she loved what she was doing.

The vibration made his balls draw tight and his eyes roll back in his head. Wyatt barely remembered to choke back his moan, seeing stars as he came in that hot fucking mouth of hers.

Leah sat back on her heels when he was done, smug as a housecat in the sun. He scanned her face, dropped his head back, and groaned again.

God *damn*, she was beautiful.

"Are you okay?" she laughed softly.

He was not okay—he was wrecked.

"Babe, that was not the kind of orienteering I was talking about." Then he startled, grabbing his t-shirt and pushing it at her. "Do you need to spit? Use this."

Leah laughed a little harder at him. "Thanks, but it's a little late for that."

A blush crawled up his neck, prickling Wyatt's overheated skin. "Sorry. I think…my brain went offline for a minute."

"That's good, though. Right?" Her voice shook the tiniest amount, like some nerves might be kicking in.

Wyatt snorted at the sheer absurdity of the question. "Uh yeah. Are you joking?"

"No." Leah shrugged, her shoulders brushing his splayed knees. "Just trying to make sure I'm not too rusty. As I said, it's been a while."

"Girl, please," he scoffed. "There is no part of a guy dumber than the dumb handle. It's impossible to screw that up."

She made a face, and not a good one.

He blinked. "What'd I say?"

"You can't screw that up? What kind of praise is that?"

Wyatt stared at her in foggy confusion until his sluggish brain finally caught up. "Ah. Right. Come here." He tucked himself back in his shorts and pulled her off the floor and into his lap.

Once she was straddling him again, like she had downstairs, he brushed along her cheekbone with his fingertips. "You are spectacular and amazing—including your oral game—and what I meant to say is that this is a very inconvenient development."

"Is it?" She still looked a little salty.

"Look, I was having issues before this," Wyatt explained. "No lie. It was beginning to affect my work. But now…" He shook his head. "You're gonna get my ass fired."

"What? Come on."

"Seriously. I think about you all the time. Thinking about Leah as I fall asleep, as I wake up…day in, day out, daydreaming. Even dreamed about you once or twice."

She laughed in his face. "That sounds like a you problem."

"Except now, I know what this mouth can do." His gaze dropped to her lips. He reached out and stroked them with his thumb, and she bit him. *Little brat.* He eyed her in challenge. "Fair warning: now that I know what I know, there's going to be no dealing with me at all."

Leah preened, very pleased with herself. "I don't know, I'm feeling pretty good about myself. I think you might just be a big baby."

He narrowed his eyes, the cocky defiance in her voice something he couldn't stand down from. Wyatt gripped her luscious ass and stood, pivoting toward the bed and dropping her onto it.

"We'll see about that." He hooked his fingers in the waistband of her yoga pants and tugged them down her hips and farther, until they slipped off her legs and he could toss them on the chair.

The loose top she was wearing was the next to go—it'd been sliding off her shoulder every few minutes anyway, taunting him with glimpses of smooth, golden skin all night. Knowing her, she'd probably worn the thing to torture him on purpose, damn it.

Leah braced herself on her elbows as she smiled seductively up at him, the ends of her shiny brown hair pooling on the comforter behind her. Wearing nothing but a mismatched sports bra and sensible underwear, she looked utterly delectable.

Wyatt whistled as he eyed her from the crown of her wavy hair to the tips of her painted toes, paralyzed by the wealth of choice laid out in front of him. *Where to begin?*

Unfortunately, before he could do much more than kiss his way up one long, toned thigh, Leah let out a jaw-cracking yawn. He froze and looked up at her face.

"I'm fine," she lied, blinking quickly.

Wyatt rolled his eyes and checked his watch. It was late and getting later—and if Teddy was anything like he'd been as a kid, he'd be up at the crack of dawn. "I should get out of here so you can get some sleep."

"What?" she cried in dismay. "No! I just got you up here."

Wyatt brushed his fingers across her soft stomach, smiling when goosebumps erupted across her skin. "You'll get plenty of other chances, I promise." He kissed one of the thin, silvery stretchmarks radiating out from her belly button, then another on the other side.

He'd bet everything that Leah had been a gorgeous pregnant person. *There were probably photos around here somewhere. He ought to look one of these days.*

"But you didn't get to do any orienting." She tried to suppress another yawn, but it seemed to be a losing battle now that she was horizontal.

Wyatt eased up and kissed the swell of each of her breasts, cupping one dreamily as he pressed a kiss to her soft lips. "Orienteering. And while I don't want to leave you hanging, you are about to fall asleep on me. I want you wide awake when I devour you."

"When? Not if?"

"*When*," he retorted. There definitely needed to be a when, and soon.

She sighed, but she didn't fight him, which probably meant she was even more tired than she was letting on. That wine they'd had couldn't be helping.

"I'd ask you to stay over, but…"

He waved her off. "I get it. We'll get there when we get there." Wyatt hooked a thumb toward the stairs. "Want me to let myself out so you can crash?"

"No, I'll meet you downstairs in a sec. Let me get dressed and I'll walk you out."

He nodded, ghosting downstairs to put on his sneakers. As he did, he noticed that they'd left their wineglasses and dessert plates on the coffee table, along with the melting ice pack. Wyatt rounded everything up and took it to the kitchen. Then, as quietly as possible, he loaded the forks and plates in the dishwasher, dumped the ice pack in the freezer, and quickly washed their glasses.

He was upending them to dry on the dishtowel next to the sink when Leah reappeared, hovering in the shadows near the stairs and watching him with a soft smile.

"Thanks for that," she whispered.

"Didn't want your kid sampling merlot before school," he murmured. "Next thing you know, he'd be coloring outside the lines and flirting with kindergartners, and then where would we be?"

She laughed and beckoned him to the front hall, where he got a good look at what she'd put on to see him off.

Upstairs, Leah had worn some of the plainest underwear Wyatt had maybe ever seen on a woman, but her pajamas now were a whole new tier of dull. Ratty old t-shirt, thin shorts with a print too faded to decipher—it looked as if dorm chic and Depression-era hobo had met and had a raggedy love child.

The dissonance of her cover model looks ensconced in such blatantly unseductive apparel was jarring. Ludicrously so. He couldn't quite hide his snort of amusement.

Leah picked up on it immediately.

"Sorry," she gestured weakly. "I know this is not very sexy. Jesse didn't think I should, quote, dress like a harlot in front of the baby. It's been eighteen months and I'm still trying to deprogram and figure out who I am without that noise in my brain all the time."

Wyatt's jaw locked in knee-jerk fury. God, he wanted to drag that prick back to life just so he could plant a fist between his eyes and knock him cold again. Maybe more than once. Or…okay fine, once for each infraction Wyatt had mentally tallied up, ever since Leah decided to trust him with her secrets.

She shifted uncomfortably. "I'm sorry. Probably the wrong time to blurt that out."

"No, I'm sorry." He shook off his red haze and refocused on her. "And don't even sweat it," he murmured. "You'd look gorgeous in a paper bag, and what matters is whether you're comfortable."

Leah let out an unsteady chuckle. "I am, but I also don't want you to think I'm trying to repel you on purpose. Especially after I worked so hard to get you to stay tonight, then almost sacked out on you."

Wyatt was abruptly reminded of how suspicious she'd been when they first met. "I'm pretty sure I'd know it if you were trying to get rid of me," he smirked. "And, breaking news, if you are, you're going about it all wrong."

She fiddled with her thin t-shirt, surreptitiously plucking it away from her chest—perhaps so he wouldn't notice she wasn't wearing a bra.

Too late. He was in possession of very recent and vivid knowledge that her breasts were perfect, and therefore now they would be perennially hard to miss.

"That being said, I look forward to tearing those relics off you in a frenzy of passion next time," he said. "I'll try not to rip anything, but given the state of them…"

"No promises, right?" Leah snorted, grinning sleepily and looking more relaxed.

"Right. And it will definitely have to be next time." Wyatt gave her a long, lingering kiss, then pulled the door open and stepped out before he could lose his will.

Up and down the street, every house was dark…except the place next door, where lights seemed to be shining from both levels.

"Neighbor lady's a night owl, huh?" he commented.

Leah frowned and stepped out, looking nervous as she peeked over. "Not usually."

"Should we check on her?"

"No. I'm sure it's nothing," she said quickly. "She'd knock if it was something important."

Wyatt studied her expression and didn't like what he saw there. "So why do you look concerned?"

"Biddy can be testy about noise," Leah whispered anxiously. "I'm just wondering if we could've woken her somehow."

He cocked his head. "Your walls would have to be pretty thin, no? We were already being quiet because of Teddy."

"Yeah. You're probably right." She looked unconvinced, though.

"Leah…is there a problem with this lady?" He tucked a finger under her chin and urged her to look at him. "Is she bothering you guys?"

His question seemed to snap her out of her unease. "No. No, it's fine. Don't even worry about it. Drive safe and let me know when you get home, okay?"

The sheer motherliness of the question made him grin. "Will do, sweet thing. Now go back to bed."

Chapter Twelve

Leah

A S LEAH PULLED into her driveway and noticed Biddy standing on her front walk, tapping her foot impatiently, she was relieved that her landlord had at least waited until after she'd taken Teddy to school to appear. Otherwise, they might've ended up arguing in front of him, and heaven only knew what he would've overheard.

The morning had dawned bright but chilly, so Mrs. Daniels was wrapped in her usual tan cardigan, arms folded tightly across her stomach and lips pursed like it pained her to have to deliver another scolding.

In truth, Leah suspected she fed off these little chats. She was just that awful.

For a second, she considered driving straight into the garage and pretending like she hadn't noticed the woman. Biddy would only stomp up the stairs and ring the bell, though, and then she'd be twice as peeved as she was already.

Leah's morning had been rough enough—it would be counterproductive to prolong the agony. So, with a heavy sigh she parked, gathered her purse and empty travel mug, and got out of her car.

There was breakfast, a hot shower, and another steaming cup of coffee waiting for her inside, she told herself, as soon as this was over. And *this*, she had no doubt, was going to be about Wyatt.

She approached Biddy with what she hoped was a neutral, curious smile. "Good morning, Mrs. Daniels. Happy Monday. How are you?"

She'd considered—and immediately discarded—the greetings *you're up early* and *you'll catch a chill out here in that housedress.* In her current state, Leah wasn't confident she could deliver them without an edge, and both comments would only remind her neighbor of the difference in their ages. Leah had figured out the hard way it was a point of great resentment.

Unfortunately, even her supposedly safe greeting was met with contempt.

"I am not well," Biddy announced, "Which shouldn't surprise you, considering your guest kept me up half the night last night."

Leah smothered the urge to roll her eyes. She would've *loved* for Wyatt to keep her up half the night, but *no*—he'd insisted on being a gentleman and making her get a decent night's sleep. When she'd had to pry herself out of bed this morning, she'd even been grateful to him for it.

Now, however, she wished she'd been left with more to show for this stupid reprimand.

She gritted her teeth, aiming for calm and not quite getting there. "I apologize if he woke you when he left. He tried to be quiet."

"He wasn't," Biddy spat. "That vehicle is a menace. And what kind of 'friend' visits a mother at all hours? Or were you lying to me about him being a friend?"

"I wasn't lying to you." Leah was worried, though, that Biddy might have seen or overhead something that would refute that.

She reluctantly added, "Things have progressed into romantic territory since then."

"As I suspected."

She sighed and gestured toward her door. "Once again, I apologize for the inconvenience, and we will attempt to be quieter in the future, Mrs. Daniels. Now, if you don't mind, I have to get to work."

She needed food, she needed a shower, and she needed to go inside and earn money to keep a roof over her kid's head. What Leah patently did not need was this visit from the morality police.

Biddy's lips thinned in distaste. "I require another moment of your time," she said, marching over to her front stoop.

For the first time, Leah noticed the folder that had been placed there, and the fine hairs at the nape of her neck prickled in warning.

"When we spoke before, I informed you that you were not to entertain men inside the premises again. You defied me. I have cataloged the violations. You'll find the addendum with that list attached after section two." Biddy handed her the folder, lifted her chin, and stared Leah down with watery gray eyes.

"Mrs. Daniels, with all due respect," Leah sputtered, "This is inappropriate. I am a grown woman. You can not dictate to me how to conduct my personal life."

"I also suspected that you would not read over your lease as I instructed," Biddy continued. "That was certainly a mistake. The Lord does not take kindly to harlots, Mrs. Burke. As you'll see in these documents, I will be initiating eviction proceedings this week."

Like that, all the blood drained from Leah's head. "Ex...excuse me?"

She'd certainly *intended* to pull out her copy of the lease the last time they'd spoken, but then life kept happening and she'd forgotten. Besides, she hadn't thought a grouchy old woman's threats could amount to much.

She'd been wrong.

"You heard me. I gave you fair warning, Mrs. Burke. You chose to ignore it, and here we are."

"When are you planning to file these?" Leah asked, flipping quickly through the pages without really seeing anything.

"My nephew will be driving me to the lawyer this afternoon."

"And how much time will I have to respond?"

"I have requested that you be out by next weekend. I will require time to inspect the condition of the home so we can ready it for new tenants."

Leah choked as the impossible words sailed around her. "Next weekend! Mrs. Daniels, I have a four-year-old child living in this house. That is not nearly enough time to pack and find somewhere else to live." Then, another panicked thought occurred to her. "Not to mention, Teddy has preschool until the end of May. I can't uproot him in the middle of the term. We were on that waitlist for months."

Biddy's eyes gleamed in what Leah could only describe as victory. "Perhaps you should have considered those factors before you chose to disregard my advice, Mrs. Burke. I did warn you there would be consequences. This is merely the outcome of your recklessness."

Leah knew arguing was not going to help her case, but she couldn't seem to stop. This was so patently unfair. "And where, exactly, are we supposed to go? There's nothing affordable for rent around here. The real estate market is atrocious right now."

"That is not my problem. I only rent to modest Christian families—*not* to jezebels and tarts. I see no need to bend my morals for your convenience now."

Leah flushed with resentment. If she was going to be labeled a slut, she should at least be getting laid regularly. Instead, she and Wyatt had barely managed to round third base, and while she hadn't minded that when she got up this morning, it was beginning to feel like a tremendous lapse in judgment.

Frantically, she reviewed what she could remember of her last conversation with Biddy, and came to a shaky conclusion. "This is because I'm a single mom now," she demanded defensively. "Isn't it?"

Biddy scowled and looked away.

"Mrs. Daniels, correct me if I'm wrong but you are a widow, too. We didn't choose this. How can you turn us out for something so completely out of our control?"

Her neighbor's severe eyes landed back on Leah, and the woman looked her up and down with distaste. "I am a widow, yes, and I have never once betrayed my marriage vows in all these many years. I knew some women who eventually went on to *discreetly* court and remarry, but after all my Walter sacrificed for us, I refused to dishonor his memory that way. It's frankly disgusting what you girls get up to nowadays, sleeping around with all and sundry like your husbands never existed. Not a one of you seems to feel an ounce of shame."

Leah's breath sawed in and out of her lungs in short, raw bursts. The universe had gifted her with one tiny slice of happiness in Wyatt, and this was the price of it? *Absolutely not.*

"Jesse would not want Teddy and me to mourn indefinitely," she told her landlord. "He would want us to be happy. To go on living."

That wasn't precisely true, but Leah wasn't about to split hairs out here with Biddy the Baleful.

The woman sniffed, utterly unmoved by her pleas. "You have one week. Unless you magically find yourself married by a man of God within that time, you and the boy need to be out no later than next Monday."

Biddy spun on her sensible shoes and took a step toward her door. Leah's heartbeat pulsed in her ears. One week was *impossible.* She needed to buy herself some time.

"Mrs. Daniels," she called, "Wait."

The woman stopped and turned, and for the life of her, Leah would never be able to explain the words that exited her mouth next.

"I don't need to read through these papers," she said shakily, flipping them back and forth in her hand. "Because you are wrong about Wyatt. About us. He's a good man, loyal and kind and true. You saw what he did for our yard. Yours, too, I might add, completely on his own. I didn't ask him to do that. He takes good care of Teddy and me, just like you say a man should."

And completely unlike Jesse did, she added silently to herself.

"I fail to see how your opinion of his worthiness is pertinent to the situation, Mrs. Burke." Biddy took another step away.

"It is pertinent." Leah steeled herself for what she was about to do. "It matters because…"

Her landlady eyed her, somehow even more pinched and disagreeable than before. "Because…?" she wondered dubiously.

Leah swallowed down her apprehension. "Because the reason he was here so late last night, the reason he continues to visit us despite what you said, is that—"

"Mrs. Burke, this is unseemly. I really don't think—"

There were going to be reasonable questions, and Leah was going to have to figure out unassailable answers to them very, very soon. She'd do it once she'd had a minute to pull herself together, once Teddy was back home and down for his nap, once she could explain what had happened to Wyatt.

She'd get right on it. Leah would call him as soon as possible, and she prayed he'd be available and would understand.

"You don't need to file the eviction papers," she blurted out, "Because soon we will be married, just like your lease requires. You see, Wyatt was here late last night because he…"

She tried to take a deep breath, but it felt as if her lungs could only hold a fraction of the air they were supposed to. Leah's head spun, and her gut roiled, but there was nothing else she could think of saying.

"Mrs. Burke, please get to the point. What are you trying to say?"

Leah stared at the woman and straightened her spine. "I'm saying, last night Wyatt proposed to me. Your complaint has no basis. We're getting married."

Chapter Thirteen

Wyatt

AFTER A LONG day spent combing through publicity photos, movie industry publications, DC and Texas society blogs, and more, Wyatt had never wanted to see another photo of the Doggett family unit again.

So many smarmy smiles. So many hangers-on.

He was under no delusion that politics wasn't a dirty business, but being confronted with the visual evidence for hours on end had made him wish he had access to a high-grade decontamination chamber.

He'd felt tainted.

Noah, of course, had been as meticulous as ever, so it'd seemed as if he'd compiled a dossier on every person Senator Doggett or his family had ever known. Despite his work, though, they'd only been able to trace a scant few back to Pendleton or Echo Company.

Now, the team just needed to develop a plan to approach the people, one that would give them the best chance of extracting the information they needed. He'd only left once it became clear that several of the ideas up for debate involved him playing the role of honeypot.

Wyatt knew the guys saw him that way, and maybe a little of it was understandable given some of his exploits…but that didn't mean it hadn't rankled.

He should be allowed the chance to change. To grow up and evolve. With Leah in the picture, Wyatt didn't want to be cast as a player anymore. It bore only a passing resemblance to the truth, anyway, and had been an increasingly ill-fitting costume for some time now.

Too bad he was the only one who seemed able to see that.

Well, he and Leah, that was. When her text had popped up on his phone, asking if he had time to stop by tonight, he'd jumped at the excuse to leave. She never wanted to meet two nights in a row, much less three.

Maybe she'd been plotting revenge for the way he'd left her hanging last night.

The thought made him smile. *All's fair.*

He looked down at their joined hands, resting on his thigh as they sat on her cozy couch. Wyatt ran his thumb lightly across her palm and murmured "Four dates in one week, Ms. Burke? What a scandal. People will begin to talk."

She flinched, then muttered, "Calling Biddy Daniels a 'people' is a bit of a stretch."

"And yet she looks so human."

"Look harder," Leah retorted. "There's nothing but ice behind those cold, gray eyes."

Wyatt chuckled, but there was an undercurrent to her words that made him wonder, "So, what's the deal with her, anyway? Just nosey, or is there more to it?"

Her face scrunched up and she pulled her hand away. "Oh, there's definitely more to it than that. And I need to tell you about her, but…I was hoping to tackle that in a little while, if that's okay. I'm trying to figure out the best way to explain."

He frowned, trying to make sense of her mood. "Sounds serious."

"It's not great," she admitted. "But I'm really grateful you could make it up here tonight. Thanks for that."

"No thanks required. Though next time I need to come by a little earlier. The grass is getting long. I should cut it again."

"Okay," she snorted, "but at the rate we're going, your friends are probably going to file a missing persons report on you."

Wyatt shook his head. "Why, so I can return to festering on the couch, watching the football draft with them? Pass."

"You don't like football?"

"I'm not a fan of pro ball. I like the college game better," he told her.

Leah tilted her head, eyeing him curiously. "Really? Who's your team?"

"The OU Sooners," he chuckled, by now used to the reaction that usually got.

"The Sooners? Why?" she looked him over like she might find the answer somewhere on his person. "I thought you grew up near La Jolla."

"I did. My dad was from Oklahoma, though. For some reason, my mom kept watching, even after he was gone. I guess she made a fan out of me." It was a simple explanation, easier than trying to explain how little of a connection he'd felt to the man who'd sired him, and how desperate he'd been to grasp at any little thing to prove there'd once been a father in his world at all.

Leah accepted it readily, though, and murmured only a distracted, "Huh," in reply.

Wyatt studied her expression again, but she'd wiped it clean of feelings. "Do you follow football?" he prompted.

"Not really." Her eyes skated around the room, avoiding him. *Something was up.*

"You gonna tell me what's going on?" he wondered. "Or do I have to guess why you're stalling?"

Leah slumped back, turning just her head to look at him. "I've got to tell you something and I'm afraid you're going to be mad," she sighed. "I accidentally involved you in something stupid without talking to you first, and I want you to know I'm so sorry."

Wyatt tried to suss out what she could possibly mean. "Was it for a good reason?" he asked.

Not that he doubted her. Leah was a responsible person—no way was she mixed up in anything hinky.

"Of course," she insisted. "I just blurted out something dumb in the heat of the moment. But now that I've had time to think about it, I can't help worrying that…" She sighed again, her frustration clear. "I don't know. Maybe there was something else I could've said. If you've got any great ideas, I'm all ears."

"Okay, so let's talk it through," he told her reasonably.

This was good. Leah had come to him with a problem and invited his opinion. It felt like cooperation and teamwork. Like good communication, which his mom had always assured him was the basis of a good relationship.

Wyatt was all ready to wow Leah with what a great partner he'd been trained to be. Until, that is, she whined, "Do we have to do it right now?"

Oh well. Baby steps were still steps.

"I mean, if you'd rather wait, I can certainly come up with other things we can try," he chuckled.

Leah's dark brows arched high on her forehead, and she smirked at him knowingly. "Why don't you follow me, so we can discuss them upstairs?" She got to her feet and tugged him up as well.

"Don't have to ask me twice." She'd taken the bait readily, which meant she *really* didn't want to tell him whatever she had to say.

At least he could be sure she wasn't about to kick him to the curb—Leah was definitely not the love 'em and leave 'em type.

As Wyatt tiptoed after her down the upstairs hall, his eyes landed on a framed photo on the wall, positioned innocuously among a set of others, but highlighted by the slash of light coming from her bedroom. Wyatt froze, staring at it with a knot in his throat.

"What?" she whispered.

"I know this picture," he murmured, pointing.

"You must've seen it last time you were—"

"No. I saw it last year. It's one of the ones Jesse showed me in Dubai."

Leah looked like a million bucks in it, her incandescent smile aimed straight at the camera as she balanced baby Teddy on her hip. Even after all this time, Wyatt probably could've described the photo in his sleep. It'd made that big of an impression.

"Oh." She made an uncomfortable sound. "Buzzkill. Sorry."

"No, it's okay," he whispered. "Look at you guys. You look so beautiful. So happy."

Leah pulled him into her room and shut the door, her face a storm of unwieldy emotions. "You want to hear about that picture? All week, Jesse had been on my case that I was letting myself go. He said we'd promised each other we wouldn't be *those people*, the kind who gave up looking nice once they got married and had kids. We were supposed to be on vacation, but with every bite of ice cream I took, and every sip of wine, I got the look. All because I tried on a skirt in a tourist shop and had to ask him to get me a bigger size. I'd just had a baby, for Christ's sake."

Wyatt blew out a long breath, taken aback by her anger. "The absolute audacity of that prick."

"I wasn't even smiling at him. I was talking to a lady about Teddy." She shook her head. "I can't believe that was the picture he was out there showing people. What a piece of work."

"You do look hot in it," Wyatt shrugged, trying to divert her. "Asshole clearly knew he was a fucking liar."

Leah spun on him with a smirk, her unhappiness evaporating like she'd flipped a switch. "I looked hot, did I? Do you have a little thing for MILFs, Mr. Oaks?"

He backed her toward her bed. "Now why did you have to put it that way?"

"Hey, if the shoe fits…"

Wyatt bent to kiss her, loving the eager way she wrapped her arms around his neck and melted against his body. He loved the hot slide of her tongue against his. He could kiss her for hours. He tried to set aside his misgivings about her earlier uneasiness.

Her legs bumped against the bed, and she broke away with a gasp. Shooting him a coy look, Leah swept her t-shirt over her head, shimmied out of her gym shorts, and sank back on the mattress.

Her bra was lacier this time. It still didn't match her underwear, though, and for some reason, that made him grin. The girl was real, he'd give her that.

Wyatt climbed over her as she shimmied backward, taking his time, dropping open-mouthed kisses on whichever part of skin caught his eye.

There was a lot to pay attention to. Long, toned legs, a tanned stomach, those gorgeous breasts, rising and falling as she took shuddering breaths.

After teasing her for a few minutes, he knew there was only one place he wanted to be. He inched down, stroking her smooth, soft skin, reveling in her warm scent, and running his tongue along the top edge of her underwear.

Leah shivered, widening her legs so he could sink between them. He could not wait to taste her. Wyatt flicked his tongue along her inner thigh, smiling at the sexy whimper she let out.

He dipped his fingers under the thin strips of material at her hips and inched her underwear down, drawing it out, making her wait despite his heart pounding with impatience.

When she shifted restlessly, he stopped and gripped her by the hips, holding her in place so he could nip her enticing inner thigh.

"Be patient," he warned, brushing his lips against her skin.

"Wyatt, please," Leah whispered. She arched her back, urging him on.

"I got you," he promised, pulling her panties a fraction lower and pressing kisses to the skin he'd revealed. "Now be good."

The change in her happened in the space between one breath and the next. Wyatt looked at the breathtaking woman pinned under his hands and froze, trying to understand what happened.

One minute, Leah was right there with him, and the next she was... *not.*

Disconnected, checked out—he wasn't sure what to call it, or even how he knew she was gone. His senses were on high alert, though, and when he pulled back Leah's eyes were squeezed shut and her head was averted on the pillow.

The tendons in her neck looked strained. Her hands were balled stiffly in the sheets, like she was shying away from something awful. *Shit.*

Wyatt did a quick rewind in his head, but nothing he'd done so far should've spooked her or hurt her. Not one freaky kink was introduced. No consent boundaries were pushed.

He hadn't been rushing or getting creative, and a moment ago Leah was absolutely buying what he was selling. Yet somehow, he'd stumbled onto a trigger of hers. That much was clear.

Except, he hadn't even said anything particularly dirty, he'd only told her to...

All at once he knew. *Jesse.* Had to be. That bastard.

If he weren't already dead, Wyatt would almost definitely have to go out and end him for all the mind-fuck things he'd left Leah to deal with.

He pushed himself up to lay next to her and stroked her tense jawline. "Hey sweet thing," he said. "How we doing up here?"

"Good," she lied. She held herself still—too still.

"Babe. Is everything okay?"

Leah nodded, but she didn't open her eyes. "Yup."

Wyatt didn't want to make things worse, but at the same time, he had to know where he'd gone wrong, so he didn't make the same mistake again.

"Who's here with you right now?" he asked gently.

That got her. Her eyes popped open, and she scowled darkly at him. "You," she murmured, but she looked…wrecked. *God.*

Wyatt swallowed hard. "I'd like you to say it, please."

"What?"

"Say my name. So I know, and so…so you know, too."

Leah blinked slowly, guilt seeping into her expression. "Wyatt," she whispered.

"I'm not him," he told her softly. "I'll never be him."

It was a risk, bringing Jesse up in this space that felt like it should be sacred between the two of them. He didn't want to contaminate it, but clearly the man's shade was already here. The only way to destroy it was to shine a light on it.

"I know," Leah whispered, barely a breath of sound. Her eyes welled up, but she managed to give him a watery little smile. "I know it's you, Wyatt. I got lost for a minute, but I'm okay. And you shouldn't…I don't want you to stop what you were doing."

"You sure?"

"Very."

She was running the show, but he had his reservations about letting her have the opportunity to slip back into whatever memory she'd gotten stuck in. "If it's all the same to you, I think I'd like to hang out up here with you for a bit. How's that sound?"

"I'll manage." She smiled wider, and her arm muscles relaxed under his stroking hand.

"Will you tell me what happened?"

"I don't want him here. I want him to leave us alone."

"It's worse if you try to bury it. When you pretend like it's not there, it grows," he murmured back. "Let it out, so it loses its power."

Leah stared at him for a long time. Then she whispered in a rush, "You don't know what he was like. No one knows what Jesse was really like."

Wyatt's blood froze in his veins, thinking of the way she'd gone from excited to enduring. "Then tell me. What was Jesse really like?"

She thought a moment. "In public, he smiled and laughed, while his fingers dug into my arm hard enough to leave bruises the next day. He made me feel like I was the one doing everything wrong." She pressed her lips together, suppressing whatever else she'd been about to say. "Jesse was cruel," she said at last. "And he was an expert at hiding it."

"So were you, it sounds like."

She nodded. "True. Except now, I can't remember why the secrecy felt so important. You should've seen it—at the funeral, everyone looked at me like I was this paragon of virtue. *Look how brave she is. Standing so straight and tall. Not a single tear.*"

Wyatt swallowed, hating that for her. Good thing he hadn't attended—not that he would've known, back then, what he was witnessing.

"You have no idea how hard it was to do that," she whispered.

"To not cry?" he wondered carefully.

Leah snorted, derision sour on her tongue. "God, no. To not show how euphoric I felt to be set free. To know that Teddy was free, too."

Her lovely brown eyes welled up, and he stroked her cheek softly.

"Jesse is gone. For good. He can't hurt you anymore," he said. "Be as happy as you want about that."

He had a hard time forcing the man's name past his lips, though, and no power on earth could've made him refer to the guy as Leah's husband at that moment. What kind of person went out into the world with a shit-eating grin on his face, making friends in bars halfway around the world and boasting about the wife and kid he had at home—and never let on what a stain on humanity he was?

How could Wyatt have missed it?

Jesse had been more worried about some stranger's opinion than he'd been about his own wife, and looking at Leah struggling to suppress her tears now—realizing the burden she'd had to bear in silence while everyone had fawned over her extroverted husband—he felt something sharp twist in his chest.

Why hadn't her brother, at least, done something to help her?

Wyatt had been drawn to this woman because of his memories of Jesse—his sorrow that a devoted family man hadn't made it home to this woman and their child.

Now that he knew the truth, he would've liked to teach the man a lesson or two about what it meant to *have and to hold*. See how he liked it.

While he was busy stewing, Leah's thoughts had apparently moved on.

"I have something else to tell you," she admitted grimly.

"Okay." *How much worse could it get?*

"Wyatt, I did something stupid, and I need you to know that I don't expect you to do anything about it. I will figure it out somehow, I promise—but I had to tell you in case it comes up."

"Alright well, no time like the present. Spit it out. Let's hear it."

Leah took a deep breath. "This morning, you and I got engaged to be married."

"Pardon me?"

"Surprise?" she smiled weakly.

Chapter Fourteen

Leah

W YATT'S EASYGOING EXPRESSION turned comically blank at her news.

"Come again?" he asked, sitting up slowly.

"Okay sorry, let me back up," Leah told him. "You really don't have to do a thing differently, I swear. I was just trying to buy a little time, but as soon as I can find somewhere else for Teddy and me to go, it will be a moot point, and we can stop pretending."

"Pretending?"

"Yes, obviously."

"Maybe you need to start at the beginning," he suggested.

"Ah. Right. It seems my lease has some kind of morality clause. My landlord didn't like that you've been spending time here, so she said she was going to file eviction papers unless I magically ended up married. She gave us a week to get out."

Wyatt considered her explanation for a minute or two, then asked, "What about a ring?"

Leah had figured that part out, at least. "Easy. I ordered an inexpensive one online. It should be here in a couple days." When Wyatt looked a little miffed, she explained, "Biddy asked why I wasn't wearing one. I told her it was too big, so you had to get it sized."

"I see."

"Like I said, you really don't have to do a thing."

She couldn't get a handle on what he was feeling. Was this strange lack of reaction anger? Was he strategizing? Or something else entirely?

"Are you…okay?"

Wyatt nodded, but he seemed curiously deflated. Almost as if…he was disappointed. Leah was certainly used to that feeling. She'd disappointed her former husband for years.

"Wyatt I really am sorry," she tried again. "I panicked and just blurted it out. I know you must be so mad but—"

"No, it's not that." The hand he held up was steady, forestalling any further groveling.

"Okay. Then what is it?"

He stared into the distance for a moment more, before he finally met her eyes. "It's just… this isn't how I imagined this going, you know?" He looked sheepish, two stripes of red blooming high on his cheeks. "I always pictured like, picking out the ring myself, and planning out the perfect proposal and whatnot. It feels weird that there's nothing for me to do."

Leah swallowed, somehow feeling even guiltier at the admission. "I mean, you still have to pretend to be the happy groom," she laughed weakly.

"No pretending required," he murmured back.

"And you'll still get to do all that stuff for real one day," she consoled him. "It's not like this counts, right?"

Wyatt held himself strangely still, looking inward, a peculiar half smile frozen on his face. "No, you're right," he agreed quietly.

Leah wasn't sure what was happening. She felt like she had ruined something important to him, something special, and coming on the heels of her triggering out about Jesse—when Wyatt innocently told her to 'be good,' and didn't have any idea the way orders like that had been weaponized against her—it was all too much.

She needed to think. She couldn't ask him to leave, though, not with what she needed him to do. *What a mess.*

Leah told him, "I feel like I brought you here under false pretenses and now I've done a horrible bait and switch on you."

Wyatt was shaking his head before she even finished. "No. No, don't worry about that at all." His eyes cleared, and his gaze bored into her. "I'm glad to help. Seriously. But there're a few things we need to take care of as soon as possible."

"Okay. What?" Leah relaxed at his tone. This was the kind of action-oriented response she'd been desperately hoping for. She needed him to be a partner, not an adversary, and to help her figure out how to sell this farce properly.

"First, I need a copy of your lease. I want to have someone look at it, to make sure what she's trying to do is even legal." He nodded to himself as he listed things off. "Not to make it awkward, but I should probably move in to make this look better, at least temporarily. I'm fine couch surfing, don't worry," he rushed to add. "I'm not trying to be weird."

"No, uh…no you're right," Leah stuttered. "We can figure that out."

He hesitated. "I'm slightly concerned that me being here could make the situation worse," he admitted. "Morality police don't exactly love when people shack up before marriage. I just thought that if this was real, I'd be here in a heartbeat. So, if it makes sense to us, it should look more believable to her."

She'd had hours to think this over, but Wyatt was already ticking off important points that hadn't even occurred to her. Leah had basically only thought of the ring—the least critical piece of the puzzle. She wanted to hide under the carpet in disgrace.

"You know her best, though. What do you think?" he wondered.

She thought about all the snide things her landlord had said to her over the years, and the way the woman's distaste had come to head at perhaps the lowest moment of her life. Like that, Leah's worry ebbed, and indignation took its place. "You know what? Screw her," she said. "She's trying to evict a struggling mother for no freaking reason. She can die mad for all I care."

"You're sure?"

Leah's bluster wavered in the face of his dubious look. "I mean…she's probably going to kick us out no matter what we do, right?"

"It's possible," he conceded.

"Then we should commit to the bit. Like you said, if we were really getting married, we'd move in together. We wouldn't be divvying up our money and time between two households, when we both know they're both in short supply."

Wyatt studied her, as if he was gauging whether she really believed what she'd said. Leah held her breath until he abruptly relaxed and continued on with his directives.

"Okay. You'll have to give me some direction on what you want to tell Teddy. Maybe just saying I'm coming for a visit will work?"

Leah nodded again, trying to keep up. Should she be taking notes?

"I also think it'd be smart to have a backup plan about where to move you and Teddy if the ruse doesn't hold. Let's think about how far it's practical for you to drive for the rest of his school session, and what other things you need to be close to."

"I've been trying to do that," she answered weakly, "But it's been hard. I need to stay in the same budget range, but there's not a lot available right now. Teddy isn't done with school until May, either. The last year has been such an adjustment, I don't want to uproot him."

"Yeah, real estate sucks right now," he agreed. "But don't sweat it—you've got options. Even if we can't find you something else to rent, I know of a few places we could stash you guys if it comes to that."

Stash? Leah shivered a little, wondering what that meant exactly.

Wyatt extracted his phone from his pocket, either to text someone or make some notes of his own, she couldn't tell.

She pulled the blanket folded across the foot of her bed closer and wrapped it around her shoulders.

"Last thing," Wyatt announced when he was done, "When is the wedding?"

"W-what?" she stammered. He really was taking this all the way, wasn't he?

"We can't hold your neighbor off forever with a fake engagement," he shrugged, "So how long do you want to wait before we claim to be married?"

"Uh, I don't know…maybe a month?" It seemed laughably short, but no more ridiculous than any other part of this performance, she supposed.

"We'll need photos," he announced. "But that's easy enough. We can probably stage them with my roommates. I also have some women who can fill in as bridesmaids if you don't want to involve your friends."

"Oh. Okay, yeah, whatever you think."

With Wyatt at the helm, their stupid fake engagement was going to end up looking more real than half of the Army marriages Leah had helped facilitate. What on earth would he do with an authentic wedding to plan?

"You're really leaning into this, aren't you?" she chuckled uneasily.

He looked up from his phone, hesitated when he noticed her expression, and set the thing aside. "Don't we…want this to look believable?" he wondered carefully.

She laughed. "I mean, I thought we just needed Biddy to believe me long enough for me to move somewhere else. Right? I kind of thought me wearing a fake ring and you lying if she asked you would do the trick."

"But if she's filing eviction papers…" he countered.

"She might not, if she accepts the engagement is real," Leah told him. "Don't get me wrong, I very much appreciate the, uh, the enthusiasm you are bringing to this project—but do you suppose you might be getting a little *too* into it?"

She glanced around, feeling uncomfortably exposed. *Where was her shirt?*

"I'm gathering that meticulousness is not what you wanted," Wyatt replied. He reached toward the armchair, found her shirt in the pile of clothes there, and handed it to her as if he'd read her mind.

"I'm not saying your ideas are bad. I'm just saying maybe we don't need to go quite so far," Leah said gently.

"But if we take care of everything ahead of time and things go sideways, we'll have our next salvo lined up and ready to go," Wyatt countered. "We can deploy each tier when and if it's needed, without having to scramble in the moment for the right response."

"Will having it all planned out make you feel better about participating?"

"Yes," he said flatly. "I don't like loopholes."

Leah studied him, from his stony determination to the stubborn set of his jaw, and frowned as an unnerving thought occurred to her.

"Wyatt…I know I sprung this on you, but the way you're responding is making me wonder what this is going to do to you."

"I'm just trying to help you, like you asked," he said.

"And I appreciate that. But do you think that your…intensity might have less to do with helping me and Teddy out of the goodness of your heart, and more to do with going back in time and somehow fixing things for you and your mom?"

She didn't know where the odd thought had come from, but once her words were out there, Leah wondered how long they'd been brewing under the surface. Longer than the last few minutes, certainly.

She was suddenly anxious to hear his answer, because it felt like everything hinged on what he'd say.

Wyatt blinked, taken aback by her accusation. "The past is done, Leah. I'm clear on the fact that we don't get do-overs."

"And yet, it feels good to be the savior you and your mom probably needed, doesn't it?" Leah bit her lip, shocked at her nerve but also unable to let it go.

"Of course, it does. What's wrong with that?"

"Well, I'm not your mom," she pointed out. "And Teddy is not you. We are our own people, and our situation and needs are different."

He looked confused. "As I said, I get it."

"Do you understand why I had to ask, though?"

"I do." His nod was slow. Thoughtful. "I don't love that you felt like you had to, but I get it."

"Okay." She'd think through his answers again later, but for now Leah took a deep breath and tried to defuse the tension she kept causing. "Then thank you, again, for taking this so well and for your excellent scheming. I know it doesn't sound like it, but I am exceedingly grateful, and I will repay you somehow. I don't know how, but I will."

"Please don't think about it like that," he murmured, shifting closer and tucking his face into her shoulder. "You make it sound so transactional."

"Then how should I think of it?" she whispered, running her fingers through the soft hair curling at his neck, touched by his need to seal their truce with affection.

He turned his head and pressed a kiss to the side of her neck, then slipped an arm around her waist and pulled her into a hug. "Think of it as me taking care of my wife as she deserves," he rumbled next to her ear.

Chapter Fifteen

Wyatt

S O… I'VE GOT a situation," Wyatt announced. No one seemed particularly surprised by the statement—he had called the team together for specifically this reason, after all.

He was uneasy about how this was going to go, but he still forced himself to look around the room, taking in faces and not quite meeting anyone's eye. As dispassionately as he could, he relayed the pertinent details of his conversation with Leah, then waited staunchly through the ensuing smothering silence for the inevitable break in the dam.

As he'd expected, Joe was the first to crack. "Are you fucking nuts?" his buddy bellowed eventually. "That had to be the fewest words I've ever heard used to describe the most fucked-up shit."

Uncomfortable heat pricked at Wyatt's neck. "You're one to talk," he grumbled. "You—"

Buck cleared his throat, cutting off what could easily have turned into an hour or more of bickering. "Stitch, what do you need from us?"

"I'm going to crash with them for a while," he replied, "to make the engagement look legit. I figure I'll need a more family-friendly vehicle, and probably a car seat for the kid. Documents would be helpful, in case the landlord wants to see proof." He brandished the papers Leah had given him and dropped them on the kitchen table. "I also promised I'd get the lease and eviction papers looked over, to see if they are even legal."

Buck nodded, rubbing his jaw as he studied the assembled group.

Seeming to come to a decision, he nodded again. "Okay, as I see it, Noah and Bruiser need to keep working on the Pendleton church group stuff. There are a fuck ton of connections that have to be traced out and we can't pull them off that right now. I do think Noah can hook you up with a better ride by this afternoon, though."

"You can use one of the Black Watch SUVs," Noah agreed, "And store your car at the hangar if you want. It'll be secure there. If you get me the kid's height and weight, I can make sure you have the right booster seat for it."

"Got it." Wyatt fired off a text to Leah before he could forget.

Buck pointed at Easy. "Bennett, look into Leah's landlord. Find out what her deal is. And you know what? Take a look at that nephew she mentioned, too. Stitch, you got a name on that guy?"

"I think Leah said his name was Luis? I don't have a last name, but I can check to see if she knows."

"Good. I'm on documents." He spared Leah's papers one dismissive glance as he snagged them off the table, then tucked them under his arm. "I'll get this shit looked over, and arrange for whatever else you might need to sell the ruse."

"Thanks, man."

"Do you need a ring?" Noah wondered, not bothering to look up as his thumbs flew over his phone, presumably getting a jump start on their preparations.

Wyatt felt his cheeks warm. Somehow, that felt like the most humiliating detail of all. "No. Leah said she ordered something online."

Silence fell like a shroud. He waited for more—a thrown can, a sarcastic barb…anything that might make this insanity feel the slightest bit normal—but nothing happened. Nothing but sharp, heavy stares, boring into him. Could they see how that one thing had stung?

Was he *that* transparent?

He scratched his neck. "So…thanks. I appreciate the help, and I know Leah will be grateful, as well."

Buck squeezed his shoulder, sent a speaking glance at Bennett, and left without a word.

Easy grinned and slapped him on the back. "Brother, we got you," he drawled. "And hey, let me be the first to say congratulations, alright?"

"Fucking A," Wyatt muttered. This was so emphatically not how this was supposed to go, it felt borderline obscene.

Bennett laughed, though. "You'll be fine. Two weeks and this thing blows over like it never happened." He looked around with a relaxed grin, clapped Wyatt on the shoulder again, and told everyone, "See y'all," before sauntering out the door, too.

Two weeks. Like it never happened. Wyatt's mood grew dark.

Joe eyed him dubiously, no doubt tracking the shift. "That's some bullshit right there. We won't see him for two weeks, probably. That asshole knows good and well the only person seeing him regularly is Kim."

"You blame him?" Wyatt grimaced. Easy's fiancée Kim was a beauty, on the inside even more than the outside. Not his type at all, but perfect for Bennett.

"Nah. But someone needs to keep giving him shit." Joe checked his watch and sighed, "Look I got a thing I have to do, but you and I are going to talk about this later, you got me?"

Wyatt nodded for what felt like the hundredth time. Bruiser might talk a big game, but he was a salt of the earth dude—when it came down to it, he'd never steered Wyatt wrong. He'd die before letting any one of them down, and nearly had.

It was partly why Joe had been taking his recent troubles so hard. He felt like the weakest link, and refused to acknowledge that any one of them would've done things the same.

Regardless, Wyatt could certainly use a dose of the guy's medicine sooner rather than later, because his own head was a mess.

Joe hustled out the door after the others, leaving Wyatt still rooted to the tile and Noah at the kitchen table, staring into his soul.

"What?" Wyatt asked irritably. It was discombobulating to be so relieved and grateful for everyone's help, yet also so inexpressibly embarrassed by the nature of what was required. He'd promised Leah, though, and he was not going to disappoint her. The fact that she was letting him help at all was huge.

Fortunately, Noah was a good egg, as his grandma used to say. Wyatt liked him a lot, apart from the inconvenient fact that the guy routinely saw way too much to make him comfortable to be around in a situation like this.

"There's more to it isn't there?" the guy said, once they were alone. Calm as the surf on a balmy summer morning, damn it.

"Dude…" Wyatt sighed, feeling unaccountably glum. "Everyone is saying it's no big deal, because none of this is real."

Noah pushed up his glasses and set his phone aside. "But?"

"But what if it is? And what if this farce ruins the real thing I think…might be happening?"

To his credit, Noah didn't laugh, and for the first time, Wyatt realized that *not* having a long, involved history with the guy might actually be a benefit.

He'd been pigeonholed as so unserious about relationships for so long now, that Wyatt had no idea how to make anyone understand that Leah was different. Except Noah didn't seem to buy the notion that Wyatt was some love 'em and leave 'em fuck boy. He didn't have the context to write him off that way.

At this moment, it literally made him the only person Wyatt could talk to about this.

He pulled out a chair and dropped into it.

"Are you saying you think Leah could be the one?" Noah asked carefully.

The question felt dangerous—too dangerous to agree with completely. Wyatt hedged, "Possibly. But the problem is, she's already done the whole engagement and wedding and marriage thing. Hell, she's even done the procreation thing. I obviously have not, and for some reason, agreeing to this fake coupling crap feels like I'm neutering the experience for myself."

"Have you tried telling her you don't want to do this?"

"I do, though."

"Then tell her you'd like it to be real."

"Three weeks after meeting her? She'll think I'm insane. And what if I'm wrong? It's not like I have a ton of experience with commitment."

"You don't strike me as the kind of person to rush recklessly into something like this," Noah commented.

Wyatt let the thought settle in him, wanting so much to believe it was true. "Leah's got trust issues, though. Like…we haven't even talked about it that much, but I get the sense that her husband was a total fuckwad and left her with loads of baggage. I can't figure out how to convince her I'm different. That I'm not like him and never will be."

Noah nodded thoughtfully and as Wyatt scanned his face, he realized abruptly that his roommate no longer seemed quite as young as he'd come off previously. In fact, he seemed…weirdly wise.

Perhaps a guy could pick up a lot of knowledge with the power of the internet at his fingertips.

"So… full disclosure, my mom is a couples' therapist," he began.

Or he could pick up a lot by knowing the right people, Wyatt amended to himself. "Convenient," he chuckled.

"Yes and no," Noah smiled back. "But this reminds me of a book she talked about once. More of a fad, pop-psych thing than peer-reviewed research, but hear me out."

"Okay…"

"Have you ever heard about love language theory?"

"Noah. Look at who you're talking to."

"People can have hidden depths," he shrugged, then gave Wyatt a brief overview. "Anyway, I wonder if maybe you've been rolling up on Leah with a barrage of Acts of Service, and she can't interpret them because she's looking for Words of Affirmation or Thoughtful Gifts, or something."

"Well, how am I supposed to know what language she wants me to speak?"

"She could be using the one she wants on you. Or you might need to do a little trial and error and see what sticks."

Wyatt sat with the idea for a minute, reviewing their interactions. Had Leah's behavior fit into any one of those categories? She hadn't given him gifts, unless he counted meals—and Wyatt definitely thought he should. Perhaps quality time? Or physical touch? He was down for any and all of those.

But what did Leah want?

Noah was a genius on many fronts, it seemed.

"Dude, thanks," he said, slapping the table. "MVP of the day. Seriously, helpful as always."

The guy gave him a hesitant fist bump and a crooked little smile. "Good luck," he said. "Not sure what I did, but have at it, I guess."

GIVEN THE CIRCUMSTANCES, Wyatt ought to have expected the call he received later that afternoon, but somehow hearing the bossman's genial voice still managed to startle him. Orders from on high usually filtered through Buck or Noah. *Not this time.*

Wyatt had caught Tate's attention, and he futilely wished it had been for anything other than this. He'd been a Black Watch employee for, what? Several months? Not long enough to feel safe as the team outlier, that was for sure.

"I hear congratulations are in order," Monroe said drily when the call connected.

"Not really," Wyatt muttered. "But I guess." He hated saying it, like the words were a direct insult to Leah. Like she'd know, and count him down for it.

"Real or not, it's a distraction that will take time to navigate, and the team needs you mentally and physically present on the current op. You think you can go through with this and still keep your head in the game?" Tate didn't sound angry, per se. More curious, if Wyatt had to guess.

"Of course. This is nothing, I swear." He immediately hated that denial too, as soon as it exited his mouth.

"Not *nothing*—it sounds as if Ms. Burke was neck deep in the Pendleton church groups that Noah found."

"It sounds as if that was mostly her husband's gig," Wyatt protested.

"And yet, we will need to keep digging," Tate countered, "both to confirm her noninvolvement and to sift out whatever details she might have picked up that could help us."

"I know." Wyatt's brain was in overdrive, trying to pin down why the man was calling and what he was aiming to communicate. "I hope you know I've reported back to the team the second anything pertinent has come up."

"I do. I just want to make sure you understand how hard it can be to face trouble that's right in front of your face when you don't want to see it." Monroe paused, then went on, "You can't ignore red flags with this woman, just because you're catching big feelings. Not until we're one thousand percent sure she's an innocent bystander."

Wyatt's jaw locked so hard, he felt his temples pulse. Still, the man wasn't wrong. "Message received and understood. Sir."

Tate snorted at the appellation. "You moving into that house with her is going to draw notice. I'm assigning a detail to keep an eye on things, alright? Wanted to give you a heads-up so you didn't get an itchy trigger finger or something."

Wyatt zeroed in on the word notice. *Interesting.* Whose notice were they worried about drawing, exactly?

Instead, he asked, "Who's it going to be?"

"I'm thinking Kendra and her squad, but I'll confirm once everything is in place. I still want you to go over the interior, make sure there are no cameras or listening devices on the property."

"Roger that. And…thank you for the extra support. I like knowing someone will have eyes on them when I'm not there."

"I bet you do." Monroe's tone was dry as dust.

Wyatt hesitated. This might be his boss, he reminded himself, the owner of the entire Black Watch company, but he could not let the dig go unanswered. "What's that supposed to mean?"

Tate chuckled. "It means that ten weeks of intense demonstrated interest in Ms. Burke and her child indicates this is more than a passing fancy for you."

"And yet I'm only half of the equation."

Another laugh. "You're the first person she came to when she needed help, and she's letting you move in with her and her kid on very short notice. I think we've got a good idea about her half, too."

His flippant tone—hell, this whole conversation, actually—made Wyatt bristle. "And yet you're still assigning me babysitters." No matter how Tate tried to sell it, Wyatt had no doubt that's what they were.

"Consider it backup. There if you need them, easily ignored if you don't."

He rolled his eyes. "Sure, boss. Whatever you say."

"Stow the attitude, sailor. I'm giving you a lot of rope here. Be a shame if you hung yourself with it." Even delivering a low-key threat, Monroe's tone never diverged from calm friendliness. Like he got what was going on, and wasn't *truly* threatened by any of it.

Wyatt shook his head, trying to clear the haze of frustration clouding his thoughts. He was acting like an ass, with the fucking head of the company. What was wrong with him?

"Sorry," he managed. "I'm not trying to break bad. I don't know what's going on with me."

"I, and at least two other men on your team, have a pretty decent idea. Just try to stay calm and don't kill anyone. You'll get through it and find the other side."

With that, Tate hung up.

He blinked in consternation. He hadn't spoken to the man a ton, but he didn't remember Monroe being quite so cryptic. Had he always spoken in riddles, or was Wyatt suddenly daft?

Chapter Sixteen

Leah

W
ELL, LOOK AT this," Leah called, holding the front door wide and smiling at Wyatt as he stepped out of a gleaming black SUV she hadn't seen before. "If it isn't my new fiancé."

He grinned back at her as he pulled a large, military-issue duffle and a grocery bag from the backseat and bounded up the steps.

There'd been a part of her that hadn't quite believed he would really go along with this crazy plan, but all that melted away when she saw his light-hearted mood.

When Wyatt reached her, Leah tipped her face up to his and murmured, "Welcome home."

He dropped his bags, took her face in his large hands, and kissed her hard. "I like the sound of that. Like kissing you, too."

Was she blushing? *Possibly.* "Me too," she told him.

Wyatt moved his things into the foyer, then turned back to his truck. He stopped, hesitated, and darted back for another quick kiss. "One more."

Leah returned the peck with a laugh, then scanned the street as he retrieved an overstuffed rucksack and sleeping bag from the truck and hoisted them onto his shoulder.

"Can I grab anything for you?"

"Nope. This is it."

"That's all you brought?"

The yard was clear. So was the street. She wondered if Biddy had witnessed any part of this production.

"I left most of my stuff at home," Wyatt told her quietly. "But I tried to bring enough to make it look believable. How'd I do?"

"I'm sure it'll be fine," she reassured him. "But where did the truck come from? I would remember if I'd seen this one before."

Wyatt smirked as he pulled her front door shut behind him. "Company car," he explained. "I even got a car seat installed in the back for Teddy."

Leah blinked. "Seriously?"

"Yep. That's why I needed to know how big he is."

The thoughtfulness of his gesture shouldn't have surprised her so much. The same went for his apparently ready access to such a vehicle.

"We are going to have a talk one of these days about what you do for a living."

"Sure thing," he grinned again, eyes twinkling. "Now where do you want me to stow these bags?"

Leah squinted at him. When it became clear he wasn't going to share more, she shook off her suspicions and told him, "Leave the sleeping bag down here, but you can put your clothes and stuff in my room. We'll have to share my bathroom."

He cocked an eyebrow at her, and a shiver raced down her spine.

"Teddy's is all childproofed and I don't want him to take a shine to your razor or anything. And we have a third bedroom, but it's tiny," she rushed to explain. "I use it as my office, but I don't think there's enough floor space for you to lay out a sleeping bag in there, anyway."

"No worries."

"So, like I said," she rambled on, "you can use my bathroom to shower and everything, but I think we have to stick you on the couch to sleep. If that's okay."

He glanced at the furniture in question and shrugged. "Sure. Completely fine."

Leah looked between him and her sofa and frowned. Wait…was he even going to fit?

"I'm sorry, it's just that Teddy sometimes climbs into bed with me when he wakes up in the morning," she explained guiltily. "I feel a little weird about him seeing you in there. Otherwise—"

He set a warm hand on her arm and caught her eye. "Leah, it's fine. I completely understand."

"I mean, we haven't even…you know. Yet."

"I am painfully aware that we have not yet you-knowed, believe me."

She laughed at his wry tone. "Sorry. I'm a total dork. Hashtag momlife."

"Don't apologize. It's all good, I promise."

"You sure?" She bit her lip, searching his face for any sign that he found this as awkward as she did.

"Positive. I know this feels strange, but we'll do our best," Wyatt told her. "Just make sure to tell me if I overstep or upset the normal order of things, okay? I don't want to be a burden. I can make myself scarce during the day so you can work, and I'll help clean up. I can help with Teddy, too, if you need me to. Like I said, I have the car seat, and everything now."

"Wyatt, I don't know what to say. *Thank you* truly doesn't seem to cover it."

"It covers it fine. Let me put my stuff upstairs and then I'll say hi to Teddy, okay?"

Leah nodded. Once he'd disappeared up the stairs, she hurried into the kitchen. Teddy was right where she'd left him—absorbed with his sand table on the back porch. He was probably ready for a snack by now, though.

She'd taken two steps around the kitchen island when a dark smudge moving across the tile floor caught her attention. Her brain took another couple of seconds to decode what she was looking at, before an ear-splitting shriek whooshed out of her lungs.

Wyatt's heavy tread banged down the stairs and stuttered to a halt somewhere behind her. Leah whined incoherently, backing away from the wriggling snake and nearly jumping out of her skin when she connected with Wyatt's solid bulk.

"Snake!" she wailed. "Alive!" She flinched when it curled an inch in her direction. "Holy shit why is there a snake! In my *house!*"

Wyatt took her by the shoulders and moved her aside, then leaned down to peer at the thing. It had to be two feet long, maybe more. It looked pissed, too, probably because of all her screaming.

"Okay, let's try to stay calm," he chuckled, as she edged behind him and whimpered some more. "It's just a baby. Probably a gopher and definitely not venomous."

"But why is it here?" Leah sobbed. "Get it *out.*"

Wyatt scanned her counter and pointed to the far end. "Hand me that box. I'll have this little guy out of your hair in two minutes."

"I do not want that thing anywhere near my hair," she warned.

Wyatt laughed at her again. "Roger that."

She sidled toward the box slowly, emptied the plastic cups she'd ordered from inside, and shoved it toward his outstretched hand.

The morning had been chilly, and the tiles were still cold. Maybe that made the snake slow, but Wyatt watched it for only a moment before he grabbed it behind the head and dropped it in the box. He closed the flaps and strolled past Leah to the sliding door.

"Wait. Whoa. Where are you going with that?" she demanded.

"To the yard?"

"The one where my *kid* is playing?" she growled. The same poor kid who must've scrambled off the porch when his crazy mother started screaming in the kitchen, she realized. *Oops.*

Wyatt glanced outside. "Ah. Right. Can I at least show him first? I bet he'll love it."

"Mr. Oaks, you will not foster a love of reptiles in my child. Do you hear me?"

"Just a quick peek, I promise."

Her admonishment didn't seem to register as he walked across the porch and down the stairs. Leah gripped the frame of the door and wondered grimly, "And then what?"

Teddy looked up as Wyatt approached, his little hands gripping his toy cars on the grass, his eyes wide and watchful, as if Wyatt had been the one to cause all the yelling. Like her, it was going to take him a while to process that not all men were like Jesse.

Leah wanted to cry.

"Hey, bud," Wyatt said easily. "Wanna see what your mom found?"

Teddy's eyes flashed to hers, and as much as she hated to do it, she nodded. He got to his feet and waited for Wyatt to come closer.

"You can look, but don't touch, okay?" Wyatt told him. "We have to set him free soon, so he can go find food and stuff."

Wyatt jostled the box a little, then opened the flaps and squatted next to Teddy, bringing things down to his level in a way that seemed to come so naturally to him. A pang hit her square in the sternum, and Leah rubbed at it distractedly.

Teddy's eyes went round as moons when he saw the snake, and he shuffled back in alarm.

"It's okay. It won't hurt you. See his fancy spots? That means he's a gopher snake. They like to live all around here, but they don't bite people unless they're really scared. What do you think?"

Leah crept over to the porch railing. She could see the snake curling up the inside of the box, checking things out. Checking *her child* out.

Maybe Teddy had picked up on her unease, or maybe he truly was scared, but he shook his head quickly, bent down to snatch up his cars, and complained, "I don't like it."

He was still saying his Ls like Ws, but she couldn't find it in herself to correct him. It sounded cute as could be, and he'd figure it out eventually.

Wyatt must've agreed, because he peeked at her with a small, crooked smile. "You don't want to say hi?"

"No." Teddy edged to the side, like he was considering a run for her.

Maybe herpetophobia was a genetic thing.

Fortunately, Wyatt didn't seem that disappointed. "Okay, then I'm going to let him go." He stood and looked around, weighing his options.

Leah and Biddy had neighbors on either side, one with dogs, but the back wall abutted public land and was high enough to keep Teddy in, and any wild creatures out. Wyatt apparently agreed, because he walked back there, reached up like he was making a slam dunk, and upended the box over the wall.

Teddy raced for her, bouncing on his toes and holding up his arms until Leah swooped him up and nuzzled his soft hair.

Wyatt double-checked the box and turned back with a grin. "All gone," he reported.

"We're saved!" Leah cried, giving Ted a little bounce. He buried his face in her shoulder with a giggle and she exhaled, forcing herself to relax.

"So, I guess we won't be spending much time in the snake house at the zoo," Wyatt commented, strolling back.

Since when were they going to the zoo? "I think we're more monkey people," Leah told him, amused when he checked the box a few more times to make sure the snake was gone.

"It really was harmless. I wasn't just saying that."

"Immaterial," she fired back. "I'm still traumatized, and we should probably napalm the whole place to make sure it never happens again."

"It was probably just following a mouse or something. I'll set down traps this weekend. You'll be fine."

Leah gave him another once-over, then beckoned him onto the porch. "Sir, I must say, I'm impressed by your reflexes. Just waltzed up and snatched a snake off the floor like it was nothing. What do you have, ice in your veins?"

"Occasionally. Not usually around you, though."

Leah rolled her eyes, but she couldn't help the grin splitting her face. It was nice to have a helpful guy around to run interference. With a little practice, maybe she'd even stop wondering what the catch was.

Looking at Teddy, she reminded herself that Wyatt wasn't playing a long game or trying to trick or con her. What would be the point? He just liked them. That was all.

* * *

DINNER WAS WINDING down when Wyatt suddenly pushed back his chair, motioned for Leah to stay put, and took a few silent, gliding steps toward the front door.

"What's going on?" she wondered.

"Going on?" Teddy echoed, doggedly chewing the same bite of salad he'd been working on for a while now. He didn't usually love raw spinach, but Wyatt had been attacking his own salad with enthusiasm, so here they were.

Monkey see, monkey do.

"One more bite and you can be done," she smiled.

Wyatt glanced over his shoulder. "I thought I heard something out front."

Leah frowned. She hadn't heard anything out of the ordinary. Nothing except a muffled thump she'd probably heard a thousand times, followed by telltale engine revving.

"I think a package was delivered," she explained. "I'm sure that's all it was."

"I'll get it," he offered, jumping at the excuse to check for himself.

Leah shook her head in amusement. Wyatt wouldn't yet know all the normal sounds of her house and neighborhood, but were all former SEALs this paranoid?

Unless…maybe he was involved in black ops now that he was out of the service? It wouldn't be unheard of for someone with his skill set. He'd been cagey about his job, after all, and there was also the blacked-out SUV in her driveway to consider.

Could be Homeland Security, she supposed. *CIA. Something like that.*

Leah pushed some salad across her plate and bit her lip as she watched him. Would they be extra safe with someone like that in the house, or did she need to be concerned that bad guys might come hunting for Wyatt here?

The notion made her chuckle. Wyatt working as some super secret spy type seemed completely at odds with his open, genial personality. It'd make for a good cover, perhaps, though she could already tell he'd never put her and Teddy at risk in pursuit of that.

"You were right." He wandered back in, showing her a small stack of parcels before setting them on the coffee table and reclaiming his seat, and his fork.

Leah eyed the pink bubble mailer on top and abruptly lost her appetite.

"I think I know what that envelope might be." She moved her plate to the island, grabbed the shears out of the knife block, and brought the mailer back to her seat.

Two layers of tissue paper and a stretchy gold string fell to the side as she cut into the wrappings, and soon Leah was left staring at an unmistakable jeweler's ring box.

Wyatt's next bite hovered an inch from his mouth, suspended in space. Teddy gripped his small plastic spork like a royal staff, kicking his feet against his booster seat as he waited to see what was going on.

Wyatt swallowed and set down his fork. "Is that…?"

Leah nodded quickly.

He pushed out of his chair and reached her in one stride. Before he could say anything else, she braced the bottom of the box in one hand and pried open the hinged top.

"Welp, that's a fake engagement ring all right," she chuckled nervously.

It looked much bigger than it'd seemed in the website photos, and she suddenly couldn't remember if she'd checked the description for a carat size or not. She also couldn't decide if it truly looked like a faux, or if she was biased because she knew it was.

People see what they're expecting to see. Don't overthink it.

Wyatt didn't say anything. Teddy watched them, rapt.

"It's too big," she sighed. "Is it tacky? I can return it and get something different if—" Leah groaned under her breath. She'd been so taken with the setting when she'd ordered it. Why did it feel so mortifying now?

"No, it's pretty," Wyatt assured her. He took the box from her frozen fingers and inquired softly, "May I?"

"It's obviously simulated," she blathered as he extracted the ring and set the box aside. "I saw the ad on social media. The band came with it, like a buy-one-get-one deal."

Wyatt took her hand in his big, warm palm, and slowly slipped the ring on her finger. He didn't let go, though, just stood there holding her hand and staring at the glinting stone.

She tugged, feeling an instant of resistance before he dropped her hand. "Perfect fit," he winked, but it didn't quite carry his usual air of mischief.

"Yeah. Whew." Leah couldn't sit there another second. She jumped up, grabbed her glass, and darted for the sink. "Gonna be weird getting used to wearing one of these again, but that's one thing done, at least."

"And my guys are working on the papers. They'll be done soon, too. Don't worry."

Teddy stretched out his hands. "Mama, I see?"

Wyatt went to him and murmured, "You all done, buddy?" before carrying Teddy's plate to her at the sink.

Leah slipped past him before their gazes could connect. "I got a new ring, see?" she told her son. His pudgy little fingers touched it carefully, his soulful brown eyes wide and impressed. "Isn't it fancy?"

"I can wear it?" Teddy asked.

Wyatt's voice sounded from over her shoulder, his arm brushing hers. "Rings like that are special," he began. "They mean—"

Leah cut him off before he could get too sentimental. "Not this one. This is just a ring. Here, try it." She pulled it off and handed it to Teddy, who tried it on several fingers with a silly grin.

"Sorry," Wyatt whispered in her ear.

Leah shivered, annoyed by how uncomfortable she felt. "It's okay. It's just…this is one woman who is not going to be racing back to the altar anytime soon."

Present farce excepted, she supposed. She'd considered only putting the ring on when she was likely to see Biddy, but thought the chances of forgetting it too often were high. She was going to have to wear it full-time, or not bother.

Wyatt backed off, his expression carefully neutral. "That surprises me. I can't fathom a catch like you staying single for long."

"With my baggage? Are you kidding?" Leah spun away and stalked to the counter. "Who in God's name would want to take us on?" She stacked and restacked the pile of bills on her counter a bit too aggressively. "We're better off alone."

Wyatt looked her over, his handsome face an unreadable mask. *Probably thought she was a total jerk. Maybe she was.*

After a moment, he cleared his throat. "If you want to take Teddy upstairs for a bath, I'm happy to clean up the kitchen."

She wanted to escape more than she wanted to argue, though, even as Wyatt's helpful act worked its way under her skin like sandpaper.

Leah unbuckled her kid and swooped him into her arms, barely managing to blurt, "Thanks," before she fled for the stairs.

She was a coward. What had made her think she could do this?

BY THE TIME she led Teddy back down to say good night, Wyatt had his sleeping bag set up on the couch and was stretched out on top. His head rested on one arm of the sofa and his feet were propped on the other as he scrolled on his phone.

Leah winced when he saw her and jumped up. Wyatt was definitely too tall to sleep comfortably there, but he was also too polite to complain about it. Where else could she put him, though?

Before she could work out a better plan, Teddy marched over to him in his dinosaur pajamas, took his hand, and led him back to the stairs, saying, "Okay, we read stories now."

"Really?"

"Oh. Teddy?" Leah rushed to intervene. "Maybe Wyatt doesn't want to—"

"No time to talk, Mom," Wyatt smiled crookedly, "We've got books to read."

He didn't look like he needed a rescue. He looked absolutely delighted. Leah trailed after them, waiting in Teddy's doorway as they selected a stack of stories.

Once they finished, Teddy climbed into his bed and looked at them expectantly.

Normally she and Teddy snuggled up together while they read, until he fell asleep, and she could slip out. She had no idea how Wyatt was supposed to fit into the equation.

"Mama, come," Teddy instructed impatiently, patting the bed next to him.

"Okay, I'll pull up the chair—"

"Uh, that's really heavy—"

Wyatt moved the glider next to the bed like it weighed nothing.

Leah slammed her mouth shut, impressed despite herself. "Okay, then."

They traded off reading duty, book by book. By the sixth title, she motioned for Wyatt to dial down his performance to a more sedate level, and by book ten, Teddy's eyes finally drifted closed.

Wyatt reached to turn off the lamp and in unspoken agreement, they stayed in place, making sure her kid was going to stay asleep.

Eventually, Leah whispered, "I'm sorry. I think it's probably safe for you to leave now. I might stay a few more minutes, though."

"It's okay, I'm good," he murmured back.

"Don't be a hero. Save yourself."

"I swear, I'm good. This is nice."

She rolled her eyes. "Right."

In the soft glow of Teddy's nightlight, Wyatt set the pile of books on the floor and frowned at his hands. His fingers were tense, gripping his knees like he was trying to stay calm.

"Hey," she whispered again. "What did I say? Why do you look perturbed?"

Teddy's breathing was soft but audible between the ticks of his robot clock.

"I don't know," Wyatt sighed after a long moment. "It's like…I'm doing everything I can think of to help you guys, to show you that I care, and you can count on me. But it never seems to make a dent in your…" He pressed his lips together with a pained flinch.

"My what?"

"Your…walls, I guess? I know it hasn't been long for us, but I can feel the way you hold yourself back. You don't trust me all the way, and I'm not sure how to prove that you can. It throws me off sometimes."

Leah blinked at him. She hadn't guessed she'd been so blatant. "I've told you what Jesse was like."

"I know, and I get it. I'm not confused about why you're locked down, I just can't figure out how to breach the barrier. But I want to, Leah. Just so you know."

"And I'm not saying no. I appreciate you wanting to try. I need time, though."

His eyes flicked to her hands, where she fiddled with her new ring. "Do I even have a chance with you?"

"You wouldn't be here if you didn't."

Wyatt nodded, then changed course. "If you don't mind me asking, why'd you stay with him? If he was that bad?"

She sighed, shrinking into herself even though he didn't sound accusatory. "That's always the question, isn't it? But Jesse wasn't always a bastard. It happened gradually, and it took me a while to catch up—to figure out that it wasn't just a bad day, or a rough patch, or battle fatigue, or whatever else. It took me a long time to realize it wasn't going to get better and I probably ought to leave. But by then…" she paused, heart aching painfully.

"By then?" He looked between her and Teddy. There was only one *by then*. Wyatt was a *by then*, himself.

"By then there was Teddy," she confirmed. "And I had to think about what was best for him. He deserves to have both parents, and financial stability, and a safe home, and good role models…" Her voice broke. *Life was hard, and then people died. And then, hard didn't even cover it.*

"He does," Wyatt agreed, "but he mostly deserves a loving upbringing, and sometimes that can only happen with one parent."

"I didn't want him to have only me," Leah confessed sadly. "I get so tired and short-tempered sometimes. I'm not fun anymore. I used to be fun."

"No one is fun all the time. And you're human, not defective. We have down spells, but we bounce back. Besides, being raised by just your mom isn't the end of the world. Look at me—I turned out okay."

She eyed him pointedly. "Jury's still out on that."

He chuckled quietly, checking Teddy's face to make sure he hadn't disturbed him. "It's going to be okay," he told her, "One way or another. All anyone can do is their best, and you're hardly tapping out on that front. Teddy will be a better person for not getting belittled by his father all the time, he'll be better not having to watch his parents duke it out every day, and once we get this house situation figured out with Mrs. Daniels, his life will settle right back down to normal. And Leah?" Wyatt reached across Teddy to grip her hand. "You're an amazing woman, and Teddy is a really great kid. If you don't want to be alone, you won't be."

Chapter Seventeen

Wyatt

WHEN IT BECAME clear that his attempt at a big feelings talk had petered out without gaining him much ground, Wyatt took a moment to see if he could place any of what they'd discussed into the context of Noah's "love language" lesson. No dice there, either, so he supposed it was time to put the pin back in the grenade and call it a day.

He leaned over Teddy and scooped Leah up and out of her kid's bed, abandoning the cozy family fantasy they'd been ensconced in to carry her into the hall.

She slid seductively down his body to find her feet and her lips quickly found his.

Frustration boiled through him. Was she going to be yet another woman who wanted a physical connection with him, but would reject the emotional one he craved?

No, Wyatt assured himself. *Leah wasn't like that. She'd explained how she felt. She said she wanted to try.*

His issue was time. Now that he'd finally found someone he wanted to pursue a deeper relationship with, Wyatt didn't want to waste *any.* He was impatient by nature, but his line of work also meant that he'd been trained to capitalize on opportunities as soon as they presented themselves.

Here and now was all anyone truly had, anyway, and what was possible today might not be tomorrow.

Perhaps that was why he let himself kiss Leah back now, and hummed low in his throat at her addictive taste. Wyatt had to set aside the nagging feeling of settling for less than he wanted, to accept the small slice of happiness she offered.

"Mmmm, can't say I hate this part of the sleepover," she murmured when he finally pulled away.

He took a second to admire her features in the soft light of the hall, the curve of her cheekbones, and the fine dark fringe of her lashes. He told her, "Good night, Leah," and knew he'd likely dream about her.

She sighed forlornly. "Good night, Wyatt."

His brows knit at her tone, and he touched her cheek. "What's wrong?" He hadn't meant for her to pick up on his angst. She had her own burdens to bear.

"It's going to be torture having you here all the time, isn't it?" she smiled faintly.

Oh. She was still on the physical train. Of course.

"Yes," he agreed, matching her teasing tone as best he could. "It will likely be torturous to gaze upon my hideous visage so often. I can wear a bag over my head if it helps."

Leah laughed softly. "Your face isn't the problem, and you know it. I'm more worried about resisting copping a feel every time you walk by."

"Is that all? Cop away, sweet thing. I live to serve."

"So kind. And I would take you up on that, but I'd rather not traumatize my poor kid." She winced. "…more. Traumatize him more."

Wyatt waved her off, striving for a careless flirtation he couldn't quite access. "Say no more. I'll speak to him."

"And say what exactly?"

"Theodore, your mother is emerging from a long, terrible drought. Please be sure to heed all flash flood warnings, cough before rounding corners, and knock before opening doors."

Leah laughed again, and the raw joy of it illuminated her face. Wyatt wanted to give her that always.

"He is not going to understand any of that," she said. "Thank God."

He laughed with her, her lightness working to assuage some of his torment. "Fair enough. Hands off the merchandise and keep it G-rated. No sweat. That'll be super easy."

Her eyes raked over him and her tone turned sultry. "Easy. Sure."

"Off I go, then." He edged toward the stairs.

Leah took a couple of steps toward her room. "Wyatt…are you sure about sleeping on the couch? I'm afraid it's going to be very uncomfortable."

It was *definitely* going to be uncomfortable. "Don't even worry about it. I've crashed in way worse places. Besides, there's always the floor," he winked. "Plenty of room there."

It couldn't be worse than the demons Leah was wrestling with, certainly, though he wondered how long he'd have to wait for her to come around—or if she ever would.

Wyatt immediately felt like an ass for that rogue thought. He'd wait as long as it took. She was worth it.

"You could always—"

He held up a hand before she could voice it. "You don't really want that."

Leah didn't argue but she did look crestfallen, so he added, "How about this? If I'm really suffering and you play your cards right, maybe I'll pay you a little visit later. How's that sound?"

"That sounds very acceptable," she grinned. "Easy, some might say." Indecision dispensed with, she ducked into her room and shut the door, and Wyatt hit the stairs.

Easy. Her comment seemed eerily prescient. Leah didn't know that was Bennett's longstanding nickname, not his—not least because the moniker fit Wyatt about as well as a child-sized wetsuit. He was difficult. Complicated. Wanted the wrong things at the wrong times.

He swallowed down his trepidation. Nothing about this temporary shack-up was going to be "easy". Not keeping his hands to himself, and especially not keeping his stupid hoping heart in line.

THE SUN WAS not yet up when Wyatt finally caved and gave into the magnetic pull drawing him upstairs like a beacon. Without a sound, he ghosted down the upstairs hall lit with its little train nightlight, and on into Leah's dark room.

She was sleeping deeply, her breaths slow and even. He stripped off his sweatshirt and slid into bed behind her, then pulled her pliant body back against his chest.

"Mmm," she murmured softly. "When did you get here?"

At least she knew who he was. He'd been worried about scaring her.

"Just now," he whispered next to the delicate shell of her ear. "Want to sleep some more?"

"Maybe. I tossed and turned half the night. Must've been after two by the time I drifted off," she lamented groggily.

Wyatt froze, concern overtaking his plans for seduction. "Do you have a lot to do today?"

"Not too much." Leah stroked his forearm with lazy fingers.

He kissed the top of her head. "Then go back to sleep. We can feel each other up later."

She was quiet for a minute or two, and he held still, hoping she'd drifted off again.

But then, she suddenly huffed, "Shoot. I think I missed my window."

"And that's my bad. I'm sorry I woke you up so early."

"No, don't worry about it. I'm happy you're here. Grounded me in reality."

Wyatt knew what that had to mean. Leah had told him she had frequent bad dreams, and if they were anything like Joe experienced—he hoped like hell they weren't—then it was a good thing he'd come after all.

Instead of addressing it head-on, though, he kept his tone light and murmured, "Happy to be of service. And now, we can work on a project I've been wanting to tackle."

Leah snorted faintly, catching on quick. "Dare I ask?" *Second-guessing her decision to stay awake, no doubt.*

"Nothing major," Wyatt assured her. "Just wanted to find out how many times I can make you come before you'll agree to blow off work and chores and stay in bed with me all day."

"Oh, is that all?"

"Isn't that enough? There's no time to waste, though. We should really get started."

At the mention of time, she craned to peer at the alarm clock on her nightstand.

Wyatt plowed on, trying to distract her, "Records don't get set on their own, Leah. It takes real commitment to bring home the gold."

"Don't you have a job, too?" she complained, giggling as he tickled her neck with light kisses.

"Job, shmob," he murmured.

Unfortunately, his stomach—awake for an hour now and clearly not on board with the mission specs—chose that moment to emit an alarmingly loud growl. Wyatt cleared his throat, but it was a pointless cover. Too little, too late.

Even if Leah had somehow *not* heard, she had to have felt the vibration against her back.

He cursed himself, disgruntled with his poor planning. He should've eaten something before coming up here, but he'd been snared in thoughts of her silky, warm skin and sleep-deepened voice. He hadn't wanted to delay even five more minutes.

Leah let out a small huff of amusement. "Be that as it may," she commented, sounding far too alert and feeling far less languid in his arms. "Duty calls."

She pried herself free, and before Wyatt could so much as blink she flicked on a light and began shimmying into a coordinated outfit of blue workout clothes that fit her like a second skin. As she stepped into a pair of flip-flops in the corner, she grabbed an elastic off her dresser and wound her disheveled mane of glossy brown hair into a sloppy bun on top of her head.

She looked perfect. Her heady scent was all around him, clinging to her bedding and permeating the air. Wyatt's chest grew tight with something he didn't dare name.

"Teddy is going to be up any minute," she explained, her face soft with apology. "Let me make you some breakfast."

He sat up and ran a hand over his skull, his thoughts disjointed. He'd had such plans. *Great* plans. He rubbed at his sternum and tried to will the rest of him into compliance.

"At least have some coffee," she urged, no doubt picking up on his regret. "If you want to wait while I run him to school, I can hop in the shower as soon as I get back. And *then*..." Leah trailed off meaningfully, giving him a pointed look.

"Then?" He peered at her, afraid *then* might entail a trip to Target instead of O-town.

Leah winked, exaggerated and comical, and all his nerve endings fired instantly back to life. "*Then* we'll have three uninterrupted hours for your sex Olympics." She sauntered into the bathroom and laid out her toothbrush, like she hadn't just strafed him.

Wyatt swung his feet to the floor and reached for his sweatshirt, griping, "Three hours is not enough time," though it kind of made him sound like a sore winner. He'd come up here expecting what? Maybe thirty or forty minutes?

"You get what you get, and you don't get upset," she commented drily.

As she blithely brushed her teeth, he eyed her in consternation. How could the woman operate under these conditions? By her own admission, she'd barely gotten any sleep, they'd been cock-blocked yet again, and here she was acting cheerful about it.

If he'd learned anything about her these last few weeks, however, it was that appearances with her were often deceiving. Maybe under that unassailable surface beauty, she was as frustrated as he was.

Wyatt narrowed his eyes as she came out of the bathroom wearing lip gloss and a smile. "Okay fine, but the shower is a group effort," he conceded.

She squinted at him. "You drive a hard bargain, mister."

Right on schedule, a small voice sounded from down the hall. *Teddy.*

"I get the shower, too," he reiterated, standing and straightening his shorts as she set her hand on the doorknob.

Leah cracked her door and stuck her head out. "Coming!" she called.

"Not even close," he grouched.

She pulled back in and made a face at him.

"Do we have a deal?" he pressed quietly, stalking closer. He reveled in the feel of her delectable ass under her running tights.

Leah pulled a jacket off her chair, grinned mischievously, and whispered, "Deal." Then she darted out the door before he could grab her again.

Wyatt glared at the space where she'd been standing for a full minute before flopping back on the bed. It still smelled, deliciously, of Leah, and her ceiling held no answers for how his plan had gone so awry.

Who was he kidding?

He knew. Of course, he knew. In his haste to see her—to touch her, to taste her—Wyatt had once again neglected to factor in Teddy.

It wasn't that he'd forgotten him, exactly, or that Leah was a mom, first and foremost. Spending time with them together had been one of the things that had made her seem more accessible, made him see past that carefully constructed reserve and unreal beauty to her warmth and vulnerability within.

Not to mention, he'd have to be an ogre to not love her son. Teddy had to be the best, sweetest, smartest kid around, with those big, watchful brown eyes, and ever-present train engine clutched in his tiny fist.

Wyatt supposed he simply hadn't thought much about what their morning routine might look like. Leah was so infernally unflappable, and made everything look so easy and run so smoothly, that a dumbass such as himself could easily underestimate the amount of effort she expended behind the scenes.

That ended now. If Wyatt intended to be her man—and he did—then willful obliviousness would not fly. He not only needed to learn the routine, he needed to know it backward and forward so he could pitch in as necessary. Participate instead of spectate.

Speaking of 'ate,' his traitorous stomach growled again, and Wyatt remembered the bacon and sausage he'd picked up at the grocery store on his way here yesterday. Leah might've gotten a jump on him this time, but there was no way in hell he was going to pull up to her kitchen table expecting to be fed like another child.

In order to join this team of hers, he needed to get smarter, and faster. He studied himself in the mirror over her dresser. He was going to be her star player. The goddamn MVP.

With that, he nodded to himself, checked that the hall was clear, and snuck down to the kitchen.

Role models mattered to kids. He knew that better than anyone.

And so, while Wyatt had no idea if Teddy had ever witnessed anything untoward between Jesse and Leah, or if he was even old enough to remember if he had, hell would freeze over before the kid caught even a whiff of disrespect from him.

He squared his shoulders in front of the fridge, took a deep breath, and extracted what he needed to cook them breakfast.

If the kid picked up anything from him at all, it was not going to be how to become some woman's liability. Wyatt would show him what a real man looked like, and he'd make that lesson stick.

Chapter Eighteen

Leah

"TEDDY, IF WE don't leave now, you're going to be late for school. Then Miss Katie will miss you," she wheedled. To no avail, as it turned out. Teddy's only response was to whine and cling harder to Wyatt's leg.

Wyatt met her frantic stare over her kid's head, not the least bit perturbed, frenetic, or frazzled. "I have an idea. Teddy, come upstairs with me for a sec. Mom, you leave those dishes alone. I'll clean up later."

He hoisted Teddy into his arms like he weighed nothing and strode purposefully up to her room. Leah followed and lingered just outside the door, watching curiously as Wyatt set Teddy on the end of her bed and crouched to rifle through his rucksack.

If this man knew some trick she hadn't thought of yet, she was all ears—but he also had little experience with small children, so she probably needed to make sure he didn't give her kid a pocketknife to bring to school or something.

A few seconds later, Wyatt announced, "Here he is." He presented Teddy with a little building block figure, silver all over and small enough to fit easily in Teddy's hand. "This guy has been all over the world, but he has never been to preschool. Do you think you can take him with you today and show him how things go?"

Teddy accepted the toy carefully, eyes wide as he nodded.

"You need to keep him safe, though, okay? He likes to sneak around without anyone knowing he's there." He made a whooshing sound and fluttered his hand. "Like a *ghost*."

Leah flinched. Teddy had been worried about ghosts for all of October and November last fall, so much so that he'd started to freak *her* out.

But her son simply nodded, and softly whispered, "Whooo-ooo."

Wyatt glanced at the clock, and then at her. "Okay, bud—time for us to skedaddle. Let's get you in the car so I can see how your booster seat works." He scooped up Teddy before he could protest, and strode downstairs.

They waited for her in the foyer. "Mom, do we have everything we need?"

Leah's head spun at how easy he was making this. *But Wyatt made everything easy, didn't he?*

"Uh…shoes. His shoes are next to the kitchen table. His lunch is already in his backpack. I'll get my purse and meet you outside."

They disappeared into the back of the house and Leah grabbed her purse from the coat closet near the door. When she straightened, she noticed Biddy out front, pacing in her driveway and shooting sour looks at Leah's door.

Waiting for me, no doubt. Foreboding raised the hairs on her neck, and some instinct made her reverse course, sending her into the kitchen instead of outside.

The ring box was still where she'd left it last night, smack in the middle of the kitchen island. Leah angled herself to hide it from the guys and slipped the wedding band out of the box and into her pocket. *Just in case,* she told herself.

Behind her, Wyatt was busy tying Teddy's shoes and buttoning his little toy into one of Teddy's cargo pockets. Once that was accomplished, he saluted her and carried her son out to her car.

The extra set of hands and steady, calming influence was…God, it was so nice. Leah hoped he'd stick around long enough for her to get used to it, especially since Biddy had retreated to her front step upon sighting Wyatt.

"I know you're short on time, but give me the down and dirty on how his seat works," Wyatt said, gently putting Teddy into his booster once she'd unlocked the doors. "In case you ever need me to drive him for you."

"Teddy can buckle it himself, can't you, honey?" Leah watched him do it, then showed Wyatt how to make sure everything was properly latched and how to check for correct strap and buckle positioning.

Wyatt stepped back and whistled in appreciation. "Whoa. Five-point harness, kiddo. That is so cool."

Teddy examined himself dubiously, patting the straps like they might have changed without him noticing.

"You want to know a secret?" Wyatt leaned in conspiratorially. "Sometimes I get to ride in helicopters for my job."

Leah peered at him, looming lateness and lurking landlord forgotten. "You do?"

He winked at her. "Sometimes I even get to fly them."

"You…do?"

He turned back to her son, very smug. "And let me tell you, the seatbelts in helicopters are *exactly* the same as this."

Teddy's eyes went round as dinner plates. "*Oh*," he breathed.

"Okay, time to go." Wyatt clapped his hands and stepped back. "Make sure you learn as much as you can and have fun too! When I see you later you can tell me all about it. I'll be back in time for dinner, and I want to hear everything."

Leah had questions—so many questions. Instead, she smiled at Teddy and mimicked Wyatt's chipper tone, "Say bye!"

"Bye Wyatt." It came out sounding a bit like *Bye Wy*, but close enough.

"Bye guys!" His grin was incandescent.

Leah got behind the wheel and saw Wyatt do a double take when he noticed Biddy marching down her stairs.

He ducked to catch her eye, forehead creasing in concern. She cracked her window and hissed, "Don't worry, I got this. I'll text you if it's anything major."

No reason to have the two of them mixing it up first thing in the morning—there was not enough coffee in the world for that. After lunch, though…she might pay money to see that.

Leah waved Wyatt off, watching until he was safely back inside.

A split second later, her landlady rapped on the passenger side window, hugging her sweater around herself while she waited for Leah to open things up.

"I'm sorry Mrs. Daniels, but we're running a little late. I need to take Teddy to school."

"I couldn't help but notice that man appears to have moved in," Biddy spat, ignoring her completely. "Did you misunderstand our last conversation?"

"About the lease? I don't believe so."

"And yet you've decided to live in sin." She peered into the back at Teddy, lips pursed like she was looking at some filthy stray. "With a child in the home."

Leah slipped her hand from her pocket and placed her hands prominently at ten and two on the steering wheel. Her ostentatious new rings glittered in the sun, impossible to miss.

"We are not living in sin, Mrs. Daniels. We are married. You can't expect us to maintain two households when our lives are together now."

She was pretty sure she delivered the lie convincingly, lightning didn't strike, and Teddy was too intimidated by Biddy to make a peep to the contrary. *So far, so good.*

"Moving fast, aren't you? A few days ago, you claimed it was just an engagement."

Leah shrugged, striving for carelessness despite the feeling that everything was upside down and out of control. "Why waste time? We knew what we wanted. Besides, military folks know better than most that life is short. You know."

"Don't make the mistake of assuming we have anything in common, Mrs. Burke—or is that still your name?" Biddy sucked her teeth like she'd tasted something foul. "You seem to believe you have this all figured out, but let me remind you, once again, of the terms of your lease. No one is permitted to live in the home that is not named on the rental agreement."

Leah couldn't resist a dig. She was late, she was tired, and she was so, so fed up with this mean, miserable woman. "You mean like Teddy?"

Biddy's eyes narrowed, and anger bled off her like a palpable thing. "What's more, if a man staying over at all hours was a violation, then you can *believe* that a couple living in sin is most certainly grounds for immediate eviction."

Leah felt sick but she managed to stare Biddy down as she tapped the sparkling band on her finger on the wheel. She wanted to say that she hadn't seen this coming, but here she was, flashing fake diamonds all over the yard.

"Mrs. Daniels. No one is living in sin, and I really need to take my kid to school."

"We will discuss this further when you return."

"Fine."

With that, Leah backed out of the driveway and drove away, rolling her eyes and smiling at Teddy so he wouldn't worry.

She was worried, though. Very much so. Panicked thoughts swirled like bees in her brain.

What if Wyatt refused to put his name on the lease? What if the lease term was restarted when they added him, and they had to live together for a year or more? What if they broke the lease and moved out, and Biddy dinged them with big fees? Worst of all, what if he couldn't produce the documents they'd need to plead their case?

Leah couldn't decide what to do. It was one thing to ask Wyatt to pretend—another for him to ask his people to fabricate the support of the lie. He'd been agreeable about those things, likely because they were things he could control.

Asking him to sign Biddy's lease was different. That was a real document that made him legally liable. He might already be listed on a lease somewhere else, or even a mortgage. What if Biddy or her nephew Luis ran a background check, or a credit check, and he didn't qualify?

Leah barely saw the passing streets, caught up in her spiral until Teddy called out from the back, "Mama! Treat!"

She blinked and glanced in the rearview, then out the window to see where he was pointing. Her favorite coffee shop. If there was ever a day she could use a treat and a pep talk…

"I'm so sorry, kiddo. We don't have time today."

He kicked his feet, disgruntled.

"Besides, how do even have room in your tummy after all that breakfast Wyatt made us? We had a feast!"

Teddy grinned and shrugged, and when Leah glanced back again, he had Wyatt's little figure held up to the window, showing it the passing scenery.

Her wary little boy was already getting so attached. She couldn't blame him—she was too. Would Wyatt still come around after all this was over? Yet another question she had no answer to.

She roared into the school lot and hustled Teddy down the now-empty hall. Her face burned as she cracked his classroom door and waved at his teacher, Miss Katie, but once Teddy was safely settled, Leah hurried back to her car and texted Wyatt.

Breaking: Mrs. Daniels now thinks we already got married. Details when I get back.

His response came quickly.

I noticed your wedding band was gone. Guess I'll need one, too?

Of course he did. Why hadn't she thought of that?

Send me your size and I'll stop on my way home.

A silicone gas station band for him, and fake diamonds for her. What a pair they made.

Her rings felt like a blinding strobe light beaming from her hand, and the deeper she and Wyatt fell into this hole she'd dug them, the crazier her lies felt.

As long as he coughed up those documents, like he promised, everything would be okay. Leah had to believe that.

THERE WAS NO sign of Biddy when she got home. Inside, Wyatt was just getting off a call, and looked burdened. Leah swallowed uncomfortably. *She'd done that.*

While she'd been gone, he'd…he…it struck her suddenly how tidy the house looked. The dishwasher was running, and the kitchen sparkling. His sleeping bag was folded and neatly stowed beside the couch. Wyatt had showered and dressed, and smelled like heaven—all while she'd been out there digging them a pit it would be a nightmare to climb out of.

Tears sprung to her eyes. What was she even doing to this poor man?

He sprinted to her in seconds. "Hey. Hey, what's going on? What happened?"

Leah swiped at her face, the waterworks streaming in earnest at his kindness. "It's okay, I'm okay. Biddy just caught me off guard, that's all. I just need to shake this off and I'll be good."

"It's okay to be upset," Wyatt said, "What she's doing to you guys is mean and unfair."

"But that's life, right?" Her tears kept coming. "Life isn't fair. Whining about it is a waste of time."

"Some might say burying your feelings without processing them is not a judicious use of your time, either."

An unsteady laugh huffed out of her. "Judicious? Who are you and what have you done with Wyatt Oaks?"

He didn't rise to her bait, staying as staunch and solid as ever. Like an oak, come to think of it. Such a perfect name for him.

"The thing is, those feelings will only come back around later, and hurt you then—sometimes worse. The only way out is through."

"Stop being so nice. I can not afford to break down right now!" Her voice cracked, and Leah paused to try to get control of herself. The more words that tumbled out of her, though, the more turbulent she felt. "I am the only thing standing between my sweet baby boy and a big cruel world, and feeling a bunch of stupid feelings is not something I have the luxury of doing when we're about to be out on the goddamn street!"

Wyatt's easy expression didn't waver. He seemed oddly unperturbed by her outburst—not irritated, not offended, not anything other than calmly understanding. *He wasn't real. Couldn't be.*

She had no idea what to do next.

He gave her a minute, then carefully reached out to hold her by the arms. "I know you're scared right now, but I'm here and I can help. I *will* help."

"I can't ask this of you," she sniffled. "It's too much."

"And yet, I'll do it." He closed the distance between them and wrapped his arms around her. "No strings attached."

His hold wasn't tight enough to make her feel trapped, but it also wasn't too loose, like he was afraid of her exploding. Wyatt's hug was, in fact, perfect.

Leah sank into his warmth and felt a new wash of tears soak the t-shirt under her cheek. The gratitude and relief she felt were dangerous.

"You're not a wizard, though. You can't magically make a new, affordable home appear out of thin air for us," she sniffled.

He was quiet for three steady beats of his heart, and then he said quietly, "What if I could?"

She pulled back and peered at his face. "Do you know somewhere?"

"I might. I need to check with some people to sort out whether it will work. I'll do that today."

"Okay. Will you…let me know? If you hear something?"

"Whatever happens, you will not be out on the street. I can promise that, at least."

Leah nodded.

"So…" he rubbed her back, hesitating a moment over his next words. "We got hitched, huh? Is that what Mrs. Daniels waylaid you about?"

"Yes. Every day she's dragging out some new clause in her lease from hell. Jesse died a year and a half ago and we've had no problems until now. I don't know why she's suddenly being such a cow about getting rid of us."

Wyatt looked away, frowning in thought.

Leah smacked her forehead and darted for her purse. "Oh shoot, I forgot. Here's what I got you. I don't know if it will work, but we can always get you something else if you prefer."

Wyatt accepted the box she shoved at him, and extracted the charcoal gray sports band like he was defusing a bomb. He held it in his fingers, but he didn't put it on.

Unable to endure his stormy expression, Leah pushed forward and took it from him, then tried to slip it on his finger the same way he'd done for her. It didn't slide smoothly, though, the pliable silicone bending at his knuckle and getting twisted.

Wyatt smiled a little sadly, pushing it the rest of the way for her and dropping his hand like he didn't want to look at it. "Look at us. Man and wife, just like that."

"I'm so sorry I dragged you into all this," she said quickly. "If you need to back out, I will totally understand."

"Leah, please stop apologizing. I'm fine, I swear."

"You don't look it. So, if you're not upset about this, then what is it? That call you were on when I got back?"

He nodded. "I can't say a lot. The job I'm working is getting hotter, though, and to move things forward, we need to…take a few risks. It could backfire, but it's important. There are bad people we need to…stop." He clammed up and rubbed his jaw. "Much as I'd rather not, it has to be done."

Leah studied him. Wyatt and his team had already lost their SEAL careers because of some blowhard politician. She could only imagine the kind of powerful opposition he was facing now.

"And I'm over here whining about my grouchy old neighbor," she told him.

"There's no worse, only different," he retorted. "But I probably do need to dip out on our day date and go take care of some stuff. Can I get a rain check on consummating this sham marriage for now?"

Leah followed him to the front door. "You bet. And Wyatt?"

He hesitated with his hand on the knob. "Yeah?"

"If you're going to raise hell, remember—don't be part of the problem."

He looked uncomfortable, like that was something he simply couldn't agree to.

"Be the whole problem," she smiled.

His face split into a delighted grin. He spun from the door, grabbed her around the waist, and dipped her over his arm. "And that's why I married you," he laughed, then kissed her senseless.

THE REPRIEVE IN tension didn't last long. Two hours later, when Leah went outside to go retrieve Teddy from school, her landlord was waiting for her again.

"The mail came," the woman said, offering Leah a stack of envelopes. Prominently placed on top was her survivor benefits check. Opened.

Leah's gaze flew to Biddy in betrayal.

The woman tapped the check, indifferent to her own treachery. "That's called stealing from the Army."

"You know the wheels of the bureaucracy turn slow," Leah said, snatching her mail and tucking it into her purse. "I'm sure they just haven't caught up yet."

"They turn slow *except* when it comes to money. You're a scam artist. A con woman. I should report you right now."

"Mrs. Daniels, that's completely unnecessary. Why are you doing this?" Her heart felt like it was beating at twice the normal rate. How did this day keep getting worse and worse?

"You've clearly lied to someone. Was it me or the Army?" The woman sniffed in disdain. "Never mind, I suppose it doesn't matter. Either way, you're out. No more delays. You have one week, no more."

Chapter Nineteen

Wyatt

BACK AT THE apartment, Wyatt kicked back on the couch as Joe brought him up to speed. After his call earlier, it was clear the team needed to make some decisions about what came next.

They'd already known that Senator Doggett had been using a shell company to hide the backdoor contracts he'd been funneling to his wife and stepson's arms company, Landry Cox, via his position on the Armed Services Committee.

However, while researching the true owners of the estate where Bennett's fiancée Kim had been held hostage a few months ago, Noah had come to the conclusion that Roy might also be using that company to launder other income—perhaps even what he was earning from his part in the trafficking network.

The question was, what were they prepared to do to shake loose the proof they needed?

"As I see it, the solution is to put that bastard in a position that forces him to react off the cuff, without the benefit of consulting his PR team or the more cautious members of his camp," he told

Bruiser. "My guy is far too arrogant and touchy to keep his cool, and will definitely end up saying more than he intends to."

"If he feels like he's been cornered? For sure."

"We need to surprise him. And we have to hit him where it hurts."

Joe looked thoughtful. "Doggett thinks he's untouchable. Smarter than everyone else, more powerful…he thinks his people are absolutely loyal, and will do anything he asks."

A narcissist, through and through. Wyatt was convinced they wouldn't need to lay a finger on the guy. All they needed was an airtight attack on his perceived image—something that would build on the angst he was carrying around thanks to his recent loss in the presidential primaries.

"Powerful people make lots of enemies," Wyatt pointed out. "And once the tide starts to turn, we're going to find others who are willing to talk." His knee bobbed as he thought it through, drawing Joe's gaze…and his irritated frown.

He propped his feet on the coffee table and crossed them at the ankles in an effort to keep still. "If we can get the media to confront Roy with allegations of financial improprieties, we can see who he tries to pin it on. Dollars to donuts, that person can be flipped, and will lead us to where the real dirt is."

Follow the money, find the missing girls. It would work, Wyatt was sure of it.

They volleyed a few more ideas back and forth, until Wyatt glanced at his phone to check the time and noticed Leah's text.

> *I had to tell Biddy we got married but she knows we're lying. I'll explain when I see you. We have a week to move.*

"The fuck? How can she do that?"

"Do what?"

He showed the message to Joe.

"Who the fuck is Biddy?"

"Her landlord," Wyatt explained. "The one who helps run those church groups. We need to get her and Teddy out of that house and into a better situation ASAP."

Joe didn't argue, which was fortunate—Wyatt couldn't have said how he might have reacted if he had. Leah's distress made him feel things that were in direct opposition to his normally easygoing nature.

Possessive. Territorial. Murderous.

Wyatt could not exact vengeance against a bitter old lady, though—he could only do his best to help find Leah and Teddy somewhere new to live, and help them get on their feet once they were safe.

So, even though he hated to leave her alone when she had to be freaking out, he nodded at Bruiser and made the call, summoning the team so he could make his case.

LEAH'S CAR WAS back in her garage by the time he was able to return and, if he had their schedule memorized correctly, Teddy was already down for his after-school nap. Wyatt scanned the street as he got out of the Black Watch truck he'd been lent, but the area was as quiet as ever.

Midday residential suburb, everyone at work. Everyone, that was, except Mrs. Daniels, who was not trying terribly hard to be discreet as she peered at him through her front window.

It took less than a breath to decide what he wanted to do. Wyatt diverted his steps and advanced on her front door instead of Leah's.

She took a while to answer, though they both knew she'd been standing right inside. But eventually, Mrs. Daniels cracked the faded panel and glared at him with watery blue eyes.

Though it galled him to extend even an ounce of friendliness, he tried to lay on the charm.

"Hey, I'm Wyatt Oaks. Nice to meet you." He extended his hand. She eyed it like she might a scorpion before touching her fingers to his.

"Hello." *So suspicious.*

"Leah tells me you're our landlady. I thought I should introduce myself, and tell you if you need anything done around the place, I'm at your disposal."

Mrs. Daniels gripped her doorframe with white knuckles, as if a violent home invasion could be imminent. "I assure you my nephew takes care of my needs perfectly well."

"Oh, right." Leah had told him about a nephew. "He's at Pendleton, right? What's his name? Maybe I know him."

"I fail to see how that is relevant."

Wyatt suppressed an eye roll and tried a different angle. "Leah told me you volunteer on base. Were you an Army spouse, too? I was Navy myself but—"

Biddy cut off his babbling with an angry huff. "Mr. Oaks, I do not have time for idle chatter. I am on my way to church and then to my lawyer."

"I see. Well, let's get down to business then. It sounds like you need me to sign the lease, now that Leah and I are married. Would you like to sit down and do that together one of these days, or would you prefer for me to make an appointment with your lawyer?"

Wyatt wouldn't have thought it possible, but Mrs. Daniels managed to scowl even harder. "That will not be necessary. I am proceeding with the eviction, as is my right."

"On what grounds?" He strove to keep his tone curious, despite wanting to punch a wall.

"Fraud."

"Fraud? What do you mean? We're happy to give you copies of our marriage license or whatever else you require."

Biddy—such a perfect name for her—shook her head and pulled further back into her front hall. "I've already discussed this with Mrs. Burke, and it sounds as if you should, too. Please remove yourself from my steps immediately, or I will have you removed."

Wyatt examined her, trying to understand where the vitriol was coming from. "Did I do something to you that I am not aware of? I am here trying to be polite, and you seem to be—"

"Mr. Oaks, I do not want trouble from you. Your…*wife*…can explain everything. Do not come here again."

Then she closed the door in his face, leaving him fuming on her stoop.

So many accidents could befall a person of her age, living alone. Sooooo many.

Wyatt played out the evil fantasy for only a minute before he shook it off and headed next door. He found Leah huddled around a cup of coffee in the kitchen, her face pale.

"Hey. So, I talked to the neighbor," he told her.

"You too?"

"She's still calling you *Mrs. Burke*. Tried to sweet-talk her. Didn't go well."

"There's no sweet-talking Biddy Daniels."

"Tell me about it." Wyatt looked her over, and didn't love the way her fingers were trembling. "Leah, tell me what's going on."

She looked at him through damp lashes, her gaze agonized. "She's kicking us out."

"So, I gathered. Why now, though?"

"She gave us a week. Wyatt, how am I going to get this whole place packed in a week? Where are we going to go?"

"Okay, hang on." He went over and set her cup aside, and took her carefully by the arms. "First, on what grounds is she evicting you? That fucking morality clause?"

"That, and she said I'm perpetuating fraud."

"She mentioned that. How so?"

Leah pulled away to fuss with Teddy's sippy cups in the drying rack next to the sink. "This is such a mess."

"Leah. What fraud is she accusing you of?"

"Well, you know how I told her…" She groaned and ran her hands through her hair. "I told her we got…we got married, but she didn't believe me."

Those words, *we got married*, did weird things to Wyatt's chest. He did a quick check of his systems, making sure he wasn't in danger of clocking out or something, then refocused on her face. "Did she look for our license or something?"

"Not that I'm aware. It would be like her, though." She gave up her haphazard organizing, sagged against the counter, and stared gloomily over his shoulder. "Biddy looked through my mail and found my benefits check. Can't still draw those if you get remarried, or even if you pretend to be married. She had a fit."

"Wait, how does she even know that?"

"Probably because she's been drawing them half her life. I hear about the sainted Walter all the time, believe me."

"Ah."

"Apparently I should've stayed loyal and mourned better," she added. "Longer, for sure."

"Let me guess—forever would've been appropriate?"

"It's worked for her." Leah's gaze finally connected with his, and the fear he saw there hit him like a punch to the sternum. "Wyatt, if she reports me, Teddy and I will lose our benefits, our insurance…he's even supposed to get money for college. I can't afford to pay out of pocket for that stuff! And he needs stability right now, not more upheaval. He still has three more months before he's done for the summer."

"We will worry about that when and if the time comes. Right now, your neighbor's main priority seems to be getting you guys out of here. So, tell me: would you rather fight the eviction or move to a new place with a less-unhinged landlord?"

"I…I don't know!" she moaned. "I've been trying to sort it out, but my brain feels like Swiss cheese right now."

"It's been a tough year," he agreed. "And none of this is your fault."

"I guess. There's just never enough time. I've been trying to look for places ever since Biddy started making noise about this, but rent is so high. I don't know where we can go."

Wyatt watched her, trying to decide what to say to guide her in the right direction without coming on too strong. "I checked with my people earlier. They said your lease looks enforceable. Mrs. Daniels won't even have to refund your security deposit if she says you're in breach of contract."

Leah shook her head glumly. "It doesn't matter. She has us screwed either way. Even if we could fight her to stay, I wouldn't be able to afford it once she gets our benefits taken away."

He took a deep breath. "I have a viable option for you if you want to hear it. It's not perfect, but it's something." Would *she* think it was doable? He suddenly wasn't sure.

Leah reached for her coffee, but she didn't drink any. She only stared into the cup before putting it aside again. "Anything is better than what I've got, which is a whole lot of nothing."

Wyatt nodded and leaned on the counter next to her. "I have another place I'm working on but until that comes through, I think you guys should come stay with me."

Her silence was tough to swallow. The laugh that followed, even worse.

"Wyatt, your roommates do not want me and my kid to move into your bachelor pad," Leah scoffed. Like he was dumber than a box of rocks.

It was the best solution they had, however, and he had to make her see it. "I already talked to them, and they're fine with it."

She wheeled on him, squinting suspiciously. "No. No way."

"You're my wife," he shrugged. *Simple, as if it explained everything.* To punctuate his words, he gave her a little smile and a small kiss.

He could fix this for her. She just had to let him.

She stared at his face for a few moments, the wheels behind those wild brown eyes thankfully beginning to turn. "You realize I'd need to actually see where you live before I agreed to move in there. And meet the people I'd be exposing my kid to."

And there was the finish line, swimming into sight. Wyatt exhaled as subtly as he could.

"No problem. We'll go as soon as Teddy wakes up from his nap. Pack a swimsuit and you can take him to our pool. It's heated."

"You have a pool."

"Yes. And a community playground, too. There is a catch, though."

She narrowed her eyes and scrunched her nose, and Wyatt had never seen anything so cute in his life. "And what's that?"

"We'd have to share a room," he shrugged again, and this time he couldn't keep the smirk from his face. "And there's only one bed."

MUCH TO HIS relief, the team welcomed Leah and Teddy warmly. He'd worried, after the debates they'd had earlier, that wouldn't be the case—but he'd barely made it past introductions before his new fake wife and stepson were settled in at the apartment community's pool, having a snack and chatting easily with Bennett and Noah.

He'd picked his two nicest friends to babysit and help butter them up, and fortunately it seemed to be working perfectly. So once Wyatt was certain they were happy and comfortable, he slipped back to the apartment to quickly hammer out a plan with Buck and Joe before they all reconvened for dinner.

"So, this Daniels broad is really off her rocker?" Joe wondered, leaning in from his spot on the couch. "She wants them out *now?*"

"I'm telling you, something is off about this. She gave them a week to get out, didn't want any kind of proof that Leah got married…she just keeps finding new things to bitch about."

Buck lounged in one of the recliners, looking pensive. "Living there for years with no problem, plus another year and a half since Burke died—and now you show up and suddenly Daniels has all kinds of issues with them. I don't like this."

"Me either. If the safe house isn't available in time, though, I'm going to move her and Teddy in here. You okay with that? Joe and Noah signed off earlier."

Joe nodded at Buck. "We'll probably need a day or two to kid-proof the place, but we can swing it, no sweat."

"Kids are curious," Buck reminded them. "They explore. So, you can't leave anything lying around. No gear, no booze, no meds, no nothing. Late nights are out. Might want to rethink overnight guests. You all are sure about this?"

Wyatt glanced at Joe again, then nodded. "The landlady gave her a week, but I'd like to move them sooner if we can—this coming weekend, if she can swing it. I don't want to risk Biddy coming up with some new thing to hold over her."

Buck eyed Joe. "Bruiser?"

"Fine. We'll be ready."

"Assuming Leah agrees, I want help to pack up her house and put most of her stuff in storage. I'm sure she's a pro at PCSing, but it's been a while and she's kind of shaken up. She could probably use a hand."

Buck made a note on his phone, murmuring, "Shouldn't be a problem. I'll link up with Monroe and Noah and let you know what we got."

Wyatt looked between them with a frown. "So, that's it? We're a go on this?"

"Yes."

"It seems too easy. Three weeks ago, you guys were giving me shit about her. I thought for sure I'd have to lobby every one of you to go along with this."

Buck shrugged. "Things change."

"Uh-huh." He watched them, but neither seemed inclined to offer more of an explanation for the official change in position.

"Just like that."

"Dude, yes. Just go with it, for Chrissakes," Joe griped.

"Okay!" Wyatt chewed his lip and cast around for a topic that might help him recover some semblance of seriousness. "Where are we on…Linedance Holdings? We gonna spill that to the press or what?"

"Monroe liked your plan best," Buck replied. "He cleared us to run with it. While you were up in Solano, Noah leaked the company name and tax filings to the media, and it's beginning to gain traction. Some major outlets are already starting to question the Doggett camp about why they've never reported it on his official tax filings."

"Has he responded?"

Buck nodded, "His people are deferring to the Linedance CFO, who in turn is blaming the omission on a lower-level employee named Kathy James. She's been let go, but we need to find her, and fast."

"Okay…?"

"Yeah, she's gone dark," Joe commented dourly. "It stinks to high heaven. Not a soul seems to know where she went."

Wyatt didn't like the sound of that. They'd learned the hard way not to put anything past the senator and his cronies. "We need to make sure she's okay, and not in trouble."

"Correct. You were right, though—this turned out to be exactly the lead we've been hoping for," Buck said, then glanced at Joe. "It's also why we agreed to help get Leah and her son to safety as soon as possible."

"Need?" Wyatt zeroed in on Buck's face, but those icy blue eyes, as always, gave nothing away. "What do you mean, need?" he demanded.

"Well…turns out Kathy James isn't just some random finance lackey. She's got connections that are very interesting. For example, guess where she lived before Texas?"

Wyatt looked between them, not liking what he saw on their faces. "I don't—"

"You do," Joe countered tersely. "Ms. James's husband bit it in a training accident at Pendleton just about two years ago. And before that…"

"Before that, she was a regular member of a bible study group called Cavalry Coalition," Buck finished quickly. "I'd bet the farm your new girl's landlady is neck deep in this mess, Stitch."

"*Shit*," Wyatt muttered.

"Everywhere we look," he agreed.

Chapter Twenty

Leah

LEAH COULDN'T REMEMBER the last time she'd taken off work to simply relax and have fun with her kid, but their day playing hooky had turned out to be exactly what they'd needed.

It'd also been the perfect opportunity to find out more about Wyatt from the people who knew him best, so when he left them alone to go shower before dinner, she'd turned to his roommates and said, point blank, "Just tell me if I can trust him."

Joe had laughed at her comment, though it seemed like something he maybe didn't do too often. "I can understand why you'd ask that," he'd said. "Wyatt has the ability to put on that surfer dude persona like a second skin, and believe me when I say, he uses it to great effect. Puts people at ease like that."

"But he can drop it in a heartbeat, too," Noah had assured her. "And behind that façade, his brain is always working a million miles an hour. He's like…like one of Teddy's toys, hiding a supercomputer inside." He'd paused, his eyes far away. "Ask me how I discovered *that* this week."

Leah had smiled at those assessments, telling them, "He's been nothing but wonderful to us, but people can be weird. I needed to know if I should be waiting for the other shoe to drop before I get too invested, you know?"

Wrapped in his Spider-man towel, draining a juice box like his life depended on it, Teddy had looked between them with big, watchful eyes. Joe had pulled on a Celtics cap and winked at her kid.

"There is no other shoe," he'd explained. "What you see is mostly what you get with Wyatt. He's loyal as the day is long, hardworking, smart, considerate, freaking nice as…as…uh, super nice." He'd cut eyes at Teddy warily, like he'd been trying to decide if he'd actually cursed or not. "Literally the best human I have ever met. He'll look out for you or die trying."

Noah had looked on, a little misty at Joe's description, but he hadn't disagreed.

In the end, Leah had decided she liked them a lot, and for his part, Teddy had seemed to love them as well. The feeling was decidedly mutual. He'd gotten more attention in a few hours than he'd probably gotten in months, and if those were the type of people Wyatt chose to be closest to, he had to be as decent as he seemed.

The only thing that had given her pause, she remembered, was the jokes hinting at Wyatt's romantic exploits. She'd guessed he was no stranger to the ladies, true…but she'd also come to the conclusion that he wielded his charm judiciously. He didn't say things he didn't mean, and Leah wanted to think she got to see a side of him that none of them knew.

But she'd known him for a few weeks, and they'd known him for years. Maybe she was kidding herself. Everything was moving so fast.

She looked into Wyatt's face, propped inches away from hers on the other pillow of her bed, and saw nothing but honesty.

"You're positive your roommates don't mind us moving in?" she asked, curling into his warmth. "I promise we won't stay long. Just until we can find something else."

"Are you kidding? You're my fake wife. They're all for it. They said they were planning to go shopping for snacks and toys tonight, to help smooth out the adjustment for Teddy. You should stay as long as you want." She felt his breath of laughter against her hair.

"They are a bunch of overgrown children," Leah commented. The way his roommates had played with Teddy in the pool had shown her that. "All this time, I assumed single men were different. Feral. More depraved, at minimum."

"I beg your pardon. We are not like other guys."

"I'm beginning to see that, trust me."

"Good." Wyatt stroked a hand down her back, so much more relaxed now that she'd agreed to the move.

And truly, once she'd seen the layout of the apartment and met his friends, she hadn't needed to debate much. They were good people. It was a safe place with lots of room. Teddy had already won them all over, and would probably love being 'one of the guys' for a little while. Even with the longer drive to his preschool, Leah could manage this.

Not to mention, she was quickly growing addicted to these moments of quiet time with Wyatt at the end of each day. Jesse had never been like this, of that much she was sure.

"So tomorrow, while you and I sort out what's coming with you and what's going to storage," he explained, "the guys are going to make sure anything potentially dangerous in the apartment is secured and out of reach. Joe wants to move a few things around to make sure Teddy has enough room to play in the living room, but if you think of anything else we need to do, just text it in the group chat."

Leah nodded, so grateful that they'd thought of arranging help for her and wouldn't hear of her paying for it. With movers coming to do most of the packing and all the heavy lifting, all she had to worry about was throwing some clothes and toys in bags to use at the apartment. Maybe she'd bring Teddy's cups and plates, too, but everything else was already there.

Getting away from Biddy by Monday might actually be doable, just like Wyatt had said. And oddly, now that the decision was made, it felt right to leave.

The past was gone. It was time for her and Teddy to move on.

"I can't believe they set up a group chat," she mused. "Why does that make me laugh so much?"

"As my grandpa used to say, many hands make light work," Wyatt said primly. "Fair warning, though—I think your kid is about to be spoiled rotten by a mess of rowdy fake uncles and a couple of fake aunts."

Leah squeezed him lightly, but a pang seared through her. Teddy's one real uncle was gone forever now. Would her son even remember Theo when he got older? Or would he only know him through her stories? He'd been so young when Theo died. Still was, actually.

"I need to stop thinking about this," she said abruptly. "Otherwise, I'm never going to get to sleep. Do you mind if I turn on the TV for a bit?"

"Not at all."

Leah flicked through a few channels, and eventually settled on a serious anchorwoman speaking into the camera with the kind of droning voice she would have no trouble tuning out if she started to drift off.

Wyatt switched off the bedside lamp and shook his head at her choice. "Ah yes. Nothing says restful slumber quite like the evening news."

"Would you prefer true crime? I'm halfway through a documentary about these unsolved murders in Arizona back in the 80s."

He shot her a wry look. "This will be fine."

As they watched, he ran his fingers gently through her hair, over and over. Leah's muscles gradually relaxed, and she was moments from unconsciousness when something about the report caught her attention.

"Wait. Did she say Roy Doggett? Isn't that the senator who hates you guys?"

Wyatt nodded. She disentangled herself from his arms and propped herself up with her pillow. "Did I miss something? What did he do now?"

"Some financial stuff with one of his companies. Those guys are all grifters, I swear. Nothing surprises me anymore."

Leah squinted at the screen, and the photo of the former employee they were discussing. "That woman looks like someone."

"Who? The reporter?"

"No, the other one. Kathy James?" Leah watched the report for another minute. "Why does her name sound familiar?"

Wyatt's expression was strange in the flickering light. "Seems like a common name. Do you know someone with a similar one?"

"No, I…" Leah shook her head, something important tugging at the edges of her brain. "Ugh. I can't place it."

"Could be someone you saw in a movie, maybe. That happens to me all the time." He took the remote and clicked off the TV, then pulled her down next to him. "Don't worry. As soon as you stop trying to think of it, it'll come to you."

"This is going to drive me crazy."

He chuckled, but it sounded off somehow. His trailing fingers in her hair lulled Leah closer to sleepiness again. His voice was soft and thoughtful, when he wondered, "Can I ask you something?"

"Sure."

"When you were doing that premarital counseling stuff…you said you thought half the couples probably wouldn't last a year."

"True. Unfortunately."

"I know you said Kandace was maybe stepping out on her man, but why did you think that about the others? Did they just not know each other very well, or what?"

"Afraid our fake marriage won't go the distance?" she laughed.

"Not in the least," he chided. "Just curious, I guess."

A smile lingered on her lips as she considered his question. "Well…sometimes it was that the couple was so awkward with each other—like they didn't know each other very well, or were acting the way they thought they were supposed to, instead of how they really were. That seemed like it would be an exhausting way to live."

"Probably, yeah."

"For others—and maybe this is a military thing—but other couples seemed to be rushing into things way too fast. There'd be red flags flying everywhere, but everyone was ignoring them. Cultural differences, religious differences, clashing temperaments. We saw it all, for sure."

"Did you ever try to dissuade them from going through with it, or was that a faux pas?"

"I don't know if dissuade is the right word. I definitely arranged to have coffee with a few women, so I could delicately try to make sure they weren't heading into a dangerous situation. I suggested actual couples counseling to a few before they made things official. The church didn't really have anything that serious, but I used to print out a list of base resources for them. Mental health numbers, emergency DV lines. Anything I could think of."

"Yikes."

"Yep. Kind of hard to escape from an abusive situation when you're stranded on a base, hundreds or even thousands of miles from home, surrounded by your spouse's armed and dangerous friends and coworkers."

She heard Wyatt swallow and peeked at him. He was watching her carefully, half his face outlined by the dim glow of her nightlight. Suddenly, Leah felt too exposed, like she'd revealed more than she'd intended.

"But what do I know," she murmured awkwardly.

"More than most, sounds like. Did you keep in touch with any of your couples? So you could see how things turned out?"

"Not really. A lot of them were young—much younger than we were. Too young to get married, in my opinion."

Wyatt nibbled his lip, seeming troubled.

"You look like you want to go save them all right now," she smiled gently.

He didn't deny it. "You're sure you don't know where they are?"

She shook her head. "I figured out fast I couldn't save people from their poor decisions. Look at me—I couldn't even save myself."

"Leah—"

"No, it's okay. One foot in front of the other, right?" She yawned so wide her jaw cracked.

"And that's my cue," he said. "Try to get some sleep. Tomorrow's gonna be busy."

Leah sighed. Talking to another adult at the end of the day was nice. Cuddling was even nicer. It'd been so long since she'd experienced either, and she hated for him to leave, even if he was only heading downstairs.

"I hope Teddy doesn't miss this place too much."

"He's young, he'll adapt fast."

"Here's hoping."

"What about you? Are you going to miss it?"

"No," she admitted. "A lot of good things happened here, but a lot of awful things too. I'm ready for something different."

"Onward and upward," he murmured quietly.

Leah closed the inches between their faces and kissed him softly. "Lead the way."

The kiss he gave her back lingered on her lips. She nestled closer to his large, solid body and tucked her leg between his, unable to remember why she'd been trying so hard to keep him at a distance and move slowly.

"You know," she murmured. "Since the TV didn't do the trick, we could always choose the nuclear option to get tired."

Wyatt kissed her cheek, then her jaw. "Do I even want to know?"

"Oh, I suspect you know. It's an activity older than time."

He pulled back and studied her. "You sure? After last time…I wasn't sure if I should hit on you again after that."

Leah winced with embarrassment. The poor guy had tried to get sexy, and she'd rewarded him with a meltdown. No wonder he'd been keeping his hands to himself.

"Last time was a weird anomaly, I promise." She ran her lips up the warm column of his neck and brushed them along the shell of his ear, gratified when Wyatt shivered. "We only have a few more nights of privacy like this," she coaxed. "After we move, Teddy will be in the room with us. We'll have to get really creative."

Wyatt's big hand landed on her ass and yanked her tight against him. "I can be creative."

"Show me now," she grinned.

Chapter Twenty-One

Wyatt

THE THREADBARE BOXER shorts Leah wore as pajamas provided no barrier at all between them. When Wyatt pulled her on top of him, it was all he could do to not grind up into her.

Not that he thought she'd mind. Leah stretched sinuously against him, searching for contact. This was their first time, though, and he wanted to make a lasting impression—but that was a dicey proposition given how much he'd been envisioning exactly this scenario. Expecting him to be 'creative' on top of that was a big ask.

This time.

"Take this off," he whispered, tugging up the hem of her tank top. He noticed her sports bra a second later, and snapped the shoulder strap. "This too."

"I will if you will," she smirked.

When he took off his t-shirt, they'd be skin to skin. The thought of it was almost too much to endure. *Almost.*

Wyatt wrestled free of the offending garment and was met with his first full view of Leah, bare from the waist up, luminous with an otherworldly beauty.

His mouth went dry.

She grinned at him, and he had the most irrational urge to wipe that smile right off her face. They'd held off on this moment for a while—longer, certainly, than he usually waited to sleep with a woman he liked—but Wyatt didn't find any part of this experience amusing.

He wanted Leah desperately. It was more than that, though. Making love to her felt important now. Significant. He wanted her to feel that too.

"You're so pretty it hurts," he confessed, wishing he could see if it made her blush.

"You're one to talk."

He shushed her. "Eyes on me, princess. Pay attention." No way was he going to let her mind wander to another man this time. This was about the two of them, and *only* the two of them. He raised his knees, holding her in place where she straddled him, and held onto her hips.

"Who am I?" he demanded.

"Some bossy version of Wyatt that I'm not sorry to be meeting."

So much sass. His jaw ticked, but he wouldn't give in yet. "That's right. And what am I about to do to you?"

"Hopefully fucking me into the next century," Leah snickered.

"That's what you want?"

She nodded semi-seriously. "More than pizza and winning the lottery."

Wyatt fought back the manic laugh that wanted to bubble out of him. "Then that's what I'm going to do. And I want to hear my name on your lips when you come. Can you do that for me, pretty girl?"

"Yes," Leah agreed, her core growing impossibly hotter against his stomach. "I am definitely going to do that."

He touched her lips, then traced a line down her throat, between her breasts, to her navel. She was so soft. So lush. He wanted nothing more than to make her scream, if only to prove that she was as insane for him as he was for her.

He couldn't, though. Not this time.

"You're going to be so quiet for me, aren't you, Leah? No one to hear but you and me."

She tried to bend forward, to snuggle against him, but Wyatt held her in place with a hand on her stomach. She searched his face, then answered, "Yes. I'll be quiet."

"Good. Come here." Wyatt traced the undersides of her lovely breasts with his thumbs, then pulled her down to devour her mouth, the mint of her lip balm a faint shadow compared to the dark, delirious taste of her wicked tongue.

Much as he wanted to, he couldn't keep his urgency at bay. He shoved down her shorts and underwear with rough, jerky movements, and somehow got free of his own despite her legs tangling with his.

Leah's scent was everywhere, drugging him, making him frantic. He couldn't get enough of her mouth, her skin, her warmth seeping into him.

"Wyatt," she whimpered when he filled his hands with her magnificent fucking ass and pressed her against him.

She was soaked and hot as lava, sliding along his cock. He hissed at the sensation, nearly losing it right then.

"Wyatt, please," Leah whispered in his ear, then peppered his jaw and neck with wet, sucking kisses.

"Now?" he managed shakily.

He was so far under her spell, and there was so much to revel in, he forgot he intended to stay in charge. Her breast was full and heavy in his palm. Her hair, thick and silky, twined in his fist. Her mouth, torture itself, landed everywhere Leah could reach.

"Now," she urged, her thighs bracketing his hips, her skin like living flame. "Please, now."

She rose up, he braced his feet and tilted his hips, and then Leah's body was engulfing him in glorious heat and Wyatt was lost.

He couldn't take his eyes off her as she planted her hands on his chest and rode him, couldn't look at anything but his hands on her body, and the column of her neck as her head fell back and breaths picked up speed.

His heart felt like a racehorse, trying to pound out of his chest. He grabbed Leah's hand and sucked her fingers into his mouth, but they were nothing compared to her tongue.

He wanted her tongue.

Wyatt sat up, wrapped his arms around her, and plastered her against him as they moved, in perfect sync as he found her mouth and swallowed each of her ragged breaths.

His balls drew tight. His cock pistoned into her like a fucking cannon. He was moments away. *Too close.*

"Come for me, Leah," he instructed. "Come so hard for me."

She moaned into his mouth, picking up her pace and adjusting her angle. Wyatt drove into her, hard and deep, and felt her tremble under his palms.

He broke first, his climax feeling like his soul was leaving his body, and praised every deity he'd ever heard of when Leah came apart a mere moment later, the exquisite grip of her body something he never wanted to leave.

Her hot breath washed across his ear, his name like a secret between them.

A clock ticked somewhere in the room. Wyatt's skin cooled, Leah's too, and still they stayed there, entangled, unwilling for it to end.

THE NEXT MORNING, Leah called him from the car, on her way back from dropping off Teddy.

"Hey, I'm on my way home. Do you have a minute?"

"Yeah, of course. I was just about to put some stuff in the truck. What's up?"

"So, remember that woman we saw on TV last night? Kathy James? I said her name sounded familiar."

Wyatt's pulse kicked up. "Yeah…?"

"I just remembered where I know her from."

Know. Not 'heard of.' So much for wishful thinking.

He kept his tone light. "Really? Where?"

"Wyatt, she was in our counseling group, and then in Biddy's bible study." Leah's voice was breathless. Excited.

It took him a minute to holster his trepidation. Buck had warned him, but even as he'd encouraged her to talk about the group, he'd wanted there to be some mistake. Apparently more than he'd realized.

"Seriously? That's crazy," he told her.

"I know! I can't believe I didn't remember it before. Kathy was so different from the other girls that I should've. My brain's been mush for months, I swear."

Wyatt could hear road noise over the connection. The sound of engines and the occasional horn, Leah's music playing softly and her turn signal clicking on. It felt surreal to be thinking about anything other than dragging her back into bed with him, but he had to find out what she knew.

The mission was the mission, and it was separate from how he felt, he reminded himself.

"Different how?"

"What the hell, dude!" she cried angrily. "Use your freaking signal!"

He waited, but not terribly patiently. She grumbled, but he couldn't make out what was going on.

"Leah?" he prompted eventually.

"Sorry! Some guy cut off me and about nine other people. Uhh…where was I?"

"Kathy James wasn't your average bible study woman."

"Right. Most of the people we counseled were young, so they were all over social media, right? A bunch of the girls got into all that *clean girl, trad wife* bullshit you see, but once their marriages went through, we never really saw much of them. Probably too busy canning green beans or whatever."

Wyatt checked his watch, gauging how long before Leah would pull in. "But not Kathy?"

"Nope. not Kathy," she agreed. "She popped into our women-only meetings now and then, but every time she'd be so disturbed by the tradwife stuff. She was always trying to convince the girls they needed to have something of their own—something just for them, you know? She couldn't understand the regressive mindset. Said God didn't want them to be dependent and vulnerable."

Wyatt snorted. "I bet that was super popular."

"They didn't like her, but Kathy was sharp," Leah explained. "Really sharp. Like, a high-level accountant, or something."

The confirmation that she was talking about the correct person pierced him more than it should have. "Was she married?" he wondered.

"Briefly. I think they met in college. Her husband was a tank gunner, I want to say. Something with the infantry."

"Briefly?"

"He died. There was an accident on base. He and another guy were crushed by some equipment."

Wyatt winced. "Ah, that sucks."

"Yeah, it wasn't great. Kathy was in a dark place for a while." Leah fell silent for a minute, the sounds in and around her car a soundtrack to his unhappiness that she was, even tangentially, involved in anything to do with the team's op.

"Understandable," he murmured, to himself and to her.

Leah went on, "The other girls kept trying to fix her up, to get her to meet some guy they knew, but her grief was awful. It was way too soon." She paused, and then gasped, "Oh my god, I'm just now wondering if it was that same person Kandace was always with. Wyatt, what if it was that guy you showed me a picture of?"

He'd bet his favorite surfboard it was, but he wasn't going to tell her that. "Who knows. What happened to her, though? Did she stick around base for long?"

"No, her husband had family out west. Texas, I think. Kathy had found a job out there, but she didn't think she'd stick with it. Said the company was a little iffy, whatever that means. It was only supposed to be something to tide her over until she could get her feet under her."

Wyatt didn't want to ask. *He had to ask.* "Leah…do you know if she's still out there?"

"Probably? We kind of dropped off after Jesse died. I had a lot on my plate, and I don't think she was in a good place to help me." She sounded distracted, though she had to be getting close to home by now.

"Seems like people really need to find her and talk to her, though," he explained. "Do you think she'd answer if you reached out? Maybe meet up with you?"

"I'm sure she would. But between Teddy and the move, it's not like I could go see her anytime soon."

"Maybe you wouldn't have to," he said. "If you could get ahold of her, other people could take it from there."

"I don't know. Maybe. Anyway, there's more. Or maybe…I think there's more." Leah fell silent for a moment, then went on in a rush, "Listen, I could be spiraling here, but remember how I told you Biddy has a nephew? She's really proud of him. Like…*really* proud. Brags about him all the time," she scoffed. "Anyway, he'd pop into her bible study once in a while, and we'd never hear the end of it…you'd think Jesus himself had graced them with his presence. But this one time, right before Kathy moved, Luis showed up and I saw the two of them in the parking lot after, having a pretty heated discussion."

Wyatt frowned. *That was interesting.* "Do you know why?"

"No, but it's weird, right? He never seemed to notice her one way or another before that, and suddenly they had beef? What was that about?"

"I can't imagine," he said.
A lie, but how he wished it wasn't.

Chapter Twenty-Two

Leah

LEAH LAY ON the couch in the dark family room, watching the muted TV without really seeing anything. Her lids were heavy. Her body was exhausted from a last-minute flurry of packing once Teddy went to bed, but her brain wouldn't shut off.

It was just as well. She needed to wait up for Wyatt, anyway.

He'd ferried a couple of truckloads of her and Teddy's things to his apartment that afternoon, then stayed down there for dinner, and to make sure everything would be ready for them to move in tomorrow.

Leah had stayed put and attempted to keep to their routine. She'd tried to make a game of packing for Teddy's sake, but she couldn't decide how he was taking the move.

She couldn't decide how she was handling it, either. Was she really going to be able to commute to Teddy's school every day? How was she going to find somewhere permanent to live? What was this going to do to her and Wyatt's relationship, and were the roommates going to get tired of Teddy?

Was Wyatt?

As of tomorrow, she and Wyatt wouldn't have to pretend to be married any longer, but they would effectively be living like they were. They'd be sleeping side by side in the same bed, for who knew how long. And Teddy would sleep right next to them in his portable crib, undoubtedly putting a damper on any sexy times.

Probably even more than her stupid Jesse baggage had.

Leah huffed in annoyance at herself, checked the time on her phone, and tossed it back to the table. Wyatt had said he'd be back in an hour, give or take, and then she could go to bed.

In the morning they'd pack up the last of the food, and she and Teddy would head straight to the apartment so he wouldn't have to witness the only home he'd ever known being emptied by strangers.

Wyatt would stay with the movers, making sure everything went smoothly and doing any necessary spot cleaning or repairs once they were done. Later, Joe had offered to babysit while Teddy napped, so Wyatt and Leah could go and organize the storage space. She wanted to make sure she could access anything she might need in the short term, anything she'd forgotten to bring with her.

Then it would be done.

She swallowed nervously. Hopefully she wasn't making a giant mistake, because there was no stopping it now.

On Monday she'd call Biddy to let her know they were out, though the odds were stellar that she'd already be aware of what had transpired. Leah's crotchety landlady would undoubtedly be watching the entire process from her window, furious that she was being robbed of the chance to put a mother and son out on the street.

She snorted. Anything that came after that, Wyatt insisted, should be handled through lawyers and she couldn't say she disagreed.

What a mess. At least she had his help, though.

She rested her eyes for a minute or two, then pried them open with a start. Maybe she should call it quits and go to bed, and let Wyatt find his own way into the house.

Movement on the wall caught her eye. Two big shadows, cast by the streetlight outside her window. Was someone out there?

Leah froze, holding her breath until she heard it—the tiniest *snick* from the hall—and she knew. Whoever had been outside had made their way in through the garage.

It couldn't be Wyatt, however. He always came straight to her front door and knocked, and he'd never asked for a key.

Leah tried to think through her best move. Normally she would run, straight out the back and right to a neighbor, but she could not leave without Teddy. She would not. That meant she had to get to him without being seen, though, and then hope they could hide until they had a clear shot at an exit.

The intruders moved into sight between her and the stairs, clad in dark clothes and slipping stealthily toward the kitchen. Males, she decided, but otherwise indecipherable.

She watched them through slitted eyes, hoping they'd assume she was asleep, if they'd even noticed her. Once they'd passed and turned away, she silently slid her phone off the coffee table and into the pocket of her robe.

They rifled through the papers she had stacked near the phone on the kitchen island. Bills, appointment reminder cards— nothing that should interest anyone.

"Nothing here," one guy said.

"She said she works from home, but there's no desk down here. Maybe an office upstairs."

She who? And why was that second voice familiar?

"Don't people work at the dinner table? That's a thing, right?"

"I guess. We'll look for a computer on the way. Come on." The taller shadow headed for the front of the house.

The second hesitated near the arm of Leah's couch, whispering, "What about her?"

"Probably the sitter," came the soft response. "The chick who lives here is pretty hot. That one ain't it."

Leah held herself still, trying not to scowl. *Assholes.*

The burglars spent no more than a minute in her front room— which contained Teddy's train table and remaining toys instead of the formal dining set they seemed to be expecting—then made their way upstairs.

Leah rolled to the floor and crouched in the space between the couch and coffee table, quickly texting Wyatt with numb, shaking fingers.

911 Break in 2 guys HELP

He would understand that. He would believe her. He had to.

Now came the hard part—getting to Teddy. Heart in her throat, Leah tiptoed to the foot of the stairs, sticking to the deeper shadows cast by the banister until she heard the creak of her office door. She swallowed down her nerves and crept up the stairs one at a time, keeping close to the wall so she wouldn't make a sound.

At the top, she dropped low, listening. One seemed to be opening drawers in her desk, and the other sounded like they were in the closet, moving boxes around.

With any luck, neither would be watching the doorway.

Leah sidled right up to the frame, took a deep breath, and chanced a peek—then crossed the opening in one long stride. *No sound. No sound.*

She backed into Teddy's room a few steps later and halted beside the door, silently breathing in and out, trying to calm her galloping heart. No one had grabbed her. No one had yelled. She'd made it. *So far, so good.*

She watched Teddy for another second or two, gauging whether he was sleeping deeply enough for her to lift him without waking him. He seemed to be. Leah peeled back his covers, pushed her hands under his solid weight, and scooped him up against her chest.

He curled into her like a little shrimp, warm and solid, resting his head against her shoulder and popping his thumb into his mouth. His eyes stayed closed, his breathing even.

Leah grabbed his blanket, cradled his limp form in her arms, and eased into his closet. Thighs screaming, she sank slowly to the floor, then gasped in pain when the corner of a shelf dug into her hip.

She froze, waiting for the inevitable reaction, but Teddy stayed mercifully asleep. Leah draped his blanket over him and prayed he'd stay that way. If he awoke, there'd be no end to his questions, and no amount of shushing would keep them from being found.

Pressed into the furthest back corner of the closet, she leaned her head against the wall and held still, feeling Teddy's heartbeat against her chest, a rapid echo to hers. Every adjustment she made felt over loud, like it was being broadcast through a PA system. Even when she didn't think she'd moved a muscle.

Realization came all at once. It wasn't her that was making noise—it was *them*. Leah could hear everything they were doing in her office next door. Everything they were saying.

She'd known the walls were thin in this house, but this? This was crazy.

Then she saw it, tucked behind the wire cubbies crowding her knees—a circle of light the size of a softball, cut completely through the drywall. Coaxial cable for the internet connection fed through it, needing no more than a quarter of that space.

Leah rolled her eyes at the crappy workmanship and fumed. She'd paid that guy $250 to run the line to her office and this was how he'd done it? *Seriously?*

Peepholes worked both ways, though. She eyed the portal warily. It let her hear what the intruders were saying, but it would also give away her position if Teddy so much as made a peep.

She chewed her lip anxiously. What if she'd forgotten to turn off her ringer and someone called?

Leah checked her phone—still no response to her text. She checked that the ringer was truly off and fiddled with the volume again, then stared at the screen in indecision.

Nothing ventured, nothing gained, she finally determined. She was never going to get out of this closet on her own, and the way those prowlers had talked about her looks…she didn't want to find out what they'd do if they realized who she really was.

Leah closed her eyes, pressed her lips to Teddy's hair, and raised the phone again. Praying for a miracle, she tapped Wyatt's name and kept the line open, hoping he'd pick up and **understand**.

"What's with all the boxes," the guy complained through the wall. *"How are we supposed to find anything if it's all taped up?"*

"Just look for anything that might have address books. Or records from the counseling groups. If we're going to find an addy for this Kathy James chick, it'll probably be there."

"Couldn't we have just stolen the woman's phone? What is this, the dark ages?"

"That's not a bad idea. Look for electronics, too. She might have kept Jesse's phone or computer. Wives get sentimental like that."

"You hang out with your grandma too much, bro. These days women sell that shit before the dirt settles."

"She's my aunt," he retorted. *"See if you can find anything that looks Army. It'll probably be all together. She would've kept stuff for the kid."*

"This is stupid. I can't see anything with my flashlight. Turn on the light."

"We can't. Someone could see it from the street."

"And think she was doing stuff in her own house? Come on. Let's come back during the day when we can see shit."

"Swear to God, soldier, your short-term memory leaves a lot to be desired."

"Well pardon me not at all. What's that supposed to mean?"

"It means we talked about this a hundred times. One of those SEAL jokers has been sniffing around here for weeks. I'd bet my left nut he's gunning for the same shit we are, but we have to find it before him. You understand? It's not fucking negotiable. We can not let them find that woman before us."

Leah stared at the hole in the wall in horror. Moving with excruciating care, she maneuvered her phone to the carpet and leaned it on the wall next to the opening.

"Well, we aren't finding jack diddly now. It's dark as the inside of my ass in here. We're gonna end up back here in a week, mark my words."

"No, we fucking aren't. She'll be gone by then."

"So, we go through her shit when we pile it out on the curb. What's the difference?"

"Besides every fucking nosy person on this street recording us sifting through her possessions, you mean?"

"But what if she comes home? Or that sitter wakes up and decides to check on the kid? Those bitches will be screaming their heads off and calling for the cops faster than you can say boo. I got kids, man. I don't need that kind of heat."

"Then why the hell are you here right now?"

"Like I had a choice."

"Whatever. Just... just shut the fuck up and keep looking. We don't have all night."

"We'd have a hell of a lot more time if your aunt hadn't decided to kick this bitch out for fuck all reason."

"She had her reasons."

"Fine. Then what about those bins in the corner?"

"They say Winter Clothes. *What makes you think that's remotely important?"*

"Because no one would think to look in there for the stuff they wanted to hide? You don't label secrets as secrets, *man. Come on."*

"Look around you. Everything is fucking labeled. The woman is getting evicted, for Christ's sake. Look for a box that says church *or* counseling *or something."*

"I don't know. Winter Clothes *seems sus to me. Why are they in her office? Shouldn't they be in the bedroom?"*

"How the fuck do I know? Maybe this is her staging area. Maybe she magically foresaw you'd be coming when she started packing and decided to screw with you. You watch too many movies."

His response was too low to hear. Leah watched her phone screen. The call was still live. Was Wyatt listening? Was he on his way, or possibly here already?

"You want to look? Fine. But you're wasting time."
A long pause, full of muttered curses and rustling.
"It's just a bunch of coats and shit."

"Imagine that. Now look for office stuff. Papers. Devices. Anything military that might've belonged to her husband or brother, or even that frog motherfucker. Use your fucking head." She bit her lip, her anxiety like a living thing inside her.

"What about her room? People hide stuff in their underwear drawers all the time."

"No, they fucking don't. Come here and help me with this."

"This is stupid. That guy probably found whatever was here the first day. They're badasses. You ever see Lone Survivor?*"*

"Those guys aren't shit. Besides, think it through. If he'd found anything, he wouldn't still be hanging around."

Leah blinked back tears. *No.* She refused to be affected by one thing these knuckleheads said. They didn't know her, or Wyatt. They were just a couple of stupid criminals.

"I thought you said they were getting married. Got married. Whatever."

"I'm not buying it. Pretty boy like him? He could pull whatever babe he wanted. Why would he saddle himself with some other asshole's brat?"

Pretty boy? He knew what Wyatt looked like? Had they been watching her house?

"You're the one who said she's so hot. Maybe he likes hitting that azzzz, bro."

"Dude, stop. How do you even have kids? Do you know any women at all? They're mean as shit once they have a kid. You know that dude is looking for what she knows, same as us. Here, check this one."

Leah choked back her rage. Her doubt. Her *fear.* With her phone silenced, she had no idea if Wyatt had said anything or could hear what was going on, but he hadn't hung up so that was something, at least.

Next door, the men were getting frustrated.

"Let's finish up in here. We'll do the other bedrooms and then you can go home to your mommy. Prick."

There was a flurry of murmuring and the thumps of boxes being restacked.

And then the one who seemed to be in charge sighed irritably. *"Fine, take her room. I'll do the kid's."*

Leah clutched Teddy closer, gaze swinging to the crack in the closet door. Light from the hall slashed across the rug in a sudden, terrifying line, but then, like an answered prayer, the unmistakable sound of a car door slamming came from outside.

The men in her office heard it, too. Through the hole in the wall, everything went still, and the demand came fast. *"What was that?"*

Another pause. The clack of window blinds. *"Shit. Someone's here."*

"Move," came the immediate command. *"Back door, go, go, go."*

"Should we take—?"

"Just go!"

They didn't bother to be quiet as they fled. Their feet hammered down the hall, and then down the stairs.

The doorbell rang as Leah fumbled for her phone, feeling for the volume button with trembling fingers.

She had to clear the knot clogging her airway a couple of times before her voice would work. Her hands shook as she put her phone to her ear.

"Wyatt?" she whispered. "Are you there? Please be there."

Chapter Twenty-Three

Wyatt

WYATT DIDN'T HEAR his phone so much as feel the vibration in his pocket, because Joe and Noah had a hockey game blasting in the living room, and he was playing music as he emptied drawers and made space for Leah in his closet.

But when he glanced at the screen and saw it was her, his heart lifted.

"Hey, babe. I'm almost done and then I'll be on my way. What's up?"

Nothing. *Maybe a butt dial?*

"Babe. Leah?"

No response. Wyatt checked the screen again, but the call hadn't dropped.

"Leah? Can you hear me? Leah!"

He pressed his phone to his ear, hearing some rustling but not much else. Wyatt psyched himself out, thinking he could make out her heartbeat. Something felt wrong.

This call wasn't an accident. Somehow, with that spooky extra sense that Easy had all the time and the rest of them were graced with only rarely, Wyatt *knew.*

A chill raced down his spine, slimy with foreboding.

He navigated to his texts and saw the one he'd missed.

911 Break in 2 guys HELP

Wyatt lunged for the main room, collared Joe, and shoved his phone in the guy's face.

"The fuck?" Bruiser barked.

Wyatt dragged him out of his chair and toward the door, snatching his keys and wallet off the table on the way.

"Dude, I'm coming. Let me get my shoes on for fuck's sake."

Noah shot out of his seat. "You need a third?"

"Stay here, in case Leah calls one of you. Roust Buck and Ben. Someone's in her house."

"Roger that."

Leah's call was still going, but Wyatt couldn't hear much more than the soft shushing of fabric, and possibly…the murmur of voices in the background? He growled in frustration.

"Leah, I'm on the way, okay? Fifteen minutes tops and I'm there. Whatever is going on, stay where you are and hold on."

Joe scowled over his shoulder as they booked it to Wyatt's car. "Fifteen? Dude, no."

He barely glanced at him, feeling wild and afraid in a way no mission had ever made him. He fired off a text to Kenya, clueing her in.

"How'd someone get past the team watching the house?" he wondered. He unlocked his car and caught Joe's uneasy gaze over the hood.

"Fuck if I know. Buck said Kenya's team is the shit. They would've caught most anybody, I have to think."

"They wouldn't have gotten us."

Joe gaped at him. "You think these are pros?"

Wyatt ignored him as he yanked his door open. "Why did I leave? God damn it. I should not have left them alone."

"Like you knew this would happen."

"I should've. We all should've."

"How, dude? How are we supposed to account for every possibility under the sun at all times?" Bruiser dropped into the passenger seat and began arming himself with the weapons he pulled from under the seat and within the glove box.

Wyatt didn't argue with his heavy-handedness—he'd use what he had stashed in the trunk. "This is my fault. I brought this heat to her door. If anything happens to her or that kid, I swear to God—"

Joe shook his head, muttering, "Fuck me," as Wyatt hit the gas, and the car jumped forward.

Bruiser didn't try to stop him, though. He knew better than that. He just grabbed the door handle and hung on for dear life.

THEY WERE SEVEN minutes out when Leah's soft voice finally drifted over the open line broadcasting through his car's sound system. "Wyatt?" she whispered. "Are you still there? Please be there."

"I'm here. Leah? I'm here," he answered frantically. "You guys okay?"

"Someone's at the door. They scared off the men in the house when they rang the bell. What do I do? Is it you?"

He glanced at Joe, who nodded. "It's okay. The people at the door are friends of mine." *Probably hoping to make it look like a social call.* "Do you know which way the guys went?"

"They said the back door, but I don't know for sure. I don't want to leave Teddy," she whispered.

Wyatt's chest ached, but he couldn't give in to it. *Mind over matter.* He had to formulate a plan. "Where are you in the house?"

"Teddy's closet."

"Good girl. Stay put. I'm almost there." He checked his mirrors and veered onto a side street to cut around a slow-moving street sweeper up ahead. It was a miracle law enforcement hadn't pulled him over by now.

"Relay her location to Kenya's team," he instructed Joe, then refocused on Leah's shaky breathing. "Okay, now I don't want you to worry, but my friends are going to come inside, okay?"

"Okay."

"We told them where you are, and they're not going to come in Teddy's room. They're just going to sweep the rest of the house and make sure there's no one else there. Got it?"

"Yes," she said.

"How's Teddy?"

"I can't believe it, but he's still asleep. Thank God."

"That's great," he told her. "Now just hang tight for a few more minutes. I'll come get you as soon as I get there."

"Please hurry," she begged softly.

"You got it." A few more turns, a few blown stop signs, and her duplex came into view near the end of the street.

One unremarkable sedan was parked in the driveway beside Leah's car, but Kenya's team had undoubtedly entered through multiple doorways. There'd be four operatives inside now—maybe more.

Wyatt pulled up to the curb, permit be damned. "Tell Kenya we're here," he told Joe, grabbing what he needed from his trunk and lunging for the stairs.

* * *

"TELL ME AGAIN what happened. Start from the beginning. You said you were watching TV?"

They'd transferred Teddy back to bed at least twenty minutes ago. Since then, Leah had been attempting to recall every detail of what happened while it was still fresh in her mind.

She was bleary, though, tired from the long day and probably also hitting a bit of shock. Wyatt had tried to get her to rest while Joe and Kenya's team finished sweeping the house, looking for prints or anything else the intruders might have left behind. She'd refused.

"Yes. Teddy was already in bed, so I turned on the TV for a little while to wait for you. I was having a hard time staying awake. I think I probably dozed off once or twice."

"And then you heard them come in? Is that what woke you up?"

"No, I saw their shadows first." Leah stopped and rubbed her eyes. "On the wall. I heard them come in from the garage soon after."

"And you could see them from the couch."

She nodded. "Sort of. It was dark, and they were decked out in dark clothes. The only light was from the TV."

Wyatt studied her distant expression. She looked like she was watching the scene unfold in her mind. "Tell me what you see."

"Two men. Average height and weight." Leah hesitated as she thought it through. "One was slightly taller than the other, I guess. But I could tell they were guys because...because of the way they moved, I think? And by their voices, too."

"What about age? If you had to guess."

"Younger. Maybe twenties or so. Although one guy—the one who was complaining a lot—said he had kids. Plural."

Wyatt nodded and added a note to the descriptions he was compiling on his phone. "Okay, what else?"

"They didn't find what they were looking for down here, so they went upstairs. They thought I was asleep. The babysitter, they said. I followed them up, and when they weren't looking, I snuck into Teddy's room. I got him out of bed as carefully as I could, and hid in his closet."

"And he stayed asleep."

Another nod.

"Is that when you texted me?"

"I texted you before I followed them upstairs. I silenced my phone and called when I realized I could hear them talking through the wall. You really couldn't hear anything?" Her bloodshot eyes welled, and Wyatt rubbed his jaw so he wouldn't punch something.

"Sorry," he told her again. "Just, like, fabric moving around. That's it."

"Damn it." Leah blinked several times, fighting back the tears. "I should've thought to record them instead. Maybe that wouldn't have worked either, though."

Wyatt wanted nothing more than to crawl into bed and wrap his arms around her so she could sleep, but she'd insisted on seeing this through. *Brave girl.*

"Did they give you any indication of who they were?" he wondered.

"Well, like I said, I might have recognized that one guy's voice—the one who seemed like he was in charge. I haven't been able to place it. I think he could be a native Spanish speaker, though. He has a slight accent when he says certain words. Just…a hint of something. They bickered and gave each other shit a lot. Used slang I'd associate with younger guys. Their attitudes, too—they talked about the woman who lived here being hot, but the supposed babysitter wasn't. Not particularly mature, you know what I mean?"

Wyatt looked to the ceiling, breathing slowly. In through the nose. Out through the mouth. *Serenity, now.*

His weapon rested comfortably in the holster under his arm, where it'd been ever since Joe had retrieved it from his hand and snapped it into place. He would not free it and go looking for those fuckers.

Not yet, anyway.

Wyatt rested his hand on the arm of the couch, inches from hers, but Leah looked at it like it was an alien thing. "Anything else you can remember about them, specifically?"

"Umm…the dumb one…didn't want to get caught. He said he didn't need that kind of heat because he had kids. He was agitating to come back another time, but they knew I was getting evicted. So they couldn't."

"Right."

"But then the leader wanted to know why he'd come along at all. And he acted like he had no choice."

"Interesting."

Leah nodded. Still distracted. Still almost…vacant.

"Okay, so one last summation, and then we should finish up for tonight," he said firmly. "You said they were looking for an address for Kathy James, and that they had to find it before me."

"Yes." Her eyes flitted to his, then skated away.

"They were also looking for anything to do with Jesse or Tank."

"Or you," she added meaningfully.

"Or me," Wyatt agreed. He took in her expression and the way she was holding herself. Something was off, something more than exhaustion and upset. "And then Kenya rang the bell, and scared them off."

"Yes."

"The one guy, the one with the accent. You think he was in charge?"

"He definitely was. He was ordering the other guy around, telling him where to look and what to look for, but also…his voice had authority. It had…" She waved her hand a little, like she was trying to find the word she wanted in murky air. "It had…command."

A ripple of foreboding wriggled in Wyatt's chest at her choice of wording.

Leah wondered, "Did anyone get a look at them? When they took off?"

Some of the Black Watch team had relayed that the pair had been wearing all black—but not just hoodies they'd pulled from their dressers. Both had been in head-to-toe tactical gear, and had virtually disappeared after exiting the back door.

They'd been pros, not hooligans, but Wyatt wasn't going to tell her that.

"It was dark. They must've slipped out the side." They'd made it past Kenya's team to get in and then eluded them again on the back end. The only way they could've done it was if they'd used Mrs. Daniels' home as a base.

Yet more information Leah did not need right now.

"Wyatt…" her voice sounded uncharacteristically meek. "Does this mean Jesse or Theo were involved in something bad?" The words dropped between them like IEDs.

"Hard to say," he hedged eventually. "And we may never know the full truth, either. So many soldiers in Echo didn't make it through Nabarut."

She pinned him with another pointed look. "Promise you'll tell me if you find out something."

"I will." He frowned at her, though, wondering what he was missing. "Of course I will."

Leah only nodded faintly, clutching her arms tightly around herself and looking away.

"One more thing," he said, and waited for her to meet his eyes.
"What?"

"What aren't you telling me?"

Her throat bobbed, and he knew his instincts were right. "I don't know what you mean."

"I mean, there's clearly something else that's bothering you, but you don't want to tell me. So, do I need to grab someone else for you to tell, or do you want to fess up to me?"

Her eyes went wide, and her hands fluttered in front of her, her fingers lacing together in a white-knuckled grip.

"Leah, whatever it is, it's okay. Please let me help."

She was silent, staring at him for an uncomfortably long time. Eventually, she forced the words out, but it seemed to pain her to give air to each one. "They knew about you. That you were a SEAL. What you looked like. They said…"

He waited. Her lashes grew wet again. The murderous fury burning in his veins turned somehow hotter.

"They said…?"

"They said you wanted the same information they did," she admitted in a rush. "That if you'd already found it, you wouldn't still be wasting your time on some mean widow with a brat to feed. They said you were using me, and once you got what you wanted, you'd be gone."

The way that missile must've hit its mark stole the breath right out of his lungs. Those morons couldn't have planned it better if they'd tried. He and Leah had *just* had a conversation about Kathy.

"And you believed them?" he asked, as gently as a man contemplating homicide could do.

"I don't know what I believe right now."

"Leah, listen to me. They're lying. They do not know me. I can not express right now how categorically untrue everything they said is, but it is."

She shook her head and refused to look at him. "I can't do this right now. I'm so tired, I can't think straight. I want to go check on Teddy."

Wyatt tamped down his frustration, stood, and held out his hand. "Come on."

He led her upstairs, ushering her into her kid's room and taking a minute to confer with Joe on their next steps. Taking a few more minutes to get his head straight.

His feelings didn't matter. She needed him to take care of her right now, not the other way around.

When he returned to her, she was in the glider with her son sleeping in her arms. Wyatt eyed the purple smears under Leah's eyes and the way she startled the tiniest amount each time one of the operatives bustled down the hall, going in and out of her home office, and he knew he had to get them out of there now.

He crouched next to her and pitched his voice low, so Teddy wouldn't wake. "Hey. You doing okay?"

"Mm-hm. Yep, fine," Leah said quickly. Vaguely. Her gaze skated around, tracking nothing in particular.

"Listen, I was thinking," he murmured. "These guys are going to be at it for a while longer here. Why don't I bring you and Ted down to the apartment so you can get some sleep?"

He could see her refusal hit the tip of her tongue, so Wyatt squeezed her knee. "Joe and Noah will stay with you, and we have a great alarm system. Not to mention, no one will have any idea you're there. You'll both be safe."

Leah looked down at Teddy, wavering.

He tucked an arm around her shoulders, feeling microscopic shudders trembling through her. "Come on. Let's get your bags and get you out of here. Everything else will go exactly the way we planned in the morning. We're just running a few hours ahead of schedule, that's all."

Wyatt's brain raced ahead, too, wondering if he should have Doc Tom look at her for shock. Trying to remember whether he'd set up the portable crib or just propped it beside his bed. Thinking about the fastest route home at this time of night. *Morning. Whatever.*

She blinked at him slowly, considering. "If they follow us…"

For the first time in hours, Wyatt felt a smile threaten. "They can try."

That seemed to be all she needed to hear. She rose out of her seat, carefully readjusted Teddy in her arms, and rotated in place, looking around the room with glossy eyes.

He wondered what she was thinking. She'd lived a lot of life here.

When Leah finally looked at him, her nod was jerky, but it was firm.

"Let's go," she whispered.

Chapter Twenty-Four

AFTER TOO MANY hours spent thinking instead of sleeping, Leah had come to a number of conclusions. First, after one night she already missed her blackout curtains and the weight and softness of her own bedding. Next, there was not going to be enough caffeine in the world to tackle how tired she was going to be today.

Most importantly, however, she knew she would not be able to spend a second night in Wyatt's bed without begging him to run the A/C—or, at minimum, the ceiling fan. That was entirely because Wyatt turned into a clingy, snuggly barnacle in sleep, which might've been cute if not for the fact that he ran hot as an inferno while doing it.

Leah dabbed at her damp upper lip with a corner of the sheet and wondered if this might be the way that she died.

Wyatt had peppered her face with light kisses when he'd returned from her house sometime in the wee hours—her *former* house, she amended quickly—and she could still recall the way the last one had landed on her forehead and lasted a few seconds longer than the others.

He'd whispered that her skin was soft. That her hair was pretty. That *she* was pretty. On the heels of the break-in, however, his quiet affection had felt overwhelming instead of reassuring. So rather than try to come up with a suitable reply she'd merely smirked, told Wyatt he was pretty right back—because annoyingly, he was—and presented the man with her back.

She felt a flare of shame at the way she'd pretended to fall asleep, but he hadn't been the least bit put off by her prickliness. He'd simply scooted close, draped his arm across her waist, and buried his face in her neck with a contented sigh.

In moments, his breath had been as even as the tides, and Leah still couldn't believe how quickly he'd dropped off. Eventually, the steady rise and fall of his chest had lured her under, too.

She'd tossed and turned, though, with bad dreams of dark, faceless men snatching her baby from his bed. Each time she'd willed herself awake to check, Teddy had been sleeping soundly, of course, his portable crib tucked neatly into the space between her side of the bed and the wall.

And now…now she was cranky, tired, and melting. How could one man give off such an outlandish amount of heat? Was that even normal?

Leah ran a hand over her face and felt more sweat beading on her upper lip. Damp hairs stuck to her forehead. Was Wyatt radioactive? Did he have a fever?

She craned so she could see over the side of the bed, reaching down to touch Teddy's hip. At least he was still safe. *They* were safe.

Her movement jostled Wyatt, and behind her, his chest rumbled with a deep, satisfied sigh. His arm tightened around her, and his hips edged forward, nudging her trunk with his clearly awake junk.

Leah stifled the crazed snort that tickled the back of her throat. How in hell was she supposed to sleep like this? How was she supposed to get up and parent, or crack open her laptop and work with this hot, horny man invading her personal space all the time?

The truth was…

The truth was, she admitted, that if she could only reach the switch to turn on the overhead fan, she might never want to leave this bed and face reality. Wyatt, irrepressibly cheerful optimist that he was, felt like a sunny spring day breaking over her winter of a life. It was straight-up foolishness to believe his interest in her would last, but there was no denying how sweet it felt to bask in it now.

She didn't believe that he was lying and cheating his way into what she knew about Nabarut, as those intruders had implied. Unfortunately, the more she got to know Wyatt, the more she wondered if his infatuation with her and Teddy had more to do with him getting a do-over on his own childhood, than with any lasting feelings for them.

Her feelings felt real, though—real inconvenient and real unwieldy. *Damn it.*

Wyatt squeezed her gently again.

"I can hear you thinking," he rumbled quietly against her neck.

His voice was rough with sleep. Leah liked it. She liked his comfortable mattress, and his solid frame guarding her back.

She peeked over the side of the bed again, and there was Teddy, still sound asleep and blissfully unperturbed.

He liked Wyatt, too.

"No, you can't," she whispered.

"Your brain is *loud*," he chuckled quietly. "And you feel hot. Did you sleep okay?"

"Occasionally. I'm sorry if I woke you. You could probably stand to get a few more hours."

He'd made it back so late, and crashed and slept so deeply, that Leah was worried she'd have to go meet the movers herself—movers he'd found and arranged for her, she remembered suddenly. She'd never even spoken to them.

Wyatt was reliable, however, or maybe just committed to his cause. Either way, letting herself depend on him felt like a novelty, if not an outright risk.

"I'm okay," he murmured, stretching and groaning softly. He inched back from her, discreetly shielding his erection under a bunched-up corner of the comforter.

Leah worked to keep her eyes on his face, and not the delectable expanse of torso on display. So much hard, tan muscle, inches from her fingertips.

"Do you want me to go meet the movers?" she asked quickly, before she forgot what the day had in store for her, "So you can go back to sleep?"

"No, I'll go." He turned his head on his pillow so he could study her. "First tell me what you're worrying about." His gaze was as warm and clear as ever.

Could she trust it? Could she trust herself?

After some internal debate, she admitted, "I keep thinking about what those stupid prowlers said. About you using me."

"I figured that would stick with you. But Leah…think about it. I was smitten long before I knew how much your life and my job might overlap. Tell me you recognize that, at least."

She thought back to all those times she'd spotted him lurking in random vehicles on her street. "Weeks of stalking," she scolded him primly.

His smirk was smug. "Months," he corrected.

Leah squinted into his guileless green eyes. "No one but the most depraved, soulless degenerate would willingly take on all that yard work," she mused, "Or all those bedtime stories."

"True," he murmured. "Except, perhaps, a guy who was down bad and hoping for a home-cooked meal."

"Tomayto, tomahto," she smiled.

Wyatt smiled too, tracing her arm from shoulder to elbow. "I'm sorry I have to go. I don't want you to worry. We can talk more later if you want."

"Don't be sorry." She reached out to pat him on the chest, but her traitorous fingers lingered on those hard pecs. "You're doing me a favor."

He held her hand against his heart and kissed her nose. "Make yourselves at home, okay? Have breakfast. Watch cartoons. Just chill. I left donuts and bagels on the counter for you."

Leah peered over his shoulder at the clock on the nightstand and flinched. "Where did you—when did you—?"

Wyatt kissed her again and pulled away. "Never you mind. I have my ways."

"Please let me know if you have any trouble. You have the list?" If he stuck to her list, nothing would get lost or left behind, and finding things in storage would be easy later on.

He padded across the room, the gym shorts he'd apparently slept in riding low on his hips. A soft expression crossed his face when he caught sight of Teddy in his crib.

He watched him for a long moment before whispering, "It's gonna be fine. I promise."

Before he could disappear into the bathroom, Leah asked, "Hey, Wyatt?"

"Yeah?"

"You know eventually you're going to have to tell me what you do for a living, right? What you and your boys are up to? Because not once has anyone mentioned calling the police or filing a report of the break-in."

"Later," he promised, ducking into the bathroom with a devastating wink, and leaving the indelible image of his ripped body scorched into her brain.

Wyatt was gorgeous. Sweet. Helpful. Attentive. It couldn't all be a lie. Right?

WYATT RETURNED LATER that afternoon to do his best mother hen impression, leading Leah around the apartment to show her where everything she might need was, nerves on full display as he manically chattered and overexplained the obvious.

Teddy remained happy as a clam, lounging on the couch after their day at the pool, eating his snack, and watching cartoons with Joe while Noah prepped dinner in the kitchen.

It wasn't precisely how Leah had imagined Single Guy Life, but what did she know? She'd been married for the last several years.

She shook her head at Wyatt as he emerged from his closet, still talking. *So much talking.*

"I cleared out space for you guys in the closet," he rambled, all business, "and emptied a couple of drawers in the dresser and bathroom."

"Thank you. You didn't have to do that, but I appreciate it."

"Like I mentioned, all the external doors and windows are wired to the alarm system. Noah has some other things in place, too, so…" He hesitated. "Just know that you and Ted are safe here. No one's getting in or out without us knowing."

"Great." Given his shiftiness, she wondered how much, if any, of Noah's *system* was sanctioned by the property manager. "Will you let me know when it's on, so we don't trip it by accident?"

"He's putting you on the system, so you'll get the alerts. He'll walk you through all that later." Wyatt stopped to take a deep breath. "Also, if you hear someone moving around in the middle of the night, it's probably Joe. He's got pretty bad insomnia."

"Okay." Leah frowned in sympathy. "That sucks."

He gave her a quick nod, like he agreed but didn't want to discuss it more. *PTSD*, she thought. In her experience, *insomnia* was almost always the common codeword.

Wyatt peeked into the bathroom and flushed a little. "Ummm. If you noticed the prescription cream in the medicine cabinet, it's not for anything sketchy. I met a cloud of sea lice in San Onofre last summer and the results were pretty gnarly for a few weeks there. All good now."

Leah smirked. "Okay. Didn't notice but sounds gross."

"Don't worry," he barreled on, "The entire apartment has been kid-proofed. Teddy is free to roam at will. Anything medicinal, alcoholic, toxic, or sharp is either up high or under lock and key. Same for—" Wyatt glanced at her and looked away just as rapidly, "—things that go boom."

She laughed at his sheepish expression. "Is that the technical term?"

"One of them." He still looked nervous, however, and Leah froze, realizing exactly what he'd meant. Three former SEALs with paranoia complexes weren't storing fireworks under their mattresses.

"Wait. You mean guns? Do you have guns in this place?" she screeched. "Are there *bombs*? Around my *child*?"

Wyatt held up placating hands, trying to shush her and stem her panic. When she spun around, scanning the room for danger, he reached forward and took her by the arms.

"Leah, look at me. No one under this roof would do anything to endanger you or Teddy. The apartment is absolutely safe for both of you. Do you understand? I won't lie. There is…stuff here. It is inaccessible to him and to you. You have to trust me on this."

She blinked at his earnest face and swallowed. Trust was hard for her. Had he earned it?

On the other hand, did he deserve her suspicion?

This man, who'd swooped in to save her and Teddy from what could've been a total eviction disaster, who'd opened his home to them, upending his life to make them comfortable?

Wyatt couldn't possibly be going to these lengths simply to probe her for information. There would have been some hint of his perfidy by now, some slip that gave him away, because no one was that good of a liar.

Especially Wyatt.

She had to trust him. With *everything*.

Leah swallowed again, steeling herself for what she had to do. "Wyatt, we need to talk." The words emerged barely louder than a whisper. She tried again, "We…need to talk."

"I know. I'm sorry. I'm stalling." *Right. Because he had stuff to tell her, too.*

Perhaps it was better to start with him, she thought. "So…in the short time I've known you, you've managed to infiltrate my home, get me evicted, broken into, and moved into your place, all in the space of a month. That's some fast-acting poison, guy. Can you understand why I might need you to tell me exactly what you do for work?"

"I can, yes."

Wyatt sank onto the foot of the bed, clasped his hands loosely on his knees, and laid it out for her. Once he'd finished, she couldn't do much more than stand there blinking like a stupid owl.

Out in the main room, Teddy's happy voice rang out in glee, followed immediately by laughs from Joe and Noah. Here in Wyatt's room, the atmosphere was decidedly more intense.

"What, so it's revenge?" she wondered unsteadily. "You're gunning for the people who wrecked your careers?"

"No. No, not at all. Leah, there's a crooked United States senator using his position to enrich himself and his family," Wyatt pleaded.

A crazy laugh burst out of her. "And you think that's unusual?"

"We think he's working with someone dirty in the chain of command," he tried. So solemn. Begging her to understand.

Leah sobered a little, but her strange laugh burst free again, tinged now with confusion. "Again—probably not the first time."

Wyatt pressed his lips together, but seemed determined to tell her all of it. "Twelve girls and young women went missing during last year's skirmish in Nabarut. We believe Doggett is part of a larger trafficking organization with ties to the Army. We have to trace this to the top and break it, Leah. We *have* to find those girls."

The blood drained from her head as the full impact of his words registered. "Wyatt, it's been eighteen months." Her voice cracked as horror took hold.

"I *know*. God, you don't think we know?" He looked utterly anguished.

Leah stared a while more, feeling like a husk of a human. She had to tell him now. *Had* to.

He squinted at her, eyes narrowing abruptly. "Leah, what's going on?"

"I think…" she swallowed, and it felt like gargling gravel. "I have something I should tell you."

"Which is?" he growled.

She wilted under his focused gaze and went to perch beside him. "I think…I might know why those guys were searching my house. I wasn't sure I should trust you and your friends before, but now…you probably need to know."

"Leah. Know what?"

"I got a call from my brother right before the…the ambush. I didn't see his message until later. I must've been in the shower or something, I don't…" she stopped and tried to pull herself together.

With another quick glance at his face, his expression scrunched with concern, Leah went to shut his door and pulled her phone from her pocket. Then she called up the voicemail she'd saved so many months ago.

"Just…listen," she whispered, and waited for her brother's voice to fill the room.

"Leah. You hear me, kid? Fuckin' A, I hope you get this—"
Voices in the background gradually grew more distinct.
"…Dan?"
"Yeah, he said his dad wanted something more exotic for this project. We're supposed to find the ones in the pictures, and he said we'll know when it's time."

"That one's Jesse," she told Wyatt, pausing the recording in case he couldn't tell. He nodded, so she hit play again.

"How am I supposed to know? He just said, 'You'll know when it's time.' Then we grab 'em."

Crackling over the line obscured his companion's response, but Jesse's answer came quickly. *"Beats me. He's gonna tell us later."*

More hurried rustling, and then Theo's urgent whisper, *"Listen, Lee—something is going down here. I'm not sure what, but it ain't right. Just…just save this message somewhere safe. And keep it private. Okay? Don't tell anyone, and save it in case I need it once we get back."* Her brother cleared his throat, his voice so deep and so familiar. *"Okay. Anyway. I should go. Kiss that little man for me. Love you. Bye."*

That wasn't all, though. Leah braced herself for the worst of it, and sure enough, her brother's voice came to life again, as if he couldn't help one last complaint.

"Fucking Jesse…listen, kid. Put aside my feelings on this guy—I heard something I shouldn't have, and I think they know. These jokers…shit, forget I said that. Just…know this is some real fucked-up stuff here, okay? Promise me if anything happens to me, you won't raise a stink."

Her lips moved around Theo's final words, a memorial she'd never wanted. *"I know you're wondering, 'What about Jesse?' He's somewhere he shouldn't be. What else is new? But that's the thing. Promise you'll accept it if anything happens to me. I'm begging you. This is a whole shit-show you have to stay far away from. Promise, if I don't make it through this, you'll ditch your skeevy husband, too. He's a shitbird and I can't stand the thought of you and that baby…"* More inscrutable background noise, and then the final words she'd ever hear her brother speak.

"I gotta jet. Love you, Lee. And Mom and Dad and Ted. Make sure you tell them. See you soon."

And that was it. The message ended and Leah uncurled her cramped fingers, closed out her message app, and set her phone beside her. It was possible Wyatt had stopped breathing.

"Ok, wow," he said eventually. "So, that is…"

"My brother saw something," she agreed, though he hadn't gotten the words out yet, "and whatever it was had to do with my husband. Someone, who is still alive and here in San Diego, knows that."

He pulled up one knee and turned to face her. "And wonders if you do too, based on last night."

Leah nodded mutely.

"Why did you keep the message? He told you not to make waves."

"And I haven't. Theo was a big bonehead, but he was my brother, and you heard what he said. Keep it somewhere safe. Save it for him."

"He also said to stay far away from this mess."

"Wyatt, I can't just forget he left that message. Even if there's nothing I can do, I can at least honor his memory by holding space for the truth."

He stared at her, his expression unreadable.

At last, he pointed out, "And this whole time I've been coming around, you knew this."

Leah nodded.

"You knew who I was. You knew I was there, too. You told me so."

"Yes."

"Weren't you worried I was involved?"

"You said you'd only met Jesse that one time, before...before *this* happened. And I knew your team was only extracting the senator, not...not on the ground like Jesse and Theo. I just thought it was a crazy coincidence. I mean, the stuff those burglars said made me wonder, I'm not gonna lie. But..."

"Leah—Echo Company supposedly went into Nabarut only because Al Kadir did. But this message makes it sound like..."

"...they planned it ahead of time. I know. Someone *planned* that fight, Wyatt. Someone knew it was going to happen."

"Al Kadir's fighters must have been the diversion," he mused. "So, they could grab the girls."

Leah shrugged. "Or Jesse and his friends assumed they were, and dragged everyone else along with them."

He blew out a weary breath. They both knew Echo Company's losses had been heavy that day.

"Who was the other guy talking? Do you know?" he asked.

Leah shook her head. "I'm sorry. I can't hear him well enough to tell."

Wyatt sat thinking for another few minutes, and Leah wasn't surprised when his question eventually came. She'd been expecting it—had mentally prepared for it. "Would you be willing to forward that message to me? So I can share it with my team?"

Leah nodded, tapping her phone and firing it off without a word. It was terrifying, sending it out into the world, but sharing it also released something weighty inside her.

"Are you okay?" he wondered carefully.

"Wyatt..." Her stomach roiled with unease, but she admitted, "I didn't know what to do with it. When Jesse and Theo didn't come home... I didn't know what to do."

"You hung onto it and waited for the right moment. You did good, Leah."

She shrugged. "I can't stop wondering if..." It felt too dangerous to say.

"What?"

"What if they died because of this?" She stopped and shook her head, her voice dropping to a whisper. "What if they were *killed*, because of this?"

He ran a hand through his shaggy hair, staring into space while he considered her words. It was a shock when his sea-green eyes snapped back to hers, focused and intense. *Lethal.*

"What's your brother's legal name?"

"Theodore. Why?"

"Theodore what?"

"Oh," she sniffed, embarrassed, "Sorry. It's Margulies. Theodore Andrew Margulies."

Wyatt was texting someone before she even got the full name out.

"Did you receive his effects after he died?"

"No, my parents did."

"Do you know if his phone was among them?"

"It wasn't. I checked, in case he'd left another voice note or took photos or something. Wyatt, what are you gonna do?"

"I'm going to pick up this ball and run with it," he declared. "Can you text me a photo of him, just in case?"

"Yeah. Sure," she shrugged. "Just tell me what you're going to do, first. Theo said I shouldn't make a fuss. If it'd just been me, I'd have ignored him. I've got Teddy, though. I can't do anything that will put him in danger."

"Leah, the danger came to you. Do you really think I'm going to let that go?"

Wyatt looked fierce in a way she'd never seen him before. Leah shivered at the dissonance from his usual easygoing demeanor.

There'd been a part of her—maybe a big part—that'd wondered how he could possibly have been a SEAL, or at least, any kind of a good one. That part sat right down and clamped its mouth shut.

The Wyatt sitting beside her now could wreak vengeance. He could—he *would*—keep her and her child safe.

She grabbed her phone with shaking hands and navigated to her photo stream. "What kind of photo do you need?"

Chapter Twenty-Five

Wyatt

"THEODORE ANDREW MARGULIES. Killed in action…" Noah trailed off and frowned. "Army has it listed as friendly fire. Surprised they admitted that much."

Joe snorted, "They're assholes. They don't care."

"Yeah, friendly, my ass," Wyatt agreed. "Leah thinks it was fragging."

The Black Watch bunker was characteristically dim and cold, the A/C working overtime to keep both electronics and explosives happy as an unseasonably warm day blazed outside. It felt like zero dark thirty inside, though, as Noah seemed to prefer it.

Joe was fidgety this morning, and Wyatt wondered how long he'd been up and stewing. There'd been a fresh pot of coffee already brewed when he'd gotten up, but there was no telling if it was the first one. It could've been Joe's fourth, for all he knew.

Next to them, Noah pushed up his black-framed glasses and turned back to the bank of computers. "Leah might be right. I crossed the photos she gave you of her brother against the footage we have from Nabarut. Facial recognition came up blank."

Bennett sprawled back in his rolling office chair, his weight making it squeak in protest. "Probably because Echo only moved in after shit hit the fan."

"Except I definitely remember uniforms in some of those documentary stills," Joe argued. "We should be looking for Jesse, not Tank. He was the one who was up to something."

Noah nodded thoughtfully, and sure enough, after several bursts of rapid typing, the guy smirked in triumph. "Bingo," he murmured, enlarging several stills on his screens, side by side.

Jesse Burke and two other soldiers were grouped loosely beside an unmistakable image of Dan Cox, holding up papers like they were comparing them to something out of view.

Bennett came to stand shoulder-to-shoulder with Buck, peering closely. "What're those fuckers doin'?" he drawled, suspicion heavy in his tone.

"The photos," Wyatt realized, shooting out of his chair. "The supposed modeling headshots Cox showed Kim. A thousand bucks says they knew which girls they wanted and were trying to pick them out."

"Except they couldn't," Noah pointed out. "With Joely's documentary cameras rolling and so many strangers in the village, all the girls were veiled. Qahat may be progressive, but Nabarut is still out in the sticks. No one was playing around."

Joe frowned and reared back. "Wait, then why did Rohaan give *us* their pictures? Isn't that *haram*, too?"

"I think it might be okay because we don't have bad intentions," Bennett explained hesitantly. "We needed to see their faces so we could help find them. It's a necessity in the same way a legal ID picture might be, right?"

Buck agreed, adding, "Noah keeps the physical pictures locked up and any digital versions encrypted. No one can access them unless it's absolutely critical. That's the best we can do to protect them for now."

The team pondered that information in uncomfortable silence until Joe suddenly slammed a hand on the table in front of him. "The way I want to bury these fuckers. It's just violation after violation with them. Those girls should be home with their families!"

Bennett rested a hand on his shoulder. "We're getting close," he assured him. "I can feel it."

"But in the meantime, Doggett walks free. He holds public office, and enriches himself and his cronies while real people suffer. Meanwhile, those poor girls are still out there somewhere, being subjected to who knows what—" Bruiser's voice cracked, and he jumped up to pace around in frustration.

Except…then he did a double take at one of Noah's monitors, and darted closer with a scowl.

While they waited to see what Joe would say, Wyatt looked around at his teammates and thought about trauma. The generational kind, between mothers and sons, families and daughters, soldiers and innocent bystanders—all caught up in the unpredictable tides of human violence.

One person could heal, if they put in the work over time. But how did dozens of hurt people heal their psychic wounds? How did a whole village recover? Or a whole nation?

The weight of it seemed, quite abruptly, insurmountable. No wonder Joe couldn't sleep half the time. He was a painfully sane man, stuck amidst a world gone mad.

A sour taste stung the back of his throat, the remembered screams of Nabaruti villagers in his head taking on a decidedly teenaged tone. Wyatt bolted from his chair and took a couple of shaky steps toward the door at the shadowy end of the warehouse. The bunker closed in on him like a tomb.

He needed air. *Right now.*

"You guys need me for anything else?" he wondered, trying to maintain an outward calm. "I've got a thing." Or he would, as soon as he could round up Leah and Teddy and find some sand and some waves.

Bennett raised a brow, dubious. "And by thing, I assume you mean the 5'9 brunette with shampoo commercial hair that's moved into your room."

Buck laughed, but he tipped his chin toward the door. "Go on. We'll holler if anything else comes up."

Wyatt glanced at Joe, then froze when the man's expression registered. "Wait. Bruiser, what're you thinking?" He strode over and looked between his buddy and the monitors, trying to see what had caught the man's attention.

"Dude, blow this up," Joe barked at Noah.

With a few taps, the photo of Jesse and his companions holding up the headshots grew bigger, then bigger again.

"This guy," Joe indicated, tapping the man to Jesse's left. He narrowed his eyes. "Make him clearer."

Noah shook his head, but his fingers flew into motion, and the face gradually transformed, the pixelation refining into definition.

"You know this guy?" Wyatt asked.

Joe's nod was faint. "I've seen him somewhere before."

The others moved in, crowding around to study the image of the man, maybe mid-twenties in age, kind of homely in the face. A scrawny-looking white guy like so many others, plain and forgettable.

Joe Doherty, however, never forgot a face. "Show me…" he paused, then gripped Noah's shoulder. "Show me Kenya's report from the break-in at Leah's."

"There was nothing from the SDPD database. She did get a DNA hit for a soldier at Pendleton, though," Noah mumbled. "Corporal William Miller. Not associated with any of the church groups, as far as I could tell. No connection to any of our other notables, either. We figured he was recruited as a one-off—"

"*Show me,*" Joe insisted.

Noah pulled up the man's USMC ID photo and dragged it next to the picture from the event in Nabarut. "Okay. So—"

"There!" Bruiser exclaimed. "The fuck I say!"

Wyatt shared a look with Bennett, impressed. "Leah said he'd acted like he didn't have a choice about being there. Remember? Guess this is why."

"Yep," Buck agreed. "Noah, show me everything you can find on Corporal Miller. I want to know where he grew up, where he had his first kiss, who he bunks with, who he drinks with, who his dad plays cards with—you name it. There's a link in there somewhere."

"I don't understand," Noah grumbled to himself. "He's not in Echo Company. He shouldn't have been in Nabarut. What's he doing there?"

"Find that out, too," Bennett suggested with a lopsided smile and a friendly nudge.

"Mother*fucker*," Noah muttered bitterly. "How'd he slip by me?"

Buck grinned at his break in composure. "Stitch, you go ahead. I'll keep you in the loop if Sherlock here finds anything new."

Wyatt clapped Joe on the back and headed for the door. As he stepped into the bright sunshine, he heard Noah hiss behind him, "*When* I find something. 'Cause I'm pissed, now."

LEAH WAS READY and waiting with towels, chairs, a cooler, and a bag of Teddy's gear by the time Wyatt got to the apartment to pick her up. One quick kiss later, he had his board strapped to the roof, and they were on their way to Solana Beach. Preschool dismissal was at 12:30, so he drove fast, not wanting to be late.

He may have driven a little *too* fast.

"Wyatt, we're half an hour early," Leah laughed when he pulled into the school lot, feeling smug. "What are we going to do for thirty-five minutes?"

"I'll park under those trees," he offered. "We can make out."

"In a preschool parking lot, with your loud muffler," she commented drily. "Try again."

He tugged at the collar of his t-shirt, stretching it. *Must've shrunk in the last wash.* Abashed, he turned off his radio and put the car in park, in an exposed spot close to the doors.

"I didn't want him to have to wait," he grumbled.

Leah squeezed his thigh. "And I appreciate it. But it takes them a little while to get their stuff together, so we have some time. Come on, let's go down the block. I'll show you my favorite coffee shop real quick."

They ditched his car and hoofed it. In minutes, Leah pointed out a small, freestanding building with a vivid mural covering the entire side of the structure, depicting positions of the sun over a tiny beachside cottage. Wyatt looked around curiously—it was clearly a neighborhood favorite.

Inside, the lunch rush was in full swing, the tables filled and a steady stream of customers and waitstaff milling around. The ringleader directing the chaos was a heavyset Black woman behind the counter, with a megawatt smile and charisma for miles.

She spotted Leah immediately, calling out, "Okay, Miss Leah! I see you! And you brought a friend." She eyed Wyatt semi-critically. "Who's this?"

"Liz, this is Wyatt," Leah beamed, pulling him forward. "Wyatt, this is Liz. She's the owner."

"Nice to meet you." He stuck out his hand and the woman immediately enveloped it in her iron grip.

"Likewise," she twinkled. Then she beckoned Leah a couple of feet to the side and muttered not-very-quietly, "Have you seen the eyes on that guy? Damn, girl. You in danger."

Leah ducked her head, but her words were clear, "Tell me about it."

Wyatt wrapped a hand over his mouth, smothering his grin. The barista at the register got his attention, but she was smiling, too, like this was an everyday interaction at this place. "What can I get you guys?"

As he placed their order, he overheard Leah murmur, "Actually, Teddy and I had to move kind of suddenly. We're much farther away now, so we might not be able to visit much anymore." Her face was forlorn, and his chest pinched to see it.

Wyatt pulled out his wallet to pay, and hoped the afternoon they had planned would help assuage at least some of her dejection.

Liz drew her in closer, grumbling, "I don't love the sound of that."

"It's not great, but we're figuring it out. Once he's out of school, though…" Leah shrugged, apparently out of words.

The shop's proprietor wasn't buying it. She straightened her spine and huffed, then reached across the counter to grab Wyatt's arm. "You'll come back here and get your girl her treats. Right? I'll fix you up, but I expect to see you two regularly."

"Deal," he assured her. Whatever it took to make Leah happy, he was down for it.

"See?" Liz demanded. "There's no problem."

Leah shook her head at them. "Introducing you two might've been a mistake," she sighed, before adding, "Listen, I wanted to thank you, in case we don't see you as much. For everything. You were…sunshine when I really needed it."

"Leah, you do not have to thank me," the woman scoffed. "You just take care of yourself and your baby, and the universe will figure out the rest." She glanced behind them at the line and shooed them away from the counter. "Okay, now go make eyes at your pretty man, and Mari will bring your order over in a minute."

They claimed a table near the window that an older couple was vacating, and Leah launched into a recitation of all the things she'd packed for their outing, trying to impress him with her operational efficiency—or, more probably, changing the subject in the hope that he wouldn't want to talk about it.

Wyatt couldn't take his eyes off her. Her golden skin glowed. The sun caught on caramel highlights scattered in her hair. Leah was, in a word, luminous.

Even as she stopped chatting and frowned at a testy confrontation erupting at the register, he wanted to lean in and kiss her. If only she wasn't completely distracted by the man who'd barged into the shop, cut to the head of the line, and raised an angry ruckus with the cashier.

Wyatt glanced over to see if there was anything he could do to help, and heard the guy ask if they'd seen Leah Burke, or knew where she was.

"I know she comes here," he bellowed.

Wyatt got to his feet and put his body between the man and Leah, murmuring, "How does he know that? You know that dude?"

She shrank in her seat, nervous and worried. "I have no idea."

"Stay here," he told her. "I'll go move this joker along." *And get a better look at him.*

Wyatt strolled up to the counter just as the guy slammed his hand down, making the barista jump.

"Whoa," he said, stopping an arm's length away. "One thing we are not going to do is lose our shit over a danish. Okay? Let's cool down, man."

He spun toward Wyatt, prepared to argue or worse, but his gaze shifted over Wyatt's shoulder and fell on Leah, across the room.

"Luis?" she squeaked, her face going pale. She slowly got to her feet. "What's going on?"

"*You.* What the hell do you think you're doing, moving out on my aunt without a word?" He bumped Wyatt's shoulder, trying to get to her, so Wyatt wrapped an arm across his chest and held him in place.

"I did her a favor," Leah scowled. "She was about to evict us."

"Doesn't give you the right to——"

Liz caught Wyatt's eye from behind the counter and mouthed, "He's been here three times already. I was going to come tell her."

Wyatt nodded and turned Luis toward him, keeping a grip on his arm. "You been coming here looking for her? Why?"

The guy eyed him like he was scum. "Who the fuck are you?"

"None of your business. Answer the question."

Luis stared over at Leah, then back to Wyatt, studying his face more carefully. All at once, he seemed to register the threat he posed. "You the fake husband? 'Cause she skipped out. She owes my aunt money."

"That's not true!" Leah cried, glancing around at the other customers. She took a step toward them, then halted when Wyatt shook his head. "I paid through the end of the month. Plus, she was *trying to evict us* for no good reason."

"You owe damages," Luis claimed.

Wyatt had overseen the movers himself, and then cleaned up afterward. That was bullshit.

Leah beat him to the punch. "Since when!" she demanded, turning red.

"It's in the lease."

"Like hell it is."

Some folks had slipped out the instant things turned salty, but many stayed, hanging on every salvo with wide, avid eyes. A scruffy kid in the corner had his phone up, no doubt recording.

Luis spotted him a second after Wyatt did, and shifted on his feet. *Uncomfortable with the attention. Good.*

"Where are you staying?" he asked Leah. "We need to be able to contact you."

"Also none of your goddamn business," Wyatt growled before she could answer. "Now step outside before I make you."

Luis jerked his arm out of Wyatt's grip, spitting mad now. "Fucking frog. You ain't shit."

We'll see about that.

As Luis stalked toward the door, he glared daggers around the shop, daring someone to challenge him. Wyatt glanced at Liz, who also looked like she was recording, and Leah, gripping the back of a chair like it might be keeping her upright.

There were several other witnesses in the place, not counting the staff. At least two had gotten video. Wyatt gave Leah what he hoped was a reassuring nod, then herded Luis outside.

The guy wasn't getting the message. He kept staring back at Leah, kept trying to say shit to her.

"Hey. You don't talk to her," Wyatt reminded him. "You're talking to me now."

"She owes—"

"Your aunt needs something else from her, she can request it through the lawyers. Leah's attorney will send notice this week. Have her respond to that."

Luis craned around Wyatt's shoulder to see Leah, still not understanding he was two-point-five seconds away from getting pummeled. Again, Wyatt put himself in his line of sight and said, "No. You don't look at her. You don't talk to her. Leah Burke has ceased to exist for you."

"Or what?" the punk sneered.

"I would love to show you. Fuck around and find out, my guy," Wyatt smiled.

After that, Luis wasn't too keen on sticking around. He moved boots to a car parked near the street, a boring sedan made tawdry with metallic paint, an oversized spoiler, and gleaming rims. It looked fast and sounded loud as it tore off, but Wyatt knew at a glance his car could lap it without breaking a sweat.

His car, which they'd left back at the preschool.

He tamped down the fierce desire to get it and teach the fool a lesson as Leah edged up behind him.

"Any chance you happened to get a plate number?" he wondered.

"No. I'm sorry."

Liz had been monitoring the situation through the windows, but she came out now, hands on her ample hips and dress fluttering in the breeze.

"We having fun yet?" she chuckled.

"Not exactly," Leah told her. "I'm sorry about all that."

Liz shook her head. "Girl, that had nothing to do with you. You guys see his plates?"

Wyatt shook his head, frustrated with himself. He should've. It'd been right there in view, but his attention had been divided between Leah's presence behind him and fantasies of how easy it would be to incapacitate the fucker. Eternally.

"Hang out for another minute," Liz said, "I'll be right back." She scanned the street, then ducked back into the shop.

Leah slipped her hand into Wyatt's, looking everywhere but at him.

Liz came out a second later with a bag and a piece of paper. "Here's your order, and here's your plate number," she announced briskly. "Have a nice day."

"Wait, what? I thought you didn't see it," Leah exclaimed.

"I got it off the security camera," the woman shrugged. At Leah's incredulous expression, she explained, "Look, I was a young mom once. Got evicted, too, and it took me thirteen years to get back on my feet. You don't need that kind of struggle."

"Thirteen…" Leah looked up above the café's doors, where a hand-painted sign read *Thirteen Suns*. "Liz, thank you."

She nodded. "Thirteen turns around the sun, but look at me now. You can't tell me nothing."

"There you go," Wyatt said, squeezing her arm. He pulled their receipt from his pocket and stole the pen from Liz's apron pocket. "And don't listen to Leah—we'll be back all the time. Call me if you ever need anything, too. Okay? I know some folks."

Liz arched a brow at him and turned to Leah. "He knows folks, huh."

A smile broke across her face. "He does."

"Alright. Well…" Liz hesitated, then brushed herself off and squared her shoulders. "That's enough excitement for me. You all go get that sweet baby and do what you have to with that plate."

Leah's voice was shaky as she dragged him down the sidewalk. "We're going to be late getting Teddy now," she said.

Wyatt grinned as he fired off a quick text to Noah. "Says you."

"There's something else," she whispered.

Her tone caught his attention, and he stared hard at her profile. "What."

"Luis's voice. Wyatt, when he was arguing with you, I realized…" she slowed to a stop.

"What?"

"I think he was the other guy in my house. I think he was the one who led the break-in."

He blinked at her. She was white as a sheet, breathing in weird little gasps. "How sure are you?"

"Almost certain."

Wyatt faced forward again, gripping her hand a little too tightly before setting off again. "Well, that is really fucking interesting."

* * *

WYATT SHOWERED OFF the afternoon's sea and sand while Leah got Teddy settled down for an early bedtime—but the routine must've gone faster than usual, because the next thing he knew she'd cracked the door to the bathroom and slipped inside.

Huh. Apparently, a few hours of running around like a wild man had taken something out of the little guy. He'd been so excited and hyper, Wyatt had eventually brought him into the cold shallows to bob on his surfboard for a while, just to give Leah a break.

The fact that she'd let him still inflated his chest with something like pride. Maybe gratitude, too.

In any case, by the time they'd hit a drive-through for dinner, Leah's mood had turned…effervescent. No sign whatsoever of the anxiety she'd grappled with after the dust-up with Luis, and now here she was, slipping off her clothes until nothing remained but skin and her glowing grin.

Wyatt rinsed off the last of the soap and stepped out of the tub, and even though he was dripping wet, Leah moved forward to plaster herself against him. His hands didn't know where to land—he'd been transfixed by her body all afternoon, every enticing curve on display in her athletic two-piece.

"Thank you," she said softly. "We had a great time today."

"Me too." Before he could capture her mouth, she slid down his body until her knees hit the mat.

"Wait," he told her urgently. "Wait, wait, wait…"

Leah was too quick for him. She already had him deep in her mouth, working him like they didn't have much time. Hell, maybe they didn't—she'd know better than him what the situation was out in his room.

She pulled back slightly at his words. Her lips smiled against his sensitive skin, and her warm breath tickled when she asked, "Wait? Are you sure?"

"I want to…" Wyatt shook his head, trying to clear it. "I want to make you feel this good, too. I want us to come together."

"Later," she retorted.

"But…"

She silenced him with a bone-melting suck from root to tip. Wyatt groaned as her fingers followed her mouth, skimming lightly along his length, tracing a vein. Who was he kidding? It was already too late for protests. Lava sang down his spine, and there'd be no stopping it now.

"No. Fuck," he admitted. "Don't stop—I'm right there," he gasped.

He wanted to hold her and her wicked mouth in place with both hands, make sure she didn't quit until he was well and truly emptied. The ferocity of the urge was a little alarming. Wyatt reached back with one hand to grip the cold counter, and tried to relax the fingers he'd buried in Leah's silky brown hair.

Tried, and failed.

Her lips tightened, her tongue cradled the underside of his dick and, impossibly, she sucked him harder. It was intense to the point of rough. Darkly perfect.

She cupped his balls, and he couldn't tear his eyes from her as he came in a rush. Wyatt didn't think he'd ever been quite so destroyed by an orgasm, by a woman, and when her steady, amused gaze flicked up to meet his, he heard a sound rumble out of his chest he was certain he'd never made before.

Jesus, what *was* it about her?

Leah gentled her touches, guiding him back down to earth for a moment or two before she got to her feet and reached for the bottle of water he'd left on the counter. She swished a mouthful around and swallowed it down, looking enormously satisfied with herself.

"You okay?" she wondered, when he couldn't quite speak.

"Wrecked, but good. So good." He shook his head, still mesmerized. "But that came out of nowhere. What was that for?"

"A-plus for effort today, Mr. Oaks. A. Plus," she said.

Chapter Twenty-Six

Leah

LEAH WASN'T ABLE to pin Wyatt down for a serious discussion until much later, after Joe and Noah had come home, eaten dinner, and headed out again—and after Teddy had woken up and had to be coaxed back to sleep once more.

She couldn't exactly blame him. Wyatt didn't technically *know* she wanted to talk more about his job, and he was still a bit starry-eyed from their little tryst in the bathroom. She had to admit it'd been some of her finer work—though ogling Wyatt on the beach, followed by Wyatt in the shower, had proved to be plenty inspiring.

Leah shook off the mental images creeping back in and refocused on the matter at hand. She could not let her questions go, because weird and scary things kept happening in Wyatt's orbit, and it was long past time for him to fill in the blanks.

"So, Noah ran the plates from Liz," he commented, as if he'd just remembered. "The car is registered to a Ricardo Luis Flores, kicked out of the Marines three years ago, no known association with Pendleton, no aunt named Biddy Daniels…" He set down the TV remote and trailed off with a frown. "Nothing. SDPD picked him up this morning on an outstanding warrant for an old D.V. complaint. That's all they had."

Leah tilted her head, studying his casual posture on the couch next to her. "An outstanding warrant. How convenient." Was he too casual? Too practiced for a man who'd likely tipped off the cops about Luis's whereabouts, or made someone he knew do it?

Wyatt shrugged, unconcerned. "Don't do the crime if you can't do the time."

"So…you have contacts in the SDPD, then? Is that why you guys had me hold off calling the police after the break-in? Or when we saw Luis yesterday?"

"We have contacts where…it is helpful to know people," he hedged.

"I see." Leah shook her head and looked away. She let her thoughts settle for a moment, then admitted, "I searched for you, you know. That first time, after you showed up at my house—I hit the internet to figure out what your deal was. There was nothing about what you do *now*, though. Only a lot of news stories about Nabarut, and the Congressional inquiry after."

Wyatt didn't outwardly react, but something about his demeanor grew stiff. Wary. Leah clocked his discomfort and knew she'd hit a nerve. *Interesting.*

"It's not how they made it look," he said carefully. "I swear."

She waved that off. "I figured. I've known guys like they described. That's not you and your friends. My brother Tank…and Jesse, too, maybe. They were that way. Not you."

He sat still. Held quiet. *Waiting to see what she said so he could give her nothing more, and nothing less.*

"So, now…you guys are looking into what happened over there, and the trafficking thing you told me about. Except…you already took the fall. Why would they keep coming after you? Their work is done. Unless…they know or suspect what you're up to."

Wyatt stared, not moving an inch. Leah stared back.

"You're looking into that senator. Roy Doggett, right? The one that's always squawking the loudest about you." She got up and paced around, feeling something important teasing the edges of her brain.

"But you're also curious about Kathy James, and the other Pendleton brides, too. What do they have in common with a senator? With Qahat, or kidnapped girls?"

She glanced at him, not surprised that his face was blank. Not even the shadow of an expression crossed its surface. It was as if he'd turned into a statue of himself, carved there on the couch.

That was okay. Leah was getting close to something. She could feel it. Hell, maybe he could too, and didn't want to jinx anything.

So…what was the connection? Senators usually worked in DC, but Doggett seemed like he spent a lot of time out here in California, rubbing shoulders with Hollywood types at various functions.

California wasn't his home state, however—she knew her representatives. No, Roy Doggett came from…

"Texas," she said suddenly, spinning on Wyatt. "Doggett's home state is Texas."

His sea-glass eyes grew sharp, cataloging her every move. He nodded, one short quick dip of his chin. Leah often thought of him as golden, gilded around the edges like a Disney prince, but now—now there was nothing fanciful about him. He looked severe. Deadly.

She stepped closer to him, knee-to-knee as she looked down into his handsome face, etched from stone. "Who do you really work for? Who *are* you?"

"Leah, I am exactly who you think I am," he assured her.

"No, not just that. You're something more, Wyatt…" She peered into his eyes, like she had recently acquired Superman sight and could see beneath the layers of façade to the truth beneath. "Are you CIA? NSA?" Neither of those felt right. "Homeland Security?"

He swallowed, but his gaze didn't waver. "It's what I told you. I work for a private security company. Normally, we'd be doing hostage rescues, that kind of thing, but our current assignment is something of a special project," he explained. "Call it a…hiring bonus. The company's owner—our boss—also has a vested interest in the outcome."

"Why? Did Doggett cut his funding or something?"

Wyatt's stern expression broke a little as he chuckled. "Nothing like that. No, uh…our exalted leader has a small ax to grind because, believe it or not, he was once in Echo Company."

Leah couldn't mask her surprise. "Seriously? What's his name? Do I know him?"

"You might?" he looked astonished, too, as if the thought had never occurred to him. "His name is Tate Monroe. He wasn't at Nabarut, though. He was home recuperating from a TBI at the time."

She sank to the cushions beside him, trying to think. "I've…maybe heard of him? The name sounds familiar, but I can't…I can't put a face to it. I feel like Theo mentioned him."

"He started Black Watch after the Army finally discharged him because of his injury. Word kind of made its way around, and when Doggett got us called before the inquiry board, Buck reached out for help. Monroe ended up hiring our whole team— Buck, Bennett, Joe, and I—when we got discharged. We weren't supposed to be." He winced. "Still looking into how that happened."

"How does Noah fit in?" she wondered.

Wyatt shrugged. "No idea how Tate found him. He did a stint in the Marines, and was already juggling grad school and the job by the time we came on board."

"Okay." Leah nodded, thinking it through. "Okay, so the five of you have the backing of your employer to pursue Doggett and whoever he's working with. And you're looking for those girls. But in order to do that, you're sniffing around Pendleton and the church groups because—"

He held up his hands, encouraging her to finish.

"—it's all connected," Leah finished.

"It's all connected," he agreed.

"How?"

Wyatt turned cagey between one blink and the next. "I can only tell you so much. You're already more exposed than I'm comfortable with, thanks to that message your brother left you, and your marriage to Jesse."

"And now to you…" Leah trailed off, stroking her braid as her mind turned things over.

"The less you know, and the further I can keep you and Teddy from this op, the better I will feel," he said. "I know you feel invested because of Jesse and Tank, but believe me when I—"

She held up a hand to stop whatever he was about to say. "Listen, I can't explain it, but I feel like there's something significant about Texas. The fact that so many of our counseling girls just happened to be from there, and Kathy moving out there and taking some strange job…and then the senator who screwed you over being from there. There's probably more, but it's all swirling around in my brain and I keep missing whatever else connects it."

Listing it all out loud helped order things, however.

He smiled at her, and she thought of how anguished he'd looked when he'd told her about the missing girls from Nabarut. Abruptly, it all simply *clicked*.

"Wyatt, listen to me. Kathy James…" Leah thought another moment, ticking names off in her mind. "Kathy, Kandace Schuler, several others…they all came from Texas. I don't think they were just saying it, either. They knew stuff. So, I bet whatever those women have to do with Senator Doggett—it's not just in DC and out here. I'll bet you anything it starts or ends in Texas."

His expression turned thoughtful, and Leah paced toward the sliding door to the patio, satisfied that he was mulling over what she'd said. There was something else, though, something about…

"Kandace!" Leah blurted, spinning back to him. "Kandace and that guy she met up with. You said he was Doggett's stepson. There's another link."

Wyatt nodded, slowly getting to his feet. "I know I asked you this before," he said, "but it's even more important now."

"What?"

"Are you able to contact Kathy or Kandace and find out where they are now? Can you send them a message and sort of…vouch for us? We really need to talk to them."

"Of course. Whatever you need."

"Wait to send anything until I talk to the guys. If we can help draft the message, and track the back-and-forth on our server, it will help."

"So…do you or don't you want me to stay far away from your mission?" she grinned.

"Far," he smiled back. "Far, far away. Just as soon as this one part is done, crazy woman."

"Then let's do it. Go talk to your people and tell me what to write."

"You're sure you don't mind? We will keep you and Teddy safe, I promise."

"I know. And if this helps get justice for my brother, then I don't mind at all. "

He backed toward the door, searching her eyes like he could see inside her soul and examine her veracity. Excitement, or maybe anticipation, lit his gaze. "I should go find them."

Leah let a swell of victory bubble through her chest. She'd helped, she could see it. She was finally going to avenge Theo. "Good luck."

He lunged for the door then stopped, came back, and grabbed her face in both hands so he could press a kiss to her lips. "Thank you," he said in a rush. "You're gorgeous and smart and so, so sexy. I'm already fucking crazy about you."

"Good thing you married me," she joked.

"Got that right." And then he took off before she could parse how serious he looked when he said it.

Chapter Twenty-Seven

Wyatt

NOTHING LEAH HAD said had been news to Wyatt, per se, but watching her work through it all had wrought some magic in his brain, firing his synapses to life in a way that sitting around in a dim warehouse had yet to do.

No surprise there. No one but Noah found Black Watch's bunkers—nestled in forsaken industrial parks and no doubt dark and freezing this time of night—inspiring.

Still, when the idea for a three-pronged stakeout had suddenly come to him, he'd sent out his summons fully expecting to end up in one of them for the next few hours.

Instead, Bennett had offered up his and Kim's luxury condo as a meeting spot, and by the time the entire team convened, Wyatt had had plenty of time to refine his plan.

Thankfully, Buck and the others had so far been gratifyingly receptive—though the posh accommodations couldn't have hurt his case. *Something to remember going forward.*

"Okay, let's run through what we know," Buck called out over the chatter, crossing his arms over his chest. Framed by the perfect view of Coronado outside the floor-to-ceiling windows, he cut an even more imposing figure than usual. "We can not take this risk if it's not going to bury him."

"Especially since we still don't know everyone Doggett's working with," Monroe's voice pointed out from Buck's phone, laid carefully in the center of the coffee table, and set to speaker.

"Tailing the guy makes sense," Bennett said. "I can even get behind watching his skeevy brother. But is staking out his wife really what we should be spending effort on? Why not look at our buddy Azevedo, from the inquiry board? He lives in Texas." Bennett stopped and took a long draught from his beer. "Heard he grew up on Fort Cavazos, too."

"Dude, you're from Texas, too. And we can surveil you from the comfort of home," Joe bitched, no doubt cranky he'd been pulled in from wherever he usually was this time of night.

Dozing off in his car, probably. Making friends at the Dunkin'. *Whatever.*

"Lena is pertinent," Wyatt insisted, side-eyeing his friend. "She could easily have been the source of those headshots, and it's her supposed modeling agency that poses the likeliest place for the stolen girls to have landed. If this op helps us rule her out, then fine—we move on. It's still a box we need to check."

Buck nodded. "I agree. Noah, run us through what we're looking at in terms of potential charges for Roy."

"Okay, so right now we have some conflicts of interest and ethics violations for the back-door weapons deals, and possible criminal charges for involvement in the trafficking ring. Tank's call means he could potentially be nailed for aiding and abetting the enemy, or possibly for planning and inciting the battle. Nabarut killed dozens of United States soldiers. If we could make all this stick, it would ensure Doggett's permanent removal from politics, and probably also some lengthy jail time."

"Alright. So how do we accomplish that?" Monroe wondered curtly.

"I'd like to run Tank's voicemail against the recording of Leah's call to Wyatt, and see if I can get a voice match to one of the intruders."

Wyatt set aside the long-neck Corona he'd been nursing. "I'll send you a copy."

Noah waved him off. "No need. I have it already."

Wyatt cut eyes at Joe, who shrugged. "Work phones all upload to his little NSA setup. It was in the employment contract, fella."

"And then?" Buck prompted.

"Proving a link between the planners on the ground in Nabarut, and the suppression efforts happening now should—"

"Should? What do you mean, should? This has to be enough," Bennett interjected. "If this isn't the kill shot, then we need to hold off."

Wyatt could understand the man's apprehension. Thanks to recent events, they'd all learned exactly how much Easy had been at the mercy of powerful men as a kid—and Roy Doggett was exactly the breed Bennett despised the most. Before Kim, he would've been plenty happy to go hunting, regardless of the repercussions.

Now, he was in possession of newfound caution, and Wyatt, he realized abruptly, felt the same.

Noah contemplated the computer on his lap thoughtfully. He was not the type to spew empty platitudes. He dealt in facts, and at the moment they were short on those.

"He's got a point," Joe offered. "All Dan's weapons dealing did was knock his stepdad out of the running for the presidential nomination. Dude's still sitting pretty in Congress, for fuck's sake. It's going to take a lot to ruin him altogether."

"True. But his reputation's been tarnished now," Noah said. "If we can layer on a provable accusation that he's part of a trafficking ring—and hopefully, one or both of those other charges relating to the ambush—we *can* sink him for good. He won't be able to wriggle out from under the allegations, and won't just be expelled from politics. If we do this right, he'll be cooling his heels in the pokey for a good long stretch."

Bennett nodded grudgingly, but trust, understandably, came hard for him.

Wyatt asked the question he knew Easy wanted to. "How much time are we talking?"

"Potentially decades, maybe even life if the case is airtight. And the guy's 68, so even with appeals he's not seeing daylight anytime soon, if ever."

Buck massaged his neck, looking tired as he eyed each of them in turn. "We cannot miss on this," he pointed out. "We need more than Tank's voicemail to hold this up. We need incontrovertible proof from these stakeouts."

Murmurs of agreement rumbled from the team.

Buck looked around at them, nodding. "While Noah works on making connections between the church groups and the ambush, the rest of us will try to lock down the Doggett's trafficking connections. Here's what I propose. Doggett is in DC all this week for committee meetings. If we can get him mixing with young women or talking about either the missing girls or Nabarut, great. He's slick, though—slick enough that we're going to need to visit some other people, too."

"Per my suggestion," Wyatt bowed, earning an elbow from Joe.

As they debated their particular assignments, his phone buzzed with a text from Leah, reporting that Kandace had already gotten back to her. He relayed her message to the group reluctantly, knowing what it likely meant.

"Okay, given that information, here's where we're at. I'll head up to LA to shadow Roy's brother. Tate, you still think you can get a ticket to that awards thing?"

"Affirmative."

"Great. Then Bennett will go to Dallas to trail Lena, and make it look like a visit home."

"Dallas ain't my home, man." Easy paused, then wondered, "Can I bring Kim? She could visit her friends."

"That's playing with fire," Buck said. "Lena knows her—Kim dated her son for what? A few months?" He frowned. "Bad idea drawing the woman's attention like that."

"Kim stays home," Monroe pronounced. "As does Doherty."

"What the fuck? Why am I getting benched?" Bruiser squawked.

"Because Oaks is going to DC to watch Doggett and win Ms. Schuler over. We need you to stay put and keep watch over Leah and her son. Plus, you know the operatives working under Kenya best. You'll be able to coordinate effectively, if it comes to that."

And there it was. Wyatt had pulled the short straw, and had to be the one flying cross country. *Damn.* Leah and Teddy had barely moved in, and he already had to leave them.

DESPITE HIS RELUCTANCE, he could hardly argue about an op that had been his idea. So in a matter of days, Wyatt found himself leaving the safehouse Monroe kept tucked away blocks from Capitol Hill, with a selection of electronics Noah had packed for him, an address in his pocket, and a name to give the doorman of The Violet Lounge.

Kandace, it seemed, was now a dancer in an exclusive men's club favored by members of Congress, a job she'd told Leah had been procured for her by none other than Doggett's stepson, Dan Cox.

Wyatt had never been particularly comfortable in strip joints, snooty or not. He didn't find it enticing to get aroused amidst dozens of horny strangers, and he'd never been able to separate the people who worked in them from their identities outside the workplace.

He wasn't able to view them simply as objects, or avatars—all Wyatt saw were daughters, and sisters, and mothers. Some of them were caregivers of family members and pets. They were…people who maybe would've preferred another path if they'd had the option.

Whether that was actually true or not felt irrelevant—the fantasy simply wasn't there for him, so what was the point in going? His imagination served him well enough when the dating world came up short.

In any case, thanks to Leah, Kandace had agreed to deal with him and only him, so right on schedule he straddled his borrowed motorcycle and picked up Doggett's car as it left the Executive Office Building, tailed him to the same club he'd visited every evening that week, and waited in the alley for the good senator to slip discreetly in the side door.

Wyatt parked in the cramped employee lot out back, gave it a few minutes, then rolled up to the back door of The Violet Lounge like a real VIP, passing the name he'd been given to security like he'd done it a hundred times.

As the bouncer led him silently to the dressing area where Kandace was waiting, Wyatt peeked around a curtain and watched Roy order drinks from a large booth in the shadows against the wall.

Over the phone, Kandace had explained that Roy had been meeting with girls all week, and that the club's manager would be introducing her to him tonight, after her set on stage as Kandy Kane.

She barely resembled her photos now, as she applied the finishing touches to her makeup. She wore a short, pink satin robe and what had to be a wig, though it was a great one if so. She looked up when the bouncer brought Wyatt over, giving him a brief perusal before turning back to her false lashes.

"You're Leah's new guy?"

"I am. Thanks for doing this."

Kandace shrugged. "Gotta make it quick. I've only got ten minutes before I need to clear my new music with the manager. It's that guy from Texas, right?"

"Also known as Senator Roy Doggett, yeah," Wyatt smirked. She rolled her eyes. "He's a perv."

"He been hitting on you guys, or what?"

"Not me. He likes the ones who look really young the best. He's real pushy. Been giving everyone the creeps."

"Like I told you before, if you do this, you can help us catch him, and protect the other girls. Where do you want to wear the wire?"

"Not too many options, as you can see. It's either my hair or my bikini. What do I do if he figures it out?"

"He won't. But you have to act like you like him. Get him talking about the things we discussed."

Kandace snorted and shook her head. "I'll try. But prepare yourself for half an hour of him talking about my boobs." With that, she stood and shucked her robe as carelessly as if he were there to perform her annual mammogram. Arms outstretched, she announced, "Do your worst."

WYATT SET UP the rest of his equipment in the manager's office, behind another curtain in the long dressing room. As the conversation kicked off, he realized Kandace needn't have worried. She was a natural.

She started off by apologizing for not meeting Roy before her set, claiming she'd been late for work.

"You know why I'm here?"

"Maybe. You're not who I expected, though."

"The others weren't available. This time y'all get the big dawg."

Wyatt wished like hell he could see Kandace's expression.

"I know you, though. Right?" she prodded. *"You look familiar."*

Roy chuckled. *"Do I? Even though I'm old enough to be your daddy?"*

"Someone's maybe, but not mine. I never knew the guy who donated the sperm that made me."

Wyatt shook his head, marveling at how Kandace could sound jaded and seductive, all at once. Roy was in over his head.

The man's voice sounded closer when he murmured *"He must've been one handsome fella, whoever he was. Look at you. Pretty as the day is long."*

Kandace sniffed, and there was some muffled shuffling. *"Shoot me straight, Daddy. Do you have something new for me, or are all the spots spoken for already?"*

"No beating around the bush, huh? That's alright. I've got four upstanding soldiers in Texas who'd be happy to make an honest woman of you. Terms are the same as before. Minimum four years before you call it quits. Your new husband will probably be deployed half that time anyway, and you'll get all the usual benefits and whatnot. You'll have to convince at least three of your friends to come along with you, though. It's a package deal or nothing. What d'ya say?"

Wyatt hung on her answer, surprised—and yet, not—that Kandace hadn't seen fit to mention she'd agreed to something similar before.

"I'm gonna need to think about it," Kandance hedged. *"I've got some regular customers, now. They take good care of me."*

"I'll bet they do, Ms. Kane," Roy chuckled warmly. *"What're they paying you? Do the same for me and I'll give you double. DC is a cold and lonely town."*

"I gotta pass tonight, baby. There's a bunch of us working, though. Ricky will hook you up."

"Turning me down ain't gonna help your case, girl."

There was a loaded pause, and then some revoltingly wet sounds that made Wyatt grimace in distaste. *"I bet you'll figure it out for me. Won't you, Daddy?"*

Kandace let out a throaty chuckle as she slid out of the booth, and her towering heels began clicking across the floor. Then she stopped and gasped. *"Wait, I know who you are,"* she exclaimed, *"You're that weather guy, right? The one on Channel 6?"*

Wyatt bent over his equipment with a laugh, completely missing whatever Doggett's answer to that was. He could only hope it'd made it onto the recording.

Kandace strolled into the dressing room a few minutes later, swiping her robe off its hook and wrapping it around herself before dropping heavily into her chair.

"Well?" she demanded. "Is that what you wanted?"

"That was quite the parting roast," Wyatt grinned. "Attacking a man's vanity? Does that work for you a lot?"

"You'd be surprised," she scoffed. "But you know what? Fuck him and his vanity. That guy's a scumbag, preying on vulnerable girls who can't do for themselves. They got so many of us from foster care, and those young undocumented girls coming up from Mexico and Central America? *Shit.* He can go be someone's pretty boy in jail for all I care."

THAT NIGHT, AFTER Wyatt uploaded his notes and the recording to Noah's servers, the team pulled him into another conference call so they could bicker some more about whether they'd really have the goods to ruin the career of a US senator.

"I'm still coming up empty on a familial connection between Luis Flores and Leah's landlady," Noah reported. "So, they're still a mystery. I can't find much on Daniels. Not a marriage license, not survivor benefits, not a birth certificate, no state ID, nothing. Are we sure that's her real name?"

"I'll check again with Leah," Wyatt sighed.

Buck had come up empty in LA—there'd been a bevy of young women in Leon Doggett's orbit, but they'd all been starlet types vying for roles in his next production.

As well, Bennett reported that Mrs. Doggett had kept things basic in Dallas, visiting the spa and lunching with other society wives.

Wyatt was the only one who'd uncovered anything remotely helpful, and he was ready to call it a day.

"An extramarital affair, Doggett could maybe survive," Noah said over the line. "But affairs with possibly underaged sex workers will be tougher to beat. Coupled with the improper contracts awarded to his stepson's gun company, and a slew of campaign finance violations from the failed presidential run…that gets us farther."

"The bad press alone will probably piss off Lena and her father," Bennett mused. "And if they withdraw their support, Ole Roy will be left high and dry."

Joe's voice patched in next, gravely and dry as sand. "Which will be the perfect time to drop the trafficking ring and abetting the enemy allegations. It's gonna stick. It has to."

Wyatt rubbed his face and glanced at his watch. He still had time to catch a few hours of shuteye before he had to move boots to the airfield for his transport back out west. "So, we're a go?" he asked, trying to hustle the conversation along.

"Have you seen the dude's voting record?" Noah complained. "If nothing else, we do this for the guy's constituents."

"We stay the course," Buck affirmed, "And we bury him."

Chapter Twenty-Eight

Leah

LEAH WASN'T QUITE sure how it'd happened but somehow, she and Teddy had gotten roped into a barbecue with what seemed like every one of Wyatt's friends and coworkers—without Wyatt, who had yet to return from his trip east.

It should've been awkward as hell, and yet…it wasn't.

In the backyard of Buck and Peyton's cute bungalow, she'd met Wyatt's boss Tate, who she was both saddened and relieved to find wasn't the least bit familiar, despite his association with Echo Company. His wife Lyla had been chatty, though, giving her about five book recommendations over the course of their conversation in case Leah ever found time to sit and read a book again.

She had a slew of new contacts in her phone, along with invitations to get lunch, coffee, and drinks. She'd also garnered three separate babysitting offers, because apparently everyone also loved her kid, in addition to her.

Shy as he was, she'd worried Teddy would get overwhelmed, or that people wouldn't react well to the presence of a four-year-old at a grown-up party. However, Teddy had surprised her, almost immediately upon arrival launching into a crusade of cuteness the likes of which she'd never seen from him.

Her son, it seemed, loved a party. *Who knew?* He'd charmed the socks off one and all, then crashed about an hour ago, sleeping like an angel in the guest bedroom with Bennett's fiancée Kim watching over him while she snuck in some work for a client.

After checking on them yet again, Leah sighed and took a sip of her lemonade. It was a beautiful evening, and nearly everyone had been so nice. It was shaping up to be the most fun she'd had at a party in years.

If only Wyatt could've been there with them.

On cue, her phone rang in her pocket, and a quick glance confirmed that her thoughts had somehow summoned him. Leah shot to her feet with a delighted, "Oh!" only to upend her folding chair and get her foot tangled in the legs.

With a sheepish laugh, she attempted to right the chair and recover her dignity, but it was hard to miss the pointed looks her new friends gave each other when she hurriedly darted for the back stairs. *Oh well.*

To be fair, she'd gotten quite a few looks already. She'd left on her fake wedding rings for the party, and had no idea who knew the real story and who didn't. No one had brought it up directly with her yet, but maybe it was better Wyatt wasn't there—he'd likely be catching hell if he were.

She ducked into the kitchen, hoping for privacy, and the music and noise of conversation grew softer as the door swung shut behind her. She was going to look like she was down bad for him, but so be it. They were supposedly newlyweds. Her seeming smitten would only support the ruse.

"Hey," she whispered as she connected the call and checked to see if she was alone. "You doing okay?"

"Fine," Wyatt assured her. "Thought I'd call and hear my wife's voice."

"Very funny," she said, though his words felt like a direct hit. She liked being his supposed bride. Maybe a little too much.

"Not to me."

Her either. Leah cleared her throat, determined to act normal. "So, you coming back soon?"

"I actually got back a little while ago, but I've got some loose ends to tie up before I can leave. Sorry. This is the first chance I've had to tell you."

Why did it make her nervous, knowing he was likely nearby? She'd been missing him, and now he was close. He'd probably even get home tonight. She should've been ecstatic.

And yet, despite all of the thinking she'd been doing about him and their relationship, she still had no idea what she was going to say to him once they were face to face again.

How was she supposed to admit her feelings were changing? Already, they were almost too big to manage, and playing the role of his new wife at this party had only made it worse.

People said you could judge a person by who they kept company with and so far, Wyatt's friends had been fantastic. *Just like him.* Not one person had a bad word to say about him.

"You still there?" he prompted.

"Yeah!" Leah shook off her panic and lowered her voice. "Don't worry about it. I'm glad you're back, though. It's getting a little awkward crashing at your place without you there. Joe and Noah have got to be sick of Teddy's cartoons by now."

"What if it was just us? Just the three of us somewhere. Would it be awkward then?"

"W…what?" Leah stammered. "You mean like before we moved?"

He laughed softly, like he was trying not to be overheard. "Forget I said that. Anyway, what's going on in the background? You guys having a party without me?"

"Oh, you can hear that?"

"Hard to miss. Guess my invite got lost in the mail."

"Joe brought us to Buck's earlier this afternoon," she explained. "I thought it was just going to be something small, but there is a full-blown cookout happening right now. There's a lot of people here." Leah laughed, a little taken aback by how easily she'd been absorbed by the group.

Like Teddy, she tended to be reserved around people she didn't know well, but Wyatt's friends didn't seem to do *reserved*, and that had been…kind of great, actually. It felt nice to have conversations again—to feel part of a group, instead of on her own.

"That happens," Wyatt mused. "You having fun?"

"Yes. I mean…I think so?"

"That wasn't even kind of convincing," he chuckled. "People aren't being cool to you?"

"No, they are. Peyton and Kim have been really sweet with Teddy, so he already worships them. And Joe brought lawn games, so for a while everyone was taking turns teaching Teddy how to play. Honestly, everyone has been incredible. Really."

"Except…?"

"Well, everyone with the exception of this one woman, Amanda," Leah admitted.

Wyatt snorted. "Okay, if that's who I think it is, she's probably a bit peeved to meet you. I took her out a few years ago and she's been gunning for a replay pretty much ever since. I can't imagine her being thrilled to meet my wife unexpectedly."

"I see." A frisson of jealousy sizzled through her, but Leah filed it away, figuring she'd examine it later. She needed to look at it carefully too, she told herself. It wasn't right to be critical of his life before her while carrying the kind of baggage she had.

For now, Leah admitted in a whisper, "Wyatt, I kind of feel like a fraud. They're treating me like I'm one of you, and we both know I'm really not. Once this is all—"

Wyatt cut her off. "Who says you're not one of us? Whether we're technically married or not, we're still together. They're welcoming you as a nod to me. I'd do the same for them."

Leah bit her lip, uncertainty flowing through her. "So, they don't really mean it? People have been inviting me out for drinks and stuff. Are they just asking because you'd be mad if they didn't?"

And why did that sting so much?

"Of course not," he scoffed. "They wouldn't ask if they didn't like you. But you might also look at it from their perspective. Couple weeks ago, I was rounding up several of them in nothing short of a fury, asking them to watch over a woman I barely knew. Then I fake-married her. I'd be buttering you up, too, if I were them."

"Wow, my hero," she retorted drily. "So romantic."

Wyatt laughed at that. "Don't be fooled. I'm not nearly as noble as I appear. I acted like a complete caveman after that break-in, and I own it."

"I thought you were very professional."

"Get real," he snorted. "They've been roasting me constantly about that, as well as the weeks where I was nearly unfit for human company before you and I met officially. So trust me when I say, not one of them is confused about where I stand. They're smart people. They've got my number."

"Um," she hedged, afraid to believe what he was implying.

Their marriage was a sham. A ruse. A fake. *Wasn't it?*

"Even if, for some painfully male reason, my teammates hadn't been able to figure shit out," Wyatt continued, "you can believe Peyton and Kim would've gotten the message. Nothing, and I mean *nothing*, gets past those two."

Leah contemplated that in silence. Had everyone at this party been able to see through her, too? *All* the way through? Could they tell that the silly marriage sham was maybe not...such a sham anymore?

"Leah," Wyatt murmured gently, "Don't be worried, okay? I'm going to see you soon, and I can't wait. There are so many things I want to say, and do with you." He made a low sound in his throat. "Being apart from you is an ache that just won't go away."

Leah pressed her phone to her ear. He'd said it so quietly, and she desperately wanted to hear what else he would confess within the safety of their soft, stolen conversation.

Except, Bennett was coming up the back stairs, laughing and calling over his shoulder to someone on the patio. Leah leaned against the counter, trying to look casual despite the frustrating interruption.

Wyatt's teammate swung open the back door open and marked her presence with an easy grin. "There you are," he drawled. "Hey, have you seen—" His gaze drifted past her and his eyes danced in amusement.

Then Bennett backed out of the kitchen smoothly, yanking the door closed and herding whoever was behind him back down the stairs.

Leah wheeled around and searched the dark dining room for whatever he'd seen—and there was Wyatt, his form unmistakable as he silently stalked closer, nearly invisible in the shadows but for the glow of his phone. He shut it down and stuffed it in his back pocket, then pulled her toward him.

"Surprise," he whispered, a breath before his lips landed on hers. Tucked out of sight into a corner of the quiet, empty room, it was several minutes before they came up for air.

"I think I like how you do homecomings," Wyatt finally rumbled against her hair.

"You were only gone for a few days," she smiled.

"Felt like a lifetime."

"How was Kandace?" Leah asked, "Did she look okay?"

"Couldn't say. I tried not to look too hard for obvious reasons." He gestured awkwardly in the direction of his torso and cleared his throat.

"Ah. Right," she chuckled. "Well did you at least pick up any ideas for date night? Assuming we ever get one of those."

"Oh, we will have many of those, and *yes*. I think if I install a pole in my room, Teddy can play fireman on it when he's home, and when he's not you can—"

"Oh, no you don't," she protested. "I am far too uncoordinated to work a pole, private or otherwise. If anyone is going to be busting a move, it's you."

"Well, now the plan's just falling apart." He slipped a hand under her hair to cradle her neck and pressed her close, growling low in his throat as she sighed.

"Wait—" Leah pushed him away when she felt something…odd pushing into her stomach. She poked the lumpy mass in his pocket with a frown. "Is that an…an extra shirt, or a…Wyatt, what is in your pocket, because you can not be that happy to see me?"

He grinned, but before he could answer they heard a scuffle down the hall, and when he peeked around the corner, a little body hurtled toward them and wrapped around his knees.

Teddy.

"Hey, little man! How we doing?" Wyatt exclaimed.

Teddy tipped up his chin and grinned from ear to ear. "Hi, Wy!"

With bedhead and sheet marks pressed into his cheek, he looked like a sleepy, feral version of his usual self, and Leah had to laugh. He'd given this party his *all* today, but Wyatt's return clearly topped everything.

Ben's fiancée Kim trailed after him down the hall, tablet in hand.

"All good?" Leah wondered.

"He slept like a champ, *and* I got my proposal done," Kim waved her tablet in the air then tucked it into a tote bag she'd stashed on a chair. "Win-win, if you ask me."

"Thank you so much for sitting with him."

"Are you kidding? He's adorable. You two should make five more just like him." With a cheeky wink, she sauntered through the kitchen, and then outside.

"Five seems excessive," Leah joked shakily, once she was gone.

Wyatt looked merrily unperturbed. "I'm game. When do we start?"

While she gaped at him, he hoisted a squealing Teddy into his arms, attempted to smooth down his crazy hair, and headed for the kitchen, too. Along the way, he grabbed a juice box off the counter and extracted a large stuffed frog from his pocket to hand to him.

"You hungry?" Wyatt asked her son. "If I know Miss Peyton, she's probably working up some s'mores out there."

Leah squawked in alarm. "Wyatt! Omigod, no. Well-rested plus sugar is a bad—"

He opened the back door, smiled widely at her over his shoulder, and leaped off the back stoop, Teddy cradled carefully in his arms, laughing wildly as they soared through space.

"Damn it," she muttered, wandering after them. *Guess the party was just getting started.*

"SO, YOU WORE these to the barbecue, huh?" Wyatt murmured later that night, taking Leah's hand and twisting her fake wedding rings around her finger.

She flushed, but it wasn't like anyone else was listening. Once she'd gotten Teddy into his pajamas, he'd crashed like a load of bricks, and she wasn't even sure if the other guys had come home from Buck and Peyton's yet.

For her part, she hadn't made it much past brushing her teeth and collapsing into bed next to Wyatt.

"I'm sorry," she told him, "I hope that doesn't turn into a big headache for you. I wasn't sure who knew the truth or not, so it seemed like the safest choice."

"You like them, though."

"I do."

Wyatt smiled. "Did anyone say anything?"

"No. But there were looks, for sure," Leah winced. *Death glares from Amanda, especially.*

"I'll bet. Not to mention that zinger Kim launched at us."

It took Leah a moment to remember what he was talking about. "You mean the five kid thing?"

"Yep," he laughed.

She tried to hold it in, but curiosity got the best of her. "Do you…think you want kids eventually?"

"Yeah, definitely. What about you?"

"I mean…sure." she shrugged. "It'd be nice for Teddy to have siblings." A few months ago, she wouldn't have thought that was even an option, and now look at her—dancing around the topic like a high schooler with a raging crush.

"So how many more do you want?" Wyatt prompted, kissing her on the nose.

"I don't know. I'd have to see how it goes," Leah hedged. Picking an exact number felt too much like playing with fire, but the truth was, she hadn't minded being pregnant. She could definitely see herself doing it again someday. "Why? How many sounds right to you?"

"Five more seems good," he said, oh-so-casually. "Counting Ted, that would round out to an even six. Nice even number."

"Says the guy who won't have to carry or birth them." *And why was he acting like they were going to do it together? Because that seemed like a critical detail to gloss over.*

"True. I'll just have to work harder after they're here to balance the scales," he smiled softly, eyes bright.

Leah shied away from his intense gaze and searched for something else to talk about. Her eyes fell on Teddy, curled around his new stuffed animal. "I noticed you brought Teddy a souvenir earlier. Didn't bring me anything, I see," she teased.

"Oh no, I did. It's in my pocket."

"Liar."

"I'm serious. Check and see."

Leah slipped her hand into the pocket of his shorts, fully expecting Wyatt to turn the move into some kind of pass. Instead, her fingers found a folded piece of paper.

Look in my top bureau drawer. (turn over), it said. When she flipped it, she saw that she'd scrawled *TOMORROW* on the back in all capitals.

"What's this?" she smiled.

"It's a scavenger hunt," Wyatt grinned back. "One clue a day. Way better than a stuffed frog, wouldn't you agree?"

"I don't know. Depends on what the prize is at the end."

"I guess you'll have to wait and see." He leaned in and kissed her again, soft and lingering.

Leah couldn't begin to guess what he was up to, but it was time to change the subject again, before Wyatt's kisses—and her heart—strayed into more dangerous territory.

She held him back with a gentle hand on his chest. "So, how did your trip go? Did you accomplish what you needed to?"

"Little by little, we're making progress," he said. "Once we find Kathy James, I think we'll make more." He didn't pressure her, though, trusting that if she'd heard anything new from Kathy, she would've told him.

It was that trust in her, that easy acceptance, that gave her the resolve she needed.

Leah stared at him for a long moment, then took a deep breath and looked away. When she met his gaze again, she was a little scared, but she trusted him, too. That felt big.

"Wyatt…Kathy got back to me while you were gone. She said if I trust you, she will, too. She said she'll talk to you."

Chapter Twenty-Nine

Wyatt

KATHY JAMES WAS smart, and she was wary—both excellent qualities for a person in her position to have, and undoubtedly why she'd managed to stay hidden as long as she had.

It also meant she was far more difficult to win over than Kandace Schuler had been, so when Noah reached out through an encrypted message it took several levels of convincing before she agreed to meet at a neutral location.

In Texas, naturally. *Where else?*

Once on the ground, the team reviewed the aerials Noah had obtained for them and made the decision to stow their vehicle on the dirt lane bordering the sprawling property where Kathy was hiding, and move in on foot. The tiny farmhouse she'd directed them to was tucked fairly deep in the acreage of the run-down ranch, with not much to cover them as they moved in.

It was a quiet evening, too. Not a soul around, no work vehicles tilling in the distance, no animals in the decrepit barns. The air was still. The birds, if there were any, were silent.

Wyatt didn't think he'd ever seen a situation that looked more like a trap, either in real life or the movies.

He froze as Buck held up a fist, stopping their forward progress in a small stand of trees—their last bit of cover before they'd have to cross the front yard. Blinking through his night vision binocs, he tried to see what the hold-up was.

Wyatt hadn't heard anything, but Buck had point and was the one tasked with letting Kathy clock their position and give her signal.

They waited, Joe getting antsy when nothing happened for several seconds.

But then the porch light flashed, once, twice, three times, and Buck waved them forward. Coast was clear. Time to move.

On the porch, a mountain of a man let them cool their heels for a while before he cracked the door and gave them a scowling once-over.

"Who are you?" Buck demanded.

"I could ask the same."

Bennett stepped forward, posture easy and voice smooth as molasses here on his home turf. "Friend, we are both invited and expected. You, however, are a surprise."

The man scanned them again, and ducked inside for a quick whispered conversation before reluctantly allowing them entry.

"Back here," he grunted, gesturing them toward the kitchen at the rear of the house, then jockeying with Joe, who obstinately refused to give up the rearguard position.

Kathy James herself sat at the ancient, scarred kitchen table, gripping a sweating to-go cup of iced tea and looking like she fully expected someone to start shooting.

Still, she managed a small smile and said, "I'm Kathy. Obviously. This is my brother-in-law, Austin. I hope you understand why I wanted him here."

Buck and Bennett shared a look. Noah had speculated that Kathy might've gone to ground with her husband's brother,

Austin James, when he'd discovered the man had gone AWOL from Fort Bliss around the same time she'd disappeared.

Here, it seemed, was their confirmation.

Austin folded thick arms across a broad chest and scowled some more. Wyatt smirked. As guard dogs went, he was doing great. *Perfect casting, 10 out of 10.*

"You can call me Buck. This is Bennett, Wyatt, and Joe. Thanks for agreeing to talk to us."

She nodded once. "Leah seems to think you can help me. Sounds like we're stuck in similar boats at the moment."

"We'll do everything we can to get you back on land," Buck assured her. "I'm gonna need him to disarm first, though," he said, indicating Austin.

"Like hell I will."

"Austin, come on," Kathy murmured. "There's four of them. The faster you do it, the faster we get this over with and get out of here."

He stared down at her like he was cataloging every freckle on her face. Kathy blinked and took a shaky sip of her tea.

"Why are you doing this?" he whispered.

"We talked about this. If Leah trusts this guy——" At that, she tipped her head toward Wyatt. "——enough to get married again, then we can trust them, too. Roy ruined their careers. They want to see him fry as much as we do."

Wyatt fought back a smile at the call out. Apparently, Leah was still keeping up the marriage sham. Not that he minded.

Kathy and Austin stared each other down for a few weighty breaths before he pulled a gun from his back waist and slammed it on the table.

Buck smirked. "Let's have the one on your ankle, too."

Once Austin complied, Bennett slid the two Glocks across the table and nodded.

The guy probably had other things stashed on his person—Wyatt certainly would've in his position—but they weren't going to press him. He was fuming enough as it was.

"Appreciate that," Buck told the guy, then pulled out the chair opposite Kathy. "Now, let's get started."

AS KATHY RELATED it, she'd realized fairly quickly that she was working for a shell company, but she'd assumed it was a run-of-the-mill variety, shielding assets or skirting taxes. It wasn't until she'd begun keeping her own records, documenting what she saw, that a darker supposition had emerged.

"I think…" she hesitated, looking to her brother-in-law before she continued. Austin James stood like an oak at her shoulder. Kathy searched his face, but as far as Wyatt could tell, his expression betrayed nothing.

She must've seen something there, however, because she nodded and turned back to Buck. "I think they were selling people," she admitted.

She picked at her nails as she described documents referencing "individuals" obtained from specific locations. "I thought that was a weird way to phrase real estate, but I thought they meant individual parcels of land. Individual properties. Linedance did a lot of investing in low-income areas, buying up cheap, abandoned, or condemned properties and flipping them for a big profit. Nothing landlords don't do all over the country."

She stopped and looked at each of them in turn. "It wasn't until I saw the headshots that I realized I was wrong." At this, her voice cracked, and her brother-in-law reached out to squeeze her shoulder. "They'd obviously been left in the file by mistake. By the time I got it back, they were gone."

"Who had access in between?" Buck wondered.

Kathy let out a long breath. "There was a big meeting that day. The only people who touched that file after me were the bosses and Mr. and Mrs. Doggett."

Bennett shot Wyatt a look that could've frozen over half the continental US. He couldn't say he disagreed.

"Do you remember anything else about the deal? Anything that stood out besides the headshots?"

"Yeah. Up till then, all the deals I'd seen had been in the States. This one was in the Middle East, though. Qahat. The numbers were bigger, and…the whole thing just smelled wrong."

"Is that why you started keeping copies?" Wyatt asked her.

"Originally, I was just trying to cover my ass, in case regulators caught on and Linedance got in trouble. But once I saw those photos, I started thinking about filing a complaint myself. Like, a whistleblower thing to force them to look into the company. I wanted to get out of there first, though, and it's not a great job market right now. It seems like all the open jobs are either entry-level or C-suite."

Bennett inquired, "Do you think they knew what you suspected?"

"I didn't think so at the time. I'd been collecting proof for a while before it all hit the fan. But then the story hit the news, and I got called in and fired, all in the space of a couple of hours. Why me and no one else?" she wondered, "Why me and not someone more important? It makes no sense, unless they knew."

Buck frowned. "Was there anything else that made you different, besides what you were doing? Any other reason you might've gotten the ax?"

Kathy shrugged and shook her head. "I don't think so? I wasn't the most junior person in the office, or even the newest hire. I don't—"

"She's too smart, that's what," Austin grumbled, interjecting. "Smarter than all those assholes put together. Can't be havin' that when you're cooking the books and trafficking kids."

Kathy swallowed, considering her cup for a long time before pushing it away and rubbing at the trail of moisture it left behind. "I thought getting canned was going to be the worst of it. I went home and kept looking for another job, but then the calls started."

"Media found you?" Wyatt wondered.

Bennett shook his head. "No."

"No," Kathy agreed. "Well, yes, they did—but there were also threats, all times of the day and night, warning me to keep my mouth shut. I called Austin after the third one. I didn't know what else to do."

"Were you who suggested she go into hiding?" Buck asked him.

He glared at the wall. "Only after they paid her a visit."

Buck turned back to Kathy. "Anyone you knew?"

Austin answered for her, an angry flush creeping up his neck as he related, "Oh, she knew him. Little punk and his friend. They're lucky I wasn't there when they showed up. I would've—"

Buck cut him off, keeping his voice level and his face neutral. Loose cannon vibes were bleeding off Austin in waves, making all of them wary of tipping the barrel.

"Can you give us a name?"

"Luis. I'm not positive what his last name is. His aunt ran the bible study at the church we used to go to in Pendleton. He was always kind of a jerk, but when he broke into my apartment out here...he scared me to death."

"Him again. Dude's like a bad rash," Joe complained.

"You know him?" She seemed relieved by that. "He got chesty with me right before I moved out here, when he found out about my new job. I didn't understand half of what he was ranting about then, but this time it was clear: if anything got out about Linedance, it was going to be my neck on the block."

Buck nodded, pulling his phone from his vest absently and glancing at the screen. He did a double take just as Wyatt felt his own phone buzz, and saw the others reaching for theirs, too.

Hostiles incoming, Noah had texted them.
2 vehicles traveling NNW approx 15 clicks from ur location, ETA 9 mins.

"What is it?" Austin demanded instantly. "What's going on?"

"Looks like company's coming," Buck replied, getting to his feet.

At his signal, Wyatt and Bennett headed for the windows, while Bruiser moved to flank Buck.

"Give me my sidearm."

Joe balked. "Negative."

Austin looked between Kathy and his guns frantically. "God damn it, give me my weapons, now! Let me get her out of here."

Buck stared him down for a few long heartbeats, then finally gave the nod to Joe. Bruiser tossed Austin the Glocks, but kept his own weapon trained on the guy's chest.

Wyatt shook his head at his buddy's show of aggression. Austin wasn't going to do anything stupid—against them, anyway. He was smitten with his sister-in-law, and panicking about her welfare. That was all.

Noah switched to comms and asked, "Want me to send local law enforcement to intercept?"

"Newsflash, that *is* local LEO," Bennett announced, finally picking up a visual from his position. "Now what are they doing here?"

The rest of them turned to Kathy and Austin, but she was too terrified to be guilty, and he gave them only a quick, disgusted shake of his head in his defense. He was hovering over her like he was ready to shoot his way out if he had to, and Wyatt supposed that was answer enough.

Someone else was responsible for the interference, and that raised all kinds of questions about who might be tracking their movements, and how.

"Noah, we're gonna need an ark, buddy. Whatcha got?" Buck asked, skirting their contacts to scan the property out the back door.

He glanced at Bennett, then prompted, "Easy?" when his partner wouldn't peel his eyes from the approaching cops. "Opinion on these two?"

Bennett nodded briefly over his shoulder. "They're good. Cut 'em loose before this gets salty."

"Y'all got somewhere else to go?" Buck asked the pair. "Hidey hole no one knows?"

"Yessir. This place is clean, too."

"Alright, then get her out of here. We'll deal with this."

"Copy." Austin grabbed Kathy's hand and towed her toward the door.

"Watch for my call, man," Buck warned. "We're going to set up a secure location for y'all to stay long term, and I'm going to arrange for her to transfer copies of whatever proof she's gathered. But don't make us come looking for you when the time comes."

Austin looked wary, but he still nodded before hustling Kathy out the back. With one foot over the threshold, he hesitated. After what appeared to be some heavy internal debate, he leaned back in.

"The owner of this ranch is a guy named Braddock McMurtry," he said. "Tell the law to call him—say you met him at a vet thing in Peru. He'll vouch for you."

"He better not have a connection to either one of you," Joe grumbled.

"None. Not that anyone could find, anyway."

"Thanks, brother," Wyatt called. "Appreciate that."

He shrugged impatiently, keeping an eye on Kathy as he waited to be dismissed.

"Y'all go on, git," Bennett drawled, wandering over to clap him on the back, then shoving him toward Kathy, hovering in the shadows of the back porch. "We got this."

After they'd made it safely into the trees and out of sight, Wyatt asked, "You think she knows her brother-in-law is in love with her?"

"Unclear," Buck answered, taking up a new position at the front window. "I suspect the feeling's more than mutual, though."

Chapter Thirty

Leah

ONCE TEDDY WAS asleep for the afternoon, Leah opened Wyatt's top bureau drawer and rifled around. She didn't have to dig deep to find his note—it was nestled right near the top, tucked under a neatly folded pair of gym socks.

The universe is strange, he'd written on the front. On the reverse, he'd scrawled, *Tomorrow, find your next clue inside my pillowcase.*

Leah spun toward the bed and eyed Wyatt's pillow. He'd said one note a day, though. If he came home early and discovered she'd cheated, he might call off the game.

She winced, impatient and fighting off the impulse to test him. She couldn't begin to understand where he was going with this scavenger hunt idea, but she had to admit she was intrigued.

Leah clutched his clue in one hand and headed for the main room, where she could examine it further without waking Teddy. He'd been a trooper all morning while she'd hurried to do what she could to prepare for the big dinner tonight.

She and Wyatt had planned it together to thank his roommates for letting her and Teddy crash at their place, and for whatever else they were doing to look into the circumstances surrounding Jesse and Theo's deaths. But Wyatt was supposed to be home to help her by now, and he was still nowhere to be found. Finding his note for the day made him seem close, though, like maybe he hadn't totally ditched her to cook for a crowd that might not even be coming.

Unfortunately, Noah was home and working at the kitchen table, so with a huff of frustration Leah stuffed Wyatt's note in her pocket and resolved to peruse it later.

"Hey, Noah," she said, pleased that her voice sounded fairly normal. She'd been feeling awkward that he'd apparently pulled the short straw and got left home to babysit her and Teddy while the rest of the guys went to see Kathy in Texas.

"Got her," Noah exclaimed under his breath.

"Sorry?"

He looked up and saw Leah standing there, and without missing a beat explained excitedly, "Your old landlord was Senator Doggett's live-in housekeeper at their big family property in Temple. As far as I can figure, Roy had a fling with her daughter at some point. She lived there, too. With her mom."

"Gross," Leah said, abandoning her vague intention to make a snack in favor of some sordid gossip.

"Seriously," Noah agreed. "To no one's surprise, it looks like the daughter kept clear of the Doggetts once she left for college, but get this—her son stayed with Biddy, not her."

"I mean…that's not too odd, is it? Lots of grandparents help raise their—"

Noah was still talking, fairly bursting with his discovery, "No, that's what's interesting. When Roy won his senate seat and moved to Dallas, Biddy stayed in Temple and kept raising the kid. You might know him as Luis Flores."

"Oh my God," Leah gasped. "Really? He's her grandson, not her nephew?"

"Yup. Once he graduated and joined up, she relocated to this teen halfway house near the border and stayed around there up until about ten years ago, when she popped up in the townhouse next to yours. Luis washed out of the Marines a few years after that."

"But if they are tied together like that, how come you couldn't find her before?"

He grinned. "Because her name isn't actually Biddy Daniels. It's Bedelia Alvarez."

Leah pulled out a chair and sank into it. "What?"

"Can you remember if either of them ever slipped? Did they ever say anything that didn't quite fit their supposed roles?"

Leah tried to think back, but knew she wouldn't be any help. The only thing that she remembered from that time was Jesse's barbs. "I don't think so. As far as I know, she only ever called him her nephew. But I'm probably not the best person to ask. I had a lot on my plate."

Noah's fingers paused on his keyboard, and behind his clunky glasses, his kind eyes flicked to hers. "I'm sorry."

She shook her head, not wanting to delve into it. "How could Biddy Daniels be on the deed, though," she wondered. "If that's not her name?"

"Because…that's not her *name*. Biddy is a different kind of name," Noah said.

Leah's face must've betrayed her confusion, because he went on to clarify, "Biddy Daniels, it turns out, is the name of a small subsidiary within a larger corporation. It's not a person's name, it's a *company* name, with only three assets in Solano Beach. The two townhouses, and another apartment across town. They did the same thing with the estate up in Montecito, where they held Kim."

Wyatt had filled her in on the recent travails of Bennett's fiancée, as well as those of Buck's wife Peyton last year. In comparison, her troubles hardly seemed to rate.

Still, Leah gawked at Noah, stunned nonetheless by his revelations. "Jesus."

He nodded sagely. "They're clever, I'll give them that."

"Not as clever as you," she pointed out.

She looked him over from his floppy, overgrown hair, to his black-framed glasses, to his faded NASA t-shirt. His laptop looked like it'd seen better days, or perhaps just hard duty. Noah could've been any nerdy-cute college student from any one of the campuses that dotted southern California.

He wasn't, though. He was so much more. She was impressed, despite herself.

Suddenly, one of the details he'd told her registered. "Wait— why do you think Senator Doggett was the dad? Maybe the daughter had a boyfriend. Or…"

Noah hunched into himself a little, holding her gaze despite his look of embarrassment.

"Oh, damn. Someone did a DNA test, didn't they?"

His neck turned a bit pink. "Someone might also have started marital counseling."

Leah felt her eyes go wide. "The Doggetts? But how did you—"

"My mom's a therapist. I took a shot. They made regular payments to a couples counselor for three years after Luis was born, and five years of payments to a child psychologist close to Luis's mom's school."

Leah had never met the senator's wife, and likely never would. Despite that, she felt a rush of sympathy for the woman. For Luis's mom, too. Men—*husbands*—could be real shits sometimes.

"How do you know how to find all this stuff?" she asked Noah. "Is it hard—what you do?"

"No. It's just…knowing how a process works and thinking outside the box to accomplish it a different way," he shrugged, leaning back in his chair. "It's like…a kitchen cabinet. You know how it opens—on hinges, right? And you know where the hinges likely are. But you can get in other ways."

Leah nodded. She was following him. *Maybe.*

He clearly picked up on her hesitation. "Look." He pointed into the kitchen. "You could unscrew the hinges and take off the door. You could smash right through the door, or drill up through the bottom. But in order to problem solve, it helps to know how the door works, what it's made of, and what's behind it, so you can decide the best way to do what you want."

She smiled at him, impressed. "You make it sound simple."

"It is, and it isn't."

Leah turned to gaze out the sliding door at the banana trees flanking their little patio, and further out, to the bright pink bougainvillea winding up the fence of the community pool. Seeing the pool made her think of Teddy, and she checked her phone.

As her stomach growled in protest, Leah groaned. *Damn, already?*

Noah frowned at her. "Everything okay?"

"Fine." Leah pushed to her feet, feeling tired and defeated. "Sorry, I have to go wake up Teddy in a minute. I meant to eat something while he was napping, but I kind of forgot."

"That's my fault," he murmured. He glanced at his laptop in consternation. "Wait, didn't he just go down like half an hour ago?"

"Yeah, but I have an appointment to look at a few apartments this afternoon before our dinner. I was hoping he'd fall back asleep once we were in the car, so he'd behave once we got there. But now I'm probably going to have to hit a drive-through, so that kind of screws up that plan."

Noah's forehead crinkled up as he blinked at her. A minute passed. He blurted, "I mean…you could leave him here with me if you wanted. I'm not going anywhere. Just tell me what needs to be done."

"Wait really?"

He shrugged. "Sure. Why not?"

"You wouldn't mind?" Her heart rate picked up. It was too good to be true.

"No, of course not," he scoffed. "Ted's great."

Leah hesitated. Would she be a horrible mother if she took him up on it?

She'd been living with the guy for weeks, and he'd never given her any indication that he was irresponsible or creepy in any way. But the weirdos never did, did they? They were always the perfect friend or neighbor until they weren't. *Ugh.* Teddy's safety outweighed her convenience. She shouldn't—

"If it would make you feel better, I can livestream us," Noah offered. "That way you can make sure we don't accidentally take over the world while you're gone. Here give me your phone."

He tapped her screen a few times, then handed it back. "Just keep that app open, and you'll be able to watch us and even talk to us." He smiled shyly. "If that would help."

Leah pulled her jaw up off the floor and swallowed down her shock and relief. "That would help a ton, thank you."

Gratitude threatened to swamp her right where she stood, so instead of acting reasonable and making herself a sandwich, she gave Noah a hasty run-down of the snack and cartoon lineup that would ensure Teddy's cheerful compliance, grabbed her purse from the closet, and fled.

LEAH WAS TRAILING the real estate agent around the second exceedingly small and boring apartment, wishing she'd rescheduled so she could finish getting dinner ready, when her phone gave a little chirp in her hand.

She peeked at the livestream, which up until then had only featured Noah, quietly tapping away on his computer, basically ignoring her.

Now, though, he was smiling into the camera and saying, *"Hey, guess who's up?"* He beckoned off camera and called, *"Come say hi to your mom.*" Tiny captions at the bottom of the screen translated his words into text.

Teddy wandered over, his hair a rumpled, silly mess and his thumb firmly planted in his mouth. His new stuffed frog obscured the view for a moment, before Noah repositioned him further away and her son's eyes lit up when she waved at him.

"Hey, baby," she grinned.

"Mom had to run a little errand but she's going to be back soon," Noah explained. *"Are you hungry? Want a snack?"*

The agent got her attention, stepping onto the balcony and showing Leah the community playground. Leah nodded dutifully, but it was hard to keep her disappointment off her face. The playground was pretty run-down. The whole development was.

The last one had been, too, but if she had any hope of staying somewhere close to where they'd been living—and to Wyatt, too, if she was being honest—then it seemed she was going to have to suck it up and deal with the downgrade.

She looked at the livestream again, where Teddy was perched on a chair next to Noah, munching on a cheese stick and cradling a sippy cup next to his frog.

"Do you know how to use a computer?" Noah was asking him. *"Do you want to learn?"*

Teddy nodded quickly and shot the camera an uncertain glance. Leah gave him an encouraging smile and a thumbs-up.

"First the ground rules," Noah intoned. *"We don't touch other people's computers without permission, because there's a lot of important stuff on there and it's easy to mess it up or delete something by accident. Okay?"* After a murmured exchange Leah couldn't quite catch, Noah told her son, *"Here, let's type your name."*

Leah focused on the agent, following her into the kitchen while the woman explained about the HOA fees. The listing hadn't said anything about extra dues and looking around, Leah couldn't fathom what they were being used for.

She took another peek at her phone, where Noah was explaining, *"Computers are just like cars. They take us places we need to go, and where we can learn new things, but if we're not careful they can bring us to dangerous places, too, where people are doing bad things. So, we have to be careful and make sure we know where we're going.*"

The real estate agent cleared her throat, and didn't quite mask her irritation when Leah looked up. "So, do you have any questions?"

"No, uh…" Leah scrambled to think of something to say about the place that wasn't morose, but came up blank. "Sorry, my babysitter's an…engineer. He's…" One look made it clear the agent did not care one bit what Noah might be doing. "So, where's the last place? Is it nearby?"

THREE AND A half hours after she'd left Wyatt's place, Leah was finally on the freeway headed home. She'd clipped her phone into the holder on her dash, but even the sight of Noah and Teddy on the couch, giggling at cartoons like they were the same age, couldn't lift the gloom she was drowning in.

She was exhausted, Wyatt had gone dark, and she still had so much left to do for dinner.

She slammed on her brakes and cursed as a cartoonishly boxy electric truck with heavily tinted windows cut her off. Leah fumed for another few minutes, watching the truck weave in and out of traffic doing the same thing to several other drivers farther ahead.

Suddenly, Noah's face loomed large in the camera, eyes searching. "Leah? You okay?"

"Sorry," she told him. "People are being the worst, as usual. Everything okay there?"

"Right as rain." He looked over his shoulder at Teddy, then back at her. "Hey, is it okay if I start a movie for him instead of cartoons?"

"Sure." Leah checked her mirrors and merged toward the exit. "He likes the one with surfing penguins right now. It should be on Wyatt's dresser."

"Roger that." He looked distracted. "He's doing great, but uh…what's your ETA?"

Leah flushed with embarrassment. She hadn't meant to be gone for so long, but thanks to traffic, everything had taken ten times as long as it should have. She shuddered to think how much worse it would've been if Teddy had been with her in person. "About ten minutes. Sorry. Can I pick you up something while I'm out?"

"No, we're good. I'm just going to do a little work next to him on the couch if that's okay. Something just came up."

Leah swallowed down another wave of guilt and hit the gas. "Do what you have to do. I'll be there as fast as I can."

By the time she finally made it through the door, Noah's work task had clearly ballooned into something more urgent. He popped up from the couch like he'd been electrocuted, balancing his laptop in one hand as he skirted the end table and made for his room.

He paused beside her with a hasty smile, and told Teddy, "I'll be back soon, okay? Then we can ask your mom what we talked about."

To Leah, he explained, "Sorry, work call," then rushed to his room, tapping a device nestled in his ear and speaking rapidly.

Leah examined her son, who looked happy as could be. "Did you have fun with Noah?"

Teddy nodded happily. "I saw you on the 'puter. You see me?"

"I did." She set her bag on the table and dropped onto the cushion next to him. Her son cuddled into her side as she slipped off her sandals and propped up her feet. "So, what are you and Noah going to ask me later?"

"Mama, Noah gonna teach me how to *swim*," he said, eyes alight. "In the *pool*."

"Oh?" Leah smiled at him. "You don't want me to do it?"

He shook his head. *So determined.* Did he get that from her? It certainly wasn't from Jesse.

"What about Wyatt? I bet he'll want to teach you, too." And she doubted he'd trust the job to anyone else, not even one of his roommates.

At the mention of his ultimate hero, her son's eyes went round. "Wy swims, too? He'll teach me?"

"I'm pretty sure he wouldn't have it any other way," she said, stroking Teddy's soft, soft hair.

A shaft of sun refracted through the big fake diamond on her hand and splashed a rainbow of rays against the wall behind her kid's head. *Just like a real one*, Leah thought, *in so many ways.*

Chapter Thirty-One

Wyatt

B ENNETT TOOK UP his position at the side window once more, pointing his binocs out the side window so he could continue watching the narrow dirt road, just visible beyond the flat, dry pastures rolling across the landscape to the right of the house.

Thanks to his vigilance, three of them were already on the porch when the law pulled up. Buck stepped out just as the cops were exiting their patrol cars, pulling the screen door closed behind him and saying loud and clear into his phone, "Brad, I'm gonna have to let you go. Seems like we've got some company." He paused. "Nah, don't worry about it. We'll reschedule."

He tucked his phone in his back pocket and set his hands on his hips. "Officers. What can we do for you today?"

The older of the two faced them down, hand on his sidearm. "You can put your hands up and step down off that porch for starters."

Not a social call, then. With sidelong glances at each other, they complied. Slowly.

Buck wondered, "There a problem?"

The first cop knocked his hat back on his head and wiped his brow. "We got a report of trespassers out this way. Thought we'd come check it out." While he talked, the second officer made a show of looking around, checking the porch and the side yard for signs of other invaders.

Buck made a show of looking around, too, and chuckled. "From who? No one out here but us, far as I can see."

Wyatt ran through the options. *Austin or Kathy. Whoever that McMurtry character was. Someone who had a bead on Austin, or Kathy. Someone at Black Watch.*

Hell, maybe they'd done the damage themselves, and had just led the Doggett camp right to their mark. Wyatt smirked to himself. Maybe not that last one.

The cop smiled thinly, his irritation evident. "Son, how about you let me ask the questions."

Buck dipped his chin. "Fair enough."

"Who are you and what are y'all doing out here?"

"An acquaintance of ours is thinking of selling the place. Said we should meet him out here and take a look, see if we're interested. Sounds like he got the day wrong, though. Thought it was next week."

The younger officer gave them another dubious once-over. "Y'all don't strike me as ranchers."

Bennett drew himself up to his full height and looked affronted, but he didn't bother defending himself. In their comms, Noah's voice was crackling softly. *"I've got McMurtry on the line. Vietnam vet, does a lot of work with wounded service people, retreats in Peru, and whatnot."*

Buck simply looked at each of them before turning back to the cop and shrugging. "We're not. We're thinking about setting up a place for vets with PTSD to come work through stuff. Maybe get some therapy horses and whatnot. There's a need."

The first officer frowned like he was examining them in a new light, and not a better one. He jerked his stubbled chin at them with a frown. "Y'all serve?"

Noah's voice hit their comms. "*No fake IDs. Be your real selves.*"

"Navy. Just got out last year," Buck said.

No mention of special forces, Wyatt noticed. Probably for the best.

"What've you been up to since?"

Buck hesitated. Noah was quick on the jump. "*You are official employees of Black Watch Security. Give them the number. Monroe will attest.*"

"We work for a security company. Protection details, that kind of thing." He gestured toward his wallet but didn't reach for it. "Can I give you a card?"

The information didn't settle the cops down, however. It only seemed to make them antsier.

The leader waved away Buck's offer. "Anyone else in that house?" he demanded.

"No sir."

"How about that vehicle we saw back at the turn-off?"

"Also no."

"Then I'm sure you won't mind having a seat while Andy goes to check things out."

Joe brushed at his jeans and eyed the red dirt bitterly. "Here?"

Wyatt could understand his irritation. He'd promised Leah he'd be home today, to help her cook the dinner he'd suggested she make for their roommates. Here was yet another delay, and he hated—absolutely *hated*—feeling like he was letting her down. He couldn't even tell her what was going on.

The officer smiled wider. "Yep. Right there. Y'all can leave any weapons you're carrying on the porch and hand over your IDs while we wait, too."

He kept his own weapon trained on them as his buddy edged past, ambling up the creaking wood steps and going inside. One by one, the cop accepted their licenses and eyed them narrowly.

"This here's a big piece of land," he mused. "Where y'all getting that kind of money?"

Buck shrugged again. "Been saving up. Split four ways, it wouldn't be too bad. Might could get some more folks on board, too. We'll see."

Wyatt raised his hand and offered, "I taught myself how to play the stock market a while back. Just for kicks, but you'd be amazed at how you can grow a small investment into—"

The cop quelled him with a frown and an outstretched hand as his compatriot came back outside, shaking his head. The two of them backed a few steps away and put their heads together, murmuring for a few minutes before the younger one strolled down the driveway, presumably to go check out their truck.

Wyatt leaned back on his hands and glanced at the rest of the team. They looked a bit like a group of overgrown preschoolers, waiting around after recess for someone to read them a story. He couldn't help wondering which of Teddy's books they'd collectively pick.

He ducked his head into his knees, trying to stifle the laugh that threatened to spill out of him. He didn't think the law would appreciate his amusement, though later, when they were all sitting around with full stomachs and he had a chance to tell her, Leah probably would.

After an interminable wait, the partner finally returned. "Alright let's get to our feet, nice and slow," the cop announced. "We're gonna have y'all come on down to the station for a bit, while we make some calls and verify your story."

A testy negotiation and cursory pat-down later, they were eventually taken back to their truck to drive themselves, while one patrol car led the way and the other held their six.

Buck took the wheel while Bennett patched Noah through the dash and brought him up to speed from the shotgun seat. Next to Wyatt in the back, Joe trained the A/C vents on his face and sniffed at the remains of his coffee, making a face when he smelled how sour it'd gone.

Instead, Wyatt offered him one of the protein bars he'd stashed in the door pocket and ripped one open for himself.

Dinner was still hours away, and they'd missed lunch. He hoped Leah wasn't counting on leftovers later because once they got clear of this mess, she was going to have a famished crowd on her hands.

"McMurtry will back your story, no worries there," Noah assured them. "He was tight-lipped about how he knows Austin James, but the guy checks out otherwise."

"Oh yeah?" Joe demanded. "Then who the fuck ratted us out? Who else but that guy knew we were even out here?"

Wyatt surreptitiously studied his friend, worried about how he would handle what could potentially turn into an hours-long interlude through miles of red tape. Bruiser had dark circles under his eyes, and looked and sounded exhausted.

Wyatt hated that he had to question whether he was up to this—whether he was perhaps getting worse, not better—when before now Joe had been rock-solid.

"I'm working on that," Noah told them calmly. "First, let me give you the run-down on what's likely to happen once you reach the station."

WHAT PASSED FOR police headquarters in that neck of the woods wasn't much, just a smallish brick box with a drunk tank, a couple of offices, and a trio of interrogation rooms that had seen better days.

The team was split up while the officers verified their IDs, employment status, flight details, and so on. The cops dawdled over a late lunch while Buck, Joe, and Bennett bided their time in the interrogation rooms, but Wyatt had been led to the drunk tank, in which one unlucky local was snoring like a lawnmower while he dried out.

That was fine with him. He much preferred the entertainment of imagining what his cellmate's last 48 hours had looked like to the sensory deprivation of the sterile interrogation rooms. It beat stressing out about leaving Leah in the lurch, in any case.

The law made them cool their heels for a good three hours before conceding that their story checked out and they were free to go, thanks in no small part to whoever the hell Braddock McMurtry was, and to their own personal savior, Noah Kent, who'd undoubtedly worked furiously behind the scenes to ensure their release.

"Kinda nice to have a fixer," Bennett murmured, shading his eyes as they piled into their SUV in the back lot of the station.

"Ask that man for an ark, and he shall deliver," Buck agreed, buckling up. "Let's call and thank the bastard."

Bennett set about relinking their comm as they pulled onto the road behind a dusty green thresher. Joe closed his eyes and rested his head against the side windows, A/C once again full-blast and aimed at his face.

Wyatt twisted in his seat, scanning their six as a hinky feeling itched at his neck. Sure enough, Officer Andy exited soon after them, tagging pointedly along a good five car lengths back.

Close enough to be noticed, far enough away to keep things civil for now.

They'd been given clear marching orders upon discharge, after all. Straight to the airfield and the bird waiting for them, no side quests allowed. That was fine by him. The sooner he could get home, the less groveling he'd have to do.

"We have a tail," Wyatt remarked, though it couldn't have been news to any of them.

"Roger that. We should be up and running," Easy reported. "Noah, you read me?"

Wyatt thought he caught the sound of Teddy's giggles before Noah's voice cut in, but maybe it was just his imagination. He missed the little guy. *Again.*

"Hey guys, sorry that took so long. Any issues?"

Joe didn't open his eyes, but he grumbled, "You mean, other than having to watch those fuckers eat their ham sandwiches as slow as humanly possible?"

"Sounds fun," Noah commented. "Where you headed right now?"

"Airfield," Bennett reported.

"One stop before you head back," Noah countered. "I'm sending you an address for a property I found buried in some of the original licensing documents for Lena Doggett's modeling agency. Kind of out in the sticks, but Mr. Monroe wants you to make sure no young women of Qahati persuasion are in residence."

"Negative on the side quests, Arkman," Buck retorted. "We've got a nice black-and-white escort straight to our flight home. No detours, authorized or not."

"You don't say." Noah fell silent for a moment, and this time, Wyatt was certain he could hear Teddy and Leah in the background. His heart thumped against his ribcage like it wanted to push him to move faster.

He prayed the straight-home directive would stand firm. His stomach was aching with a gnawing hunger, and the rest of him was growing increasingly anxious, too.

"Arkman? That's what we're calling him now?" Joe mumbled.

"Gotta admit, it kind of fits," Wyatt shrugged.

"That's okay, I have someone else I can send," the guy said, amiably leaning into his new moniker. "What's your ETA at the airfield?"

"47 minutes," Bennett replied, "Assuming Buck doesn't get fed up with Johnny Law and pull a runner."

"Really want to know whose pocket those assholes are in," Joe added. "Arkman. Did you get my text? I sent you their names and badge numbers."

"You, too?" Noah chuckled. "Yeah dude, I got it. I promise you'll be the first to know if I find something. What else needs attention before you get back?"

"We're going to need a safehouse for Kathy James and her brother-in-law," Bennett said. "God only knows where he's got her stashed right now, but if local law enforcement is compromised—and given how fast they got to us, I have to think they are—then we can't take a chance on them getting picked up."

"On it," Noah agreed, the familiar tap-tap-tapping of his keyboard broadcasting loud and clear through the SUV's sound system. "What else?"

"Austin's AWOL," Wyatt called. The cop trailing them was temporarily obscured by a bend in the road and a small thicket of trees, but popped back into view a moment after the road straightened out. "Anything we can do to help the guy's case? Doesn't seem right for him to get demoted or whatever, just for trying to help out his family."

"Okay, yeah—I'll look into that."

"What about McMurtry?" Buck wondered.

Noah laughed. "He's a piece of work. Sounds like he actually really wants to sell that property. Mr. Monroe's assessing whether it might be useful to us or not. I'm sure he'll want to hear your thoughts."

Easy nudged Buck's arm. "You know we're gonna have to actually do that ranch idea, right?"

"Be stupid not to," Joe agreed. He'd yet to move or open his eyes, but seemed to be having no trouble keeping up with the flow of conversation.

"You got a headache?" Wyatt tapped his shoulder. "Need some shades?"

"Nah, I'm good."

Up front, Buck told Bennett, "Can't say I disagree, but let's get clear of this shit first."

"Alright, listen—if you guys are good, I'm signing off for now," Noah told them. "Teddy and I are gonna hit the pool. I'll give the pilot a heads-up on your ETA, so try not to get pulled over in the meantime."

"No promises," Buck muttered.

Giving up on watching Officer Andy, Wyatt righted himself in his seat and pulled out his phone. Leah had texted him a photo of Teddy, grinning like a loon in a yellow scuba mask and big blue flippers. His little belly was stuck proudly out over his colorful shark swim trunks, right there in the middle of the living room.

Wyatt smiled, wishing he was there to teach him Marco Polo and retrieve his toys off the bottom of the pool. *Soon enough*, he reassured himself.

"Hey, Noah," he called, before the comm cut out. "Help Leah with dinner."

"Roger wilco," came his rapid response.

He eased back in his seat. Before long, Leah would be searching for her scavenger hunt note, if she hadn't already. He'd written several before he'd left, but he hadn't hidden them all yet. *Just in case.*

The only one left in the apartment for her to find was today's:

Sometimes life leads us places we don't expect.
(like the top shelf of my closet, in the left brown dress shoe)

Chapter Thirty-Two

Leah

WYATT RETURNED LIKE a wraith in the night. One moment, Leah was listening to the steady sounds of the overhead fan and Teddy's soft breathing, and falling a little more asleep with each click and exhale. The next, Wyatt's palm was smoothing across her stomach and his lips brushing her ear.

She hadn't heard him come in, or even felt the mattress dip with his weight. The only thing that kept her from jumping clear out of her skin was the steady weight of his hand and his familiar, enticing scent.

Her relief was a heavy knot in her chest.

This, *this* was why she'd sworn off military men when Jesse died—the unrelenting anxiety for their safety when they were gone, followed by almost unbearable gratitude when they returned in one piece. How had she forgotten so easily what an agony it was?

"Sorry I'm so late," he murmured, for only her to hear.

"It's okay."

It wasn't, though. Leah wished she'd held on to a skewer from dinner, so she could stab him in the leg with it.

Okay, maybe not stab. But brandish in a threatening manner, for sure.

"Not it's not," Wyatt said. "I cleaned up the kitchen and put everything away, though."

She and Noah had run the dishwasher after they'd eaten, but there were a few pans left that'd been too big to fit. She hated waking up to a dirty kitchen, but she'd left them piled on the counter anyway, so they could wash them in the morning.

"You did?"

She hadn't heard Wyatt in the kitchen either, she realized. Not one clang, bang, or splash. *Was this guy even real?*

"Mm-hm," he chuckled, low and sexy. "Least I could do after missing the feast. I snuck a taste from the fridge here and there, but I can't wait to try everything tomorrow. It smells so good in here."

Disappointed tears welled on Leah's lashes. When she'd asked Wyatt what she could do to thank everyone for helping her and Teddy so much, he'd immediately suggested a home-cooked meal. *Surprise, surprise.* She'd been the one to propose Greek food, since that was what she could cook best without any of her recipes on hand.

Everyone had seemed so excited about it, too—though she still didn't know how to decipher the coy look that had passed between Joe and Noah when they'd picked the day.

They'd left town to go find Kathy soon after, and as they'd said their goodbyes, Wyatt had assured Leah he'd be back in plenty of time to help with the preparations.

But perhaps they hadn't been working with the same timeline, or even the same concept of time. Not only hadn't he helped, no one but Noah, Leah, and Teddy had eaten one bite of it.

It was Wyatt's absence that stung, though. He was the one who loved to eat—loved any and all kinds of food—and he'd been the person she'd had in mind as she put together each dish.

Did he have any conception of the amount of work that went into a meal that big?

Yesterday afternoon, Leah had gone to the market with Teddy after his nap. After he went to bed, she'd chopped vegetables for the kebabs, cut up the meat and put it in bags to marinate, made the tzatziki, and put together an orzo salad so the flavors would have time to blend.

This morning, before she met the realtor, she'd assembled the spanakopita and oiled and seasoned a large stack of pita. When she'd returned, she skewered a preposterous number of souvlaki—pork, chicken, and shrimp, because that much lamb would've cost a fortune—and tossed together a Greek salad.

With no one to help her, she'd given up on her intention to make dolmades, putting aside the grape leaves and ground meat and steaming a pot of rice instead. She'd worried all day about whether there'd be enough food, as every person on her dad's side seemed genetically predisposed to do.

There was always too much food, but better that than too little.

After his livestreamed babysitting gig, Noah had stayed sequestered in his room for most of the afternoon on his "work call," eventually reappearing to explain that the guys were okay, but had run into an unexpected snag in Texas and would be running late.

Maybe she should've given up and rescheduled right then, but all she'd been able to think about was how hungry they'd all be once they finally made it home. How hungry *Wyatt* would be.

Leah had kept cooking, and Noah had cast a worried look around the disaster of the kitchen and then at Teddy, ensconced on the couch and growing restless in front of his second movie.

When he'd offered to bring her kid to the pool before dinner, Leah had wanted to kiss him, and had. One brief peck on the cheek, and he'd turned such a deep red that it'd cut through her haze of concentration and made her smile, even as she'd continued powering through each successive task that needed to be accomplished before dinner would be done.

But another couple of hours had gone by, with still no sign of Wyatt. As her feet began to ache, and exhaustion set in, Leah's mood started to turn, too.

Wyatt would show up at the last minute, she'd just known, getting to be the fun host while she tried not to nod off in her orzo and kebabs. It'd felt so familiar, so much like her former life with Jesse, that Leah had wanted to throw everything in the trash and cry.

Even that crack in her resolve hadn't been enough to extinguish her hope, though. Noah and Teddy had returned as she'd put the spinach pie in the oven, her kid had washed up and changed himself into dry clothes without a peep from her, and her one remaining roommate had posted up in the kitchen with a determined glint in his eye.

"I got the grill going," Noah had told her. "Hand me the kebabs."

In the end, they'd had a nice meal, just the three of them.

Now, Wyatt curled around her, sniffing her hair and groaning softly. "Leah, you smell delicious."

A diplomatic way to say, *you smell like food*. Damn it. "I was too tired to shower after dinner," she admitted defensively.

"Not complaining." Wyatt kissed her shoulder, gently nudged her onto her stomach, and began kneading her shoulders. "You smell good enough to eat."

His hands paused, like he'd just realized his own innuendo.

"Keep rubbing, mister," she instructed, gesturing for him to massage her lower back.

As her protesting muscles loosened and Leah began to melt into the mattress, Wyatt leaned down to drop kisses on her shoulder, then down her spine.

He gave an unsatisfied sniff when his mouth passed from her skin to the cotton of her tank top, and moved his attention to her arm.

He stopped, inhaled against her skin again, and licked along her bicep. "Mmmm. Little salty. Is that butter? Or something else?"

Wyatt rolled Leah to her back and grabbed her hand, taking two fingers into his mouth and tasting them experimentally. A shiver worked its way through her, but he shook his head sadly. "Shoot. Tastes like soap. I was hoping for lemon."

"Shhh," she reminded him, giggling despite her sadness and fatigue. Leah pulled him down, so they were face to face. "You can try all the food tomorrow, I promise."

Wyatt's stomach rumbled at the suggestion.

"Did you ever get dinner?" she asked him.

"I'm about to," he retorted, undeterred. He closed the spare inches between them and kissed her hungrily. His hand cupped her neck, holding her in place while his tongue danced with hers.

Leah pulled free and hit his arm. "I'm serious. What did you eat?"

"I had a protein bar on the bird and snuck a few bites of chicken from the fridge," he confessed sheepishly. "Missed lunch, too, though. I'm very sad about it."

"Oh, my god. Come on. Let's get you some real food."

"Later," he insisted. "I want you first."

He kissed her again. Slowly. Desperately. Like the three days they'd been apart had felt as long to him as they had for her. His palm slid across her hip and moved higher, until his thumb grazed the underside of her breast.

Wyatt kissed her like he'd missed her, and Leah's eyes got misty again.

She could forgive him for standing her up. *This time.*

She held her breath as his warm lips found her ear. "So beautiful," he whispered.

How was she supposed to stay mad that he and the rest of the guys had missed dinner, when he seemed determined to be the sweetest man on earth?

"So soft," Wyatt continued. "So warm. So sweet." Each assertion was punctuated with a small kiss. His knuckles grazed her nipples, back and forth, sending jolts of heat along her nerves with each pass.

No reason to muck things up by giving in too soon, she figured. So far, his grovel was going swimmingly, and she was curious to hear what he would come up with next.

The bed dipped as he leaned closer, angling for better access to her ear. "So ticklish," he murmured ominously.

Oh no. Leah tensed, but Wyatt's fingertips were already dipping under her shirt and grazing up her side in the worst possible spot, dragging her top with them. She pulled in a massive gulp of air, squirming and letting out a muffled shriek when he fluttered his fingers along her ribcage.

He chuckled wryly. "So loud."

Leah settled in his arms as his heavy palms petted her, soothing her back into submission. "No fair," she laughed softly.

"So many things and all of them mine," he told her. "All. Mine." He pressed a kiss to her forehead and edged his thick thigh between her legs.

"Shh," she whispered again.

Wyatt's possessiveness should've bothered her, but somehow it didn't. It felt good to be claimed by him, secure instead of oppressive. Leah couldn't fathom how she'd ever confused him with Jesse. They were as opposite as sand and soup.

"This is a good welcome home," he whispered, tucking a lock of her hair behind her ear. "I like this."

"Yes, I've noticed."

"Would've been even better if the way to my heart had been paved with Greek food, but we'll just have to make do, I guess."

"Beggars can't be choosers," she fired back. Leah adjusted her pillow and traced his cheekbone, highlighted by the soft glow of the nightlight she'd left on for Teddy. "I'm really sorry you missed dinner. What happened? Noah said you *hit a snag.*"

"Couple locals couldn't get enough of our winning personalities," he explained. "It worked out eventually. I'm sorry you had to do everything alone, though. Was Noah any help?"

"Huge help. Straight A's for that guy."

"Good." Wyatt pressed her onto her back and levered his body over hers, cocking his head as he contemplated her. "Am I in the doghouse? And if so, what can I do to make it up to you?"

Leah grinned at him. "I don't know…whatcha got?"

"Well…the tickling was a no-go. After that, I've mostly got good karma and clean living."

"That's it? That's the best you can come up with?"

"Pretty much. Usually, targeted applications of brute force take care of the rest."

"Brute force?" she laughed, "I don't think that applies here." Then she started singing softly, "Which one of these things is not like the other ones, not like the other ones, not like the…"

Wyatt narrowed his eyes and cut her off with a firm kiss. "So smart," he growled. It was anyone's guess whether he meant her brains or her mouth. "Now, please focus. I'm busy cataloging the reasons why I missed you so much. Where was I?"

"I believe you were on *brilliant*," Leah shrugged. "Can't argue with you there."

"So funny," he smiled softly.

He declared her heart *loving* and her breasts *enticing* and *arousing*. Thanks to her ticklishness, she couldn't quite make out what he said to the inside of her elbow, but her stomach was apparently *tantalizing*.

Wyatt shifted lower, murmuring *delectable* as he lifted her thigh and licked a line up the inside of it. Had she been frustrated with him earlier that evening? *Who could remember?*

When Teddy sighed in his sleep, they seemed to simultaneously remember the sleeping toddler next to them.

"Oh my god," she gasped, pushing his head away at the same time he hissed a heartfelt, "Shit," into her waistband.

"*Shh*," she whispered again, pulling him up to face-level as her face flared hot.

"Did we wake him up?" he wondered, voice tight.

Leah peered over the edge of the mattress, examining her son. "No. Exciting day, thanks to Noah. Kid's still out like a light."

"And that's why he's Arkman."

"Pardon?"

"Never mind." Wyatt pulled her closer and whispered, "I'm sorry, that kind of got away from me. Should we stop? We should stop, right?"

Leah made a face. "Feels a little weird with him right there, not gonna lie."

He flopped up on his back and stared at the ceiling. "True. I can't believe I just…forgot."

"Hey. It's okay. We're new at this," she said, stroking his solid bicep. "And I don't want to stop. I just don't want to stay here."

Wyatt's head snapped to the side, and his gaze burned into her. "Really?"

"Really."

"Then come with me."

He backed off the bed on the far side from Teddy, tugging Leah to follow him into the bathroom. Wyatt left the overhead light off and silently locked the door behind her.

He pulled her close, plastering their bodies together and hiking one of her legs around his waist as his lips landed on hers. Wyatt backed her against the counter and kissed her, but it lacked his earlier finesse, unfurling like an explosion of need as he sucked and nipped clumsily at her mouth.

Eventually, he broke off and breathlessly kissed his way across her jaw.

"I missed you guys so much."

"Wyatt—"

He didn't let Leah finish, instead turning her to face the mirror so she could watch his big hands drag off her tank top and fondle her breasts. His hair was soft brown in the dim light, falling in messy waves around his forehead. Wyatt seemed transfixed by the sight of his palms moving over her body, until she released a quiet moan at the way he made her quiver.

His gaze snapped to hers in the mirror, fiery and intense. "Is this okay?"

"I missed you so much, too," Leah admitted.

He bit his lip and scanned down her body, his eyes leaving a trail of sensation in their wake. All at once, he pulled her hips back until she was bent at the waist, legs spread, supporting her weight with her hands on the counter.

He dragged two fingers between her legs and squeezed his eyes shut at the evidence of her desperation. Wyatt shoved down his shorts and took himself in hand, groaning as he entered her with a determined thrust, and his voice was strained when he told her, "There is no one on this earth like you."

She gasped as she met his steady invasion, relishing his warmth and safety at her back. *Relentless. Reliable. Reverent.* Everything she hadn't known a partner could be.

"Leah, look at me."

She forced her eyes open, a little startled to meet his scorching stare in the mirror over the sink.

Wyatt's body loomed over hers, the muscles in his broad swimmer's shoulders straining as his fingertips dug into her hips, holding her in place as he filled her.

Once he was sure he had her attention, he said, "I love you."

"What?" It was possible her heart had stopped, frozen mid-beat like every other part of her.

"I love you. I'm in love with you," he said again, dead serious. "And not just because of this. Because of everything you are."

"What are you—" Leah shook her head, trying to get her bearings. "What are you doing?"

"I think this is called communicating."

"*Now?*"

The faintest smirk played across his lips. "Also multitasking."

"Wyatt!"

He bent to press a kiss between her shoulder blades. "Don't say anything back. I just wanted you to know I'm yours, Leah. Whether I'm here with you or away for work, I'll still belong to you as long as you'll have me."

Wyatt gathered her hair in one hand and pulled it aside so he could press open-mouthed kisses to the back of her neck. Buried deep in her body, he toyed with her breast, then dropped his fingers to circle her clit.

"Mmm. Target acquired," he murmured, like he wasn't completely insane for dropping his bomb and then going back to playing her like a fiddle. Like it was nothing.

"I'm sorry—" Leah gasped.

"Don't be."

"We keep having to do this in your bathroom," she rambled, his words, his hands—his unyielding, amazing cock—making her frantic. "We can't ever be spontaneous. I need to get my own place soon. I need to—"

"Stop thinking."

She hadn't told him she loved him back. The words were jamming up in her throat, blocking everything but complete nonsense from escaping. "I'm just—"

"You're just supposed to relax and have fun," Wyatt assured her. "That's it. Just let me make you feel good."

Under his coaxing, Leah soon came apart, her legs trembling so hard the only thing keeping her standing long enough for him to find his release was his strong hands holding her in place.

Long minutes ticked by when it was over, like time itself had come to a stop. Leah pressed her forehead to the cool marble counter and wondered what was so wrong with her that she couldn't echo three little words back to the best man on the planet, even in the midst of a brain-melting orgasm.

Wyatt's breath was hot against her shoulder. He slipped out of her gingerly, gathered her into his arms, and sat right there on the mat, cradling her in his lap while they caught their breath.

She wanted to bring him to the kitchen, so he could have a snack before bed. She wanted to ask if everything had gone okay with Kathy James. She wanted to lay beside him and whisper sweet nothings until sleep claimed them both. She wanted to tell him she loved him, too.

That one, most of all.

It was as if his confession had stolen all her words, though.

Everything except one more weakly uttered, "I'm sorry."

"No more sorries," Wyatt whispered back. "You're perfect exactly the way you are. Just like this."

Later, after they'd showered and dressed and gone back to bed, Wyatt stroked her hair and looked as sublimely happy as if she *had* returned his declaration. Unable to bear her own failure, she pretended to be asleep.

After a few minutes, he pulled another note from his pillowcase and tucked it into her hand, then draped his heavy arm across her and drifted off, too.

Leah clutched it to her chest all night, and in the first rays of dawn, she read:

In a bar across the world, I saw a picture of you and Ted. You supposedly belonged to another man. (next stop, under the bathroom cabinet, behind the glass cleaner)

"Supposedly." Never had one word been so loud.

Chapter Thirty-Three

Wyatt

THE HOTEL SUITE was big and well-appointed with a great view of the bay, but it wasn't luxurious to the point of ridiculousness. It suited Black Watch's boss well—functional, comfortable, and unpretentious.

It looked as if Monroe and his wife had been crashing there for a couple of days, at least. There were wrinkled clothes hanging in the closet, his and hers. The usual ephemera of short-term travel littering the bathroom counter. The air smelled fragrant, too, like someone had showered recently.

Monroe's wife Lyla, perhaps, who they'd passed down the hall as they'd gotten off the elevator. She'd looked casual in her hoodie and glasses, and she'd greeted them with a cheerful, "Hey guys!" before stepping into the car they'd just vacated.

Tate was a decent-enough looking guy, Wyatt supposed, but his wife was on a whole other level—one of those gorgeous women who wielded her studious vibe like a weapon she didn't even know she was aiming.

She'd clearly landed a direct hit with her husband, though. The man was smitten, and then some.

In a way, they reminded Wyatt of himself and Leah. He, too, was moving through life like a besotted caricature. He hadn't been able to stop thinking about the other night. Obsessing. *Making plans.*

He'd told her he loved her as she'd detonated around him in the most spectacular way, and though she hadn't said the words back, the look on her face had told him everything he needed to know.

His tentative mission was now a definite go, and he needed to map out the finale soon. Not right this minute, though. He was technically supposed to be working.

Wyatt glanced around the room, getting his bearings again. Monroe had ushered them into the living area of the suite when they'd arrived, and a decent spread had been laid out for lunch.

Tate had initially spent some time moving around the room, making small talk as he urged them to eat, but now that their cups and plates were mostly empty, he positioned himself in front of the windows and held up his hands.

"Guys, thanks again for coming on such short notice. This isn't anything formal, but since I was in town I thought you could give me a sitrep. Hash out where we stand and what comes next. Sound good?"

Agreeable nods and murmurs sounded all around.

Wyatt snagged another meatball sub off the platter near his knees and settled back to listen.

As expected, Tate tipped his chin in Arkman's direction first. "Noah, why don't you start?"

The guy steadied his plate on his lap and took a swig of his water. "Right, so I've got some updates on the landlord from hell."

"She still sucks?" Joe wondered.

"Correct." He pushed up his glasses. "Get this—Biddy Daniels is not her real name. She's actually called Bedelìa Alvarez. Moved into the duplex shortly before the Burkes did, and as we suspected, is not the true owner."

Tate frowned at him. "Who is?"

"A property management company literally called *Biddy Daniels*. Sometimes it's listed as *BD Properties*. Together, they oversee several similar residences all over San Diego and LA counties."

Buck nodded, interjecting, "You will not be shocked to learn they are also subsidiaries of Linedance Holdings."

"Naturally," Joe commented, then tipped back his supersized cup of coffee to drain it.

Wyatt leaned to his side to grab the second cup he'd brought for him, and slid it his way. Bruiser whispered, "You're going to make some lucky person a great wife one day."

Wyatt winked, because where was the lie?

Noah spared them a smirk before continuing, "It's not surprising that Leah has had trouble finding a similar place at that price point. The Burkes were getting a pretty sweet deal on their rent."

Monroe nodded. "In exchange for Jesse facilitating the acquisition of new trafficking victims?"

"Almost definitely. Now from what I can see, Ms. Alvarez moved here from Eagle Pass, Texas, where she was last employed as the house mother at a facility for teen girls aging out of the foster system. It was run by another church group, but was shut down after abuse allegations got too loud for local authorities to ignore anymore."

"Yeah, that's not a red flag or anything," Joe muttered.

"And, what?" Bennett growled, "This gig was her retirement package?"

"Apparently," Noah agreed. "A little light duty, funneling victims back into mainstream society, fixing them up with soldiers affiliated with the Pendelton church groups. I've been tracing her contacts and family members, to see if I could link her to anyone we already know."

Tate reached for a chunk of cantaloupe, popped it in his mouth, and as he chewed prompted, "And?"

"Well…Bedelia was never married to anyone named Walter Daniels, KIA in Vietnam or otherwise. She was, however, hitched at age 15 to a Waldo Garza, currently serving life in the La Tuna lockup. They had one daughter, Isabel, who in turn eventually had a son. You may know him as Luis Flores."

"No shit." Tate reached blindly for the desk chair next to him and sat. "He's her grandson?"

"Seems to be."

"Have we been able to place him at Leah's yet?"

"Not yet. He wasn't as sloppy as Corporal Miller. Didn't leave a lot for Kenya's crew to find."

"What about the daughter? What's her deal?"

"Thirty-five years with the postal service," Noah reported. "Unblemished record. Lives in Houston with her husband. They run 5Ks a few times a year and help out at an animal rescue."

"Guess the criming skipped a generation," Joe scoffed.

Noah shrugged. "It happens."

Clearly irritated, Bennett restlessly began collecting plates and utensils to stack on the decimated food platters in the middle of the coffee table. Joe glared at the wheels of Monroe's desk chair, which emitted a small squeak each time the man shifted his weight.

Wyatt skirted Easy's piles to scoop the last few bites of fruit salad onto his plate, and had just lifted a chunk of pineapple to his mouth when Noah spoke up again.

"There's more, though," the guy said. "Would you believe, our buddy Luis is Roy's illegitimate son?"

The subtle hum of activity in the room came to an immediate, screeching halt.

Wyatt glanced around and dropped his fork. "Say what, now?"

"Luis," Noah reiterated calmly, "Is Roy's kid. Swear to God."

No one said a word. Wyatt grinned at all the blank expressions, and lobbed a softball back to him, "And you know that how, exactly?"

Arkman smiled in that coy, mysterious way of his, but before he could answer Bennett blurted, "DNA test."

Monroe jerked forward in his seat, rapt. "Really? Doggett made them take a test?"

"Sure did," Noah agreed. "Though honestly, how gross is that? Creeping on your housekeeper's teenage daughter? Is there no bottom with this guy?"

"What a fucking skeeve," Joe muttered. "I shouldn't be surprised. And yet…"

Tate sat back and rubbed his face. "Okay, so…what are we doing with this? How does this fit into the bigger picture?"

Buck got to his feet and paced to the windows, gazing at the bay for a few beats before he turned back. "It certainly ties Luis to the Doggetts, but we don't know who pulled who into the network. Was Bedelia's family already involved, or did Roy rope them in?"

"We need more information," Bennett mused. "If we can uncover more of the other players…"

"Working on that," Noah told them. "Obviously."

"In the meantime, I think we can go ahead and take Ms. Alvarez out of play," Tate announced. "Noah, let the base chaplain at Pendleton know that Biddy Daniels is not who she says she is. We'll follow up later, but I expect that'll curb her access to base while we work out some of this other crap."

"Roger that."

"Let's talk about Lena Doggett's property next. When you guys got your all-access passes revoked, I had another team head over there to take a look. They reported signs of recent habitation, but nothing conclusive. Nothing we can use."

"This was the address listed for the supposed modeling agency?" Buck clarified.

"Yep. It was definitely a residence, not a business. Out in the sticks, too, considering it was supposed to be handling a decent-sized roster of models and clients. The team said it looked like a group of women had lived there at some point. Just not currently."

"Were they able to scrape any DNA?" Bennett wondered. "Anything to connect it to one of our known victims?" With no more trash to organize, he eyed Wyatt's plate, like he was gauging his odds of snatching it successfully.

"No. They gathered samples, but so far haven't gotten any matches."

"Awesome," Joe grunted, sounding more like someone's cranky grandpa than the deadly operator he was. "So, it's another dead end."

Monroe sent him a brief, unhappy nod.

"Fuckin' A."

"Agreed," Tate said, "but it does make me think we need to pay more attention to the good senator's wife now. It's convenient to assume she's either unaware or being used unwittingly…but we have to consider that she might be an active participant in all this."

"Shitty, if true," Wyatt commented. He held Easy's eye and pointedly took a bite of watermelon, daring him to reach for his plate before he was finished.

Bennett snorted and rolled his eyes. "And yet, not unheard of."

Joe sighed heavily beside him, and Wyatt knew what the guy was thinking. After so many false alarms and dead ends, no one wanted to disappoint Rohan again. Their young Nabaruti informant, who'd been elemental to getting this investigation off the ground, was settling into his new life as an American college student nicely, but he'd never given up hope that the team would find his stolen girlfriend.

The lack of progress had been deeply frustrating, to him as well as them.

Monroe glanced at his watch. "Okay, moving on," he said brusquely, "Tell me about Kathy James. Buck, you want to take this one?"

"Yeah, sure." He pushed to his feet and ran a hand over his silver hair like he was about to give a book report to the class.

"We've received all of Kathy's promised materials, and have compared them to a timeline and list of victim names that we got from Kandace Schuler. Both accounts are corroborated by external proof, with various girls being absorbed into the network and disappearing from their regular lives, then reappearing around the Pendleton church groups as marriage prospects sometime later."

He paused and glanced around, but when no one contradicted that assessment he added, "We also found photos of both Roy and Dan on public outings with known victims. Taken with what we already know about Linedance's business activities and Landry Cox's weapons deals, we've been able to construct a solid outline of the network's processes and primary players, with only a few glaring exceptions."

"Which are?"

"Well first and foremost, where are the girls they took from Nabarut?"

Tate nodded thoughtfully. "The eternally burning question."

Joe raised his hand, reinforcing Wyatt's impression that they had somehow all regressed to high school. "I say we start with Lena. Mark my words. That chick knows something."

He met Wyatt's eyes, looking for agreement. Wyatt gave him a solid two thumbs up, because fuck that bitch—you weren't married to someone as long as Mrs. Doggett had been without getting some inkling about what kind of person they were. *Just look at Leah and Jesse.*

And that was before they even touched on what kind of son Lena had raised.

"Let's think about the economics of this," Tate mused, propping his elbows on his knees and massaging his temples. "We've mostly nailed down the supply side. Tell me who's managing the demand. Who were these women intended for?"

Joe looked pensive as he went to crouch next to Noah. After some whispered back and forth, Noah called up a photo of Roy Doggett with his older brother, Hollywood producer and dignitary, Leon Doggett, on his laptop. He held it up so everyone could see.

"I say this guy," Joe announced, pointing to the screen. "If not him, then someone close to him."

Monroe sat back as he contemplated that. "Interesting."

Buck blew out a long, tired breath, which was understandable. He'd already had a brush with the Hollywood contingent of the Doggett family, and Wyatt expected he wouldn't look forward to a renewed involvement.

"Before we go too far down that road," he declared, "there's one more gaping hole in what we know."

Wyatt knew this one. He pointed at Buck. "Who's our mole in the chain of command?"

"Bingo."

The room fell silent, but he knew there were theories. To a man, they were too sharp to not have theories.

"Anyone else thinking Azevedo?" Wyatt prodded.

Four hands shot up, besides his own. He grinned. *He was totally getting an A in this class.*

"Well, gentlemen, I think we have our path forward," Monroe said, the ghost of a smile lightening his expression. "We'll move ahead with putting pressure on Roy. I'll reach out to my contacts at DHS and the FBI. They should be able to make a case for fraud and coercion, at minimum, for the trafficking angle, and that'll be on top of the charges arising from planning the ambush. Noah and I can make sure they have access to what they need, so the evidence is all above board and admissible. They can involve the IRS if it comes to that, but I'll leave that to them."

"Do you want me to drop some hints online?" Noah wondered. "Get the media to pick up on it?"

Wyatt chuckled. Arkman did love to get the bloggers talking.

"A little public scrutiny on this can't hurt," Monroe agreed. "If anything, it might force some reluctant hands behind the scenes."

"Done."

"Any more loose ends?" Monroe looked around the room, eventually landing back on Noah. "What do we have on Flores's buddy, Corporal Miller? Any more on him?"

Noah nodded eagerly. "Turns out he's pretty interesting. Not only did he serve under Commander Azevedo when he was still back in Texas, he also used to report directly to Luis's old bunkmate."

"Well, that's cozy," Bennett commented drily.

"At this rate, we're going to need one of those corkboards with all the red yarn connecting these assholes to each other," Joe cracked.

"Don't tempt me," Monroe retorted. "Hey, what about those cops who showed up at your meet and greet with Kathy and her brother-in-law? You find anything new on them?"

"Yes and no," Noah shrugged. "Officer Andrew Buckner grew up in that area, but not much else to see there. The other guy, Clay Haskin, attended TCU with Dan Cox. That seems like the obvious connection. Doggett's camp knows we're poking around, so best guess would be they were monitoring flight traffic to see where the Black Watch bird went, then rousted an old connection to keep an eye on us."

"Wouldn't surprise me. How'd they get to the ranch, though? Did they follow you from the airfield?"

"Absolutely not," Buck bristled.

"Tracker on the vehicle?"

"No. They're swept regularly," Bennett said. "We went over it again before we left."

"So, they must've had eyes on Kathy and Austin," Tate decided. "Good thing they went willingly to the new location."

"Mmhmm," Joe muttered. He was still salty about Austin's jumpiness, no doubt.

Across the room, Buck dropped into a free armchair and rubbed his eyes. "Half these roads lead back to our boy Luis. We probably should go talk to him again."

"Yeah, about that," Noah tapped the screen of his laptop and looked around with concern. "Flores was released on bail this morning."

Wyatt's ass was off the couch before he even registered the desire to move. "What?"

Monroe stared at Noah for a long beat, then whipped out his phone. "Who do you have on Leah Burke right now?" he barked a second later. He paused, then scowled, "Why the hell not?" As he began to berate someone, he pointed at Wyatt and Joe, then jabbed his finger toward the door.

Maybe it was the recent infusion of caffeine and food, or maybe all the show-timing for the boss, but Joe snapped to immediate attention and hauled Wyatt after him.

Bruiser's demeanor was suddenly so much like it used to be that Wyatt wanted to curse with gratitude.

He was in there—somewhere under the layers of insomnia and nightmares and God knew what else—CPO Doherty, his best friend and brother, was still in there.

"Where are they likely to be right now?" Joe inquired, lock-stepping for the exit and leaving everything about that meeting behind.

Wyatt checked his phone. "Assuming Teddy still has his shirt on, and Leah has her phone, he's at school and she's at the Von's down the street."

Joe didn't react at all to the obvious, which was that Wyatt was actively tracking both of them. He simply said, "Tell her we're on our way."

"Dude, I don't want to worry—"

Joe briefly shifted his glare from the elevator doors to Wyatt, and the heat of it nearly singed off his eyelashes. "Tell. Her."

Wyatt lifted his phone. "Okay, so...text sent. Any other orders, you sexy, angry beast? A nice sandwich, perhaps?" His heart thumped like a low-rider in East LA, despite the joke.

The doors slid open, and Bruiser stomped inside, yanking Wyatt in after him.

"You're driving. Let's go get your girl."

Chapter Thirty-Four

Leah

L EAH REACHED FOR a can of ravioli on the top shelf of the grocery aisle, then pulled back when she saw the way her fingers were trembling.

She had to settle down. They had no proof that Luis would come to find her now that he was out of jail. Wyatt was only being cautious when he'd called to warn her. Besides, he'd said that he and Joe were on their way, just to be on the safe side.

With Teddy safe at school, Leah had absolutely nothing to worry about.

She reached for the can again, intent on giving her kid his favorite treat for lunch since he'd been so good about all the upheaval—but perhaps she was still shaking, or sweating, or whatever else happened when you were freaking the hell out. She couldn't quite get her hand around it.

She made herself think of something good, like the new note in her pocket where Wyatt had scrawled,

Why did you feel like mine? You weren't, but in that moment, I think I became yours. (Look for your next note in your snack basket in the pantry.)

Leah smiled a little, picturing him in some Middle Eastern bar surrounded by servicepeople, falling for a photo of a woman he'd never met. It was so like him that he'd known, on some level even then, what life had in store for them.

She let out a yelp as the can under her fingers tipped forward and tumbled toward her head.

In a series of cascading calamities she couldn't quite comprehend, the ravioli fell, and she had to jump back to avoid getting clocked in the skull. In the process, her shoulder bumped a cardboard display of toy cars and sent them clattering to the linoleum and rolling in every direction.

Leah bent to gather the ones closest to her feet, then finished off the chaos by cracking her head on the cart handle when she tried to straighten up.

Her eyes were watering, and her hand was pressed to her forehead and feeling wetness that could perhaps be blood, when down at the end of the aisle a man walking past stopped in his tracks, backpedaled with a disbelieving double-take, and bellowed, "*You!*"

It was Luis—*of course* it was. Why did the universe hate her so much?

He stalked down the aisle and her heart seized in her chest.

"What do you think you're doing?" he demanded, stepping over toy cars to get closer.

Leah tried for a bravado she didn't feel. "Grocery shopping. What does it look like?"

"Not anymore, you're not. I've got business with you now." A sheen of sweat shone on his forehead and warmth radiated from him, like he'd been exercising outside in the sun.

Or maybe he was just spitting mad.

She needed to get away. Leah abandoned her cart and tried to walk past him.

"Where you goin', mami?" Every time she tried to take a step, he boxed her out, keeping her from leaving. Her pulse throbbed in her ears.

"I don't need to stay here for this." She *needed* to find someone to help, preferably Wyatt or Joe. How long had it been since they'd called her?

"Oh no, no," Luis chided, "You're not going anywhere. Not after what you and your little fuck boy did to my aunt." He looked her up and down, crowding too close. "You like all that bible bullshit, don't you? Well, I've got your eye-for-an-eye right here, bitch."

"You mean your grandma," Leah said, hoping she sounded calmer than she felt. "And I didn't do anything to her. Whatever happened was one hundred percent her own doing."

"She is my aunt, and that's not the fucking point," he snarled, kicking a racecar away.

Leah looked around him. She needed to stall. The guys had to be coming any minute, but what was taking them so long?

"Isn't it?" she asked. "All this time she's been lying about who she is, about who you really are. About loving the lord too, I'll bet."

Luis's eyes narrowed dangerously. "Don't you dare. She is a godly woman, and you are nothing but a whore."

"Not quite. And I don't know what you think you're going to do about it." *She sounded tough, right?* She hoped so, because she was shaking in her shoes.

"You know, I had my doubts about you," he mused, scanning her face as he stroked a hand down her arm. "They were so sure you and your boyfriend were up to something, but I thought, nah—she's just some dumb bitch with an okay ass. So, she's getting laid again. Big deal. But they were right, weren't they? I just can't decide how you figured it out. How do you know?"

"Know what Luis? What the hell are you talking about?" For the life of her, Leah couldn't figure out where every other customer in the middle of the day in this stupid grocery store had gone. Not one other person needed soup?

Luis's stare cleared and his grip on her arm tightened. "Your husband. That's it, isn't it? Jesse insisted he kept you out of it, but he told you everything, didn't he? Asshole would've lied about being dead if he thought he could get away with it," he spat.

Leah searched his face, sudden alarm freezing her efforts to wrench free. It took a minute to remember that there'd been a body, and DNA, and that Jesse was verifiably, provably dead.

"You're insane," she whispered. She peeked as far as she could down the aisle, trying to see if anyone was watching them. If there was *anyone* she could call to for help.

"What are you—" He stopped, and a muscle in his jaw ticked. "Who are you looking for?"

"No one."

"Wait. He's here, isn't he? Your fucking guard dog?" He laughed in her face. "Here's *here*?"

"Yes," Leah asserted. "And he's going to lose it when he sees you. Let me go!"

Luis grabbed her by the throat before she could duck him. "No, I don't think I will. Let's wait right like this until he shows up. I want to talk to that fucker, too."

She worked her fingertips under his, buying herself more air. "Then what are you going to do?" Leah gasped. "Knock us around, Luis? There are cameras everywhere. You're just going to end up back in jail."

Tightening his grip, he shoved her back against the rows of canned soup, face flushing deep red with anger. "It'll be worth it."

"You think so?"

He didn't answer, eyes darting back and forth, keeping watch on either end of their aisle, waiting for Wyatt.

"Oh, that's right," Leah gasped, baiting him a little more, despite all her instincts telling her to stop, "it doesn't matter because your secret dad will just bail you out again, right? There's one little problem, though—Roy's about to be in the cell next to you. Can't exactly help you from there, can he?"

Luis turned a bit white around the gills, then roared with rage. He shoved Leah to the floor and lunged for her. "You little fucking cu—"

She covered her head and braced for an impact that never came.

At the sound of a scuffle, she cracked one eye to find Joe crouching near her shoulder, reaching to help her sit up. Wyatt was wrestling with Luis a few feet away.

Only now did several employees come skidding into the aisle, led by the store manager and a panting security guard— summoned by the ruckus, or the cameras, or perhaps other customers, any or all of whom had taken their sweet damn time to help her.

"You. Call 911," Joe barked, pointing at the manager, then pressing on Leah's shoulder to keep her from getting to her feet.

"This man assaulted my wife," Wyatt growled, giving Luis a shake. A dark silicone stripe on his finger caught Leah's eye, and the tears welling on her lashes began to spill over.

Like her, he was still wearing his wedding ring. Because he loved her.

And right that second, she knew without a doubt she loved him back.

She had to tell him. *Immediately.*

"Wyatt."

"Don't worry, you still have plenty of time before you need to go get Teddy," Joe assured her.

"No, I know," she told him. She tried again, "Wyatt!"

"You okay, babe? Joe, is she—?"

Luis kept struggling, and she worried that Wyatt didn't have as good of a grip on him as he thought he did. If she distracted him, things could get out of hand again.

Wyatt yelled at the manager, who was still frozen in shock, watching the proceedings. "Call the goddamn cops!"

Joe held her in place as Wyatt grappled with Luis, trying to subdue him. He'd pinned one arm behind his back and gotten him into a headlock, flushed with anger and hissing something in his ear—when Leah noticed the sudden glint in Luis's free hand.

Joe must've seen it too, because right as she gasped, "Knife," he pushed her behind him and surged toward the fray.

He was too late, though—Luis buried the blade in Wyatt's arm with a quick upward jerk.

He growled in annoyance as bright red blood bloomed on the skin below his sleeve, and did something with his foot that sent Luis facedown on the scuffed linoleum in a moment. Wyatt pinned the guy's arms behind his back and sat on his legs.

Luis howled with fury, trying to buck him off—but somehow Wyatt stayed put. Very casually, Joe leaned down and bent his wrist until it cracked, and the knife fell from his grasp.

He kicked it out of reach and gradually, Luis quit fighting.

"I had him," Wyatt complained.

"Oh, okay. So, why'd you let him stick you?"

Wyatt rolled his eyes and looked for Leah. "You're okay," he said when he found her. "Everything's okay now."

She couldn't take her eyes off that spreading stain on his arm, soaking into the cotton of his t-shirt and pooling in the crease of his elbow.

"You think she's safe?" Luis sputtered. "She's not *safe*. We'll get to her *and* that fucking kid, and you won't even see it coming. And when we're done with her, no man on earth is gonna want to touch that—"

Wyatt palmed the back of Luis's head and banged it against the floor, and Luis went limp.

"That's one way to do it," Joe commented.

Leah gripped her mouth in her hand and tried to hold in…tears or a scream, she wasn't sure. Something big was building in her throat and all she knew was that if she let it out, she might not be able to stop.

Wyatt's eyes burned green as the heart of a wave as he stared at her.

"No one will get to you. Do you hear me, Leah? They will never, *never* get past me. I will stand between you and the fucking apocalypse if I have to, but I will keep both of you safe."

A shaky breath escaped between her fingers, and she forced herself to move her hand away. "I know," she told him.

Tears slipped down her cheeks, and she realized…she *did* know.

She believed him.

She also loved him, more than she'd ever loved another human being besides Teddy. And she had yet to tell him.

Bodies flooded the aisle, legs and feet all around her as voices battled above her head. Joe yelled over them, taking charge.

Leah crawled toward Wyatt and tried to hold his gaze. "I love you," she said, but someone stepped between them, blocking her.

"Wyatt?" she cried, desperate for him to hear before that blood pouring from his arm made listening a problem. "Wyatt!"

The store's manager and the security guard murmured to each other with their hands on their hips, seeming unsure of what to do next. The stock guys were happy to follow Joe's lead, and eagerly hauled a groggy Luis to his feet and restrained him while Joe patted him down.

She shuffled past them to Wyatt, who'd propped himself awkwardly against some cans as he peered at his wound.

It looked even worse up close. In the face of all that blood, Leah forgot what she'd been about to say.

"Give me your belt," she ordered.

Wyatt glanced up and his brows knit together. He seemed surprised to see her. "I don't have one."

She scanned the waists near them, but even the security guard, in his black and gray uniform, wasn't wearing one.

She was going to have to use her shirt. Leah pulled it from her jeans and started unbuttoning, and Wyatt's eyes went wide.

"No," he squawked. "No, use mine." Before she could argue, he peeled it off his good arm and worked it down the bleeding one.

Was the blood flowing harder now? *Possibly.*

Leah snatched the warm cotton from his hand and wrapped it around his bicep, pulling it tight. There wasn't enough material to tie a knot.

His eye twitched just a little, but she knew the wound must hurt.

"Sorry," she whispered, putting all her strength into the compression.

Her tears kept coming, wetting her collar.

With his good hand, Wyatt stroked her hair off her face and wiped her cheek. "It's okay," he told her. "I'm okay."

"There's so much blood."

"Just a flesh wound."

She glared at him. "You are not quoting Monty Python right now. Absolutely not."

"'Tis but a scratch," he grinned.

Leah examined him, from his gorgeous thick brown hair to his twinkling jade green eyes, to his tanned skin and broad chest.

Wyatt wasn't breathing hard, or even pale.

He looked as gorgeous as ever, for crying out loud.

Leah sat back and threw his bloody shirt at him. "Are you kidding me? You're really fine?"

He balled up his t-shirt and pressed it to his arm, but he kept smiling. "Almost definitely."

"Unbelievable."

"What were you trying to tell me before?" he wondered. "I heard you calling me, but—"

The store manager approached and handed Leah her purse. "The cops should be here any minute. Ambulance is also on the way."

"I don't need it," Wyatt said, at the same time Leah spoke over him, "That's great. Thank you."

"Can I get you guys anything? Water? Or, uh—" He took in Wyatt's improvised dressing and gestured toward the pharmacy at the back of the store, which appeared to be shuttered for lunch. "Some bandages or something?"

"All good. Thanks, man," Wyatt smiled.

Leah rolled her eyes, exasperated. "Where's Joe?" Maybe his buddy would know what to do with him, because she sure didn't.

Wyatt tipped his chin down the aisle where Joe was talking rapidly into his phone and keeping his eyes trained on Luis, held immobile between a couple of stockers.

He glanced toward them and gave them a cursory nod.

Guess he wasn't worried either.

She took a few even breaths and sat back on her butt.

"Leah?" Wyatt wondered again. "Tell me what you were trying to say before."

The police arrived at the end of the aisle, and following them, a couple of EMTs hauling bags of gear.

She couldn't picture any setting less romantic than this one to confess her undying love, but then Wyatt fished around on the floor next to him and handed her a can.

Teddy's ravioli.

"For his lunch," he explained softly, as she took it from his hand. "He's been a total trooper, lately."

Leah laughed through the tears that started up with a vengeance again.

"I love you," she blurted out. "So much."

Wyatt's throat bobbed, and his eyes looked a little misty—though she supposed it could've been a symptom of blood loss.

He grinned wider, though, and told her, "I know."

Chapter Thirty-Five

Wyatt

LEAH WAS STILL sputtering indignantly at his joke when Joe leaned down to get their attention.

"Stitch, I've gotta steal your girl for a bit," he said. "The EMT wants to look her over and she has to make a quick statement to the cops, and then we need to go get Teddy."

Leah jolted and looked at her watch, as if she'd lost track of time. "Shit—"

"It's all good, we got time," Joe assured her. "We'll pick him up, I'll bring you guys home, and then I'll come back up to get this guy."

Leah turned back to Wyatt, anxiety etched into her expression. "You're not coming?"

Joe helped her to her feet and answered for him—which he ordinarily wouldn't like but in this case was probably a good thing, since he was starting to feel a *touch* queasy.

"Docs are going to transport him to the hospital. They need to make sure nothing important got nicked before they stitch up that nonregulation air hole he's sporting."

"I thought you said you were okay," Leah accused him.

"I'm fine, I promise. I'll be home before you know it."

She glared at Wyatt like she'd smelled a rat. "Joe, you should stay with him. I can drive myself."

He caught Joe's eye and sent him a *look*, receiving an impatient eye roll in response. But hey, at least they were on the same page.

"Sure, you can," Bruiser told her. "I'll just tag along for funsies, how about that." And then he simply led a compliant Leah away, like it was easy-peasy to convince the woman of any damn thing.

Wyatt gave her a chipper wave when she looked back at him. Joe would keep her safe, there was no doubt about that.

Joe, who had undergone some kind of fascinating transformation today. He looked notably alert—more than he had in months. It was almost as if…as if having Leah and Teddy around to protect had brought a part of him back to life.

Wyatt wasn't picking up any whiff of lovelorn competition, it wasn't that. It felt more like having someone smaller to look after had given Joe purpose.

He readjusted his position as the grocery aisle took a lazy spin around his head. Maybe they needed to get Bruiser a dog, or something. Perhaps a goldfish. A plant. Start small.

A whole girlfriend of his own felt like a bridge too far.

Wyatt rested his head against the boxes and cans behind him, keeping his shirt pressed against his seeping bicep until another cop and a medic crouched next to him. He'd explore the dog idea once this whole mess was over.

Perhaps there was a path to Joe's recovery in there somewhere. At this point, God knew, he was willing to try anything.

WHEN JOE PICKED him up from the hospital a couple of hours later, he was alone, and Wyatt was relieved. His arm was sporting a dressing the size of a small throw pillow to cover his stitches, and he didn't want Leah or Ted to be alarmed.

That went double when an orderly insisted on wheeling him outside like an invalid.

Thankfully, Joe was the type to merely shake his head at the spectacle, and crack the passenger side of Wyatt's car to usher him inside like the world's surliest chauffeur.

"Thanks for grabbing my car," Wyatt told him, once he'd rounded the hood and gotten behind the wheel.

"Thank Buck," Joe commented, checking the mirrors before pulling into the hospital's turnaround. "He's who gave me a lift to the store once Leah and Ted got settled at home."

"Are they doing okay?" Wyatt had tried to keep Leah updated on his status but at some point, her replies had slowed, then dropped off altogether.

"Seem to be. Teddy was napping when I left. Leah said she might try to close her eyes, too. The adrenaline crash probably wasn't much fun for her."

Wyatt nodded, but he couldn't fully relax until he got eyes on her himself. He knew she'd act stoic in front of Teddy and their roommates, even if she was freaking out. Because of that, the ride back felt interminable, and the rush hour traffic coupled with Joe's sedate driving didn't help matters.

When they finally made it home Joe was ready to disown him, and Wyatt's impatience was in the red zone. Neither of them expected to walk into what appeared to be an incipient dinner party.

In short order, he spotted platters piled with food lined up on the counter, Buck positioned in front of the TV with a full plate on his lap, and Bennett making his way down the row, loading up his own.

"Hey guys," Noah greeted them. "I hope you don't mind. I thought people might be hungry after the day you had."

Wyatt's stomach growled hollowly as he surveyed the spread and the heady scents of bread, lemon, and oregano hit his nose.

It seemed Arkman had reheated the leftovers from Leah's postponed Greek feast and laid them out buffet-style on the island. He'd even opened a couple of bottles of wine Leah must've bought for the occasion.

Wyatt squeezed his eyes shut and inhaled deeply. "I could kiss you right now," he said.

"Dude, seriously," Joe agreed, tossing aside his keys and grabbing a plate. "How many more ways can you find to save the day?"

"At least a few," Buck called from the couch. He pointed the remote at the TV and flipped through channels. "Monroe just texted me. Grab some grub and come see this."

On the news, an anchor gazed soberly into the camera as he read:

> *"A historic vote in the Senate today, as expulsion proceedings get underway to vacate a senator's seat, and pave the way for an emergency election for his replacement.*
>
> *Texas senator Roy Doggett was quietly placed under arrest days ago, charged with involvement in a human trafficking organization tied to at least two U.S. Army bases. Sources on the Hill tell us the Congressional proceedings are expected to move quickly, as the preponderance of evidence incriminating the senator leaves little doubt that Doggett will serve an extended sentence behind bars.*
>
> *Executives at a Doggett family company called Linedance Holdings have also reportedly retained counsel, as the firm's position at the epicenter of the criminal organization comes into focus.*
>
> *In addition, a spokesperson at the Federal Bureau of Investigation confirms that Senator Doggett may also be facing charges related to last year's ill-fated skirmish in Nabarut, Qahat—a dramatic turn of events after the senator publicly lobbied to pin the tragedies of that day on the team of Navy SEALs tasked with his and his family's extraction from the area.*

> *Viewers may remember that the subsequent trial of his stepson, Daniel Cox, led to allegations of back-door weapons deals and speculation that the family could have been enriching themselves at the expense of taxpayers for years thanks to Senator Doggett's position on the Armed Services Committee.*
>
> *Sources tell us that Homeland Security and the IRS may therefore play a role in future proceedings.*
>
> *When reached for comment, the senator's office called the proceedings a disgraceful miscarriage of justice and a political witch hunt that is destined to fail once all the facts come out."*

The split screen panned out to follow Roy as he sauntered through the crowd with a coterie of lawyers. He smiled and joked with members of the press and onlookers alike, as smug and smarmy as ever with his immaculate suit, deep tan, and pomaded salt-and-pepper hair.

"Looks like the pressure campaign worked," Joe commented, popping a Kalamata olive in his mouth as he came to stand next to Wyatt.

"So far, so good," Buck agreed.

As if he'd heard them, Doggett turned to mug for the cameras. He winked like he knew a delightful secret. Watching him move through the mass of people, he looked like he was attending a movie opening rather than being kicked out of Congress.

All of a sudden, Bennett shot to his feet. "Where are those girls, you son of a bitch?" he thundered. "Where are those goddamn girls!"

Wyatt took a deep breath and stepped forward. "Whoa there, Tex. Slow your roll. I got a kid sleeping down the hall, man."

"Yeah, Easy," Joe agreed. "Shut your mouth. What the hell?"

Bennett ran a hand through his hair, making his pale blond strands stick up at odd angles.

"I hate that they know we're looking for them," he argued, eyes a little wild. "No matter what we do, they're just going to keep moving them. Like it's a game."

"We don't know that," Buck said grimly.

"No, we don't. And we're getting closer," Noah added. "I know it."

"And yet, we might've found those kids by now, if I hadn't given up the goods when we busted Dan," Bennett argued.

Buck pulled him back down to sit again. "Not your fault."

"I know," Bennett nodded. "I guess. I just hate that look on his face. Did Dan learn that from him? Does assholery run in the family or something?"

Buck shrugged. "Seems to."

"Interestingly," Noah chimed in, chewing on a mouthful of food as his fingers flew across his laptop's keyboard. "It looks like Roy was arrested in Dallas, but he wasn't there in an official capacity, as far as I can tell. His schedule had him in DC at a fundraiser."

Joe glanced at Wyatt. "So…did someone tip him off this was coming?"

"Possibly. Which means maybe he was out there getting some ducks in a row."

"Threatening witnesses in person," Wyatt suggested, heading for the buffet before something else could waylay him.

"Or, giving the order to move some women around again," Bennett argued miserably.

"Alright, focus up," Buck commanded. "What's done is done. Now that this ball is rolling, we have a very short window of time to lock it down before that asswipe posts bail. What needs to happen next?"

Naturally, Leah chose that moment to wander out of Wyatt's room, looking groggy and a little disoriented. She sagged in relief when she saw him, and marched straight over.

When she spotted the spread laid across the counters, he wondered if she might cry.

"I have never been more grateful to prior me in my life," she gasped.

Buck took advantage of the distraction to grip Bennett by the shoulders and force him to meet his eyes. "What's going on?" he murmured. "We talked about this. This is what we expected—what we wanted."

"I know. I guess it just happened faster than I expected."

"Which underlines the fact that those agencies were probably already working their own cases against him. This guy's a stain, Ben. He needed to be taken down."

"I know," Easy agreed glumly. "I just thought…I hoped we'd be able to find those girls before Roy went down. Now they're going to have them hidden so deep we may never—"

"Don't think like that," Joe said, glancing at Leah before going over. "We're finding new leads to follow all the time. Hell, I bet Noah has ideas up his sleeve he hasn't even told us about yet."

All eyes turned to Noah, carefully choosing morsels off his plate and chewing them with marked focus. He looked up, startled, and pushed up his glasses. "I do," he nodded. "Yesterday, I—"

"I heard yelling," Leah whispered to Wyatt, getting his attention. "What happened? Is everything okay?"

"Sorry about that," Bennett sheepishly called over. "Got carried away watching the news."

She blinked a couple of times and turned to scan the TV, but the anchor had moved on to a new segment.

"Senator Doggett was arrested," Wyatt explained. "Probably getting kicked out of Congress as we speak."

Her mouth dropped open. "Whoa."

"Fuck around and find out," he shrugged.

Leah sighed and looked down, too tired, apparently, for pithy observations. "How's your arm?"

"Okay. They gave me a few stitches. It's still numb for now. I need to eat so I can take something before it wears off all the way."

"And on that note," Joe announced loudly, "how about some recognition for this woman's culinary efforts, huh? She cooked her ass off for us, and I, for one, am super grateful."

All at once, Leah seemed to notice the plates everyone was holding. An enthusiastic cheer rose up, rousing, yet respectfully low in volume. Wyatt wrapped his good arm around her back and kissed her temple.

Leah grinned and flushed an adorable pink, demurring, "I hope it's okay. It's been in the fridge for a few days."

"Everything is delicious," he assured her. "And today might be an even better day for it than what we planned. Thank you."

She scanned the counters, looking impressed by the carnage. "You guys have done some damage."

"But we saved some for you and Teddy. Get a plate. Let's eat."

"In a minute. Let me just find something before Teddy wakes up." She stuck her head in the pantry, rummaging around. "Where did it go—?"

"What are you looking for?" he asked. "We don't need more food. Trust me."

"I had wine—"

"We got the wine," he assured her.

She poked her head out and Buck saluted her from the couch with a plastic cup. "We are enjoying the wine," he smiled. "Peyton's going to be so mad she missed this."

"Oh, shoot." She fluttered her hands and darted back to the counter. "I'll make her a plate. What does she like?"

"Doggy bags can wait," Wyatt chuckled. "Come sit with me first. You need to eat."

Leah blinked and exhaled, then took another few steadying breaths. "You're right. I'm…I'm hungry. I should eat."

Once he had her settled at the table with a fork in her hand, Wyatt asked, "How are you?" He kept his voice low, not wanting to invite the others into their conversation. "Luis got pretty rough with you. Are you okay?"

"I'm fine," she said. "Might have a few bruises tomorrow but nothing too bad. What happened to him?"

"Back in the slammer and not getting out. Violated his parole, obviously. We won't be hearing from him for a while." Wyatt took a bite of souvlaki and wanted to moan in bliss. "Haven't heard a peep from Biddy, and now Roy is out of commission, too. For the time being, at least."

"Wow, okay." She eyed him with wide eyes. "So, we have…"

He nodded. "We have a reprieve. For now, at least."

Leah gazed fondly at the guys gathered in front of the TV stuffing their faces, but after a minute her expression clouded over. "Which means Teddy and I absolutely need to find our own place."

"Leah, there's no rush. You're more than welcome here. Wait to find someplace you really love."

Her eyes drifted to his, troubled in a way he didn't like.

She nodded, but Wyatt knew. His plan needed to finish up. *Soon.*

THE NEXT MORNING, the team visited the county lockup where Luis Flores, predictably, stonewalled them like the punk he was.

They didn't want to give him too much information about where their investigation was going next, and he resolutely refused to tell them anything they didn't already know about where it'd been.

They were getting nowhere, so Wyatt got to his feet to leave, irritated that he'd wasted so much time there when he could've been home with Leah and Teddy.

"Catch ya later, Flores," he called over his shoulder.

At Buck's nod, the guards hauled Luis to his feet and pulled him toward the doors behind him.

Joe snorted as he resisted. "Or not."

Luis wrenched around, laughing maniacally as the guards held his arms. "You guys really are as dumb as you look, aren't you?" he exclaimed. "You thought my dad was the worst you had to worry about? My fucking *grandma?* Good luck with that. They're a cakewalk compared to what's heading for you."

The guards rolled their eyes and carted him off, no doubt used to the empty threats of hotheaded prisoners in cuffs.

Still, Luis's rant raised some questions, and as the doors swung shut with a decisive clang, they all looked askance at each other.

"Not a word," Buck instructed. "Out in the parking lot. Right now."

In the bright, late morning sun, Joe was the first to scoff, "He's BSing us. Right?"

"That wasn't bullshit," Bennett grumbled.

"Then who's he talking about?"

"Azevedo is up for promotion," Noah reported in a rush. "Rumor has it that he's angling for SecDef, or maybe Chairman of the Joint Chiefs. Flores could mean him." He adjusted his glasses, and gazed across the lot, looking pensive. "Before we strike at him, though, I think there are targets closer to home we should look at."

Buck frowned, eyeing him quizzically. "Such as?"

"Roy's missus and his big brother," Bennett guessed.

"Lena and Leon, the terrible twosome," Wyatt groaned.

"That's right," Noah agreed. "Let's get 'em."

Chapter Thirty-Six

Leah

"HEY, THAT LOOKS nice. What's that one?"

Leah looked up from her laptop to find that Wyatt had set aside his tablet to peer intently at her screen.

"So far out of my price range it's a joke," she sighed.

They were supposed to be getting work done while Teddy napped, but neither of them was having much success. She'd been ogling mansions on a realty website for at least fifteen minutes, and she knew for a fact Wyatt kept getting pulled away from the Doggett indictment he was supposed to be reading and into the hockey game playing on the muted TV.

She scrolled down to one of the spectacular rooftop photos and tilted her computer so he could see better. "Can you imagine living here, though? It'd be so cool waking up to that view every day."

"Maybe you could swing it if you had a roommate."

Leah scoffed, "Would that roommate be a tech billionaire? Because that's the only way it would work."

He motioned for her laptop with a little smile. "Come on, hand it over. Let me see this place."

She snapped her computer closed and set it out of reach on the side table. "There's no point."

Wyatt swiveled sideways, pulling up one knee and resting his arm along the back of the couch, giving up any pretense of caring about work as he faced her. "You've been going to see a lot of apartments this week."

Leah nodded glumly. This was probably the part where he explained—kindly, because he was, after all, Wyatt—that he was tired of them crowding the apartment with all their stuff. Or maybe that one of his roommates had been complaining about having a little kid underfoot all the time.

They'd all undoubtedly begun wondering what was taking her so long to find a place. Hell, she'd been wondering the same thing. But the notion that any of them might want to be rid of her and Teddy still kind of stung. She thought they'd been getting along. Becoming friends, even.

She'd gotten too comfortable, though. She knew that. Any minute now, Wyatt was going to delicately ask how soon they'd be moving out.

"Have you seen anything you like?"

Here it comes. Except, when Leah peeked at him to confirm her suspicions, she was startled by the vulnerability she saw, just for a second, flicker in his face. Wyatt was…nervous?

A tiny ember of hope—that had flared to life sometime in the last few weeks and despite her best efforts at self-preservation refused to be extinguished—burned brighter in her chest.

Maybe she had this all wrong. Maybe he didn't want her to leave. Maybe he was worried she *would.*

So, Leah took a risk and shrugged. "Not really. They all feel so depressing."

Wyatt made an awkward little sound in his throat and eyed her curiously. The expression didn't quite sit right on his face, though, like it was masking what he really felt.

A swirl of complicated emotion made her lungs lock up. She couldn't decide what he was hiding. She couldn't decide if she could handle whatever it was.

"What's wrong with them?" he asked.

"Nothing really," Leah admitted. "I thought I would know it when I saw it, but they've all been so small. No character. Nothing particularly charming or welcoming, I guess."

"I think that part probably comes when you move your stuff in and bring it to life. Make it familiar."

"Yeah, that's the other problem. The places I've seen so far can't fit my furniture. I'm going to have to leave half our stuff in storage, I think. Or sell it. I don't know."

He reared back with a troubled frown. "You don't want to do that."

"I might have to," she groaned, frustrated. "I don't know what I was expecting. It's not like I'm going to find anything like we had before. I just wanted to get close, you know? I wanted Teddy to have some continuity after all the disruption. Something that felt like home."

"I mean…there's no rush, right? He seems like he's happy here. You do, too."

Leah watched his face as he spoke, and didn't see one ounce of prevarication. He meant what he was saying, she just wished she knew where he was heading with his questions.

She should've come right out and asked. Instead, she said, "Yeah, but I think we need more structure. Our routine has been completely off the rails."

"Ours too," he grinned, undeniably pleased.

Leah bit her lip, fighting a smile of her own. "Don't worry— I'll decide on something soon. You won't have to deal with our chaos for too much longer."

Why did hope feel like such a dangerous rebellion? She ought to be giddy, but instead, she felt like her toes were hanging off the edge of a perilous ravine. It made her furious, but also determined.

"No, that's…" Wyatt's brows knit together in consternation. "…that's not what I meant."

"It's okay. We'll be out of your hair soon." She patted his knee.

Wyatt looked a little panicked. "Wait. Just…" he stopped, closed his eyes, and took a deep breath. "Just don't make a final decision until you finish the scavenger hunt. Okay? You're almost to the end and you can choose then."

Leah tilted her head, perplexed. "What does that have to do with—"

He gripped her hand. "Promise me."

"Okay…?"

"How many notes are you up to so far?"

"You don't know?"

"Just tell me." His big green eyes zeroed in on hers, intense. Searching.

"Um…" Leah glanced away as she thought. "Five with today's, I think?"

"You found today's note?"

She pulled the scrap of paper from her pocket, on which he'd written:

> *Maybe because we were always meant to be.*
> *(I'll hand you the next note when you're ready.)*

"How many more are there?" Leah wondered.

"Just a few." His expression shuttered, giving nothing away.

Wyatt played with her hand absently, then held them up palm to palm, smiling at the difference in size. All at once, he flipped her hand around and tapped her faux engagement ring.

"Never thought I'd say it, but I'm getting used to this. I like it." His expression went soft.

How could someone so lethal be such a softie?

Leah smiled. "It's kind of ridiculous, but I do, too. I hope it doesn't bother you that I keep wearing it. I know the cat's out of the bag now."

"No, I like it."

He slid the "diamond" off her finger and slipped it onto his index finger, lips quirking as he turned it this way and that, catching the light.

"It doesn't even clear your knuckle," she laughed.

"Nope." He handed it back to her, but didn't try to put it on her. Thank God for that—Leah wasn't sure she could've held it together if he'd pulled the "I Do" move on her.

Wyatt waited until she looked at him again, then tipped his chin toward her laptop. "We should go look at that place later. Just for fun. Based on those photos, there's no one living there right now, so it should be easy to get into."

Leah snorted. "What, so I can fall more in love with a place I can't have?"

"No, but we could look at the neighborhood and stuff. Maybe we'll see other places in the area that aren't listed yet."

"I don't know. Don't you have to work?"

It felt like the exact opposite of what she was supposed to be doing, but suddenly, she wanted nothing more.

"It's pretty dense reading. I could use a break. Besides, what's there to lose?" he prodded. "Worst case scenario, we can spend the afternoon playing on the beach with Teddy after we're done. He loves that. And—" He leaned closer, eyes pleading and charming her into agreement, "I haven't gone with you to see any of these places. I want to see some."

"Except this—" Leah tapped her laptop, "—isn't reality. This is fantasy." *Once a mom, always a mom*, she supposed. *Would she ever be fun and spontaneous again?*

"Just make the appointment. I'm invested now," he declared.

"What do you care? You have a place to live."

"I care because I want the woman I love to be happy."

Leah's air supply somehow got mixed up with her salivary system, and she choked and coughed like a dork for a couple of minutes. When she could breathe again, she told him, "Oh, wow. You said that, alright."

"Sure did. What of it?" He looked smug and adorable, and she was completely, utterly screwed.

"Um. Well, what time were you thinking of going?"

"Good save," he laughed, leaping up. "Let's go after Teddy wakes up. This is going to be great. You'll see."

WYATT CHECKED HIS phone a few times as they said their goodbyes to the real estate agent who'd met them at the house, then again as he walked the lady across the quiet street to her car.

Leah bounced Teddy on her hip and kissed his temple, frowning at Wyatt's pensive expression. Something was up, but it couldn't be the house tour they'd just had. That had gone swimmingly, exactly as fun as he'd promised it would be.

When the woman pulled away, he pasted a smile on his face and jogged back, turning so Teddy could clamber onto him to ride piggyback.

"You have been very polite this afternoon," he told him. "You ready to go play now?"

Teddy bobbed with excitement. "Yeah!"

Her son *had* been good, Leah mused. He'd been wide-eyed and sweet as they'd been led from room to room, and it'd been hard not to envision how happy he'd be to grow up in a place like this. Maybe someday, she thought…in a parallel universe, or alternate reality where money was no object.

Too bad she seemed to have a thing for military men. She could've been out there haunting the Silicon Valley happy hours, and securing her and Teddy's (probably eventually unhappy) future.

Wyatt double-checked that his car was locked, then left it in the driveway and set off down the sidewalk. "Okay, let's go! Beach is this way."

Leah caught up and waited for Teddy to get distracted by a passing motorcycle before quietly asking Wyatt, "What's going on? And don't say nothing because it's obviously something."

His sidelong glance was wry. "You remember my boss, Tate? You met him at Bucks barbecue."

"Yeah, of course. He was nice. His wife was, too."

"Well…" He took a deep breath, then let it out. "He asked if he could come meet us. He wants to talk to you."

"Me? Why?"

"Nothing bad. You do have some shared acquaintances, though." Leah stared at his hands, dwarfing her son's little shins as they bounced against his chest.

And all at once it hit her. The man who'd started the company Wyatt worked for—the man leading their investigation into the ambush in Nabarut, where her husband and brother had been killed—had also been a part of Echo Company. He hadn't been a part of the fighting, and she hadn't recognized him at Buck and Peyton's barbecue, but Tate Monroe had most likely known Jesse and Theo. Maybe well.

How had that never registered with her before?

"Oh." Words felt like foreign things. "What does he want?"

"I don't know. He just said he's been meaning to catch you since that party, and I guess he was up this way tonight." Wyatt peeked down at her warily. "I didn't plan this. You can say no if you don't want to. I'll put him off."

Leah shook her head. "No, it's fine. I'll see him. Just…stay close, okay? I don't know what to expect, and if it's something crazy, I just—"

"I won't let you out of my sight," he promised. "But Tate's a good dude. You'll see."

WYATT PERFORMED A casual introduction when the man strolled up to them on the sand several minutes later, saying genially, "Tate, you remember Leah. Leah, my boss, Tate."

"Hi, nice to see you again." She kept her tone neutral, not sure what this was about.

Tate smiled warmly, though, as warm as he had at that barbecue. "Hopefully also his friend."

"That too," Wyatt smirked, then added importantly, "And *this* is Teddy. Teddy, do you remember Mr. Monroe? His wife Lyla was the lady who gave you popsicles at that party we all went to."

Teddy nodded solemnly, clearly hoping there'd be more today—but it was the pride etched across Wyatt's face that made Leah's heart hopscotch under her ribs. *Oh, God.*

Teddy hung off his arm like he was on a jungle gym, unaffected by her bout of nerves.

"Okay if we walk and talk for a bit?" Tate asked her. "I promise I won't steal you for long."

"Sure," she agreed. "As long as we can stay within eyesight." She swallowed around her dry throat. "Kids and water, you know."

Tate glanced at Wyatt, but his smile didn't falter. "Right." He beckoned her to follow him and took a couple of easy steps.

Leah glanced back at her boys.

"Mommy going?" Teddy gripped Wyatt around the neck, trusting him implicitly.

"No, she's not leaving," he answered tranquilly. "They're just going to talk for a minute. Let's go put our feet in the water while we wait for them."

She watched them amble toward the surf, startling when Tate appeared beside her.

"Sorry," she told him sheepishly.

"He's really good with him."

She nodded, even though she was unsure who he meant by "he." It didn't really matter, as both options were true.

Tate waited for her to turn away, then slowly strolled next to her along the hard-packed ridge above the waterline. "Listen, I know this is a bit overdue, and I'm not sure anyone has shared this coincidence, but I served with your brother in Echo Company. Before the skirmish. I wasn't there," he clarified quickly, "I was benched for a TBI a few months before."

"I knew you were in Echo," Leah said. "I didn't remember you weren't part of the ambush."

"It's why I started my company, and why I hired Wyatt and his buddies. But I don't mean to imply more of a connection than there really was. Tank and I weren't best friends, nothing like that."

"He was a lot," Leah smiled, "Even for his family."

"True," Tate grinned, "But that's what made him great. And I guess what I wanted to say is that, even though he and I weren't the closest of buddies, we were still brothers. You know? We went through some stuff together, and even after I was sidelined, we still tried to look out for each other. Family's like that, right?"

Leah nodded, a little numb as an onslaught of new emotion threatened to swamp her. "A lot of you came by in the weeks after the funeral. I can't remember if you…"

"I didn't. I was still dealing with a head injury, and I was working a job in New York that went a little haywire."

"Ah."

"I would've reached out if I could've. But life is funny—it put us in each other's path anyway. Like it was meant to happen."

She smiled, his rueful demeanor and the echo of Wyatt's own words putting her more at ease. "Yeah, I guess that's true."

"I'm very grateful you decided to share Tank's voicemail with Wyatt and the team. I know that couldn't have been easy, but it's going to help a ton in nailing some of the assholes responsible for the ambush. They're bad dudes, and they need to be stopped."

"I really hope that's true."

"It is," Tate assured her. "And I have to say, if you really think about it, your brother was like my brother, so that kind of makes us brother and sister too."

She laughed as he nudged her. "That's a bit more of a stretch than…"

"So, as your surrogate brother, I should definitely weigh in on this thing between you and Oaks. Since you obviously need my advice and all."

She smacked his arm, exactly like she would've done with Theo. In a weird way, they *were* sort of similar. "I do not recall asking for or needing any such thing."

"Just go with it."

"Wow, so you're really …"

He waved her off with a grin. "Wyatt's a great guy, Leah. The best of the best. I just wanted you to know. You've been through a lot, and if you're thinking of trying to make a go of it with him, I'll back you however I can."

"And if I'm not?"

He stopped and looked back to where Teddy and Wyatt were playing in the surf. "I'd support that, too, if I thought it was what you really wanted."

"I see."

"I don't think that's what you want, though."

She smirked at his lordly tone. "Theo always used to try and tell me what I was thinking, too."

"I believe brothers are supposed to be universally annoying. It's on page ten in the handbook."

THEY SAT AND talked for a while, sharing stories and memories and making plans to stay in touch so he could share photos he had of Theo with her and her parents. Despite his efforts, though, it didn't feel like she had her brother back.

However, it did feel as if he'd maybe sent her a friend.

When they eventually headed back, Wyatt and Teddy were crouched in the sand, building a lumpy, lopsided sandcastle.

As they approached, they heard Wyatt explain, "Well, Mr. Monroe knew your Uncle Theo in the army."

"Oh."

"Do you miss him sometimes?"

Teddy nodded, not noticing their arrival as he patted more mud on the pile. "He's Mommy's big brother," he explained.

"That's true. Your uncle, your mom's brother, and your grandma and grandpa's son. All at the same time."

"Are you a big brother?" Teddy wondered.

"Nope. Just me, no brothers or sisters, big or little."

Her son said in a small voice, "Me too. I'm not a big brother either."

She and Tate glanced at each other, and he looked like he'd just watched the cutest baby animal video ever made. Leah wanted to laugh—if she could bottle her kid's aww factor, she'd make a fortune.

Wyatt cocked his head as he watched Teddy poke at the sand with a stick. "But you could be," he told him. "Someday. Do you think you'd like that?"

Teddy stopped jabbing and got a faraway look as he considered it. After a while, he smiled and nodded. Then, he caught sight of her and Tate, dropped his stick, and barreled over to her.

"Mommy!"

Tate shot her an amused look, clapped Wyatt on the back, and said his goodbyes.

Leah held Teddy on her hip and looked Wyatt over. "Giving him a younger sibling already?"

"Oh, you heard that?" he smiled. When she nodded, he hedged, "I only said it in the most general way."

"Oh, you did, huh?"

He wrapped his fingers around hers and set off down the beach. "Yeah, his mom's kind of skittish. I have to be careful and play my cards right, or she might kick me to the curb."

"We wouldn't want that."

"No, we really wouldn't."

Leah set Teddy down to walk on his own, but he must've been getting tired and hungry because the protest was immediate. Before it could escalate, Wyatt swooped him up and set him on his shoulders, like it was the most natural thing in the world.

He laced his fingers with hers and kept walking, scanning the beach with a contented expression as they wandered back toward the stairs that would lead them up to street level.

"I have to admit," she said carefully, reluctant to upset their peaceful little bubble. "I kind of wondered if you might lose interest once your job settled down."

Wyatt side-eyed her.

"Well, the senator's in jail now, and so is Luis. Maybe you don't need us anymore."

"Is that something you actually believe or is it something you're using to shield against potential hurt?" he asked pointedly.

"Ouch. When you say it like that—"

"The thing is, we can't predict the future," Wyatt explained. "I can't promise I will never make mistakes, any more than you can. And life, as we know, is full of ups and downs. But to live in fear of what *might* happen…" He shrugged, and his green eyes burned with conviction. "That's no kind of life at all."

Leah studied him, then looked up at Teddy, hands in the air and giggling as he tried to reach for a seagull circling high over his head.

"You're right," she agreed.

"All we can do is try, Leah," he said more gently. "And I want to. Plain and simple. I want to more than anything else on this planet."

They went a little farther before angling inland, heading for the weathered wood access stairs that would lead them up to the street.

"Wyatt." She pulled him to a stop and looked into his face, and for a second she could see it, the three of them standing exactly there, Teddy on his shoulders, her with a new baby in her arms, the four of them a family.

Her heart skipped, and she had to catch her breath before she could tell him, "Wyatt, I want that, too."

Eyes soft, he pulled a note from his pocket and handed it to her, then started climbing the stairs.

Leah unfolded it.

With your permission, I'm going to spend the rest of my life proving it to you.
(Find your next clue behind my TV.)

Chapter Thirty-Seven

Wyatt

WYATT SMOOTHED OUT the note he'd written for Leah, spreading it open next to his leg. He still needed to hide it, but he couldn't. Not quite yet.

Last night, he'd written it quickly, and his handwriting wasn't the best. The message, however, was as clear as could be.

Tomorrow at 6 pm, drive to the house we toured and park in the driveway if you want something that belongs to you.

(Don't worry, Kim and Bennett will stay with Teddy. They'll arrive at the apartment no later than 5:30.)

When he'd busted Leah looking at the realtor website yesterday, it'd been sheer impulse to suggest they go view the house she'd been mooning over. But she'd agreed, and they'd gone, and it'd been love at first sight for all of them. Later, on the beach, had been even better.

But now that Wyatt had to decide on the final piece of his plan, he couldn't determine if his biggest obstacle was a case of nerves or possible financial insolvency.

Noah appeared out of nowhere, silently walking behind the couch on his way to the kitchen. The guy was so freaking quiet, he'd assumed he was home alone. Wyatt snapped his laptop shut, though not fast enough it seemed.

Great.

"House hunting?" Noah wondered genially.

He shook his head, the eye-watering price tag of the tall, airy house up on the hill threatening to give him hives if he dwelled on it too long.

In the next instant, however, Wyatt thought about how they'd recently started calling Noah 'Arkman,' in homage to his biblical name and all the rescues he was prone to handing out. He'd made a habit of saving them from drowning, time and again.

Wyatt decided he could probably use a rescue right now. He was paralyzed with indecision, and the guy had come in pretty clutch the last time he'd needed advice.

"Actually, you have a minute?" he said. "Look at this and tell me what you think."

Noah finished cleaning his glasses on the tail of his shirt and put them back on. "So, you *are* house hunting."

"I don't know," Wyatt groaned. "Maybe I am. Shit's expensive, though."

He came over and plopped down beside him, taking the proffered computer and resting it on his knees. "La Jolla," he said, looking over the listing. "Not too shabby."

He shrugged. "I might've seen Leah ogling it yesterday."

"I see."

"Yeah."

"It's just funny because I'm pretty sure I also saw Leah looking at this place earlier this week."

"Doesn't surprise me," Wyatt nodded. "She's pretty taken with it."

"Except she's only made appointments to go see dinky little rental apartments."

He hadn't gone with her to any of those, but the thought of Leah and Teddy moving into one of them—moving out and away from him—felt grim.

He kept nodding. "Yeah, but I convinced her to go look at this one. Yesterday afternoon. Monroe came and met us after and now…"

Now he was sitting on his couch asking advice from a friend and coworker, instead of talking to Leah directly. Because apparently, he'd regressed back to high school.

"Something happen between you guys?"

Noah looked so freaking concerned, it was impossible to stonewall him. Wyatt threw up his hands in defeat, not really wanting to, anyway.

"I don't know. I thought things were going well with us. Really well. But then she started talking about moving out as soon as possible again, and I found myself feeling kind of…"

"Angry?" Noah scanned him, watching for his reaction. "Disappointed?"

"Hurt," Wyatt admitted. "I'm kind of hurt. I've tried to make sure they were comfortable and safe, and you guys have been going above and beyond to help with Ted, but she's acting like she can't wait to get away and it's making me doubt if I'm reading things right. Between us."

"I'm not sure I'd go that far," Noah frowned. "Leah probably just wants her own space again. She probably misses her stuff, and not having her kid a foot away every night. She's a mom crashing in a three-guy bachelor pad, which might work in a sitcom but can't be nearly as fun in real life."

"That's fair."

"Not exactly conducive to having a grownup relationship either, if you catch my drift."

God, that was the truth. Wyatt hadn't minded though. He thought they'd been making it work. But what if she didn't want to make it work?

"She could be sick of me, though. Sick of my job and my whole…life."

Noah's frown deepened. "Has she given you any indication of that?"

"Not really. But Leah plays things pretty close to the vest sometimes. She says she wants to make a go of it, but what if I'm reading too much into that? She has Teddy to think about, and if I push too hard, or too fast, she might decide they're better off on their own."

"She could also be ecstatic and gung-ho."

Wyatt stared at the TV, but didn't really see it. His whole over-the-top, crazy plan really depended on Leah being ecstatic and as Noah put it, *gung-ho*. If she wasn't, everything he was about to set into motion was going to drop out of the sky faster than a Hornet with two shot engines.

"You should probably talk to her," Noah explained sensibly. "Ask her directly what she's thinking. From what I've seen, she's probably more worried about being a burden than about leaving you in the dust."

Wyatt tested that theory, trying to weigh its probability against the worries his own insecurities kept tossing out.

After a moment or two, Noah gestured to the laptop. "Tell me about this house."

"It's a couple blocks from the beach, but it's up on the hill, so the views are great. And it's got this nice rooftop deck. Leah said it'd be like a dream having coffee up there every day."

"Can't argue with her there." He clicked through a few of the sales pictures.

Wyatt nodded. "It costs a fraction of what the neighboring places do, probably because it needs updating. There's also a weird separate apartment on the ground floor that I'm not sure could even be reintegrated into the main house."

Noah scrolled down, intently perusing the listing details. "You thinking of helping her get it? Or getting it for both of you?"

"I don't know." Wyatt reached over and took his computer back, tapping into his spreadsheet of finances again. "I've never bought anything this big before. Obviously. I'm trying to figure out if I can even afford it."

"Or if she'd want you to."

"That too."

Noah was quiet for a bit, pushing to his feet and heading into the kitchen, where making a sandwich soon took over his focus.

Wyatt's eyes watered a little at all the zeroes in his figures. He had his signing bonus from Black Watch and the nest egg his mom had left him, but the down payment would still be a stretch. More than a stretch.

He didn't want to ask Leah to help, though. She had enough to worry about. If he was going to do this, he wanted her to have the option to keep her current job or not work at all if she chose. He wanted to lessen the stresses in her life, not multiply them.

So far, it felt a little as if he'd multiplied them.

Noah dropped onto the couch next to him again, and set his plate on the table.

"So," he said tersely. "Walk me through the pros and cons. Sometimes explaining it to someone else clarifies things."

"Okay, so it's really expensive," Wyatt began, "But I have this money my mom got as a settlement when my dad was killed and—"

"Freeze. Killed?" Noah asked.

"Oh." Wyatt blinked. He'd assumed the guy already knew that, given that he'd likely compiled dossiers on all of them before Monroe had hired them. "Yeah, he was in a training accident when my mom was pregnant with me."

"Ah, geez. I'm so sorry."

"No, it's alright. My mom never touched the settlement money, and when she passed it came to me and I…I built on it."

"Okay—"

"I've been playing around with the stock market. I'm doing pretty good." Wyatt couldn't seem to stop the flow of words, as if Noah was the one he had to convince.

"That's awesome." Arkman pushed up his glasses. "So, you feel like this will be affordable, then."

"I've done all the calculators they give you about ten times. I should be able to swing the mortgage payment with a bit to spare. On just my pay, I mean."

"Great."

"And look. The apartment on the ground floor, next to the garage—if it can't be reintegrated, I thought it'd be a good place for guests to stay when they visit, like…grandparents or whatever. Or if something happens and Monroe cuts me loose, we could rent it out to make some extra dough."

"Helpful."

"The backyard is tiny. But it's fenced and the beach is only a few blocks away."

Noah turned the computer toward him and clicked through to a map of the neighborhood. "That looks like a steep hike for little legs, though."

"Little legs don't stay little," Wyatt announced, like he was any kind of expert.

"True. And the school system is good."

"The weird thing is the garage," he mused. "One car wide, but it has this lift thing so you can lower one vehicle under the other and store it below ground. Not knowing who installed it makes me leery of how it would hold up in a quake."

"I mean…looking at when the place was built, it's probably already seen some action," Noah said.

"But not great in terms of accessibility. What if we needed both cars fast?"

His roommate chuckled like he'd said something funny. "Anticipating a quick getaway?"

"Preparation is survival," Wyatt intoned primly. *Geez. Jarheads.*

Noah laughed outright at that. "I imagine this was intended to store some guy's restored classic car, instead of a regular family vehicle. Something they only brought out to drive twice a year."

"Ah, yeah. That makes sense."

"Still, not terribly useful for your purposes."

Wyatt stared into space, thinking. "Not unless we used it for something other than a car. I could park on the street, and this could be storage for things we wouldn't need access to all the time, like luggage or holiday decorations."

Noah listened, then sat back and studied him. "I'm hearing a lot of *we* here."

"I guess you are."

"But you haven't discussed any of this with Leah?"

"Not yet."

"Shouldn't you?" He held up his hands when Wyatt started to protest. "Daydreams are one thing, but big plans like this require both parties consenting."

"I see what you're saying," he said.

"But?"

"But I have a vision."

"Oh…no. Dude what are you—"

Wyatt pulled his computer closer and clicked over to the other screen, the treatise he'd been attempting to commit to memory alongside everything else.

"The Four C's," Noah intoned grimly. Like it was about the four horsemen of the apocalypse or something.

"Carat, cut, color, and clarity," Wyatt explained. "It's how you choose between—"

"I know what this is," Noah cut him off. "Are we being a bit precipitous, do you think?"

"Uh…actually no. I don't feel like I'm skidding downhill too fast. I'm not spinning out on some crazy carnival ride. I feel…clear." Wyatt waved around at his skull. "Maybe I've just dated enough women to know the real thing when I see it." Saying it aloud, he knew it was true.

"Okay…"

"And a ring doesn't have to mean moving fast. People can wear them as long as they need to before sealing the deal." *Again, with the expert opinions from a complete rookie.* Wyatt wanted to laugh at himself, and someday, once this was resolved, he probably would.

"People," Noah repeated.

"Leah," Wyatt spelled out.

Arkman's eyes went unfocused as his massive brain did its thing.

"Am I missing something? Are there massive red flags that everyone sees but me? Because if there are, I need to know stat," Wyatt pointed out.

"Actually—no," he conceded. "I don't see any. Leah's a great person, and so is Ted. And incredibly, the three of you fit really well together."

"The ring's a promise," Wyatt said, grateful for the vote of confidence. "One I can make with no reservations."

Several beats passed while Noah digested that information.

"How do you—how do you think Joe will take it?" he asked eventually. "You moving out and moving on?"

Wyatt did feel some anxiety about that, but there was that little apartment on the ground floor, just in case, and…Joe would continue to get better with time.

He had to.

"Bro, how are *you* gonna take it?" he deflected.

Behind his glasses, Noah's eyes flickered. Still, he scoffed, "Dude, I made it 26 years before all you squids started complicating my life. I'm gonna be just fine."

"Arkman, you wound me."

Noah shook his head. Chuckled for a minute. Pushed up his glasses. "But like, you guys will still have people over for dinner and stuff, right? It's not like we'd never see you. There's the takeout plan to adhere to, and I know your girl likes to cook."

"Correct." Wyatt fought down the urge to ruffle the guy's hair. *Not a kid*, he reminded himself. *Not a kid.*

Noah cleared his throat. "You want me to take a look at the numbers again? See if Black Watch can make the downpayment a little easier?"

"Why on earth would Monroe do that?" Tate was already paying them crazy salaries, more money than Wyatt had ever expected to earn. So much, that he'd gotten himself more books on money management and investing, so he wouldn't screw up and squander anything.

"You're very valuable assets to the company. He wants to keep you happy because happy employees don't jump ship."

Wyatt chuckled. "That's heartwarming."

"Come on. He also likes you. He thinks of you as friends."

"Nothing like a bought-and-paid-for bestie," he said ruefully.

"It's not like that." Noah balanced his plate between them and gestured for Wyatt's laptop. "Here, let me see what we're dealing with."

Feeling shy, inferior, inadequate, and a whole host of other things…he reluctantly released his death grip on his computer and handed it over.

Because he also felt another thing, small and flickering like a candle at sea.

Hope.

After a long moment, Noah looked between him and the screen curiously. "Dude, you got this. You just need to negotiate the seller down a little bit."

"It's La Jolla, man. Things sell over asking price, not under."

"Yeah, but…" Noah—Arkman, he amended with amusement—started typing at Mach 10. "They've tried to sell this place three times in three years. They've dropped the price each time. I can find out if there's something catastrophic wrong with it. The one offer they had fell through after inspection. But the owners…"

More typing. Sandwich forgotten.

Wyatt peered at it, wondering if Noah would notice if he stole half of it. As his angst began to dissipate a little, he realized he hadn't had lunch yet.

"What about the owners," he murmured, reaching for the plate.

Noah shoved it toward him absently.

"Looks like they split up five years ago. The wife's already remarried. I'll bet you a hundred bucks they want this sale over with," he said excitedly.

"So, I should try to get it?"

Even if Leah didn't want to live there with him, he could rent to her and live in the apartment. Or set Joe up there to watch over them, and rent somewhere else nearby. There were a hundred ways to make it doable.

Damn, Wyatt thought, shaking his head. He might just pull this mission off.

Chapter Thirty-Eight

Leah

LEAH FELT AROUND behind the TV until she discovered the piece of paper she was looking for, taped to the back.

She peeked into the hallway, but thankfully she appeared to still be home alone. Every time Wyatt hid one of his clues, she worried that one of his roommates would discover her searching and think she was a nosy and suspicious weirdo, invading his privacy and crossing boundaries.

Right, because so many men hid their secrets under the bathroom sink or behind their TV. And like Joe and Noah cared.

She and Wyatt were living together in fake wedded bliss, for heaven's sake. Surely that merited some level of spatial mingling?

No, this silly worry had everything to do with Jesse's old paranoia and secretiveness and nothing to do with her current reality. Wyatt had set up this scavenger hunt specifically so she _would_ go looking for clues. Leah was supposed to be doing this.

She rolled her eyes at herself, then perched on his chair to read what he'd written.

Tomorrow at 6 pm, drive to the house we toured and park in the driveway if you want something that belongs to you.

(Don't worry, Kim and Bennett will stay with Teddy. They'll arrive at the apartment no later than 5:30.)

She sat back in astonishment. This was a definite escalation. Wyatt had never directed her to go anywhere outside the apartment before. He'd even taken the step of arranging childcare.

Whatever he had planned, it was for grownups only.

Her heart rate picked up as she wondered what it could be.

A date? A real date, at a fancy restaurant, maybe?

They hadn't done anything like that before.

Leah read over the note again. Wyatt hadn't specified whether she should dress nice in his clue, and that felt like a detail he wouldn't have overlooked.

Either it was a casual outing, or she'd really left something behind when they'd toured that house yesterday. If that was the case, though, why not just pick it up for her? Particularly if he was planning to be up there anyway?

Leah shook her head, equal parts confused and curious.

Wyatt had a good heart. She trusted him. Whatever this turned out to be, she knew he meant well. He'd undoubtedly intended for this foray to be sweet and fun, and God knew she could certainly use more of that in her life.

Besides, Teddy loved Kim and Bennett, and he'd be thrilled to hang out with them for a while one-on-one. They'd take good care of him.

Leah glanced at her watch, calculating the rest of her day. If she was going to be on time, she had to shower and get dressed, prepare for her babysitters, and stop for gas on the way.

She had to get *moving*.

KIM AND BENNETT arrived in a flurry of activity, explaining to Teddy that they'd be taking him out for pizza and then to see a new kid's movie that had just hit theaters. He was wide-eyed with excitement and raring to go, but Leah had been operating on the assumption that they were going to stay in. She got a little flustered, scrambling to install his car seat in Bennett's truck, gathering them a bag of necessities, and making sure they could reach her if anything went sideways.

With three efficient adults working together, though, Teddy was soon strapped in and kicking his feet, Kim was bear-hugging her on the sidewalk, and Bennett was smothering his grin behind the wheel.

Something was up, and they were in on it.

Leah couldn't begin to guess what, and the drive to La Jolla felt like it took forever as her mind looped through possibilities. At 6708 Camanito Corazon, she pulled into the driveway and looked around.

Wyatt's car was parallel parked on the street out front.

And, taped prominently to the garage door, lit up by her headlights where she couldn't possibly miss it, was Wyatt's next clue.

Leah shut off her car and scrambled out to grab it.

You're here! Leave your car and walk to the beach access we used last time.
Take the stairs down to the beach. (If you dare!)

Leah spun in a circle like a different clue might jump out at her, but there was nothing and no one to direct her. Nothing except the note.

She took a deep breath, locked her car, and slung her purse across her chest. Then she marched to the end of the short driveway, turned west, and started hiking.

The sun hung low on the horizon, and the view was even prettier than the last time they'd been there. As she walked, Leah took in the sleepy street, and the quiet chirping of birds hidden in the trees.

The surrounding houses had lovely blooming landscaping and large windows lit up for evening. Neighbors moved around inside, returning from work, perhaps, or getting ready for dinner.

In one direction, someone walked a dog. In another, a person jogged.

Her steps slowed as she looked around. It felt safe here. Peaceful. Leah felt a pang, wishing she could stay longer than this one night. Become a part of the community.

Three blocks passed far too quickly, and soon she reached the small lot at the top of the cliff, nothing but a low wooden fence separating the cul-de-sac from the panoramic view of the sun setting over the Pacific.

Leah stood at the head of the stairs, filling her lungs with briny air as a chilly breeze lifted her hair off her shoulders. All at once, little lanterns winked to life along the weathered wood staircase descending the hill, illuminating a red runner weighed down with scattered shells, pebbles, and fluttering flower petals.

She gasped, stunned by the beauty of it.

The lights ended at the bottom. On the beach below, people occasionally walked by and pointed, but their voices were indistinct, drifting up to her over the sound of the waves and the wind.

Leah went closer, and that was when she saw the note, tucked securely under a corner of the first lantern.

Nothing fake, faux, or sham past this point, Wyatt had scrawled.
(i.e. take off those mail order rings.)

Leah stared at her hand, her breath stuttering in her throat. She hesitated, then swallowed down her nerves and slipped them off. Once they were zipped safely into an inside pocket of her purse, she took another deep breath, stepped around the lantern, and started down the stairs.

Halfway down, on a landing, she found a kind of waystation with another note.

It said, *Time for some liquid courage?*

Holding it in place was a goblet of chilled sparkling wine with plastic wrap protecting it. Leah peeled it off and sipped it gratefully. When she glanced back the way she'd come, she noticed that the stairs behind her had gone dark.

She flipped over Wyatt's note to read, *No turning back now!*

There was nowhere to go but forward. On the bottom step, she paused. Behind her, the stairs were dark. In front of her, the beach was dim as well, lit only by the moon and stars reflected on the waves. She wasn't sure what to do next, and her pulse pounded in her ears.

A moment later, however, a circle of lanterns lit up on the sand several feet away, scattered with red petals and illuminating a careful still life in the middle, centered around a little box.

A small child with a familiar giggle scampered away, staying out of the circle of light.

Leah stared at the scene, stunned. *It couldn't be.*

Could it?

Next to her feet, a tiny lantern she hadn't noticed before came to life, illuminating another clue.

Leah swallowed and bent to retrieve it.

What do you think? Are you ready to be mine, and for me to be yours?

(If so, go get that box, holding something real and true inside it.)

Her heart hammered with irrational, unreasonable hope. The circle in the sand beckoned her.

Leah took a deep breath and stepped off the stairs.

Chapter Thirty-Nine

Wyatt

WYATT CROUCHED BEHIND a rocky dune amongst the beach grass and lupine bushes, and turned on the lanterns with the remotes in his hands. Kim and Bennett let out quiet sounds of approval, handed off Teddy, and bent to give both of them awkward half hugs. Then they left, strolling off hand-in-hand to give them some privacy.

He tucked Teddy against him, and together they turned off each section of lights as Leah passed it. Wyatt hoped the message was clear. There was no going back for them. Only forward.

He couldn't quite make out her expression as she took the leap and crossed the sand, entered the flickering circle, and retrieved the ring box he'd left there. He and Noah had found a diamond similar in style to her fake one, just a bit smaller.

She'd been complaining about the size of the stone she'd ordered off the internet, not liking the way it sagged sideways on her finger and knocked into everything. He hoped like hell she hadn't been bullshitting and he'd read her cues correctly.

Teddy clutched his hand tight and did an excited little jig next to him.

"Now?" he whispered impatiently.

"Almost," Wyatt told him.

Several feet away, Leah turned in place, searching for him. She wouldn't see them on her own, though. The only thing left illuminated was the circle she was standing in, the stars winking to life overhead, and the last little sliver of the setting sun over the water.

"Where are you?" she called softly. Panic laced through her words as they drifted to him. "Wyatt?"

"Now," he told Teddy. "Ready?"

He led him carefully out of the shadows and the kid shot over to his mom. Leah sagged with relief.

"Mommy!" Teddy shrieked. "Did you see the lights?"

She laughed, scooping him up. "You little stinker, were you in on this?"

He nodded with a huge grin, peeked back at Wyatt, and wriggled out of her arms. With a quick fist bump, he dropped to his knees next to him in the sand.

Leah noticed what they were doing with a jolt. Her breath hitched, and Wyatt had to wonder what, exactly, she'd thought all this had been leading up to.

"Leah?" he asked.

She nodded. "Wyatt."

"Are you okay?"

"I am. Full speed ahead," she urged with a smile. Her voice was a little shaky, but he'd take it.

The green light was his proof that he hadn't blown it, that this thing growing between them wasn't all in his head. Wyatt squeezed Teddy's hand and felt a grin wreathing his own face, too.

The big speech he'd planned evaporated as if it never existed. All he could manage was, "Leah, will you marry me? For real this time?"

"This is crazy," she replied, in a breathless gasp of a laugh.

"Maybe," he shrugged, glancing at Teddy. "That doesn't make it wrong."

"Mommy, you have to answer!" the little guy demanded anxiously.

She laughed again, and her shoulders relaxed a fraction. "And what should I say, since you know so much?"

Teddy leaned toward Wyatt, caught off guard. "Tell her to say yes," he murmured conspiratorially.

"You have to say yes!" Teddy proclaimed, leaping to his feet and cavorting around. "Yes, yes, yes!"

"He said it," Wyatt smirked. "Must be true."

Leah looked from the box in her hand to him, to her kid, and back again. Tears welled in her eyes. She stood there frozen, utterly mute.

The kneeling thing wasn't working. Wyatt got to his feet and gathered her close, starting to worry, just a little. "Hey. Hey, it's okay," he soothed. "No pressure. You don't have to—"

"No, it's good," she rambled, face pressed to his rapidly dampening shirt. "This is good. It's better than good. You just took me by surprise, that's all. And I want this, I really do." That part seemed to startle her, and she sobbed a little harder. "I can't believe it, but I do."

He took her by the shoulders and held her a few inches away, so he could see her eyes. "So that's a…?"

"Yes," she laughed through her tears, gripping the ring box so tightly it dug into his spine. "That's a big fat yes. Oh my god."

Wyatt pried her arm off him so he could take out the ring and slip it on her shaking finger, then bent her back for a real kiss to seal the deal. He thanked the universe for the cover of night, praying that his relief and own watery eyes might go unnoticed.

Teddy whooped and wrapped his little arms around their knees, so Wyatt pulled him up and sandwiched him in the middle for a group hug.

A *family* hug.

"Thank god," he chuckled, happiness fizzing like champagne in his chest. "Make a guy sweat, why don't you."

Leah wept and laughed and kissed them both, quick pecks wherever she could reach.

"Do you like the ring?" he wondered, once she'd settled down a little. "We can change it out, if you don't."

"Stop it, it's perfect and you know it." Rather suddenly, she pulled away and righted her clothes, swiping at her face and slapping Wyatt on the arm. "Okay, but now we have to go. We need to clean all this up and move our cars. I don't want to get towed. It's residents only up there."

Wyatt kissed the top of her head and went to retrieve his gear from under the blooming shrubs. "We're not going to get towed," he assured her. He plucked a purple flower to tuck behind her ear.

Leah and Teddy were already bustling around, picking up the lanterns and turning them off, shaking out the red tablecloth he'd laid on the sand, and shoving everything into the bags he was holding.

"You don't know that," she argued, marching for the stairs like a general. "Someone could've already reported us, and parking enforcement will be all over it."

"Leah, it's okay," he said again, trailing up the stairs behind her as Teddy took point, tossing his carefully collected pebbles and shells aside while Leah rolled up the runner.

She spun on him and jabbed a threatening finger at his chest. "I am not going to have the best proposal ever ruined by a trip to the impound lot. Do you hear me, soldier? Now, move boots."

"Sailor," he corrected, smirking, "And no one's going anywhere but home." How had all of his romantic plans gone off the rails so fast? She was dismantling his set-up like a tank brigade tearing through a field of wheat, and his head was beginning to spin.

"Right," she agreed absently.

Time to take back the reins. "Our home, at 6708 Camanito Corazon," Wyatt elaborated.

They'd reached the landing halfway up the stairs, and Leah turned to stuff one of the runners into his bag. Lit by Wyatt's phone flashlight, Teddy gathered up the lanterns and the wineglass, and handed them off carefully.

"What did you just say," Leah drawled slowly. She squinted dangerously, suspicious as hell.

"I said…" he paused, but he was in it now. *The only way out was through.* "I put an offer on the house, and they accepted it. We close in a couple of weeks. It's ours." It was a simplified version of what'd happened, but conveyed the necessary information.

"You *what!*" she squawked.

"I bought the house," Wyatt said again. "For us. So we can live there, together."

He handed Leah his bags and began rolling up the second stair runner, like he hadn't just dropped two bombs on the woman in quick succession. If she could change gears at the drop of a dime, so could he.

Teddy forged ahead, gleefully tossing away shells and pebbles, and raining the flower petals that remained on Wyatt and Leah's heads.

She shuffled up the stairs after him, looking shell-shocked. "But why would you do that?"

"Because I want to make a home with you. You and me and Teddy, together in a stable place, one we can count on, and he can return to whenever he needs it. I wanted a place for us to grow old together. A physical manifestation of a life and a love built together. Rings are great, but a home is what counts long-term."

She didn't say anything, so Wyatt turned to check her reaction. Leah was crying again, parked three stairs behind him and clutching the railing.

He set down the end of the runner and grabbed her hand, pulling her up next to him. "Is that okay?" He held her palm under his flashlight, checking for splinters.

She yanked it away and wrapped her arms around his waist, hiding her face as her whole body trembled against him.

"I'm overwhelmed," she admitted, voice muffled in his shirt.

He stroked her hair gently. "I thought we loved it, but it's okay if we didn't. Even if it's not that place, we can make a home somewhere else. Right? We're in this together now."

Leah gazed up at him, eyes misty with love and wonder. "I do love it. But you're right. We can make it any place you want," she said, gathering Teddy against her leg as she kissed him, "Anywhere at all, as long as we're together."

Epilogue

Joe

I'M NOT ABANDONING you." Stitch stared at him with wide, worried eyes.

He'd brought the team up here to check out his new digs but true to form, he'd spent the last half hour trying to sell him on moving into the nanny suite on the ground floor.

"I wouldn't blame you if you were," Joe told him. "Look at you—out here buying property and getting hitched, and I've been MIA. I should've been around for you more."

"Stop. You know I don't blame you for that."

"Maybe you should."

"Dude, no. I just want you to feel better," Wyatt said gravely. "That's all that matters."

"Whatever," Joe smirked, gesturing around. As usual, he was uncomfortable being the focus of things. "So, when do you guys close? Next week, right?"

"Day after tomorrow."

"Ah. Right." He'd probably been told that already. Repeatedly.

"What do you think, though? You like this place? You can crash here whenever you want. Or move in and decorate. Leah and I are good with either."

"I'll think about it," Joe hedged. Wyatt had already done so much to keep him going. Infringing on the guy's new marriage would be unconscionable. "We should get back upstairs. Make sure they haven't started demo-ing the kitchen, or whatever."

"Sure. Yeah." Wyatt ran a hand through his shaggy hair and tried to hide his concerned frown. "Just…think about it, alright? Offer stands."

"Roger that." Joe fled for the door, taking several calming breaths outside while Stitch locked up, then led him into the main house.

Upstairs, Leah, Peyton, and Kim were in a bedroom that had apparently been earmarked for the little guy, discussing paint colors while Teddy wheeled a toy truck around on the rug.

They found the rest of the team on the roof, asses parked in a collection of beach chairs while they admired the view and shot the shit about work. *Of course.*

The one mission of his career that he couldn't seem to shake, was destined to be never-ending.

He and Stitch pulled up their own folding chairs, while Bennett raised an issue that had clearly been nagging at him. "Listen, all I'm saying is, most of these young women are from rough beginnings. Right? But in the photos Dan showed Kim, she said the girls looked like polished models—like women intended to be public-facing companions to high-powered people."

Buck's shades reflected a shard of sun into Joe's face as he tipped his head toward Easy. "And your point is…?"

"How are they making the transition to sophisticated escorts? Who is doing that? Who's running the finishing school? Cause y'all know it ain't Dan or Ole Roy."

Noah adjusted his hat, tipping the brim back so he could see better. "Maybe the older ones are coaching the rookies. Showing them the ropes."

Joe nodded at him. He'd considered that possibility himself, before he and Wyatt had landed on their favorite theory. "Or maybe…" He scrolled through an album of screenshots on his phone and found one featuring Senator Doggett's wife, Lena, "…we start here."

Wyatt pointed at him, adamant. "Yes! Agreed."

Buck looked intrigued. "Hmm. We've danced around that a few times. You could be right."

"I think so, too," Noah said. "At the time, I feel like we assumed Dan used his mom's supposed modeling agency as a cover story for Kim. But what if it wasn't? What if it's a part of this whole thing? A way station in the pipeline, so to speak."

"Could be," Bennett speculated. "Lena funded Roy's political career. Maybe she spearheaded this side quest, too. Y'all saw those headshots of the village girls. Those weren't some amateur shots from someone's phone camera. Someone knew what they were doing."

"So did they photoshop their school pictures or take the headshots pretending they were for the documentary?"

He shrugged.

"So, Lena's our top dog?" Joe prompted hopefully.

"One problem with that is that she doesn't have the required military connections," Buck argued. "Not that we're aware of, anyway."

Joe shrugged. "We think she doesn't. Only one way to find out for sure." If the team picked up this idea and ran with it, it would be his first real contribution in what felt like way too long.

He needed the win. Far more than he would ever admit.

"I'll add it to the list," Noah said, setting aside his beer and his phone and propping his feet up on an overturned painter bucket. "Hey, I meant to tell you guys—I think I found some possible new pictures of the Nabaruti girls on the dark web. I'm trying to trace their source. Figure out if they're even real before we get too excited."

"Dude, really? That's amazing," Bennett cried. "Can you tell where—"

Joe's phone vibrated in his pocket with an incoming call, so he dug it out to see who it was. He'd been dropping balls left and right lately, and there was no telling what he might've forgotten or who he'd left hanging.

The number flashing on the screen made him catch his breath.

"Sorry. I should take this," he told the team, and made for the stairs like hell was coming.

"Hello?"

"May I speak to Joseph Doherty, please?"

"This is he."

"Oh, hey. It's Taylor Wiggins from Patriots and Paws. I just wanted to let you know that your dogs are doing really great, and as of today, I'm releasing them from quarantine. They're just about ready to transition to a home environment."

Joe's pulse ticked up. The pair of beautiful German Shepherds were young but given where they'd come from, there was no telling what they'd already lived through. When Joe found them, they were being used as guard dogs by the thugs holding Kim hostage at that posh estate up in Montecito.

The cops had taken them into custody after the raid, but Joe had informed them right then and there that he wanted to adopt if it was an option.

For a while, none of them had been sure it would even be possible, not until he'd found Ms. Wiggins and her rescue by way of a group he'd met, that paired vets with PTSD to future service dogs and retiring military and police K-9s.

Doc Tom's idea, of course. Guy was full of them.

"Hey, that's great. So, when can I pick them up?" he asked.

"Soon." Taylor hesitated. "Just to confirm, there are no children or other pets currently living in the home, correct?"

"Other than my roommate, yeah," he quipped. Now that little Teddy was moving up in the world, Noah was the closest thing he had to a kid at home, and lord knew that guy had insisted up and down he was a grownup.

"And what is that person's age?"

"Sorry, that was a joke. He claims to be 28 but some days I have my doubts."

She inhaled audibly, pausing again before coming to a decision. "Okay. So, we'll need to do a quick home inspection to make sure you have what you need in place. As we discussed, you're going to have to commit to bringing them in weekly for at least another few months to complete their retraining. I wasn't lying when I said we've had our best trainer working with them. They've got quite a bond going."

A ribbon of jealousy threaded through him. Those were supposed to be his dogs, and they were incredible animals—but now some asshole trainer was bonding with them? *No fucking way.*

On that thought's heels came another, in Doc Tom's Kumbaya voice, naturally. *No one is trying to steal your dogs, brother. They're trying to make sure they won't accidentally kill someone, or bite your face off in your sleep.*

Assuming he ever slept again.

"Uh, that's great," he managed, refocusing on the current, real-world conversation. "Is that trainer going to stick with them, or have they graduated to someone new?"

"I think it's best if we stick with what's familiar for now. She'll help you guys get acclimated to each other and assist with getting them settled at home. Continuity will be key in this situation."

Had Taylor said *she?* The fancy trainer bonding with his dogs was a *she?*

Joe frowned. Somewhere in the last several weeks, he'd missed that detail. And lately, he'd struggled with relating to *she*s.

Oh, how the mighty have fallen, his mom might say.

"You got a name for me?" he asked, wincing at how brusque he sounded.

"Of the trainer?"

"Yeah, who else?" *Jesus, he just couldn't stop.*

"Uh, yeah—her name is Sarah," Ms. Wiggins relayed. "Sarah Boone."

Joe's unease flared into something different. Sarah, like the girl he'd crushed on all through elementary school. Sarah, like his favorite aunt. Sarah, the girl's name he'd always liked best for a thousand stupid reasons.

What kind of nutcase had a favorite girl name, anyway?

All Joe could say was that *Sarah*, whoever she was, had better not try to steal his fucking dogs. He was fairly sure his life depended on it.

Up Next

Fight or Flight

(Black Watch Security, Book Four)

Once upon a time, Joe Doherty was the pride and joy of his family, a hero among heroes, and a ladies' man like Boston had never seen. Then came the mission that changed everything, but nothing so much as him.

While Joe would like nothing more than to leave the ambush that ended his career in the SEALs behind, his team is now working for Black Watch Security, and their sole job is to dismantle the shadowy network behind that ill-fated skirmish and bring home the girls kidnapped during it.

His problem is that he hasn't gotten a solid night's sleep in the two years since it happened, and his grip on life is getting worse, not better. In a last-ditch effort to return to the man he once was, Joe's adopted two rescue dogs who might need more help than he does.

They're perfect for each other, with one tiny little catch. The dogs come with baggage in the form of a beautiful trainer named Sarah, and she looks at Joe like he might be her next charitable endeavor. Even worse? She has a past that could save him—or sink him for good.

Sneak peeks and release dates will be shared in my monthly newsletter soon! Are you signed up?

FREE BOOK

Get a glimpse of Morgan, Meg, Molly, and Mina — before their happily-ever-afters take place!

Sign up for the author's newsletter to receive a free digital copy of the Lost & Found prequel story "Girls Night Out," as well as another full-length novel.

Visit Here to Get Started:

http://eepurl.com/ctGk1j

Also by Kristen Casey

The Triple Threat Series

The Titan Was Tall
The Doctor Was Dark
The Hero Was Handsome
The Triple Threat Box Set

The Lost & Found Series

Girls Night Out
Finding Home
Finding Love
Lost in Love
The Flynn Sisters Box Set
Finding a Husband
Finding Forever
Forever and a Day
The O'Connell Sisters Box Set

Acknowledgments

You guys waited a long time for this one. I hope Wyatt and Leah were worth it!

Thanks, as ever, to Deborah Bradseth for her always-wonderful cover design, and to Helen Snay for her unflagging cheerleading, excitement for each new book and hero, and extremely helpful beta reading.

To my family, who listens so patiently when I ramble about publishing ephemera, and tags along when I invariably want to visit bookstores on vacation.

To my cats, whose cute little napping poses kept me going when it felt like writing this book might never end.

And last, but never least, to my readers, who make this job the best one I can imagine. Thank you from the bottom of my heart for loving my stories about love.

About the Author

Kristen Casey writes the kind of heartfelt, steamy books she loves to read—full of relatable characters and delicious dialogue. She lives in Maryland with her family and cats, and in her free time enjoys all things crafty—especially projects she makes from yarn.

Sign up for her newsletter to receive exclusive content, sales, and new releases emailed right to your inbox.

Follow her on social media, for even more fun stuff!

Goodreads: Kristen_Casey

Facebook: AuthorKCasey

X: AuthorKCasey

Pinterest: KristenCase0461

Instagram: Kristen.Casey.Books

BookBub: Kristen Casey

Bluesky: KristenCasey

TikTok: KristenWritesRomance